SHADES OF TRUTH

—— A Matt Jamison Novel ——

James A. Ardaiz

Pace Press
Fresno, California

Published by Pace Press
An imprint of Linden Publishing
2006 South Mary Street, Fresno, California 93721
(559) 233-6633 / (800) 345-4447
PacePress.com

Pace Press and Colophon are trademarks of
Linden Publishing, Inc.

ISBN 978-1-61035-345-8

135798642

Printed in the United States of America
on acid-free paper.

Library of Congress Cataloging-in-Publication Data on file.

A Native American elder once described his own inner struggles in this manner: Inside of me there are two dogs. One of the dogs is mean and evil. The other dog is good. The mean dog fights the good dog all the time. When asked which dog wins, he reflected for a moment and replied, "The one I feed the most."

—George Bernard Shaw

Prologue

The blazing sun of summer fills the great Central Valley of California with heat until even shade provides little respite. It's not uncommon for late afternoon July days to reach 105 degrees. Nothing moves, not even the leaves on the rows of vines that stretch out along endless country roads, their wooden canes curling around wire that holds up the summer's end crop of green and red grapes. There is no wind. No breeze. Just heat. Like the leaves of the vines, nothing moves unless it has to.

Until the evening. That's when the ground begins to release the warmth it has absorbed and the onset of evening becomes a balm to the people of the Valley. The dusk sun sets orange against the rise of the Coastal Range and the horizon folds streams of crimson and yellow into the slowly darkening sky. It is a time when older people remember that as children they played in their front yards while neighbors sat in chairs watching and visiting. Even now, when in many cities across America people don't know the names of their neighbors, the evening time is when people of the towns of the Great Valley walk and wave and stop for a moment to say hello. It's one of those places that remind people from other places of how they want to think it used to be.

But memories of the past cannot push back the slowly rising tide of change. The violence that no longer leads the news in major cities is still a headline here. Like the violence elsewhere that seems to find new and different ways to crash through the sensibility of people, shocking them with what before they could not even imagine, it sometimes happens here also. And people are reminded that the life they once held on to so casually they must now hold on to tenaciously because there are more and more who would take away from the peace of others. It is the way of a changing world and even that change has come to the Valley. What once stunned its inhabitants by its uncommon violence now assaults slowly calloused sensibilities. With that progress of civilization, the revulsion that once endured in memory is now frequently only a moment's repulse. But on this warm July night, there would be one more moment, and even those who thought of themselves as no longer surprised at what predators could do, would awaken this time to horrific images conjured by the words of reporters, reporters who themselves were recoiling from what they had before not even imagined.

Chapter 1

Christine stirred fitfully in her bed, opening her eyes to the darkness. Moonlight seeped into the small bedroom, outlining the few items of furniture that provided familiarity in the daylight and became fearful shadowed objects of imagination at night. She squeezed her eyes tightly shut, pulling at the T-shirt that rode up over her belly, sticking to her small body. It was too warm even for a sheet. But it wasn't the stifling trapped heat of her room that kept her awake. It was the sounds. She'd heard them before. They were part of the three short years of her life. She pulled her knees up to make herself small, hiding in the folds of the sheet, and buried her face in the pillow.

The sounds of her life were not the noises that should be part of childhood. But Christine didn't know that because it was what she'd always known. These were the sounds of her home. Soon her mother would come and comfort her. Her mother always came, and then they would both cry, from the child the frightened tears of an innocent who needed reassurance, and from her mother the resigned tears of a woman who couldn't find her way out of despair. But tonight, her mother didn't come. Only the sounds.

The body of Christine's mother slammed against the thin wall of the kitchen, the shuddering vibration carrying throughout the long-dried wooden frame of the house. It carried even into the bed where the child lay, pulling her small body against herself. She kept her eyes closed, scrunching them, trying to keep out the resonating sound. She curled into a tighter ball, drawing the pillow up against her face, reaching for the softness of her stuffed rabbit. The worn fur of the over-loved toy yielded to the child's tight embrace, but it was unable to block out the reverberating noise which came—again and again and again.

❧

The light in the kitchen was unshielded. Any glass shade that once softened the harsh glare of the light bulbs had long ago disappeared, probably broken, certainly misplaced in time and memory. The eight-by-ten room was cramped by the small kitchen table in the center and three chairs, their plastic seat coverings splitting as age took away whatever suppleness they once had. The sink and counter were littered with half-empty glasses and plates with remnants of food drying hard on them.

For some inexplicable reason, at that moment Lisa Farrow took in the meagerness of her life as her back slammed into the kitchen wall. She felt the air leave her body. The coppery taste of blood filled her mouth where her teeth clamped together against her tongue as she tried to brace herself against the blow. Her vision closed in as her left eye began to swell. She didn't reach up to see whether the skin was broken. She needed both hands to protect herself. Experience had been a brutal teacher.

Her words came out thickly. "Rick, don't. No more. What do you want? I'll do what you want, anything you want." It didn't matter. She was long past pride. This was about survival for her, for her baby. Lisa's face turned slightly to the left, toward the hallway and the bedroom where Christine was, hoping she didn't hear. Out of the corner of her right eye she could see Rick moving toward her, his face twisted with anger, his eyes narrow slits revealing only blackness.

He stood there, his eyes darting around the room, the rage coming in waves, ebbing and flowing. *This is her fault. She made me do this. It's her fault, not mine.* The thought refueled his anger, focusing his eyes on the woman, her back against the wall, coughing and shaking. *This is all her fault.* The more he looked at Lisa's swollen face the angrier he was that she made him do this. He felt the rage rising up inside him like a tornado blacking out the light of day. His hand slid to his side, the fingers curling around the smooth dark wood of the Buck knife he carried sheathed on his belt. He didn't even sense the automatic gesture of his other hand easily pulling out the blade, the stiffness of a new knife being opened long past.

Lisa kept her face turned to the left, the swelling eye closing rapidly, forcing her to focus her right eye as she heard the dull click of the blade locking into place. Rick held it up, hesitating before he laid it on the counter, the silver metal of the blade glinting as it rattled against the cracked and aging tile. He lunged forward, drawing his hand back into a fist, shoving it into her stomach. Lisa felt her knees buckle as she gasped for air, fighting the urge to simply be still but unable to stop the slow slide to the floor. There was nothing left for her except to cover her head as Rick kicked at her. "Bitch! Bitch! What makes you think I would even want you? What makes you think anybody wants you?"

Lisa felt him standing over her, his sweat dripping down, mingling with her own fear-driven sweat and the blood from her split lips. Then he began to kick again. He kicked until she couldn't feel it anymore, and then he kicked again. She heard him shouting, but his words were a garble of sound and spit. Finally, he stopped.

She should have lay still but there was Christine. That was all that went through her mind as she struggled up from the floor, trying to raise her upper body, her side burning, every breath a racking pain, her body choosing between the need to breathe and the inevitable agony that shot through each breath. Lisa looked for Rick. She could only see his black boots. They were moving toward her again.

She felt the tugging on her pants. She pulled her legs up, trying to squeeze them against her body. One more plea for him to stop came gasping from her throat. She wouldn't resist. Her slurred words came out with effort, trying to close her swelling lips to form the sounds. Even Lisa wasn't sure what she said. It didn't matter. Begging carried its own plaintive sound.

The heavy blow only carried an instant of pain. If Lisa had any feeling at that moment it was gratitude that perhaps unconsciousness would free her from the agony.

⌒

There was vague awareness of light penetrating through the slits of her swollen eyelids. Slowly what was around her emerged from the dark images as her eyesight adjusted. He was still there and so was the throb of pain threatening the slightest movement, including every breath. Lisa raised her head, bracing against the anguish. Then she saw the glint of silver.

The blade burned through the air, its passage making the hissing sound of a striking snake. She felt it moving across her neck like a scratching nail catching skin, pulling, slicing. She felt the warm stickiness running down her chest. She was surprised. It didn't hurt as much as the kicks. A moment of clarity focused her. *What will happen to Christine?* She watched as her vision collapsed into a narrow pinpoint of light. Then she saw nothing at all.

⌒

Christine stopped squeezing her eyes shut. There was only silence. She waited. But tonight, when the sounds stopped her mother did not come.

But the man came. She could sense him over her bed as he spoke to her in a rasping whisper. She pulled her pillow and her rabbit against her ears, shutting out his voice until his footsteps receded in the darkness of her room. He came back. His breath hot and slurred. It would be all right. He told her to go to sleep. "It will be all right, Christine." As he left the room she heard him say, "It will be all right." She sank her head deeply into her pillow. It would be all right. Her mother would come. She always did.

A new sound came. The sensation was soft at first, almost imperceptible. Christine could smell something different. Something that even her young mind knew was not good. Wisps of smoke wafted into the bedroom, curling through the moonlit room. Christine pulled her stuffed rabbit closer to her, waiting and watching as yellow-orange light flickered against the shadows on the hallway. Her mother would come. She always did.

Chapter 2

Matt Jamison walked from the elevator to the double mahogany doors crested by the brass letters of the words *DISTRICT ATTORNEY, TENAYA COUNTY*. Thirty-four years old, a little over six feet tall, with dark brown hair and striking blue-green eyes, his dark features contrasted with his crisp white shirt and carefully knotted red silk tie. As he opened one of the heavy doors to enter the reception area, Jamison couldn't help feeling that after nearly eight years so far pretty much everything in his legal career as a prosecutor had gone right. Passing Helen, the receptionist, he began to say good morning but could see she was answering a phone call. "District attorney's office. May I help you?"

Matt started to move on but saw Helen raising her hand, waving it at him to catch his attention while at the same time she punched numbers into her phone and directed the call. He waited until she was finished. It was never a good idea to ignore Helen. You might find that your messages got misplaced just long enough to create a problem. Eventually you would get the message. Helen never would lose one. She might, however, hold one just long enough to make you rush around when it suddenly appeared. One of the first things he learned when he came to work as a young deputy district attorney was not to cross Helen.

Blonde and somewhere, according to her, near middle age, Helen had been the receptionist for as long as anybody in the office could remember. She was not a secretary, she would remind anybody who asked her to type a document or copy a brief. She was the gatekeeper. If there was somebody you needed to see or talk to she would let them through and if it was somebody you didn't want to see or talk to, she would make sure that they didn't get through. She knew the moods of everyone, including the district attorney himself, and Helen would let you know if you needed to watch your back in the perpetual roil of office politics. Behind her back the younger DAs referred to her as Mother Helen. And occasionally she would look at some officious young attorney and say, "Don't mess with Mother Helen." That was usually enough to keep people in their place, but if it wasn't she would make sure that eventually it would be.

Helen leaned forward, closing the space between herself and Jamison. Her hair barely moved. Helen didn't scrimp on hair spray. She wanted her hair to look the same way in the afternoon that it looked when she combed it in the morning. Jamison bent down to hear what she apparently did not want anyone else to hear. "District Attorney Gage wants to see you. He was in early and told me that as soon as you came in I was to make sure you saw him."

"Good mood or bad mood?" Jamison asked.

"I couldn't tell but whatever the reason is, he seemed anxious. I'm guessing, but I don't think whatever it is that it's your fault." She gave a slight smile. "I could be wrong, though."

"Yeah, thanks." Jamison straightened up, returning the tight smile. "Any other messages?"

Helen handed him a small pile of paper with various names, phone numbers, and messages. "These just said to call back and left the number and a message. The rest didn't want to tell me what they wanted to talk about." It wasn't just a business inquiry that caused Helen to ask if they had a message. Lawyers who wanted to get through immediately without explaining what they wanted learned quickly enough that Mother Helen liked to know what was going on and cooperation with her frequently was the price of admission or else their message might get shuffled to a different pile—maybe sitting for an additional day or two. Helen didn't like voice mail and everyone had given up on getting her to adjust. Even the district attorney didn't dare mess with Helen, but then he had the advantage of his calls going directly to his secretary. Only lawyers who had the number to Jamison's direct line could bypass Helen and leave a private message, but Jamison deliberately made sure who had personal access was a very small group. He also appreciated that Helen's screening process allowed him to say he didn't get the message.

Jamison shuffled through the sheets of message paper, quickly evaluating what had any urgency to it and what he could parcel off to one of the newer deputy DAs or an investigator to deal with. He walked through the door to the hallway where offices of deputy DAs lined the hall. The higher the floors occupied by the district attorney's office, and the closer the offices in the hall-ways came to *the* district attorney, the larger the offices were. Jamison's office wasn't very far from District Attorney William Gage's office. As chief deputy in charge of Homicide and Major Crimes, he was the lawyer who caught the big cases that made headlines and that focused public attention on the district attorney's office and on his boss, Bill Gage, as *the* district attorney.

Jamison kept his eye out for carpet edges curling up. It had been a while since new carpet had been put in, and here and there silver duct tape held down seams that had separated. The county supervisor didn't seem sympa-thetic to yearly pleas for new carpet. Jamison didn't imagine that the hallways in the county supervisor's offices had duct tape but then again, they held the purse strings. He also imagined that somebody with taste picked the color of the supervisor's carpet. It was the generally held opinion in the district attorney's office that nobody with taste had picked their carpet, the orange color maybe having been in fashion before he was born.

As he walked down the hallway first toward his office and then to see what his boss wanted, Jamison could almost measure his advancement as a prosecutor as he moved by offices he once occupied. First it had been the lowest floor referred to by young deputy DAs as "the basement," even though it was on the sixth floor of the eight-story county building that housed the offices of the district attorney. You started there and you worked your way up through the grunt assignments of juvenile and misdemeanors and preliminary felony hearings and then specialty assignments like narcotics and vice until those on the upper floors reached down and pulled you up the ladder into cases that the public actually paid attention to.

He knew his advancement had been fast even by the standards of others who had jumped over assignments and floors. Jamison had completely skipped the seventh floor to move to the eighth, the top floor. But that didn't mean that the one thing that went wrong wasn't going to be a brick wall to his career. He had never been ambitious about being something. It was doing what he wanted to do that he held on to. It didn't get much better than being chief of Major Crimes, not if you wanted to be a prosecutor. And Jamison loved being a prosecutor. He glanced up at the closed door at the end of the long hallway, the office of *the* district attorney, the top of the ladder.

District Attorney William Gage had been the district attorney of Tenaya County for twenty-three years. He was good at it. Gage understood the politics of the office and the power of the office. Now rumor had it that he had been tapped to be the Democratic candidate for attorney general of the state. In a state like California, it was fairly certain that a Democrat would be elected attorney general and if the party backed you, it was also fairly certain you would be the Democrat elected.

As one of the people with an office close to Gage's, Jamison was aware that the rumors were true. He was also acutely aware that if Gage did become the attorney general, then despite his age, Matt Jamison was considered by many a likely choice to be the next district attorney of Tenaya County. While he kept his own counsel when others asked him what-if questions, he couldn't help thinking about the big what-if. However, Jamison knew at least one thing. While he had a vague idea that someday he wanted to be district attorney he wasn't sure he was ready for that yet, leaving behind the adrenaline rush of trial to push paper and policy. For right now he loved what he did. He also knew he had time and that there were several more senior prosecutors and the chief assistant who also were counting their place in line. He could wait his turn unless, because of political pressure and plain opportunity, he had little choice. He'd been around long enough to learn that sometimes opportunity only came once and you either grabbed the ring on the professional merry-go-round or you spent the rest of your career just riding in circles.

Jamison dropped the pile of messages on the chair in his office. There wasn't an empty spot on his desk. He immediately walked back out and turned toward Gage's office. Gage's secretary caught his eye as he walked past, and in the silent body communication that people used Jamison nodded his head toward the DA's door with a question on his face. She smiled her acknowledgment with a slight nod. "He's waiting for you. I've been hearing him pace in there since I walked in this morning."

He gave a soft knock on the heavy door, at the same time opening it before there was an answer. Bill Gage had his broad back to the door, the suspenders straining across his age-expanded frame. He was staring out the window that gave him a panorama of the city, backdropped by the Sierra Nevada Mountains to the east. There were still peaks of snow clinging to the higher mountains that were visible through the building haze of spring. It wouldn't be long before the fierce Valley heat melted all the snow, the frigid snowmelt flowing down into rivers and reservoirs that would keep the Valley green and feed the thirsty fields that drove the Valley economy.

Gage could see Jamison's reflection mirrored on the expanse of plate glass window. He didn't turn, continuing to look at the view of his jurisdiction as far as the eye could see, and if fortune smiled on him, farther than he could see.

"Good morning, Matt. I've been waiting for you." He made a backhanded gesture toward a chair. Gage's voice didn't carry its usual bonhomie. There was an edge of stress and impatience. He sighed noticeably and walked behind the large expanse of mahogany desktop. Gage sat heavily in the black leather high-backed chair and placed both his hands together on the desk, staring straight at Jamison for a number of seconds before he spoke. "Something's come up and I want you to personally handle it."

Fixing his eyes on Jamison, Gage shoved a stapled sheaf of paper across the desk. Jamison could see the heading. It was some kind of order from the state supreme court. All Gage said was, "Read it." That was it. Whatever was in it Jamison could see had upset his boss. He'd been around long enough to know that Bill Gage didn't let people see him get upset very often.

Jamison scanned the crisp heading at the top of the paper, *THE SUPREME COURT OF THE STATE OF CALIFORNIA*, and the caption on the upper left side of the paper, *In Re the Matter of Richard Harker, Petitioner*. Jamison knew the name. Anybody who paid attention to criminal cases in the Central Valley knew the name and everybody in the Tenaya County District Attorney's Office knew the name of Richard "Rick" Harker. That was a name that went with a notorious murder case, the case that made William Gage the district attorney of Tenaya County. It had sparked outrage across the state of California and cost the trial judge his office after he refused to impose the death penalty the jury had recommended. Jamison scrolled down the page, skipping over the formal language that seemed to accompany anything from an appellate court and especially the supreme court, although Jamison's experience with the supreme court was rather limited. Whatever it was, Jamison knew from the district attorney's standpoint it couldn't be good, especially with the way Gage was reacting to it.

Jamison had seen petitions from Harker before. His appeal had been denied nearly two decades ago, but every few years he seemed to crawl back out of the dark recesses of the prison he was in just long enough to send another petition attesting to his innocence. This was the first one that got more than a paragraph response ending in *petition denied*. Jamison had heard there was a petition that had been filed about a year ago in the superior court that had been denied, and he had let the Harker case recede to the back of his mind like so many others. Even the Charlie Manson case that happened years before Jamison was born popped up every now and then when Manson filed a writ and got his whole case repeated in the paper. Jamison looked at notorious murderers like cockroaches who inhabited the dark but occasionally made a dash into the light. Now it appeared Harker was back.

He kept reading before Gage's impatient voice broke his concentration. "The damn supreme court has ordered that Harker get a hearing on his petition. That son of a bitch convinced those ivory tower justices, or at least four of them anyway, that maybe something was wrong with his trial. I don't need this now, dredging that case up and some ponytail defense lawyer arguing that Harker should get another trial."

Jamison quickly took in the details of the order, ignoring Gage's character-izations. "Bill, this doesn't say that the supreme court found any of Harker's claims to be true. It just found that his claims need to be looked into. He hasn't got anything. I'm surprised they even considered it, let alone ordered a hearing. So he has a hearing. It won't take long. You know that. You're the one who slammed the cell door shut on Harker when I was still in grade school." He paused for a moment before adding a more cynical observation. "Besides, the press will report on the crime and remind all the voters out there that you were the one who put him in prison. Then he'll go back to San Quentin."

Gage's hands were so tightly clasped that his knuckles were white. "He's going to make claims that the press will report and that will bring out all the bleeding hearts. I don't want any publicity that distracts from what's maybe going to happen in the next month. This is my time." Gage paused, his eyes settling uncomfortably on Jamison. "And if the political rumor mill has any credibility, this may be your time too. The last few cases you've handled along with that doctor who killed all those women has made you a press favorite. Every little bit helps."

Jamison didn't answer. He didn't like discussing the case involving Dr. Alex St. Claire. He had handled it, but the jury's justice wasn't what St. Claire deserved. In the end, St. Claire got street justice delivered twice through the chest. The shooter had never been caught. Jamison kept it to himself that maybe not catching the shooter was for the best. It was an ugly case. It didn't help that Jamison had allowed his judgment to be clouded by the surviving victim. In the end, he wasn't even sure if she was a victim. Just like the identity of the shooter, he didn't want to really know if she was more than a victim. That was past history now also. But the publicity for him and the district attorney's office had been positive, so he knew that in Gage's eyes, Jamison came out of it as a winner.

Whether Jamison thought of himself as a winner when he turned off the light at night was another thing Jamison kept to himself. But he had learned that the higher you climbed the ladder, the harder the decisions and the choices were and the less clear everything was.

He fiddled with the supreme court order. Jamison didn't want to ask the question because he didn't want to hear the answer, but he had to ask anyway. "So, what do you want to do with this?"

The words came out of Gage's mouth like the staccato burst of a machine gun. "I want it handled by somebody in this office who doesn't have his head up his ass and also understands the politics and ramifications of this."

Jamison could feel his mouth involuntarily twitching into a grimace. He had an idea where this was going. He had a major trial coming up and he didn't have time for something like this. "We've got a couple of really bright deputies that are good law guys. I can have one of them brief this up for you and then handle it. I'll personally keep an eye on it."

In every district attorney's office, there were trial lawyers and there were law guys who had a more academic bent. Trial lawyers were a lot like gunfighters. They shot what moved. Law guys thought about it and used more technical legal arguments. They tended to look before they pulled the trigger. They were the lawyers who argued dance-on-the-head-of-a-pin search and seizure motions. Most of them weren't top gunfighters but the aggressive trial lawyers needed law guys and law guys needed the trial people. It was a symbiotic relationship. Then there were a few lawyers who could do both. That trait was one of the things that had rapidly moved Jamison up. He could do both, but he preferred being a trial guy. The technicalities of the law didn't get his juices flowing. There were a few others in the ranks of the office he had been cultivating and keeping his eye on. *Maybe one of them would work for this?* He was mulling over the list in his mind when Gage's voice broke through. "I want *you* to personally handle it. Nobody else. *You*. Whatever else you have I want you to push it aside. *You*." Gage kept his large hand cupped into a fist that rested on his desk, but his thick index finger was pointed straight at Jamison.

"Bill, don't you think it would attract less attention if one of the regular law and motion guys did this? I mean, is there something to worry about here? A reporter might wonder why the chief of Major Crimes is handling a motion like this if there's nothing to it. Why not treat it as just more whining from Harker? The guy's lucky he didn't end up in the gas chamber or with a needle in his arm." Jamison dropped the gratuitous comment that always came up with discussions of Harker. "If that judge—what was his name?—yeah, Judge Stevenson, hadn't refused to impose the death penalty the jury recommended maybe Harker would have gotten what he deserved a long time ago."

Gage didn't bite. "*You*. I want *you* to handle it personally. Send that son of a bitch back to his hole in San Quentin so he can rot there for the rest of his miserable damned life." Gage raised his arm and again pointed his index finger across the desk. "You want to sit in the big chair? *You* handle it." Gage's eyes narrowed as he raised his chin, settling back in his chair.

Unconsciously rolling the order into a tube. Jamison stood up. "Okay, Bill. I'll have to move some things around. I may need to pull in an investigator."

"Pull in whoever you want. Just take care of it!" Gage abruptly swiveled his chair around and started staring again out the plate glass window.

Chapter 3

Jamison walked back into his office. He picked up the discarded messages on his chair and dropped them near the phone, hoping he wouldn't bury them under the slowly growing pile of paper that never seemed to get smaller. He unrolled the three-page order, smoothing its curling edges as he laid it on the desk. *What the hell was the supreme court doing with Harker?* It was a case that was long past the memories of those judges and almost everyone else unless you had been around at the time. But every time Gage made a speech or got introduced there was always somebody who remembered the Harker case and brought it up. And when brand-new deputy DAs came into the office and underwent their mandatory training sessions, the Harker case was always a point of instruction.

He unrolled the order and spread it on his desk. It was a writ of habeas corpus. The term basically was Latin for "bring the body." It was used when someone was trying to convince a judge or an appellate court that he deserved a hearing because something wrong happened in his case that hadn't been brought out in the trial. Most of the time they were just gripe sheets and were routinely and unceremoniously denied. Jamison knew there were guys in the joint who earned cigarettes and money from other prisoners just by writing writs.

Jamison snorted to himself. Jailhouse lawyers. Capitalism behind prison walls. Some of them had even once been lawyers themselves but now, the fall from grace complete, their hourly fee was measured in tobacco and whatever else was the currency of prisoners.

If the reviewing court decided that the allegations in the writ deserved a hearing, then the prisoner would be brought before the court, a lawyer would be assigned at taxpayer expense, and the prisoner would get his hearing. Most cases didn't involve the issue of whether the prisoner had gotten a fair trial, but a few did. A prisoner could lose his case on appeal and then file a writ arguing that his lawyer failed to bring in a vital piece of evidence that would have shown he was innocent, or at least not guilty. If the allegations in the writ were of sufficient seriousness to arguably make a difference if true, then the prisoner would get a hearing for a judge to evaluate the actual merits of the claim and use his or her judgment to determine if the new facts would really have potentially made any difference had they been presented. However, the alleged new facts had to be such that they might actually make a difference.

The problem, Jamison thought, is not the use of the writ of habeas corpus to address serious issues, but its use to complain about trivial things from the quality of the food in jail to the quality of toilet paper. Jamison had only seen a few that had any merit at all, but those that did received hearings and sometimes, although rarely, they obtained new trials.

But Harker was a different story. Harker had been in jail for over twenty-six years for a murder that people still talked about because of its brutality. At that time Bill Gage had been in a position similar to the one Jamison now held. Gage had asked for the death penalty and the jury determined that Harker should get the death penalty. In fact, the jury had returned a death verdict in a matter of hours, emphatically demonstrating what they thought of Harker.

Then after a hearing at sentencing, the trial judge had exercised his power and rejected the death penalty. That judge had ordered Harker to spend the rest of his life in prison without possibility of parole. He had spared Harker's life, and at the next election it had cost him his judgeship. That was one thing most people didn't realize about the death penalty; a judge couldn't override a jury's rejection of the death penalty and impose it, but a judge did literally hold the power of life and death because he could reject the decision of the jury to impose death.

Judge Walker Stevenson's career never recovered, and Jamison recalled that the few times he had seen the now defrocked Mr. Stevenson he had been sitting by himself at local bar association functions, serving his purgatory in the isolation of peer exclusion.

Harker had appeals that went all the way to the United States Supreme Court, with him claiming his innocence and the prosecution trying to undo what Judge Stevenson did. None had been successful. The courts closed the door on Harker's appeal and since what Judge Stevenson did was discretionary and within his power, they upheld the sentence. Harker went to prison for life without possibility of parole and now when his name came up, the face of the man himself was only a distant memory. But the facts of his crime were not forgotten. Some crimes never get forgotten and just Harker's name would cause people in the community to shudder whether they knew exactly what he did or not.

Jamison began to skip through the archaic language at the top of the writ and cut to the chase. *What was it that Harker had asserted that got William Gage so upset?* It didn't take him long. Harker alleged again of course that he was actually innocent and that he had been railroaded by perjured testimony and biased eyewitness testimony. Jamison pulled the corner of his mouth to the left side. *So far, it's the usual.* He continued to read. Harker claimed that he had told the sheriff's detective that one of the major witnesses had admitted he had lied. According to Harker that evidence had not been disclosed because the detective lied about it when he testified and so had the witness. He claimed that the witness, Clarence Foster, had ended up an inmate in the same prison with Harker and eventually admitted it.

Jamison leaned back in his chair. *Okay, so Harker claimed that detectives suppressed evidence. Convicted criminals claimed that all the time. How had this gotten the attention of the supreme court?* Jamison read a little further. From the description in the order, it looked like the petition had been filed in the Tenaya County Superior Court and the criminal law and motion judge, Judge Reynolds, had denied the petition without a hearing. Harker had filed again in the court of appeal and it got denied there also. Then it got to the supreme court and they decided Harker deserved a hearing.

The usual way these matters were handled was by looking to see if the accusations were sufficiently credible to warrant further examination. Granting a hearing didn't mean that the judge thought they were true. It just meant the judge concluded there was enough there that it should be given a hearing and the prisoner should be given the opportunity to prove in court what the facts were, if he could, assuming he could make a reasonable showing that his assertions might have some merit. The full hearing was to decide if they actually did have any merit.

Evidently some staff lawyer at the supreme court had looked at the conviction and then at Harker's writ petition and recommended that Harker should have been given a hearing.

Jamison shook his head to nobody in particular. This was why death penalty cases never seemed to end. What the public thought of as endless appeals were actually endless writs where defendants made constant claims about things their lawyer should have done or claims of evidence that wasn't introduced. The more serious the case, the greater the possibility that some sympathetic appellate staff lawyer would feel his or her sense of justice being pricked and take it to a judge who would feel his or her sense of justice being pricked—and a guy who had been convicted of the ax murder of his wife would get a hearing about whether his trial was unfair. As far as Jamison was concerned the claims were usually about as substantial as why they got a spanking that traumatized them for life and the jury didn't hear that in deciding whether they should be found guilty—or sentenced to death.

Jamison wasn't very sympathetic. He had acquired the common prosecutor's contempt for judges whose sense of justice was contemplated within wood paneled rooms with deep carpets instead of looking at savaged bodies on the floor while investigators and prosecutors like Jamison stepped around pooled blood. Intellectually Jamison knew he wasn't being fair. Those judges had their job to do and he had his. But he couldn't help thinking that maybe those judges would be a little less sympathetic if they actually had to smell and see a homicide scene or hold the desperate hand of a savagely battered woman clinging to what was left of her dignity and life while some stranger tried to collect evidence of rape.

Jamison looked at the signature at the end of the last page, the chief justice. Pretty standard stuff except the order came from the supreme court. *Okay, Judge Reynolds should have given Harker a hearing.* All the supreme court decided was that Harker had shown enough to get a hearing and reversed Judge Reynolds's decision that there wasn't a sufficient showing. Now he would get his hearing and then get sent back into his hole at San Quentin.

Jamison knew enough about the Harker case to know that there was a mountain of evidence of his guilt. The thing that tugged at Jamison was why this had gotten the district attorney's bowels in such an uproar. *There's nothing here that defendants don't say all the time. They always say everybody was lying about them. What were they going to say? Everybody is telling the truth about them?*

Jamison reached over and hit his speaker phone button, then punched in the three-digit code for Veronica Castellon in the office pool. As soon as she answered Jamison began the start of the process. "Veronica, I want you to have one of the office assistants go over to the storage room and pull the file on Richard Harker. I don't have the case number, but it shouldn't be too hard to find. It's going to be a big file, probably in three or four boxes at least. Have it brought to me as soon as it's pulled. Also send me the file on the writ petition in the Harker case that was denied last year. It should be in a separate file." Jamison paused for a moment. "Oh, and, Veronica, make sure you tell them to clean the mouse droppings off before they bring the boxes. The last time I got one of these old files I had to have shots because of the poop that was on the file boxes. Thanks."

Jamison could hear Veronica laugh. Files this old were kept in storage for years along with the evidence in the cases. While some of the cases ultimately ended up being destroyed just to make room, that didn't happen for years and cases like Harker's never got destroyed. The files just sat, moldering away in a dark corner holding the paper record of people's lives and their sins. This case had been tried before Veronica was born, and when the crime had been committed Jamison was still in grade school.

Jamison let his mind wander for a moment. Veronica was the object of constant attention by the young lawyers in the office. None seemed to ever get anywhere, but Jamison had a feeling that his attention might be welcome. However, one thing Matt Jamison realized a long time ago with a resigned sigh was that you don't fish in the office secretarial pond, not if you want to stay out of trouble. And given that most of Jamison's contact with members of the opposite sex was either with DAs or defense attorneys or secretaries in the office, the pond he had to fish in wasn't very big. And most female defense attorneys were usually in his face telling him what was wrong with his case or him rather than flirting. He was tired of his mother asking him when he was going to meet a nice girl.

Jamison pulled out a yellow legal pad, letting the momentary thought pop up as to why legal pads were always yellow. He dismissed it and wrote Harker's name at the top of the pad. Then he began to outline the things he would need to do. The first thing he had to do was read the file and that was probably going to take a few days in and of itself. Then he had to talk to whomever the court had assigned to Harker's case so the logistics of it could be worked out. And he needed to get an investigator, which meant he was going to have to pull an overworked investigator from other cases to work on this one.

Jamison already knew the investigator he was going to use was Bill O'Hara. He just didn't want to go down and deliver the news because of the reaction he would get. Willie Jefferson O'Hara was a seasoned homicide investigator who was like a grumpy old dog that basically tolerated the people who fed him. Actually, Bill O'Hara—"Willie" to those who knew him well—mostly cultivated his crusty persona to keep people at a distance until he decided whether to let them in his inner circle. Then he was only irascible depending on his mood instead of all the time.

Jamison had long ago decided that he would put his life in O'Hara's hands without a moment's hesitation and had in fact done exactly that on several occasions. Jamison did a mental nod to himself. *Yes, O'Hara's the right investigator for this.* He decided to spare himself O'Hara's reaction for the time being and read the rest of the writ petition first. Whatever was in that would tell him why the supreme court had issued the order that was sitting on the edge of his desk and, he suspected, would also tell him why the district attorney was so agitated.

Fifteen minutes later, Veronica brought in the file on the writ petition. It was stuffed with notes and the declarations and other written arguments that had been submitted by Harker's lawyer to Judge Reynolds and denied without a formal hearing. Jamison looked at the assignment sheet. One of the law and motion deputy district attorneys had handled the file, Franklin Bailey. Jamison pulled an image of Bailey from the back of his mind—young, good law school, a little bookish, liked digging through arcane legal trivia. It all fit, perfect law and motion guy. He started to pick up the phone to talk to Bailey, then put the receiver back down. It was probably best if he read that part of the file first. At least maybe it would give him an idea of what got the attention of the supreme court.

Two hours later, Jamison had separated out the declarations and notes. The declarations were written statements made under oath. They weren't subject to cross-examination and were basically statements that a judge reviewed to determine that *if* the declarations were true and *if* the information was unknown at the time of trial, whether there was any reason to question the credibility of the verdict.

The first declaration in the case was by Harker himself, claiming that while in prison, an inmate named Clarence Foster had allegedly admitted that he had lied to the police when they had interrogated him and he had fingered Harker as being at the scene of the crime.

Jamison then read Harker's declaration that he had told detectives that the witnesses, including Foster, were lying, but nobody paid any attention to him. He put the declaration down for a moment. *That couldn't be what got the supreme court to issue its order, could it?* Obviously, Foster had snitched on Harker. Anybody going into the joint with a snitch jacket would have a hard time. So Foster had an incentive to ingratiate himself with Harker since he was one of the people who put him there. Jamison considered for a moment that Foster was actually lucky to be alive given that Jamison doubted Harker was the forgiving type and prison rules were essentially predator rules with very few absolutes about the sanctity or worth of human life. This included the rule that snitches were a life form slightly above child molesters.

He rummaged through the rest of the file, but there wasn't any declaration from Foster. That didn't mean it didn't exist, but it wasn't in the file. And, in any event, he couldn't believe the supreme court would order a hearing based on some inmate claiming he lied to the police. It took more than that to get a writ hearing. First Harker's lawyer would have to show that there was some reason for the investigators to know that Foster was lying and either conceal it or ignore it. Or they would have to show that the testimony could not have been discovered by reasonable investigation.

You couldn't just go back and keep reopening cases simply because somebody now said they lied unless there was more to it. Jamison knew that there had to be a lot more. Then he saw the name on the next declaration—Christine Farrow. It had been submitted on behalf of the defendant, Richard Harker—the man who killed Christine Farrow's mother.

Chapter 4

Jamison reread the declaration of Christine Farrow for the third time. It hadn't changed through a single reread. He picked up the photograph of the child taken at the crime scene slightly over a quarter century ago. At the time it was taken she was three and Jamison would have been almost eight years old. He tried to remember what it was like to be three years old. Only bits and pieces flashed through his mind. It was almost impossible to put the pieces of childhood memory in any order, let alone relate them to how old he was when the memory was created.

Childhood memories were like a jumble of snapshots and two-second videos. It was parents or adults who put those images in context. Jamison realized that what he remembered from his childhood was a combination of how he had chosen to remember things and feelings that affected his memory. But he also realized that nothing in his life compared to what Christine Farrow had been through.

Jamison thought about what Christine's memories must be like and whether the mind would bury it as an act of self-preservation. Some things were simply so horrible that the human mind closed the door and kept such images in the dark. But Jamison knew that didn't mean the memory wasn't still there. The memories were always there, concealed in the recesses of the mind, lurking and waiting and sometimes springing out like a nighttime intruder.

The declaration of Christine Farrow was all of that and more.

Harker's appointed counsel, Samuel Gifford, had gone to her as part of a routine investigation into his client's claims of innocence and the supposed admission of Clarence Foster that he had lied. Jamison could only imagine what Gifford thought when he finished talking to a now twenty-nine-year-old woman reliving a memory that should never be a part of anybody's childhood.

Christine Farrow's declaration was written in the first person. Jamison's eyes moved back and forth over the words of an adult visualizing what she remembered as a three-year-old child.

SUPREME COURT
STATE OF CALIFORNIA

IN RE THE MATTER OF
RICHARD HARKER   *DECLARATION OF*
V   *CHRISTINE FARROW*
PEOPLE OF THE STATE OF CALIFORNIA

My name is Christine Farrow. I am twenty-nine years of age. I live in Tenaya County, California. Twenty-six years ago my mother, Lisa Farrow, was the victim of murder. I was there. I was three years old. Richard Harker was convicted of murdering my mother. I testified that Richard Harker was the person who killed my mother.

For the last twenty-six years I have believed what I was told about what happened to my mother and to me and what little I thought I remembered. I have struggled with emotions and pieces of memory, but when I tried to recall exactly what happened I would suffer from anxiety attacks. For the last five years I have been receiving psychological counseling.

Last year, with the help of my therapist, Dr. Arnold Vinson, I was finally able to bring forward my memories. Dr. Vinson helped me to cope with the images that have made my life so difficult. Now I know the truth.

All my life I have believed that Richard Harker killed my mother. I have read the police reports and understand that is what I testified to in court. I identified Richard Harker as the man who was in our home the night my mother, Lisa Farrow, was murdered.

I now realize that the man who killed my mother was not Richard Harker. I am certain I made a mistake. I was only three years old. I now understand that Richard Harker is innocent and that my testimony as a child was wrong. I am prepared to testify that I now remember that the person who killed my mother was not the man I identified in court."

CHRISTINE FARROW, Under Penalty of Perjury.
Christine Farrow

A chill went down Jamison's spine. He knew the basic facts in the Harker case, but he didn't know the details, the evidence used to convict Harker. Was the only actual witness to the murder of Lisa Farrow a child, three-year-old Christine Farrow? And now she was willing to testify that Richard Harker was innocent?

He could feel himself cringing. If Christine Farrow testified in court that Harker was not the man who murdered her mother, then the hearing would turn into a media circus. No wonder Gage was agitated. His career had been built on the conviction of Richard Harker and now the supreme court had granted a hearing that would put the entire core of that conviction in question. Jamison could see the headlines in his mind—Child-Witness Now Claims Convicted Murderer Is Innocent—District Attorney and Rumored Candidate for Attorney General Built Career on Wrongful Conviction.

Jamison had seen similar declarations before, usually in child molestation cases. Small children were asked what happened to them in the most horrible situations and asked to describe who did it to them and what they did. Jamison had worked on sexual assault cases for almost a year until he couldn't stand it anymore. He had grown to hate the people who hurt little human beings and finally asked to be moved to a different assignment. It wasn't an uncommon request. Many men had difficulty with the assignment. Women prosecutors seemed to handle it better. Jamison wasn't sure why that was, but he had quickly realized that he couldn't keep doing it and keep his sanity.

But he had also seen some of those cases come back years later, a few of those children, now adults, struggling with their memories. It didn't happen often but sometimes they recanted their original testimony. Usually it was because it was a relative who had been their tormentor and other family members prevailed on them to change their minds or made them uncertain that what they had said was correct. But sometimes they simply became uncertain, and the passage of time and unjustified guilt over what they had been through seemed to persuade them that it must have been a mistake. Jamison didn't understand the psychology of it, but he knew at the time it was reported that it was very real to those children because he had heard them say it, and he had also heard some of those now grown children say it wasn't true.

Then declarations would be filed and people who were in prison for the most awful sex crimes would find their accuser becoming their savior as they changed their testimony. Victims would again be victimized by the destructive forces of memory and the mystery of the human mind as it tried to reconcile the horror of the past with the wreckage of the present. What was real or wasn't real was blurred by time and the jumble of childhood images that had no context.

Jamison had himself fought several of these recanted testimony battles in court years after the fact. One of the issues in those cases was always the credibility of the child victims, three- and four-year-old children trying to answer questions about what happened to them and who did it. First there was the problem of a child trying to explain something that they didn't have the words for. Then there was the problem of that child, now an anguished adult, trying to explain why they thought what they testified to and believed at the time was the truth was not in fact the truth.

It had always pained Jamison that children were asked to describe sexual activity that at their age they shouldn't even begin to understand, let alone be victims of. And then there was the problem that by the time he was able to talk to the child, numerous other people, mostly well intentioned, had talked to the child, sometimes parents, sometimes babysitters, sometimes strangers just trying to help and then cops and prosecutors. And sometimes defense attorneys.

Jamison had come to realize that a child's understanding of things was a layered process of explanation and memory, context and experience. A child had difficulty relating what they had not previously experienced, and their innocence took away the context that adults had. So when an adult talked to a child, the child picked up cues and understanding from the adult asking them questions. Experience had taught him that the initial questions asked of a child and repeated questioning would affect their explanation and memory.

He had learned that years ago. When these children were first questioned by well-meaning investigators, there had been little training in how to talk to children. Now investigators were trained by specialists in the field of child and victim psychology.

Children wanted to please. It was very easy to get a child to say what an adult wanted to hear. Then in repeating what the adult wanted to hear, it became part of the child's memory, and then, to the child, it became the truth. Jamison searched his mind for the word—confabulation. Was that what he was looking at? Surely the conviction of Richard Harker didn't rest on the accusation of a three-year-old? There had to be more.

Jamison had tried death penalty cases. There had to be a lot more. Now he needed to find out what more there was.

Chapter 5

L ate in the morning, there was a knock on the door casing leading into Jamison's office. One of the office assistants had a two-wheeled dolly stacked with three boxes of files. It was obvious from looking at the cardboard containers that they had been so tightly packed the corners were strained. Moisture and time had softened the cardboard and the box on the bottom of the pile was sagging under the weight.

Jamison's only thought was that three boxes were going to take a lot of time to go through, but it wasn't as bad as he feared. Then the assistant told him that there were four more in the outer office that he still had to bring in. The assistant could tell from Jamison's reaction that the thought of additional boxes wasn't good news. He grinned. "I guess you'll have some light reading for the next few days." He laughed. "Oh, and I cleaned them off for you." Veronica had passed on his message.

Jamison stared at the two piles of stacked boxes. The DA file number and the name *People v Richard Harker* was written in black flow pen on the front and side of each box. Hopefully he wouldn't have to read the entire trial transcript. That was probably over twenty thousand pages. He knew that files like this were often disorganized. After a trial, paper got stuffed into storage boxes. There wasn't a lot of concern about preserving order and cataloging files for history or for somebody else to wade through.

As Jamison knew from his colleagues and his own experience, trial lawyers were like gunfighters; they shot and when their work was done they walked away from the mess left behind. So, cleanup was not going to be meticulous. Besides, most prosecutors went from one case immediately to the next and left the rest of it to appellate lawyers, only occasionally revisiting their old cases. Multiple hands rummaged through cases, making them even more disorganized. In big cases that came back on appeal or writs, it was not uncommon that the prosecutor who tried a case would have left the office for the bigger money of private practice or maybe even retired. Harker's trial file was twenty-five years old and the murder itself was over twenty-six years ago. Jamison was surprised the cardboard boxes hadn't split apart under the weight of more boxes that would have been piled atop them, like the slowly building accretion of a river bank or the colored striations of a canyon that created many layers with the passage of time.

He waited as long as the few seconds of passive resistance would allow and walked over to the stack. First, he needed to find the beginning. He knew that was going to be a problem the minute he opened the box on top. Manila file folders were labeled with witness names and reference designations like "blood evidence," and were filed in an order that probably made sense to Gage when he tried the case but would be a maze to anybody else. Plus, the tracking slip on the box at the top told him that the writ attorney, Franklin Bailey, as well as a few other names of deputy district attorneys from the past, had rummaged through the case, adding to the confusion. Jamison sighed and began pulling paper out, flipping open folders and closing them as he tried to put the Harker case back together.

⤻

Jamison stretched his arms. He had been at it for hours. He was tired of organizing files when he didn't know the basic story. He was still separating paper and he wasn't there yet. That would start with what the officers on the scene had found. Everything built from there, and that was where Jamison would start. But he had to find it. He knew that the investigation of criminal cases, particularly major cases, was built in layers. First there was the initial responding officer and his or her perceptions. Then there were the detectives' reports and so on until the case built itself sufficiently for there to be an arrest. And then the district attorney would take over with his or her investigator, sending out more investigation requests and breaking the case down into pieces that could be put in front of the jury.

It was like figuring out what the story was and then figuring out the best way to tell the story. At the end of telling the story the jury would write the closing line. All of that was in these boxes. Or, Jamison thought, hopefully all of that is in the boxes. Matt Jamison had been around enough of these cases to know that sometimes little pieces of files didn't get put back into the box and you had to figure out what wasn't there and then where to find it.

Four hours of burrowing through paper and Jamison finally found the initial crime scene investigation reports. He decided to quit organizing for a while and sit down and read. The aged paper bent limply in his hands but almost three decades had not softened the impact of the words.

Sheriff's reports never changed in format and the Harker case was no different. There were printed boxes on the face page for every category to ensure that vital information was cataloged. In the upper left corner there was a name, Lisa Farrow. To the right of her name was the word "victim."

There were numbers for every crime based on the penal code. Next to Lisa Farrow's name the category of crime was PC 187, murder. The reports were impersonal. There was no emotion in them. All the emotion comes from the narrative of the officer's observations and the visualization that comes with people reading, it having seen similar crimes before. If you had seen it before, you could smell it and you could feel it. But even though Matt Jamison had been to more than his share of homicide scenes, he wasn't prepared for this.

According to his report, Deputy John Kinster arrived at 9:12 a.m., responding to a dispatch call regarding a body in a house at 224 East Flower Street. Jamison knew the area. It was a poor neighborhood of slowly disintegrating wooden homes. Its pitted asphalt streets were continually put at the bottom of street crew projects so that they never reached the top. He had been there more than once on homicide investigations that some areas of town generated like weeds in the sidewalks. The thought flicked through his mind at the irony of calling it Flower Street. He doubted that any flowers were planted along the front yards of homes that sheltered people holding on to bare subsistence.

Kinster's report stated that outside the residence there were two women waiting, Maria Castillo and Nancy Slaven. Next to them was a little girl, later identified as Christine Farrow. Jamison read slowly, trying to visualize the scene.

Slaven said that she and Castillo were neighbors of a woman named Lisa Farrow. They had gone over to visit. When they walked up on the wooden porch steps they could see that there was damage to the curtains. It looked like they had been partially burned or blackened. Castillo knocked. When there was no answer they decided to open the door, which was unlocked. The first thing that hit them was the smell. Then they saw Lisa Farrow's body on the floor in the kitchen. The women were unable to further describe what they had seen. Both women were crying and extremely emotional.

Slaven did get out that Christine, the little girl with them, was Lisa's daughter. They had found her sitting on a chair in the kitchen area. She was covered with soot. When Castillo tried to get Christine to come outside with them she wouldn't leave. All she said was, "Rick did it." After that she wouldn't talk at all. Slaven had finally picked her up and carried her outside while Castillo called the sheriff. Neither woman had gone back inside.

Jamison looked at the age listed on the report for Christine. She was three.

Deputy Kinster entered the house and observed the victim lying faceup with her arms and legs stretched out. She was wearing no clothing on the lower part of her body. A red T-shirt was pulled up, exposing her breasts. Kinster could visually observe that the victim was deceased. To Jamison that meant that Kinster hadn't disturbed the crime scene by checking the victim to see if she was still alive. Anything or anybody that touched the body became more evidence to sift through and more fodder for defense attorneys to claim the crime scene was contaminated. The other thing Kinster observed was the faint odor of a flammable liquid like gasoline or lighter fluid.

He read carefully through Kinster's description of the injuries. Jamison knew that detailed descriptions would be in later reports, but the initial description by the first responding officer was important to establish the position and condition of the body. How wounds were inflicted was often critical to the process of establishing what happened.

There were lacerations on Lisa Farrow's arms that were consistent with defensive wounds suffered when she had tried to shield her face. There was a gaping wound to her neck where she had been slashed.

It was evident to Jamison that Kinster also had difficulty describing the crime scene because he said only that he quickly determined the scene needed to be secured and left out the normal details. Jamison pulled out photographs of the crime scene to look at while he read Kinster's report. When he looked at the photographs, Jamison understood Kinster's inability to convey what he saw.

Even after looking at pictures of numerous homicide scenes as well as actually being at a substantial number of murder sites, Jamison had difficulty staring at the pictures. The lower portion of Farrow's body was charred. Something flammable had been poured over the bottom area of her body and set on fire. From the appearance of the photographs, the fire had spread to a rug that Farrow was lying on and that had added to the flames until they burned off whatever accelerant that had been used and died down to a smolder. Jamison imagined that the soot that covered the child was from the smoldering rug. He shuddered at the thought that it could be from anything else.

Jamison shuffled through the pile of photographs taken by the forensic team. There were beer cans on the kitchen table and on the counter. There were several charred beer cans between the victim's legs. A full ash tray was on the table and there was a broken knife on the floor.

Carefully he laid the photographs out on his desk. Then he rummaged through the same box until he found reports labeled "Autopsy."

The pathologist's report concluded Lisa Farrow's throat had been cut in one powerful slashing motion. She would have gone almost immediately into shock and been dead in no more than a minute or two. The throat wound severed the trachea, the carotid artery on the right side, and most of the supporting muscles of the neck. The wounds on her forearms were consistent with her trying to protect herself against her attacker as the knife was swung. Her face showed bruising to her jaw and lips. She had been struck, probably at least once by a fist and likely several more times. Her left eye was swollen shut. The pathologist found evidence of burning from the knees to the waistline and determined the fire had been concentrated in the genital region. The entire vaginal area and much of the musculature of the thighs had been consumed by fire.

Pulling the reports of the first detectives on scene, Jamison concluded that apparently arson investigators had been called in by the detectives. They had moved around the crime scene but made a quick determination the fire had been intentionally set. Based on the pictures, Jamison knew that conclusion was no surprise.

There had been a smoke alarm in the kitchen, but the cover was slightly ajar. It was an old house and the smoke alarm was apparently battery driven instead of wired in. There was no battery. Jamison speculated to himself that the alarm had probably started to beep when the battery was getting low and to stop the beeping someone had pulled it out and never replaced it. Or, maybe the killer pulled it out before he set the fire, just to make sure the fire obliterated the evidence before anyone came in and discovered the body. The only problem with that plan was that he had used magazines placed under the body as fuel for the fire. Magazines were dense and they didn't burn as easily as people thought. They had probably flashed with the accelerant and then died down to smolder with the rug. That was the only thing that saved the house and the body from going up in flames. That was probably what saved the little girl.

Jamison looked at the photographs of three-year-old Christine Farrow taken at the scene. She was holding a stuffed rabbit. Except where someone had cleaned her face, she was covered by a layer of black soot, and the stuffed rabbit was also covered with grime, although it was difficult to tell how much of the grime on the rabbit was from soot or from hours of being loved. It took no imagination for Jamison to realize that the child had sat in the kitchen tightly hugging her rabbit while the smoldering rug desecrated her mother's body. He hoped that the child's age somehow would spare her the horror of what it would be almost impossible for an adult to get out of their mind.

And now the man who had done this savagery was going to get to come out of his cell at San Quentin and be in the sunlight outside of prison walls once again. Jamison leaned back in his chair. He had seen a lot of brutal murders, but the viciousness of this caused him to draw in his breath.

Most people who commit murder will panic because they killed in anger. When they realize what they've done they don't think clearly and they make clumsy efforts to conceal the crime or they simply run. Jamison could see that the person who killed Lisa Farrow was trying to conceal what he did by burning the evidence, only the evidence was a human being. It was clear to Jamison that Lisa Farrow had either been sexually assaulted or sexual assault had been attempted. Her killer had the presence of mind to try to destroy the evidence of what he had done. It wasn't the brutality of the of act of murder that shocked Jamison anymore. But in this case, it was that someone could have so little feeling for what they had done. They had set a fire, leaving that little girl in the house. Whether they knew the child was there or cared was not something that had even teased at their conscience.

Jamison pulled out a booking photograph from the stack of pictures. Staring back at him was Richard "Rick" Harker from over twenty-six years ago. Jamison wondered what he looked like now. Soon enough he would know. Jamison looked at the face of a young man backdropped by height designations on the wall behind him. Most men under arrest and being processed had to be ordered to look at the camera as they absorbed the reality of their situation. Harker stared straight into the camera. Jamison immediately noticed Harker's appearance. *Why is it that so many of these people don't look like killers, or at least what killers are supposed to look like?*

Jamison knew from experience that jurors didn't expect murderers to look like their neighbors, but so very often that was exactly what they looked like. More than one time Jamison had heard a juror say that the defendant looked like such a nice young man and they couldn't believe what he had done. Harker's face looked like that of someone you would sit next to on the bus and wouldn't give a moment's thought about. Rick Harker looked like anybody. And that was one of the things Jamison knew was most frightening about murderers: you wouldn't know one if they walked by you on the street or sat next to you on the bus—unless they were the last person you would see at your final moment of life.

He examined the crime scene photographs for a moment longer, trying to commit the images to memory. He knew it wouldn't be difficult. The sterile images captured by the crime scene photographer would etch themselves in his mind almost as much as if he had stood in the room when the photographs were taken.

Jamison shuffled the photographs back into a bundle and slid them into the manila envelope he had taken them from. He picked up the phone and punched in the three-number extension for Bill O'Hara, his investigator. The phone didn't finish its first ring before O'Hara picked up, his voice rumbling like wet gravel in a cement mixer. "So, Boss, rumor has it you got stuck with the Harker case. You dusting off old files?"

Jamison caught himself stifling a snorted chuckle. The DA's office was a constant rumor mill and the investigators were the worst, cruising through the secretarial pool and picking bits and pieces of information from their colleagues. O'Hara was a senior investigator and he was also Jamison's primary investigator, along with Ernie Garcia. In some respects, Jamison was O'Hara's boss, but O'Hara was one of those people who didn't seem to have a boss. He worked his cases and he responded to questions, but if he thought for one minute that you were ordering him around you would soon know that O'Hara was his own boss and not you. Jamison accepted that, primarily because he had no choice. He also accepted that O'Hara called him "Boss," essentially to indicate that he wasn't. It was a test of wills. O'Hara never lost. At least not so far; and that included the day they first met when Gage sent him to O'Hara's office and O'Hara had stared at him like a bug at the end of a pin. When he took over the Major Crimes Unit, O'Hara was his first choice, but nobody would call their relationship warm and fuzzy.

He responded after a second's hesitation. "Yeah, and you're stuck with it too. I'm still going through the files, but I want you to go over to the sheriff's office and have them start gathering all the forensic evidence. I need to know what there is and where it is."

O'Hara didn't let out his usual caustic comment to remind Jamison that their relationship was equal in his mind. Instead he showed an immediate level of interest and curiosity. "I was a brand-new sheriff's deputy when that case went down. Don't tell me after all these years that it might have to be retried?"

"Well, that's what we're going to have to find out. But right now, I need to know what we have." Jamison was well aware that even in big cases, evidence got shoved into corners and sometimes misplaced. This wasn't going to be simple. Basically, the way these cases were attacked by a writ of habeas corpus was to show that the trial lawyer made mistakes, and that if those mistakes had not been made, a different result might have occurred with the jury. Defense attorneys would go over the original defense lawyer's conduct with a fine-tooth comb, looking for any stone that was unturned or not thrown at the prosecution, and then they would argue that the trial counsel had been negligent. They would frequently find pieces of evidence that had not been brought in for various reasons, and when they smelled blood they were like sharks chewing on another wounded shark.

It was one thing for a defense attorney to argue that the case wasn't proven beyond a reasonable doubt. Lawyers argued that all the time. But all of them, Jamison included, knew that actual innocence was a different thing. Defendants began with a presumption of innocence and the prosecutor's job was to overcome that presumption by showing guilt beyond a reasonable doubt. But reasonable doubt was not the same as factual innocence. The law's presumption of innocence was not so naive that it did not understand that not guilty and actually factually innocent were two very distinct things. It was a distinction that non-lawyers had difficulty with—innocent because guilt hadn't been proven beyond a reasonable doubt and actually innocent, as in he didn't do it. The jails and prisons were full of guys who claimed they were not guilty because the DA or "The Man" or some other vague authority figure didn't prove their guilt. Privately most of them would slyly acknowledge that they weren't innocent. Even criminals maintained a degree of realism about themselves.

When lawyers, especially criminal lawyers, got together they would all in confidence admit that their biggest fear in defending a case wasn't losing it. Their job was to make the prosecutor prove the charge and they accepted that most of the time they would lose. Some would even admit that they should lose. Defense lawyers weren't any different than anybody else. They knew that some of their clients shouldn't be out on the streets. And even they would secretly admit to a sigh of relief when a particularly bad defendant was convicted. They looked at it as a constitutional obligation to make the prosecutor meet the burden of proof and they justified the result by making the prosecutor work hard to do it. But their biggest fear was when they believed their client was actually innocent. Nobody wanted to feel responsibility for a man being convicted who was actually innocent.

A judge would be evaluating all of the defense arguments, but there was one argument that Jamison knew he would have to win or there was no question that he would lose in the end. He would have to show that there was no question that Richard Harker murdered Lisa Farrow. No judge was going to deny a new trial if he thought that there was a serious possibility that Harker was actually innocent. With what Jamison knew was coming if the case went to a full hearing, he was going to have to open doors that nobody had looked behind for a quarter century.

Chapter 6

Jamison put the phone down. Before he gave any job to O'Hara or his other investigator, Ernie Garcia, he needed to know more about the case so he could evaluate the issues in the writ of habeas corpus and understand what he needed O'Hara or Garcia to do. He had already taken the first step, sending O'Hara to ensure that all the evidence was located and cataloged. He didn't want to think about what would happen if evidence had been lost.

He began to stack the file in sequence, deciding that he should approach the case like he would if he'd been the original prosecutor. Normally he would have been to the crime scene. Nothing gave you a sense of what happened like being there, but the photographs would have to do. Then he would read the detectives' reports sequentially, building the case in his mind. After reading the initial response by the first officer on scene, the detectives would be called in. Their reports would give him more detail. Already he knew that they had called in the arson investigators. The responding detective in charge was Mike Jensen, now retired. Jamison had met him several times at various law enforcement functions that the old boys showed up at to relive past glory. Jensen had been gone from the sheriff's department for a number of years, but Jamison had heard he still kept his hand in doing private investigation work.

According to Jensen's report, when he arrived at the crime scene the child, Christine Farrow, was still there. She was completely covered with soot and squeezing a stuffed rabbit that was also visibly begrimed. Jensen called in a female officer to sit with her while efforts were made to locate relatives. The two neighbor women had wiped off the child's face but had not done anything else to clean her up. As distasteful as it was, Jensen had forensic examiners photograph the child, and then the neighbors supplied clean clothing while the investigators bagged and tagged what she'd been wearing.

Jensen's experience showed in his report. He observed that the child was visibly traumatized by what had happened even though she was too young to completely understand it. She kept asking for her mother. He allowed the neighbor women to stay with her as well as the female officer with specific instructions that nobody was to ask her any questions until he was present.

The neighbor, Nancy Slaven, repeated to Jensen that Christine had said several times, "Rick put fire on Mommy." Slaven said that she was worried the child was in shock because she wouldn't talk except to keep repeating the same thing over and over and then asking for her mother.

Jensen walked his report through the crime scene, carefully detailing his observations. Nobody moved the body while they waited for the coroner to come in and determine officially that the victim was dead and identify her if possible. While it was obvious that Lisa Farrow was dead, the law had requirements and the coroner being the one to make death official—a legally redundant verification of the obvious—was one of them.

It was evident that the victim had been beaten and the lack of clothing was a recognizable indication of sexual assault. Jensen's description of the condition of the body and the graphic photographs that were spread on Jamison's desk made it clear that the killer had intended to destroy as much physical evidence as possible.

The reality was that this case was over twenty-six years old and forensic investigation, including DNA preservation and analysis, had by now jumped light-years in terms of use. Jamison ruefully recognized that there would have been little effort to avoid contaminating the crime scene with DNA from investigating personnel because most of them would not have known that DNA was anything more than letters in the alphabet. And how evidence was preserved now was much different than how evidence was preserved then. Jamison made a note to himself to have forensics go over the physical evidence, including the clothing and anything else removed from the scene, on the possibility that something new might be recovered.

Jensen's report indicated that a broken knife was found near the body. The photographs clearly depicted that the victim's throat had been slashed. While the knife in the photograph was a kitchen knife, whether it was also the murder weapon was unclear to Jensen because it was lying in pooled blood. Jensen had the knife separately preserved after multiple photographs had been taken to establish the precise location of the knife in relation to the body.

Jamison had been to enough homicide scenes that he knew the chaos of shuffling feet around a crime scene. According to Deputy Kinster, the initial responding officer, he had avoided walking around the body because it was evident from visual inspection that the victim was dead. There were partial footprints in blood that Jensen had directed forensics to photograph. A ruler was laid out next to each shoe print and apparently Jensen had directed that the tiles on the linoleum floor be carefully pried up to preserve the blood-etched imprints. Jamison made another note to himself to see where those tiles were and their condition.

Holding the photograph of Christine Farrow in his hands, Jamison narrowed his focus, looking at her eyes. What he saw wasn't the face of a child, at least not the face of children that people usually saw. He suddenly realized what it was that he hadn't picked up on initially. It was the face of someone who didn't have a child's trust in her eyes.

He had seen this only a few times but he had seen it. A child who realizes that not all adults were protectors—some were predators. Christine Farrow had seen a predator and no adult would ever again have the benefit of the doubt from her—or her trust.

Jensen apparently had made it clear that he wanted to talk to Christine before anyone else took a statement because there were no other initial reports that Jamison could find. That was the right thing to do. Too many people questioning a small child in a case like this and you couldn't depend on anything she said. Jamison sympathized with the situation. At that point, the only witness was a three-year-old child who was traumatized. Jensen made the decision to talk to her at the neighbor's home while they determined who the relatives were and contacted them.

According to Jensen's report, he allowed the neighbors, Slaven and Castillo, to be present when he talked to Christine in order to keep her calm. Jamison kept looking at the crime scene photographs of a little girl with a soot-covered T-shirt, tightly holding a stuffed rabbit, her face smeared with the remnants of ash. The child's huge blue eyes filled the photograph.

As he held the photograph in his hands, Jamison's anger stirred. Dealing with numerous victims had taught him of the emotional wreckage left by crimes of violence. He knew that the public had no concept of the graphic reality of crime, the cascade of visual bludgeoning that crime scenes revealed and the slow desensitizing of crime scene investigators who walked where the average person could not imagine. But most of all, the years had taught him that victims of violent crime did not emotionally heal quickly, and sometimes not ever.

He had a sense of vague uneasiness that Christine Farrow was one of those victims of violence for whom the crime overwhelmed their life. It happened more than people realized, particularly in cases like the Harker case. For the victim, it was the endless judicial proceedings and the constant reminders of the crime as the case slithered like a lethargic snake through the maze of the criminal justice system, while the defendant fought the very personal— to him—consequences of his crime. Meanwhile the victim was forced to live with the consequences caused by the defendant. In the end, Jamison often wondered, Who suffered more?

Even Jamison had lost the edges of memory of individual homicides he had worked on. There were so many that the Saturday night shootings and the robberies gone wrong all merged together in jaded investigators' minds into jumbled memory snapshots of violence. But there were a few that always managed to stay with him sharply etched. Jamison was sure that the image of little Christine Farrow would remain vivid in Detective Mike Jensen's mind until the day he died. He made another note to have Jensen come in and help place all the reports in perspective.

Detectives weren't always the most sensitive people. They had to be tough to do their job and sometimes the endless lying to them and the constant confrontation with the sludge of society made it difficult to allow themselves to see the sides of life that other people, normal people, lived in. It was one of the reasons that so many cop marriages broke up. There was a gulf that separated the lives of cops from the lives of everyone else, including their families. Some detectives and cops were successful in bridging that gulf, but many were not. Jamison imagined the difficulty for Jensen as he tried to do his job and at the same time remember that Christine was three and not thirty.

From the report narrative, when Jensen asked if Christine knew who had hurt her mommy, Christine said, "Rick did it." Christine said that Rick started the fire "because him was mad at my mommy." She told Jensen that Rick and her mother had a fight and then Rick "put fire on Mommy." According to the report, Christine repeated that same thing several times and refused to say anything else except that she wanted her mother. Jensen's report indicated that he decided to have the child taken to the hospital to make sure she was okay and not suffering from smoke inhalation.

Both neighbors said they weren't sure who "Rick" was. They knew that Lisa had been involved at one time with somebody named Rick and they had seen a white man and an African-American man go to Lisa's house the day before. Neither knew who the white man was, but they identified the black man as Clarence Foster, who had lived in the neighborhood off and on.

Immediately Jensen had contacted the sheriff's department to determine if Foster had a record. It didn't take long to establish that Foster was a longtime loser in the lottery of life. He had a lengthy record of petty crimes and had pissed off enough people with his criminal activity that he had done a short prison stretch. It was harder than people realized to get sent to prison, particularly for low-level criminal offenders, but if a small-time criminal worked at it, eventually some judge would get fed up and drop the hammer.

Before he had started looking for Foster, Jensen made sure that Christine was at the hospital. Her grandmother had been notified and was on her way. From the report, it appeared Jensen concluded that under the circumstances the best use of his time was to shake Clarence Foster and see what rattled.

Jamison decided, since there was no declaration from this Clarence Foster in the petition to the supreme court, that he would see what Foster had told the police. For the time being that was all that mattered. Whether Foster had allegedly decided in prison to recant his accusation of Harker wasn't as important at the moment as what Foster told detectives at the time about the crime, particularly if he was the only other witness besides a traumatized three-year-old.

Clarence Foster's file was lying neatly in Jamison's organized stack. This was the guy who, according to Harker, now said that he had lied to the police about him. Jamison put the gloss of his cynicism on the credibility of Foster's prison conversation—at least that's what he *apparently* told Harker, according to Harker. Jamison flipped open the file. It was thick with reports and a transcript. Jamison thumbed the pages of the transcript—an interrogation. Well, it was at least a beginning.

While the Clarence Foster file was carefully sandwiched in Jamison's sequential stack, nothing in the file itself was neatly organized. That didn't surprise Jamison. Once the trial lawyer had gone through the reports, he would normally pull them apart and create his own organization depending on his focus. Looking at the reports, Jamison could almost smell the dust from years of the paper lying within the bulging manila folder. It reminded him of the musty smell of law books preserving cases fifty and a hundred years old, the paper slowly surrendering to time.

The pages were underlined in red pen with notes on the side. Jamison was surprised at the cramped scrawl in the margins, apparently by Gage or the lawyer who was second chair in the trial. He hadn't given a lot of thought to that, the lawyer who was second chair. Almost every major trial had a younger lawyer who followed the lead lawyer around, carried the boxes of files, and marshalled the witnesses. The purpose was for the younger lawyer, commonly referred to as "second chair," to learn how a big case was tried and, if he or she was lucky, to get to stick their head into the edges of the public spotlight. In the Harker case, the second chair was Jonathon Cleary. Now Justice Jonathon Cleary of the court of appeal.

Jamison sat back in his chair, thinking about what the Harker case had done for Gage and Cleary. It had made Gage the district attorney of Tenaya County and put him on the path to probably being the next attorney general for California. And maybe, after that, governor. As for Cleary, office legend had it that Cleary pulled a rabbit out of the hat in the Harker trial and after that became the golden boy in the office.

Cleary started drawing big trials on his own, with the blessing of the new district attorney, Bill Gage. After a number of years in the public spotlight, Jonathon Cleary had been appointed to the superior court and then to the court of appeal, where he had distinguished himself on both the state and national stages. Rumor had it that he was about to be nominated by the president of the United States to the District of Columbia Circuit Court of Appeal, the pool where most justices of the United States Supreme Court were drawn. Jamison had watched with fascination when Cleary occasionally deigned to walk into meetings of the Tenaya County Bar Association as members of the bar and local judges hovered around him like moths around a flame.

Jamison allowed himself a smile as he looked at the constricted notes in the margin with lines drawn to encircled sentences. There were so many lines that Jamison thought whoever made the notes would have been better off just drawing a circle around the entire report. It was indicative of a compulsive personality. As he thought about it, Jamison decided the notes probably belonged to Cleary. He had seen Bill Gage's notes, and aside from being virtually unintelligible, he wasn't a detail guy.

As he flipped through the pages Jamison decided he would have to make an appointment with Cleary in order to tap into his memory. Right now he needed to familiarize himself with the reports as much as possible, and that meant reading about Detective Jensen's drilling down into the mind of Clarence Foster.

Jamison shuffled through the Foster reports and rearranged them by date. Jensen had put out an APB for Foster and it hadn't taken long to pick him up. According to the time notation on the reports, with the help of the deputy assigned to the area, they soon found Foster drinking in a nearby park with a few other fellow losers.

Jensen's report indicated that the sector deputy transported Foster to the detective division where Jensen was waiting. He didn't read Foster his Miranda rights, deciding that he needed to first find out whether Foster was a witness before deciding that he might be a suspect.

Foster claimed he knew nothing about the murder of Lisa Farrow. He said he only had a general idea of who she was and expressed his sorrow that somebody had killed her. When Jensen told him that he had been seen going to Lisa Farrow's house with a white man and that was why he was being questioned, Foster said whoever said that must have been mistaken. He had been nowhere near her house and claimed that "all black people look alike to white folks" so it was a mistake. Foster was adamant that it wasn't him and at that point Jensen didn't have anything else.

Jensen's report from the next day changed all of that.

Chapter 7

According to his report, Jensen had turned Foster loose after the initial meeting. He didn't have any basis to hold him and he didn't have any information that an African-American man might be involved other than what the neighbor had said. And he didn't have a photographic ID yet of the white man; the neighbors were still looking at mug shots. Then he received a call from one of the forensic techs in the Identification Bureau, or the I Bureau as was commonly called. They were still trying to identify all the prints they had lifted, but one of the beer cans in the victim's kitchen had Foster's fingerprint on it. And it was the same brand of beer as the cans that were near Lisa Farrow's body, at least one of which it appeared had been filled with flammable fluid and poured on the victim in an attempt to destroy evidence. And they picked up another fingerprint from the kitchen that attached to a mug shot that both neighbors identified as the white man with Foster. Only the name in the report was Richard Sample, also known, based on his rap sheet, as "Rick." Jamison suppressed his confusion about who Rick Sample was and kept reading.

Immediately Jensen had deputies pick Foster up, and this time there was no mistaking the circumstances. Gage and Cleary were waiting with Jensen when Foster was brought directly to a sheriff's department interrogation room, but only after Jensen had let him sit in a holding cell for two hours. Jamison had used the same tactic a number of times, telling the deputy not to remove the cuffs and letting the suspect think about his situation before beginning the interrogation.

Guys like Foster who had been to prison wouldn't like to cooperate with cops, even if they had nothing to do with a crime. But this was different. And it wouldn't be hard for even his booze- and drug-addled mind to understand that murder wasn't a short stay in prison. He had been told enough about the murder of Farrow to realize that whoever did it was probably looking at the death penalty.

Jensen would know that was a lot for a man like Foster to think about; he would want those thoughts to tenderize Foster a bit before he asked the first question.

The transcript of the interview was short. Foster said he had nothing to do with the crime, and he didn't know how his prints got on the beer can, and he didn't know any Rick. He offered that he frequently shared beers with men at the park and some of them were white. His print could have gotten on the beer can when he shared it. How the beer ended up in Lisa Farrow's house he had no idea. He said he had been loaded that day on a combination of cocaine and meth, a "speedball." He didn't know whether he was coming or going. Maybe he had shared a beer with the person they were looking for and maybe he hadn't, but he said he *"didn't kill no woman"* and *"asking him over and over wasn't going to change that."*

Jensen and Gage stopped the interrogation but made it clear that whoever cooperated first in the case was the one who was going to get the deal. The reason they stopped the questioning was clear to Jamison. He didn't need to be in that interrogation room to know that either Jensen or Gage had realized that Foster was very close to asserting his Miranda rights and telling them that he didn't want to talk anymore. They had weighed the situation and decided that Foster needed a little more tenderizing. Jensen had deputies take Foster back to the jail and put a hold on him for suspicion of violation of Penal Code 187, murder.

The next report in Foster's file was two days later, in the late afternoon. Jensen, Bill Gage, and Jonathon Cleary were all there, and the interrogation transcript made it very clear that Gage had laid it on heavy with Foster.

Apparently, the tenderizing worked. At first Foster again denied having anything to do with the murder. Now he claimed that even though he "was loaded" that day, he had a hazy memory of sharing some of his beer with a *"white guy."* The description was general, twenty-five to thirty-or-so years of age, maybe a little older, maybe a little younger, with brownish hair, and about five feet eight inches and maybe 175 or 180 pounds. Foster claimed his memory was that *"the guy was rough-looking, like he had a job that involved dirty work or something."* Other than that he didn't remember anything and claimed he had never seen the *"white boy"* before and didn't know his name.

It was at that point that Gage pointed out that the neighbor had now positively identified him as the black man who had gone to Lisa Farrow's house on the day of the murder and that he was with a white man. Gage reminded Foster that they had his print on one of the beer cans and that was enough right there to charge him with murder, which he would do *"unless I hear something that makes me believe you weren't the one."*

Jamison could visualize a younger Bill Gage leaning over a seated Foster, Gage's voice rumbling as he pushed his thick finger into Foster's chest. According to the transcript, Gage put a picture in front of Foster and asked if this was the man who was with him, and told Foster, *"I've had enough of your bullshit. You need to stop your lying unless you want a cell right next to this asshole."*

The next thing that happened jumped right off the aging pages of the interrogation transcript. Foster just said, *"That neighbor says that's him, the white boy she says was with me? She picked him too?"* Gage didn't answer.

Jamison had done numerous interrogations and he could lift the silence off the page, imagining the wheels turning around in Foster's mind as he began to shrivel in his chair before answering, *"That's who you want? That's what you want to hear?"*

Gage had immediately responded, *"Don't feed me any crap about 'what I want to hear.' I want to know is this the man who killed Lisa Farrow?"* Jamison didn't need the sound from a tape recording to hear in his mind the bite to the words coming out of Gage's mouth. There was no question that Gage's voice carried a question wrapped in an unstated threat if Foster didn't cooperate.

Foster replied, *"I didn't see him do it, man. I ran out of the house. That dude's crazy. He was like an animal. I told you, man, I don't know his name. What the fuck do you want me to say?"*

Jamison could visualize Gage pushing his chest out and pointing his finger in Foster's face as he said, *"You think we'd have this picture if we didn't know who he was, Clarence? Now I want answers and you need to give them to me. You got it? Let me hear them now. You know the name, now give it up. You want to protect this guy then you go down with him."*

"But I told you, man, I don't know his name and I didn't kill no woman."

Jensen cut into the interrogation like a razor blade. *"Bullshit and more bullshit. This is a waste of time. Let me book him and then they can share a cell together. How's that sound, Clarence? Maybe you want to share a cell with this guy, and then you two can be bunkmates at San Quentin when they get the gas chamber ready."*

The fear from Foster seeped out of the dry ink on the reports as he began to blubber. *"Maybe I heard guys call him Rick. I think so, I don't remember. I told you I was high. Man, why're you in my face? Okay, that's him. There, I said that was him. You don't need to keep pushing his picture in my face. He's just a white guy that I seen around."*

The transcript showed Gage then said, *"Okay, Clarence. No more of your shit and lack of memory. Right now, I want it all right now, and you better not hold back anymore. You understand?"*

Jamison paused in his reading. That sounded like Bill Gage in full rant. He had seen it before but this was Bill Gage almost thirty years ago. He was an imposing man now but back then it must have been like a snorting bull right in Foster's face.

Jamison hadn't read enough of the reports to know the forensic details, but Gage and Jensen clearly were convinced that the photograph they had was of the white man in that kitchen and Foster had just verified it. Whatever Foster had been thinking about in the several days between interrogations, he had apparently made the decision to cooperate and regain his memory. Foster didn't have to be a genius to figure out that whoever did this crime was somebody the system was going to swallow whole. And Foster was clearly no genius.

According to Foster he had been drinking at his mother's house and run out of beer. He walked over to the liquor store and bought two six-packs of Wild Horse Lager.

Jamison wrinkled his nose at the thought. Wild Horse Lager was only slightly above carbonated horse piss, at least that's what he recalled from college when somebody brought over a six-pack. The basic attraction was low cost and high alcohol content. It would definitely get you there quick, as long as "there" was a drunken stupor. Usually a can of this stuff was drunk out of a paper bag to avoid embarrassment. At least now Jamison had a picture in his mind of Foster. He wasn't just a drunk, he was a cheap drunk. No big surprise there.

Foster said he was walking out of the liquor store when *"this white guy"* was getting out of his truck. Foster knew him from *"seeing him around"* and they had been drinking buddies on more than one occasion when they and the rest of their drinking crew had to pool their money to achieve their daily alcohol level requirement. The guy had offered Foster a ride and he agreed. Foster kept claiming that he didn't know the guy's name, but he thought he had heard him called *"Rick."* That was all he knew. At least that's what he said.

Foster claimed they opened their first beer before Rick pulled his truck out of the liquor store parking lot. Rick drained part of his can of Wild Horse and then refilled it from a whiskey flask.

Instead of driving Foster to his mother's house, Rick said they should go over to the home of a woman he knew. When Rick banged on the screen, Lisa Farrow opened the door. Apparently, she knew Rick because he walked right in and Foster just followed him into the kitchen.

At that point, Foster claimed he didn't remember much of what happened. They started drinking beer and then he left because he had *"things to do."* Then the transcript stopped. There was a gap in time because Gage had Foster taken back to his holding cell. About twenty minutes later, according to the transcript, Jensen said that for the record they had taken a break and Foster had been put back in the holding cell.

There was no explanation for the break, but Jamison could easily infer that Gage and Jensen wanted to talk about how to push Foster into providing more details that they evidently thought he had. That his assumption was correct was borne out by the rest of the transcript.

Gage wasn't mincing any words. Jamison could almost feel the whiplash of Gage's tone of voice cracking off the transcript pages. *"Now listen to me, Foster. This asshole that you say you know only as Rick murdered this woman. Her name was Lisa Farrow and he assaulted her first and then he burned her. Your prints were on a beer can in the kitchen and you were there with him. You admitted you were there and we have a witness that puts you there.*

"So now is the time for you to choose which side you want to be on. You either start telling us what happened or I'm going to wash my hands of you and you're going to be charged with murder, just like Rick. Do you understand me, Clarence? Is this real clear to you? Because I'm tired of your bullshit and your 'hazy memory.' It should be obvious even to you that we know who he is or we wouldn't have his picture. You already identified him—you've already given him up. We have his prints. We know it's Rick Harker. So you better either get very specific about what happened or you can figure out real quick how the rest of this is going down on you like shit dropping on a bug in the barn—and you're the bug."

Jamison looked away from the aging paper for a moment, wondering how Gage and Jensen had moved from Rick Sample, whose prints were in the house, to Rick Harker, but he knew that would come out in the reports. And the forensic reports had shown that Harker's prints had also been found at the crime scene, so it was clear Harker had been in the house where Lisa Farrow died. He continued reading.

"Now you've had time to think. I'm out of patience. I don't give a rat's ass about you except for what you can give me, and if you can't give me anything then it's your sorry ass. What's it going to be, Clarence?"

While Jamison couldn't see the sweat that must have been coming out of Foster's pores, he could almost smell the sour stink that spurts out when a man breaks. He had smelled it a number of times and the odor had no color or ethnicity. It was just the smell that came with submission and the collapse of resistance when a man realized that he was cornered, and all his choices were gone. Clarence Foster must have, at that moment, felt his bladder pushing down and his sphincter tightening as he made his choice and let it all out like air hissing from a deflating tire, slow and steady.

The rest of Foster's statement read like a horror story. *"All right, it was like I told you, man, all I know is his name's Rick. We went to this Lisa's house because Rick wanted to. I didn't see no harm in it. He acted like she would be okay with it. She let us in and that Rick guy sat down in the kitchen. I was just standin' there, man. Just lookin'. Then Rick, he starts comin' on to her, telling her to let him have some. You know what I mean? And she wasn't havin' nothin' to do with it. She told him to leave her alone, that she didn't want him touching her. I told him to let it go and we should leave but he wouldn't do it.*

"She kept tellin' him to leave her be, but he started getting rough and then he hit her. Man, you shouldn't hit no woman. I don't like that shit at all. I never hit no woman just 'cause she said no. That ain't right, man. That ain't right.

"Then Rick, he started tellin' her that he brought beer and the two of them should party. He grabbed her and she pulled away and that's when he hit her again. She grabbed a pan from the sink and held it in front of her. Said she would

*hit him with it. Then he said for her to shut the fuck up or he was gonna kill her.
I mean he scared the shit out of me.*

"*I tried to stop him but that guy's bigger than me and I was drunk, and then
he hit her again. I know I shoulda stayed and helped her but I was scared. That
dude was crazy. I ran, man. I just ran. I don't know what happened after that. If
he killed her, I didn't see it and that's the God's honest truth, man. I didn't kill no
woman. I ran. I know that ain't right and I'm ashamed that I ran, but I did. I'll
testify to it, but I didn't kill no woman and that's the God's honest truth.*" Foster
showed them the scrapes on his hand and claimed he'd gotten them in the
struggle to stop Rick.

Jensen asked the next questions to fill in the gaps but there wasn't much.
All Foster said was that he had run out of the house and woke up the next day
in the park. He went to his mother's house after that and he hadn't seen Rick
since. He admitted he had heard about the murder of Lisa Farrow but said he
was scared of Rick and it wasn't his doing. He was sorry he ran but he wasn't a
murderer. Rick did it all.

There were other reports of interviews with Foster, but the story didn't
change. Jamison scanned the notes in Foster's trial file that were written by
Gage and by who Jamison assumed to be Cleary as they prepped for trial.
He would read those more carefully later but for now he pretty much had a
picture of the case. Rick Harker was convicted because his fingerprints were at
the scene, there was an eyewitness neighbor who placed him at the scene, and
there was the testimony of Clarence Foster. And then there must have been an
identification by Lisa Farrow's daughter, Christine.

Jamison closed the Foster file, visualizing how it all must have gone down.
After a jury heard the brutal manner in which Lisa Farrow had been killed and
then heard Clarence Foster, the identification of Rick Harker by little Christine
Farrow must have rung in that courtroom like church bells at a funeral. The
jury gave Harker the death penalty. Matt Jamison had no doubt that Harker
deserved it and he gritted his teeth that a weak judge had deprived Lisa Farrow
of that final justice.

As for Harker's claim that Foster had gone back on his identification,
Jamison wasn't concerned. He could already tell that Foster was a coward and
a sniveler. Inside a prison with Harker, it wasn't hard to figure out which side
Foster would pick.

But Christine Farrow was another matter. She was innocent and her life had
been ruined from its very beginning. Christine Farrow was still being haunted
by the memory of that day, a memory no child should have to live with. And
worse, somehow that memory had turned into subconscious guilt over the
bottom-dweller that had murdered her mother.

Jamison could hear the breath coming out of him as he contemplated the
raw injustice of it all. Rick Harker had ruined lives. He was still ruining lives.

And the system was letting him do it. Even his name sounded like something you'd cough up and spit out.

Jamison picked up Christine Farrow's trial file. Now he was going to have to do further damage to this fragile young woman. He was going to have to cross-examine her and he was going to have to inflict more pain on her. There was no choice. Whatever made Christine Farrow write that declaration recanting her identification of Rick Harker, Jamison knew in his heart it was simply more emotional wreckage from what Harker had done. He could feel his dislike for Harker building by the moment as he thumbed open Christine's trial file. He had to start somewhere.

Chapter 8

For the next twenty minutes, Jamison scanned the pages of reports that began with Jensen's interview with Christine Farrow. As he read the reports he had a growing sense of issues that were created by the declaration from the adult the child had become. And he had been rereading the reports that he knew were going to be the focus of the attack on Harker's conviction.

His concentration was interrupted when his investigator Bill O'Hara walked in, the smell of the cigars he smoked drifting ahead of him. As Jamison had requested, he had gone to the sheriff's office to see what they still had on the Harker case. O'Hara's skin was the color of chocolate and his closely cut hair was beginning to show strands of gray. While he hated for anyone to notice, he had stopped trying to control the bulge that was once a flat stomach. But everyone knew that it would be a serious error of judgment to make the observation that he was showing the years a bit. O'Hara glanced at the stack of boxes, his rumbling voice grinding out, "That it?"

Jamison nodded and waived his hand over the booking photo on his desk. O'Hara tapped his finger on the photograph of Harker. "Asshole." To O'Hara they were all assholes, just some were bigger than others. "If that weak-ass Judge Stevenson had done his job, Harker would be burning in hell by now."

The contempt in his voice was acid-edged. Judges were another group on O'Hara's long list of people who needed an attitude adjustment. He had little patience for the procedural considerations that the law accorded to people accused of crimes. And he had no consideration for a judge who didn't have the stomach to sentence a lowlife like Richard Harker to the death he so richly deserved.

He knew all about the Harker case. It was going on when O'Hara came on at the sheriff's department. The old guys talked about it, and they still talked about it at training sessions. But mostly they talked about the judge who let Harker spend his life eating and sleeping at taxpayer expense while Lisa Farrow lay in cold ground.

Jamison was used to O'Hara's diatribes. He knew there was no point in making fine legal distinctions with O'Hara about the presumption of innocence. He had heard O'Hara say so many times that as far as he was concerned the presumption of innocence ended with the ratcheting of handcuffs.

O'Hara took a seat and pulled out a cigar. He slid a fingernail down the cellophane wrapper with practiced skill and jammed the cigar into his mouth. Jamison turned his nose up but he knew it wouldn't do any more good than a lecture about illegal searches. He also knew that O'Hara reveled in Jamison's aversion to cigars. The only concession that O'Hara had made in their relationship was that he wouldn't light it in Jamison's office, but he would chew it to a soggy pulp, and then they both knew that O'Hara would find a way to leave the wet cigar on Jamison's desk. Another part of O'Hara's sense of humor.

O'Hara rolled the cigar around in his mouth until he found the right fit before he offered his next observation. "The sheriff's department says they got all the evidence in the Harker case locked up with the other high priority cases. I looked at it—lotta shit there. Checked on the file. It's all paper, nothing on computer, but they still have the original case file and the clerk said they also had it on microfilm. I told them we would need a copy of everything. They asked why but I said I would tell them when I knew what was going on—which I don't yet." O'Hara added the last comment with a tone that made it clear he didn't like operating in the dark. "Guess we can get it put on a computer disc. Anyway, I asked them to do that. So, what we lookin' at? Why's this case back here?"

Jamison handed O'Hara the declaration from Christine Farrow that came in the packet of papers with the writ and order from the supreme court, letting him take a moment to read it. After thirty seconds, all he heard from O'Hara was, "Shit—shee-it," the word spit out as two syllables.

O'Hara put the declaration back down on the desk with an observation borne of years of experience. "Boss, you know this poor girl's been hammered by a defense attorney. I've seen this before with kids. They get to a point where they don't remember up from down. And now almost thirty years later this girl has to be made to think she did a wrong thing? On top of everything else that happened to her? I know Jensen was the detective. He wouldn't have screwed this up. I mean, yeah, he was a rough guy. Detectives back then were tough as an old boot and Jensen wasn't any different, but this was a kid. He would have been careful with a kid. You looked at the reports?"

Jamison nodded. "Yeah, I've looked at most of the crime scene stuff. I haven't gone through the trial transcript yet, but there isn't much as far as the little girl's statement. After all, she was only three at the time—five when she testified. He summarized the preliminary reports for O'Hara before he got to the part of Jensen's additional reports that he knew was going to be the issue. He had been reading those reports when O'Hara walked in.

Apparently, Jensen had a female deputy sit with Christine in the back of his unmarked car with the intention of driving her to the hospital to make sure that she was in fact unharmed, although the child appeared physically unhurt. The neighbors had already called Lisa Farrow's mother, who showed up at the crime scene before they took the child to the hospital. Jensen had to have deputies restrain her and calm her down. Then he reunited Christine with her grandmother, Barbara Farrow.

Jamison understood Jensen's dilemma. This was a murder and he needed information quickly but he also had to be sensitive to the trauma both to Christine and to a woman who had just learned her daughter had been brutally murdered. Jensen was present when the grandmother talked to Christine so he could try to control the situation as much as possible. The grandmother asked if they knew who did it, and Jensen told her that Christine said that "Rick did it."

Jensen asked if she had any idea who Rick was, and Mrs. Farrow turned to Christine and asked if Rick was "Tommy's daddy?" Christine had nodded and said, "Tommy's daddy, Rick." Mrs. Farrow had then said that Rick was Rick Sample. Tommy was his son by another relationship. As soon as he read Rick Sample's name, Jamison's mind flashed back on the fact that Sample's prints had been found at the crime scene. He could already hear the questions Harker's lawyer was going to ask. It took flipping through a few more pages for the answer. It wasn't a good answer, but it was an answer. The problem was that it came with a lot of questions, and they weren't good either.

According to his report, when Jensen asked Christine if Rick used to live with them she said yes, and then shook her head no but then repeated that "Rick is Tommy's daddy." He decided to wait until he had photographs and had radioed in to see if Sample had a record and available mug shots. His report said that he quickly found out the answer to both questions was yes. He asked that the mug shots of Rick Sample, along with other similar mug shots, be acquired as soon as possible for a photographic lineup.

Jensen had the female deputy ride with Christine and her grandmother in the back of his unmarked car as he drove to the hospital. While he was at the hospital the photo spread he had called for was brought to him and, according to his report, after talking to the grandmother he showed a photo lineup to Christine that included a mug shot of Rick Sample. Christine immediately picked out the photograph of Sample, putting her finger on the picture and saying, "That's Tommy's daddy." She didn't say anything else and her grandmother was so distraught that she refused to allow Christine to be questioned further.

O'Hara watched as Jamison rummaged through the files looking for the photo spread that had been used by Jensen with Christine. He spread the six photographs out on his desk and put the photograph of Rick Sample in the center. Then he pulled out the booking photograph of Richard Harker. There was no question there was a resemblance. Jamison could understand why a child might be confused.

Jamison already knew that when Clarence Foster was questioned he identified the photograph of Rick Harker. From the look on O'Hara's face, Jamison knew the same thought was going through O'Hara's mind that had gone through his: Who the hell was Rick Sample and was that who Lisa Farrow was now going to say killed her mother?

Chapter 9

B oss," O'Hara said, "this little girl probably got confused. Hell, she was only three years old. You know as well as I do a kid that age isn't that reliable." Jamison nodded thoughtfully at O'Hara's observation. It was true. Children under the age of five were normally not considered competent to testify, but that didn't mean they didn't understand what was going on or they couldn't explain in their own words what they had seen or heard. The problem was that in terms of testifying, the standard was whether the witness understood the more complex concept of the obligation to tell the truth. As any parent knew, truth to a child can include what they believe as opposed to what's real. That includes believing in Santa Claus and the Easter Bunny. But as lawyers know, truth may be an obligation that witnesses understand but it does not mean that it is an obligation that is always honored.

He responded to O'Hara's comment. "Maybe so, but she isn't three years old now and in her declaration she's saying that she was wrong. My guess is she's going to say that this Rick Sample is the guy."

"Well at some point she obviously testified that Rick was Rick Harker because her declaration says she identified the wrong guy. You talked to The Big Guy yet?"

O'Hara usually referred to District Attorney Gage as "The Big Guy" and referred to Jamison as "Boss." Although Jamison was not naive enough to think O'Hara used the term "Boss" as anything but a little jibe that he got some personal kick out of. "No, I haven't talked to Gage yet. I need to finish with the reports before I start asking him any questions. If I go in there now, all he'll say is, 'Did you read the reports?'"

"Well it has to be in there," O'Hara said through teeth firmly clinching the half-chewed cigar. "Anyway, the sheriff's office is pulling the evidence out for us to look at and I have a call in to Jensen to talk to him. Let's look at the rest of the file on the kid and see what's there."

"That's what I was doing when you walked in, Bill. The next report is almost three weeks later."

"And?"

"And it says that Jensen and Gage met with Christine." Jamison picked up the report and quickly skimmed down. "Apparently, the grandmother wouldn't let Christine be questioned without her present and she wouldn't let anybody talk to her for several days. The kid just kept saying Rick did it and the grandmother said that Rick was Rick Sample."

"Then how the hell did she change, and Harker become the suspect? I know why Jensen and Gage thought it was Harker. They had the neighbor ID and a fingerprint and Foster." O'Hara pulled his cigar out of his mouth and stabbed it in the direction of the report. A small spot of tobacco juice splattered one of the manila files and Jamison shook his head as O'Hara said, "Sorry." But both knew O'Hara was seldom sorry and this wasn't one of those times.

"I haven't been through all of the reports, but it looks like Jensen and Gage finally got to question the kid outside the presence of Grandma because there's a transcript here of them talking to her. It's a little hard to follow because she was so little, but apparently she had some idea of who Rick Harker was."

Jamison smoothed the paper down that detailed the transcribed statement. When he had opened the file, he had seen a manila envelope stapled to the inside of the file and had quickly looked inside, seeing an old tape cassette with Christine Farrow's name on it and a date consistent with the one on the transcript. "We got a tape here. Maybe we should listen to it. That'll tell us a lot more than the transcript." He called the secretarial pool and asked for a tape recorder to be brought out of storage that would handle the larger cassette-type tape that had been used back then. "According to this transcript, Gage, Jensen, and Cleary talked to her and she identified Harker from his photograph."

"Cleary? You mean Judge Cleary, the guy that the papers keep talking about that's supposed to be under consideration for a federal appointment?" The raised eyebrows telegraphed that O'Hara was beginning to see the political outlines of the Harker case.

"That's him. Back then he was a junior prosecutor on the rise. It looks like Gage pulled him in to be second chair because he was present when the child's statement was taken and he was one of the trial attorneys."

O'Hara stifled a snort. "Sounds like somebody else I know, a golden boy moving up."

Jamison let the comment pass. "Whatever. Anyhow, look at the transcript. It seems like they had cleared up the identification and any confusion."

With a practiced eye, O'Hara followed the transcript, jumping over all the preliminary comments that explained where they were when the statement was taken and who was present. "I've talked to a lot of kids over the years. Three years old is tough. They don't sit still and they either talk too much about nothing or they don't say anything. You have to dig it out of them." His eyes followed the meandering twenty-six-year-old conversation. Gage had taken the lead.

Jamison focused on how Gage and Cleary had dealt with the identification trying to visualize the small child sitting in a room with three men she didn't know. "They should have had a female officer in there. We wouldn't do it that way now."

Ernie Garcia stuck his head through the doorway, a large tape recorder in his hand. "You two looking for this? Must be a tape from the Harker case to be using one of these old tape recorders. So, you two going to investigate it again?" Ernie shrugged, acknowledging that he had been sniffing around. "At least that's the rumor around the office." Ernie's square brown face broke into a grin as he handed over the recorder to Jamison.

"Nope, it's not the two of us, it's the three of us. You're going to be with us on this ride." Jamison took the tape recorder and sat it on his desk, indicating for O'Hara to plug it in. "You may as well sit down and listen. I'll fill you in on the rest later."

O'Hara slid the tape into the machine and then carefully pushed the Play button, mindful of the risk of erasing it. "I think we better get duplicates of any tapes just to make sure we don't screw one of them up, like President Nixon's secretary did with the White House transcripts."

O'Hara was not a lover of Nixon, not because Nixon was a Republican but because he got caught covering up a second-rate burglary. O'Hara had said before that anybody that let something like that get out of control didn't deserve to be president. What always puzzled Jamison was that O'Hara had been much less offended by the criminal act than that Nixon had gotten caught. But then, Jamison had learned that O'Hara had a much more pragmatic side to him about what was justified. Jamison had experienced that very clearly in the case involving a doctor that had ended up dead after committing a series of murders. Even though they never positively identified the shooter, the investigation concluded that it was a justified shooting—probably. And whoever did it was left as a dead end by Jamison's choice. Neither he nor O'Hara had discussed it since. Jamison dismissed the momentary flashback from his mind. Sometimes questions were better left unanswered. It had been a hard lesson to learn.

The tape hissed and crackled as it slowly began to unwind and release words that hadn't been heard in almost three decades. The three men listened, each letting the sound paint images in their minds as they heard the voice of a younger Bill Gage, not yet roughened by years of political speaking and coarsened by the cigars and bourbon he had become too fond of. It was in sharp contrast to the child's voice that they had to strain to understand.

Bill Gage sounded uncharacteristically gentle. "Christine, you and I have talked before, right? And you've talked to Mr. Cleary here and Detective Jensen?"

Christine must have nodded because Gage said, "You have to answer so we can make sure that is what you said, okay?"

The tiny voice came through. "Yes."

"Okay, that's good. That's very good, Christine. Now I need you to use your big girl voice."

"Where's Grandma?"

"Your grandma is waiting for you, don't worry. Remember? Grandma said we could talk to you for a little while and then you could have ice cream. Remember?" Jamison focused on the sound in Gage's voice. He had done enough questioning of children to know that it was going to be a slow process.

"Christine, I need you to look at me. Can you do that? It's important. This won't take long." The sound of shuffling could be heard on the tape as well as a muffled whimper. "Christine, now don't cry. We just need to ask you a few more questions, and then you can go with Grandma. Can you do that?"

The sound that came through on the tape was broken by the beginning of a child starting to cry and then Gage saying, "Christine, you have a rabbit, right?" Jamison could hear a door opening and then footsteps before the next words were spoken by Gage. "There's your rabbit. You hold him, okay? I need to show you something. I want you to look at some pictures. Do you see them?"

"Yes. That's Rick and that's Rick."

Gage tried to clarify what was happening. "You're pointing at two different pictures. Both of these pictures are of people named Rick, is that right? I see your head nodding. Is that yes?"

"Yes. This Rick is Tommy's daddy. This Rick is bad Rick. Rick put fire on Mommy." Now the tape filled with the increasing sound of Christine's crying. The pained expression on the faces of Jamison, O'Hara, and Garcia mirrored what Jamison could only imagine was the emotional strain for Gage and Cleary as they tried to coax the child to relive that night without leaving her with more nightmares.

Gage's voice was low and precise. "Christine, this picture of the bad Rick, is this the man who hurt Mommy? You need to answer so we can be sure. Is this the bad man?"

Christine's childish voice whispered through the span of years. "This Rick. Him hurt my mommy. He was bad. I want my grandma." The child's tears almost seeped from the tape.

"Very good, Christine. You're a good girl." Gage tried to comfort Christine and then simply said, "The bad Rick won't hurt anybody else, I promise. We're going to take you back to your grandma now. Okay? Let's shut off the tape."

The silence from the tape recorder continued for a few seconds before O'Hara snapped the Off button. "I guess that's it. According to the report, they showed her the picture of this Rick Sample who used to live with her mother and also the photo of Rick Harker and the mug shot she picked on the tape was Rick Harker—the 'bad Rick.'"

O'Hara left a brief gap of silence before uttering one word. "Asshole." He had a daughter, although they had been estranged for years. But he remembered her when she would sit in his lap at the same age as Christine Farrow. It was a memory he revisited often in his mind. It was one of the few about his daughter that he could revisit.

After her mother left with their daughter, everything else for O'Hara had been brief stopovers that simply turned into the silence of lack of contact. Now he realized, to his daughter he was just somebody that was out there, but she did not regard him as part of her. The sound of Christine's voice reminded him of what he had lost and focused him like a laser on what Rick Harker had taken from the disembodied voice of the child on the tape.

All three remained quiet for a moment before Ernie Garcia broke in. "So why are we listening to this now?"

"Because," Jamison said quietly, "Christine Farrow is now thirty years old and she says that Rick Harker wasn't the man who murdered her mother. Our job is to get that straightened out and put Harker back into the darkest hole we can find." The edge in his voice revealed how much the sound of the child's words had affected him. "That little girl has lived with all of this virtually her entire life and still she has no end to it, no peace. We have to fix that. We have to make this right. We need to help Christine Farrow and put an end to this once and for all. And we have to do it in a way that doesn't bring any more pain to her."

Bill O'Hara and Ernie Garcia stared at Jamison. Both men nodded. Sometimes cases just didn't end. They kept on going, squeezing the last drops of pain from everyone involved until nothing was left but a dry husk. They understood that they owed it to the child whose voice they had heard on the tape and to the damaged woman they could only imagine she had become to give her closure. And that meant slamming the cell door shut on Rick Harker once and for all. Each man understood what they had to do.

Chapter 10

Jamison ejected the tape from the recorder and placed it back in the manila envelope, carefully resealing the tab. "Okay, here's what I think we're going to have to do. We need to rebuild this case from the bottom up. I'm going to approach it like I'm the one trying it. You two need to start pulling the evidence together.

"Ernie, I want you to start figuring out where these witnesses are, assuming any of them are still alive. Find out where Christine Farrow lives. Go through the reports at the sheriff's office. Make sure we have everything they have." Ernie nodded. Sometimes there were reports in the sheriff's files that weren't in the DA files, incident reports and other minor investigative reports. "Also, I want you to talk to Bill and then give me a list of all of the physical evidence we have. I want to see it all so I know what we have to work with. I don't think it'll be necessary to put this case back on. I think we can beat back any claim by Harker, but we may have to show the judge that the evidence of guilt is overwhelming in case the judge starts asking questions."

"Bill, I want you to make contact with Mike Jensen. You talk to him and get a feel for what went on with the case. We're going to start with him. And I want you to find Clarence Foster."

O'Hara finally asked the question that was likely also on Ernie's mind. "Look, what's all this stuff mean? I don't understand. Just because Harker got this Clarence Foster to claim he lied and some defense attorney screwed with Christine's head or her shrink did, does that mean Harker gets a new trial?"

"No, not if we can help it. What it means is that we're going to basically have to prove that Clarence is lying and, unfortunately, we're going to have to also prove that there's no reason to accept Christine Farrow's statement. Just because somebody comes in thirty years later and claims that they have new evidence, or a witness decided they were wrong, doesn't mean the defendant gets a new trial. The defense still has to show that the evidence wasn't available to them at the time and that it has sufficient credibility that it might result in a different outcome.

"So as for Clarence Foster, the fact that now he says he lied doesn't mean all that much. The defense had the chance to cross-examine him at the time and the motive for him to lie was the same. They're going to have to do a lot better, a whole helluva lot better, than dragging out Clarence Foster to say he had a prison revelation, if that's the entire argument they have.

"But Christine Farrow's different. She was a little kid. If Harker's defense team can convince a judge that there is real reason to believe that she was mistaken and that her statement is credible, then we're going to have a major problem. And if that happens we're going to have to convince a judge that even if little Christine wasn't credible at the time, that the evidence is so strong that it wouldn't make any difference—that it didn't make any difference. That's why we have to be prepared to defend this case and that's why we need to know it from the ground up.

"The district attorney made it clear that we pull out the stops on this. I don't care how much time it takes. This case goes front burner. And that counts for me too."

Jamison watched his two investigators to see if they had any more questions. Both men shook their heads. As usual Ernie stayed quiet while O'Hara said what was on his mind. O'Hara's voice was flat and emotionless. "Matt, you know it's going to be tough dealing with Christine Farrow. She's damaged goods emotionally. I've seen this before. These witnesses start losing confidence about identifications and then somebody gets to them and makes them doubt themselves. Next thing you know, they start feeling guilty and then they think maybe they were wrong. I've had kids come back years after a molestation when they were little and say that they woke up one morning and knew they were wrong when they accused their uncle or their neighbor. And then there's all this bullshit from her shrink. I'm going to look at this guy's background and see what his story is. My guess is he's the one that pushed her over the edge."

"Maybe—probably. But first I need to know as much as possible about this case and Christine Farrow before I talk to her. Right now you guys get started. I'm going to go over and talk to the district attorney. Then I'm going to start reading all the rest of these reports. Let's do it."

He watched as O'Hara and Garcia stood and walked out of his office. He knew what they would do. Both of them would go to O'Hara's office and start mapping out their own plan for the investigation. Just because he had made the assignments and told them what they should do didn't mean they would simply do what he said. They would decide what needed to be done and how best to do it. And they wouldn't ask him before they did it. But whatever they did, he trusted their judgment. He had to.

Jamison stood up and took a deep breath. He needed to talk to Bill Gage. Before he read any more he needed to have a sense of where Gage was coming from. He looked at the loosely organized stacks of paper and the still unopened boxes of files. Regardless of how long ago this case had been tried, Jamison was confident that Gage's memory would still be vivid. It was like that with trial lawyers. Small cases and repetitive crimes of violence were pushed to the dustbin of memory but big cases were always right there, constantly retrieved and relived—those were the cases that defined you as a lawyer. Those cases you never forgot.

Gage's secretary, Sheila Barrow, saw him walking toward the door of the district attorney's office. She raised her hand. "He's on the phone. I think it's the governor. As soon as he's off I'll call you."

"I'll wait."

"Better that I call. It may be a while." Sheila had been Gage's secretary for over twenty years. She knew him better than his wife—certainly better than his current wife—and longer than both his marriages had collectively lasted. Jamison had always wondered if there was any truth to the office rumors that Sheila was more than Gage's secretary. But there were always rumors and if there weren't, then there would be rumors about why there were no rumors. He turned and started to walk back to his office when he heard her call his name. "He's off the phone. Let me see if he has a minute."

When Jamison walked through the door to Gage's office, he could tell from the satisfied smile on his boss's face that Gage must have been happy with the phone conversation. Gage was leaning back in his chair, his hands clasped behind his head. "That was the governor. Looks like the party is beginning to circle in on who they're going to back for attorney general." He waited for Jamison to ask.

"And I take it that would be you?"

Gage's smile broadened. "Looks like it. But nothing's final yet. What's up?"

"Bill, I've been reading some of the files in the Harker case, but it's going to take me a couple of days to read all of them. I wanted to quickly drill down a bit."

Gage's eyes narrowed momentarily before his expression loosened and he leaned forward, placing his hands on his desk and gave the trademark smile that greeted every constituent and every camera. "Okay. It's been a while, you know."

"Yeah, yeah. Don't give me that." Jamison laughed. "You remember every day of this case. I haven't talked to Christine Farrow yet. So, what should I be looking for here? It'll just make it easier if I know what to look for before I read a couple thousand pages of old reports."

"What've you read?"

"I looked at the interrogation of Clarence Foster first."

Gage stifled a laugh. "Scared the hell out of him, didn't I?"

"You scared the hell out of me and I was only reading it, but what's the story about this Rick Sample? O'Hara's going to go see Detective Jensen and I'll talk to him of course, but originally it looks like they thought Sample did it. I listened to the tape that you and Cleary did of the little girl, Christine. She picked Harker, but I can smell it coming. She's going to say it was somebody else and my bet is she's going to say it was Sample."

Gage was silent for a moment. "Rick Sample. That's the direction that we went at the very beginning. The grandmother, what was her name?"

"Barbara Farrow."

"Yeah, Barbara. She was a real piece of work. Is she still alive?"

"Don't know yet."

"Well, she wouldn't let us talk to Christine for maybe a few days or so. I don't exactly remember but Grandma was the one who said Rick was Rick Sample. So that's where Jensen went first and so did we. Christine didn't say much at the scene, just that Rick did it, and then Barbara said Rick was Sample. But we also had the neighbors saying that they saw two men go into the house and the neighbors identified Foster and a mug shot of Sample. Eventually Clarence Foster admitted that he was one of the men and, after he had a little time to consider the logic of his position"—Gage laughed at the memory—"he gave up that the other one was Harker. By the time we got to talk to Christine, she identified Harker as the one who killed her mother. Problem was there were two Ricks and both their prints were in the house. One was Rick Sample and the other one was Rick Harker. Those two assholes, Harker and Sample, looked a lot alike. You've seen that, right?" Jamison nodded. "So the mistake by the neighbors was understandable. Her mom had a relationship with both men at various times so Christine knew them.

"Obviously the mother had a problem with her picker when it came to men. Neither one was a prize. But the girl was definite that it was Rick Harker who killed her mother. She called him 'the bad Rick.' He was bad all right, a real class one son of a bitch. The other thing was that Sample had an alibi that was ironclad as near as we could make out. He wasn't even in Tenaya County at the time of the murder. We had Harker's prints in the house, including on one of the beer cans that was on the counter. We squeezed Foster so hard that he popped like the pimple he was on society's ass. Finally, he gave up Harker. It took a while, but he gave him up.

"At the trial Foster testified it was Harker and so did Christine. I'll tell you one thing. When that little girl got on the stand and pointed at Rick Harker you could have heard a pin drop in that courtroom. I can still see her, holding that stuffed rabbit and looking lost in that witness chair. She was so little. I think she was about five by the time the trial started. I thought we were going to have trouble with her being permitted to testify, so little and all, but the one right decision Judge Stevenson made was to allow her to tell what happened."

There was no need for Gage to explain. Jamison knew that children around five years of age were frequently not permitted to testify and children under five almost never. The reason had to do with their lack of understanding of the concept of the truth.

Gage seemed lost for a moment at the memory before shaking his head, his voice softening with a tinge of emotion. "You know, she would never talk or do anything without that damn stuffed rabbit. I remember it was pretty mangy by the time of the trial. Poor little kid. I really wanted to put Harker away for what he did."

Gage's voice resumed its usual gruffness. "Matt, you make sure Harker stays where he is." He hesitated before continuing. "Does that help? It's been a lot of years. Maybe if you show me an investigation report it will help me remember specifics. But we concluded very quickly that Sample was a dead end. Harker did it and he would have been executed a long time ago if that damned judge had any balls."

Gage looked straight at Jamison. "You shut the door on this. Maybe someday you'll be sitting in this chair. You'll find out—a thousand memories and a thousand old cases come back at you. There's always somebody wanting to pull at you—some bullshit. Forget that asshole Foster. He'll say anything to save his sorry ass." His voice trailed off as he turned his chair to the side. "Talk to Detective Jensen. He worked the case. He's the one."

Jamison stood up. He could tell he had used up his time. "Thanks, Bill. That helps. No problem. O'Hara and I'll start to focus on Christine Farrow. She's going to be the star witness. I hate to have to do this. I'm going to have to discredit her declaration. And you know, to do that I'm going to have to very carefully undermine her credibility. No choice there."

A thoughtful expression crossed Gage's face. "Sometimes, Matt, there are only hard choices. That goes with this job. Remember that."

Chapter 11

The investigators were down a hallway at the far end of the floor below the offices of the senior prosecutors and the district attorney. Jamison ignored the elevator and took the stairs, a conscious decision that it was probably all the exercise he was going to get for a while.

The nameplate outside the door said, W.J. O'Hara. Even though everyone called him Bill, O'Hara's given name was Willie Jefferson O'Hara. To call him Willie you had to be part of some cryptic intimate inner circle. Jamison had never considered going beyond calling him Bill, any more than he would consider sticking his hand inside an alligator's cage because the owner said he was friendly.

O'Hara was sitting with his feet up on his desk. The office smelled like stale cigar smoke, a blue pall lingering near the ceiling. The still-wet chewed end of a cigar was mashed in an ashtray. All smoking was illegal in the county building, but the investigator's row policed itself and no lawyer, no matter how senior, dared interfere. As Jamison had learned early on, when people said payback was a bitch, they had to have been thinking of disgruntled investigators who you needed a favor from. So, Jamison ignored the cigar smell that he detested.

"You able to get hold of Mike Jensen?"

"Yeah, he says he has plenty of time on his hands so for us to come on over. He asked what it was about and when I told him, the only thing that came out of his mouth were four-letter words. He remembers the case all right. You don't forget shit like that—ever."

Jensen's house was in an older section of town. Time and urban sprawl had left the residential area behind and Jamison could see that here and there yards were beginning to show neglect. Jensen's yard was fairly neat but little effort had been put into beautifying it. No flowers, mostly bushes and small shrubs that had been there for a long time. No woman's touch.

A voice yelled at them to come inside before O'Hara had a chance to knock. Evidently Jensen had been watching for them. Jamison guessed that like a lot of older people, a visit was going to be the high point of his day—that and a chance to relive his glory days to somebody besides other old cops.

Jensen shook O'Hara's hand and nodded at Jamison when O'Hara introduced him and said he was the attorney assigned to the Harker case. Jamison recognized the slight. He was used to it. Cops had an aversion to lawyers and often treated them like they had a communicable disease. Old cops were the worst. It took a long time to gain their trust and a very short time to lose it.

The retired detective walked over to a worn leather recliner and sat heavily. From the look of it, the chair had adapted to its owner's shape. Jensen began coughing spasmodically and took almost a minute before he could talk. It wasn't hard to figure out why. The smell of cigarettes permeated the room, giving it a stale odor. On a TV tray next to the chair was an overflowing ashtray and a glass that still showed remnants of condensation from a few melted ice cubes. Even from across the room Jamison could not only see the light brown color of the liquid in the glass but he could smell it—bourbon. It was still early afternoon.

"What can I do for you, Willie?" Jensen's use of O'Hara's given name instead of calling him Bill told Jamison that these two went way back. "I understand you want to talk about the Harker case? So that asshole is sticking his head up out of his hole again?"

The sound out of O'Hara was a cross between a laugh and a grunt, something that Jamison had heard cops make that seemed to be a kind of code noise that indicated to other cops that they were on the same page. "Like I said on the phone, Mike, the supreme court has sent Harker's case back for a hearing because this Clarence Foster supposedly said that he had lied about his identification. But that kind of jailhouse bullshit happens all the time. The real issue, I guess, according to Matt here, is that the little girl, Christine Farrow, now claims that she made a mistake in her identification. So, the DA gave the case to Matt to handle. He says we need to put it back together to see what's going on, and you were the best place to start."

Jensen's head swiveled, and he gave Jamison a long look. "You related to Roger Jamison? Willie says you're all right, so you must be worth at least the powder to blow you up—more than most lawyers." He didn't laugh when he made the observation even though Jamison gave him a tight smile in response. "What do you want to know?"

"Roger Jamison was my father."

Jensen stared at him for what seemed like a minute. "Guess there's some irony there, right? You working as a prosecutor and your old man doing what he did, defending people like this." Jensen didn't say anything else.

Jamison wasn't going to discuss his father with Jensen. They had enough issues between them before he died. Maybe Jensen thought it was ironic that he was working to put people away because his father worked defending people. Jamison didn't see it, but he wasn't going to bite at the bait. He moved the conversation forward. "Well, I think the best place to start is what happened when you got to the crime scene. Then maybe some background on why this Rick Sample showed up early in your reports?"

There was a pronounced sigh from Jensen, who picked up his drink and took a sip. "You boys like a drink? This is going to take a while." Jensen was clearly enjoying the thought of how the afternoon was going to pass. He coughed again into a handkerchief.

O'Hara shook his head. "Thanks, but we're on the clock, Mike. Tell us what you remember from the beginning. It'll give us a head start. Also, if you have any notes, I'd like to see them."

Jensen's eyes narrowed briefly. "I got notes. Keep 'em from all my old cases, especially that one. I'll look for them, but I remember it. Not something that you'd forget. I been to a lot of crime scenes, just like you, Willie, but nothing like that.

"It was a bad neighborhood, you know? It was bad then and I imagine it's only gotten worse. I walked into that kitchen and I started gagging—not just from the smell but from what I saw. That poor woman got beaten first. The only decent thing Harker did was she was dead before he tried to destroy the evidence. I've never seen anything like that. She was burned. We couldn't get any useful evidence because of the fire. If he raped her, he managed to get rid of that evidence with the fire. But we found his prints in the house.

"The little girl, Christine? She was in that house when it happened. That son of a bitch set a fire and left that little girl in there. I still can't believe that judge let him live. Maybe if that judge had seen what I saw he would have let him die like the jury said he should. I'll hate that bastard judge until the day I die."

Jamison decided he needed to get Jensen back on track. "Detective Jensen, what's the story with Rick Sample? What caused you to decide it wasn't him?"

"The little girl's grandma, Barbara. The two women who found Christine said she kept saying that Rick did it. The grandma said that Rick was Rick Sample. Apparently, the victim had lived with him for a short time and he had a little boy. I forget his name."

"Tommy," Jamison prodded quietly.

"Yeah, that's right, Tommy. Anyway, that's why we went after Sample, but that trail got cold real quick. It's in one of my reports. Have you read all my stuff?"

Jamison shook his head. "I've read some of the preliminary stuff but the reports are all mixed up. It will take me a while to get it all sequenced. I wanted to talk to you so I could get a jump-start."

Jensen nodded. "Yeah, I get it, old cases, right? The crime scene boys turned up Harker's prints in the kitchen and that's when we focused on him. We had an APB out on Sample but by the time we got to him we had circled around to Harker. Anyway, Sample had an alibi. We checked it out and couldn't find a hole. When we talked to people who knew Lisa Farrow and then went back to the grandmother, we found out pretty quick that Lisa also had a relationship at one time with Harker. You ever look at the pictures of Sample and Harker? They look like they could be brothers. No wonder that little girl was confused. Evidently her mama liked a certain look in her men—dirtball.

"The neighbors had seen a black man and a white guy go into the house. They identified the black man as a guy named Clarence. It didn't take long to establish it was Clarence Foster. I put out an all-points but he wasn't hiding. One of our boys found him in a park, drunk. I brought him in and he denied everything. At the time, we were still working on Sample, but Foster claimed he didn't know anything. I let him go so I could keep working the case without lawyers getting into it and I didn't have the physical evidence to tie Foster in—yet."

Jensen glanced at Jamison to see if he had picked at a nerve but there was no reaction. "Then we got Foster's prints, so I pulled him back in. Anyway, that's when we started squeezing Foster. We didn't find Foster's prints on any of the beer cans near the body because they were burned, but we had found them in the kitchen. Then we found Sample's prints. Eventually we also found Harker's prints, but since both men had a relationship with Lisa Farrow that didn't surprise us. And Sample had a tight alibi. So, we had Foster and we had Harker's prints. Foster weaseled around a lot but eventually he gave us Harker. Later on, we were able to talk to the little girl and she identified Harker. That was the nail in the coffin."

"Did you arrest Harker?" O'Hara asked.

"Yeah, he was working construction. When we showed up he started running. Son of a bitch made the uniforms chase him. He got a little bruised up when they took him down. Had a few cuts on him that he might have gotten when he killed Lisa but they were also consistent with construction work. That part was hard to say. Later he said that he thought we were there because he had warrants for old traffic tickets and that's why he ran.

"I interrogated him for almost six hours. All I got out of him was that he didn't know what I was talking about. He started crying when we told him what had happened to Lisa Farrow and he asked about the little girl, but between his blubbering he said he didn't do it. He'd lived with her for several months. He admitted he'd been in the house numerous times, including the day before, but he claimed he would never hurt her. He did have a prior arrest for hitting her. He said it was an argument and he got mad, but it was only once. With those guys, they always say it was only once, but guys who hit women? It's never just once. But he knew Clarence Foster; that much he admitted. Said they sometimes got drunk together. I worked him every way I could, but he kept saying he didn't do it and it was all a mistake. That's all he ever said.

"Your boss, Gage, got the case I handed him, and it made him the DA. I guess it made Jonathon Cleary a judge. I hear he's going up real high pretty soon. At least that's the rumor. As for me, I got the satisfaction of seeing that asshole

Harker convicted. I should have seen him choke to death at San Quentin, but Judge Stevenson didn't have the stomach for that. Now here we are.

"So, what are you going to do, Willie, you and Jamison here? You going to put Harker back in his hole? I'll help any way I can. Not much else to do anymore. No woman around to tell me what to do. Not that there's much to do anyway." Jensen held the drink up in his hand and motioned with it around the room. He pointed the drink at Jamison. "I hope you've learned that some of these guys are like fungus. Even when you think you've killed them there's still little pieces hiding in dark cracks. Do us all a favor and shut him up once and for all. He's been saying he's innocent since the day I put the cuffs on him."

"Well," Jamison said, "they all say they're innocent."

"And they hire lawyers like your old man to get them off." Jensen lit a cigarette and exhaled through his nose. "That why you became a lawyer?"

"I became a lawyer to make sure people like Harker get what they deserve."

Jensen waved his cigarette around. "There's real irony here, don't you think?"

"I don't see it that way."

Jensen laughed. "Really? Maybe you will, Mr. Jamison. Maybe you will someday. What does the bible say? Sins of the father and all. Yeah, that's it, sins of the father." His guttural laughter ground down into a hacking cough as he repeated, "Sins of the father."

Detective Jensen was still coughing and choking on his own private sense of humor as they walked out the front door. O'Hara waited until they were in the car before saying anything. "Matt, don't pay any attention to Jensen. He's been drinking and it's obvious he's bitter about the judge letting Harker off with a life sentence. Your dad got a lot of people off and cops like Jensen don't forgive that—ever."

Jamison didn't respond. There were a lot of things he hadn't forgiven either when it came to his father.

Chapter 12

Ernie Garcia rolled to a quiet stop outside a well-shaded house on the south side of the city. The dark green paint on the front contrasted with the faded color on the side exposed to the sun. It wasn't exactly a rest home. A cottage industry had grown up over the years where people took in older people who needed to be cared for. Most of these homes had five or six elderly residents and the board and care was paid for by the county or whatever responsible agency paid for those who couldn't afford the more elaborate senior citizen's homes in the northern part of the community. Ernie hated going in these places, and he had been in more than a few. It was the smell that got to him. Even the cleanest of them had an odor that reminded him of wet leaves that matted the ground in autumn. He couldn't help thinking that maybe the occupants weren't much different. The inevitability of life's winter. But here was where Nancy Slavin lived, one of the women who had been a neighbor to Lisa Farrow, one of the women who had gone into that house.

A neatly dressed Asian woman in her early forties answered the door. Ernie had his badge out but he had called ahead. She led Ernie into the living room area where several people were watching an afternoon game show. One of them looked up when the woman said, "Nancy, this man is here to see you." She helped Slavin out of a cushioned chair, walking her into a kitchen area before telling Garcia, "You can talk here, just keep your voice down so the residents can hear the game show. Otherwise they get mad." She smiled and shrugged. "It's their favorite, isn't it, Nancy?"

Ernie sat down at the kitchen table and took out a notebook. "Mrs. Slavin, my name is Ernie Garcia and I'm an investigator with the district attorney's office. I'd like to ask you some questions about the Richard Harker case and Christine Farrow. Do you remember that?"

Slavin's eyes brightened with recognition. "Yes, I remember. I'll never forget that. It was a terrible thing . . . that poor little girl and what that man did to her mama. Why are you talking about that now? It was over a long time ago."

Ernie nodded. "Yes it was. But sometimes questions are asked a long time after these cases are supposed to be over. It's my job to answer those questions. I won't be long and you can get back to your show, okay?"

"*Price Is Right*. I always watch it."

Ernie nodded again. "Well, can you tell me about what you remember that day when you and Mrs. Castillo found Christine?"

"Don't like to think about it."

"I understand. I know it's difficult, but I need to know what you remember. Tell me about it."

Slavin's eyes lost some of their brightness as the memory clouded her face. "Maria and me, we would go over sometimes and talk to Lisa and visit Christine. She was such a beautiful little girl, Christine. That morning we walked over. We both could tell right away something was wrong. You can just sense it, you know? The curtains didn't look right, like they had dirt on them," Ernie nodded and kept listening. "The door was unlocked and we knocked and then opened the door. The first thing was the smell. I can't describe it. It hit you in the face and I remember gagging. But we didn't go back out. We stayed because we both knew something bad had happened. And then we saw Christine standing next to Lisa. Her mama was on the floor and it was so terrible I can't even think about it. He burned that woman." Slavin stopped talking and began wiping her eyes. "That little girl, Christine, she just had on panties and a T-shirt, but she was all black and dirty, holding that rabbit. She always dragged around that stuffed rabbit. We didn't know why she was so dirty at first but later we could tell it was the smoke. She'd been in that house when the fire was set and there was smoke all over, soot you know, like a fireplace. And the smell. You could taste it. It was horrible. I grabbed Christine and Maria and I took her outside. Maria called the sheriff. Later they showed us some pictures, but we already knew one of them was Clarence. He was always in the neighborhood—another no-good. Never was no good. We told that to the sheriff."

"When did you see Clarence? You mean Clarence Foster, right? Was he with another man?"

"Clarence, Clarence Foster. I just knew him then as Clarence—no good. He was never no good. He was there the day before. Both Marie and me saw him. He was with a white boy and I picked his picture out too. There was two of them in pictures. Looked almost alike. First time I guess I picked the wrong one but the next one they showed me, I guess I got that right. That was him."

"Him?"

"Yes, him, the one what done it, you know. I identified him in court. He was the one with Clarence. Maria said it too. You should ask her. Do you know Christine? She must be all growed up now."

Ernie patted Slavin's hand. "I haven't met Christine but I will. I spoke to Maria's daughter. Her mom passed away in her sleep three years ago. I'm sorry."

Slavin nodded. "Guess she was one of the lucky ones."

Ernie had a puzzled expression on his face. "Lucky?"

"Look around. We all gotta go sometime but it's the waiting that's the worst. Sleep is the best way to go I think. You'll see. Can I go back to my show now?" Ernie walked her back to the front room. Nobody seemed to have noticed when she left and nobody seemed to notice when she returned. Ernie slipped his notebook back in his pocket and quietly shut the door as he left.

Chapter 13

You want to talk to Christine Farrow, now? Ernie got an address and a phone number." O'Hara glanced over at Jamison as he roughly accelerated from Jensen's home. O'Hara didn't show much respect for county cars, primarily because they were bare bones with the only splurge being a big police interceptor engine. Usually it was the color. O'Hara said county purchasers looked at anything normal people would reject and picked that.

"Not yet. I think I want to talk to Harker's lawyer first. I don't really know him but I've been told he knows what he's doing. What some people call a true believer." He spends a lot of his time taking low-percentage cases that nobody else will defend, either because it's a loser or there's no money. Usually because there's no money."

"Yeah, that's a problem with you lawyers, isn't it?" O'Hara waited to see if Jamison would respond to the dig.

Jamison didn't bite. He called information to get the number and then got busy punching the keys on his cell phone.

"Law Office of Samuel Gifford." The voice that answered didn't preface the conversation with hello but it wasn't unfriendly. Jamison immediately guessed that Gifford answered his own phone, which meant either his secretary was out or he didn't have one. Probably the latter.

"This is Matt Jamison from the district attorney's office calling about the Harker case. I would like to speak to Mr. Gifford."

"Speaking. What would you like to talk about, Mr. Jamison? Sorry, I don't have a secretary. With my clients it keeps expenses down."

"Not a problem. I would like some background on the Harker case. I thought maybe you and I could talk. Tell me what you have and maybe we can talk it through?"

The snort of laughter at the other end of the line caused Jamison to pull the phone away from his ear. "You just have my client's best interests at heart, right? So, Gage stuck you with the dirty end of the stick? I thought you were the golden boy over there? At least that's the rumor."

"Mr. Gage asked me to handle the writ. Do you want to talk or not?" Jamison had dealt with enough defense lawyers to recognize the ones who operated on the principle that all prosecutors were really just one step up from fascists. It wasn't much different than those prosecutors who thought that some defense lawyers were one step below gum stuck to their shoe. Jamison wasn't one of them. He didn't defend people, but he recognized it needed to be done, and while he kidded his few friends who were criminal defense lawyers, he recognized that they did their job like he did his. But he didn't like getting stereotyped and he could hear the edge in Gifford's voice—and his own.

"Sorry, didn't mean to offend you," Gifford's voice was conciliatory. "This case sets my teeth on edge. You want to come by my office or you want me to come by yours?"

"How about I come by yours. You available now? I have my investigator with me."

Jamison clicked off. "Bill, we're going to Gifford's office. It's—"

"I know where it is. Been there before." Despite his usual penchant for editorial comment, O'Hara didn't explain. Jamison felt the car speed up.

The building address plate for Gifford's law office looked more like it was holding up the building instead of the other way around. It had definitely seen better days. It was in an older part of town in an even older building. Actually, it looked like an old house. "Samuel Gifford, Esq. LAWYER" was painted on a sign hanging from the porch area. Underneath "LAWYER" was printed "ABOGADO," Spanish for lawyer, and "Habla Español," which meant Spanish was understood. Glancing around the neighborhood, Jamison imagined that many of Gifford's clients would be Spanish speaking, and judging from the condition of Gifford's office they would be poor.

"You want me to wait in the car?" O'Hara asked.

"No, you can come in. We can compare notes later."

"Gifford and I have been around the block together before. He isn't going to like seeing me."

"And that would be because?"

"That would be because I've been on the other side of some of his cases and he didn't like the way I did things." O'Hara's face didn't reveal anything.

"Well, I don't always like the way you do things either, but I want you in there with me. Whatever issues he has with you, that's his problem."

Jamison walked up the wooden steps. The clean spot on the porch was the worn path where people walked to the door. He wasn't sure about knocking and decided to walk on in. The inside of the house surprised him. The woodwork was well maintained. Somebody cared about the old craftsmanship and had made the effort to preserve it.

A voice came from behind Jamison. "You like the old wood finishes?"

Jamison turned around. Samuel Gifford looked like someone had put him together using every stereotype of an aging liberal lawyer. His hair was long and hung in gray strands starting from a receding hairline, only part of which was contained by the rubber band that brought the bulk of it into a ponytail. His face was creased and had a weathered look, but he didn't look like a man who spent a lot of time outdoors. Jamison briefly thought that perhaps the pressure of his cases had taken as much toll on him as might have been caused by hours spent absorbing the relentless ravages of the sun.

"I restored this place myself. I also live here. Like to be near my clients—at least the ones that are out of custody." Gifford paused before adding, "You know, I knew your father."

"So did I."

Immediately Gifford reacted to the sharpness of Jamison's tone. "Did I miss something?"

"No more than he did." Jamison regretted his response. It sounded churlish. He really didn't care to discuss his father with Gifford. Roger Jamison had been a famous criminal defense lawyer, even at the national level. He just hadn't been well known at home, and what had been known at home was something Jamison tried to put behind him. It was difficult sometimes with so many people remembering the great trial lawyer, not really knowing the man himself. But he recognized that someone like Gifford would probably have looked up to him.

"Look." Jamison caught the expression on O'Hara's face as he tried to restart the conversation. "I think you know Bill O'Hara, my investigator on this case?"

"Mr. O'Hara and I have met." The tone was decidedly chilly. "I'm sorry that your office has decided to approach this case this way."

"What way?" Jamison responded.

"He means by assigning me." O'Hara's gravelly voice broke into the conversation. "Maybe I should wait outside."

Jamison shook his head. "Mr. O'Hara is my investigator and he's as good as they get. You can say anything in front of him that you would say to me." He wasn't sure how the entire conversation had broken down so quickly. That was something he would take up later with Bill but he needed to get back on track. "Why don't we sit down and talk a bit about Rick Harker and why you think he should get a hearing?"

Gifford walked over to a scarred conference table and took a seat, waving Jamison and O'Hara to chairs on the other side. "Because he's innocent, Mr. Jamison."

"Innocent? You mean you don't think there's enough evidence to prove he's guilty? He went down that road when he was convicted. You and I both know you'll have to do better than that."

"I mean," Gifford said quietly, "that he didn't do it—innocent. Some people are, you know."

"Some people are, just not Rick Harker. We have his prints. We have motive— he liked to slap women around. We have three identifications: Christine, Foster, and the neighbors. All you allegedly have is a jailhouse recantation from Clarence Foster and a statement from a misguided woman almost thirty years after the fact. Maybe we should start there. How did you get her to say that?"

Gifford gazed levelly across the table at Jamison. "I didn't get her to say anything, Mr. Jamison. It might come as a surprise to you but Christine Farrow came to me. I didn't seek her out and I didn't influence what she had to say." Gifford leaned back in his chair and put his hands behind his neck, appraising the reaction. "I guess it does come as a surprise. Let's start over, shall we?

"Christine has a therapist, Dr. Arnold Vinson. As it happens, Dr. Vinson and I know one another. He referred Christine to me. I talked to her and then I went and visited Harker at San Quentin prison. Then I went and visited Clarence Foster at Corcoran. And here we are."

"Did you know Clarence Foster before?"

"My world is full of Clarence Fosters, Mr. Jamison. I didn't know him personally but I know and have known plenty like him. Petty criminals who your office rolls over like road kill."

Jamison ignored the effort to provoke a reaction. "If there's something here, Mr. Gifford, it would be in everyone's interest if you would let me know it now. I notice you didn't have a declaration from Clarence Foster, just your client. Do you have a statement from Foster that says he lied?"

"You'll have to ask Foster." Gifford slid down in his chair, appraising Jamison for a moment before saying anything else. "All right, it's simple enough. Rick Harker said he was innocent. I hear that from almost all of my clients but I'm not naive enough to believe it. Except once in a while it has the ring of truth. I believe Rick Harker. I don't know who killed Christine's mother. I have my suspicions, but then I always have my suspicions. But I don't think it was Rick Harker and neither does her daughter. That's a pretty powerful piece of evidence when the victim's daughter and primary eyewitness say the man who was accused is innocent." Gifford waited for a reaction.

Jamison had been making short notes on a legal pad. He put his pen down. "It's going to take more than that, counselor, and you know it. Clarence Foster was there to be cross-examined at trial by Harker's lawyer and so was Christine. All you're bringing up is that they should have said something different. That's not enough. You need evidence that shows there's a reason we should believe they made a mistake other than them just saying so twenty-six years later. And what I'm hearing is that you don't have it. Do you." The verbal punctuation at the end of Jamison's statement wasn't a question mark.

"Rick Harker's trial lawyer was Alton Grady. He made a lot of mistakes. Check back on him, Mr. Jamison. You're going to find that by the time Alton Grady defended Rick Harker, he was well past his prime."

"Whether he was past his prime or not, Harker's case was upheld on appeal and it's been rattling around in the courts for over twenty-six years. If Grady was ineffective as a lawyer in his defense we would have heard it by now."

Jamison softened his tone. "Tell me something that has any legal value, Mr. Gifford, and I promise I'll look at it. So far I haven't heard it."

Gifford pursed his lips; for a brief moment, he looked even older than he had looked when Jamison walked in the door. "I've been around a long time, Mr. Jamison, maybe too long. I've seen a lot in the legal system. Personally, I haven't seen a lot of what I call justice come out of your office. Even though that's what you call it. But I can tell you that I've learned that sometimes mistakes are made, and legal technicalities and interpretations don't always ensure that justice is done. That's supposed to be your job, isn't it? To do justice?"

"So, is there any problem with me talking to Clarence Foster? I assume you don't represent him too?"

Gifford looked at Jamison, appraising him without answering immediately. "No, I don't represent Clarence." He paused before continuing. "That was somebody else." Gifford's smile was enigmatic as he waited for the next question. "I have no problem with you talking to Clarence. But I doubt if he'll even talk to you and if he does I doubt there will be much that you want to hear."

"And why is that?"

"First of all, Foster's in prison and he isn't going to want to be seen cooperating with prosecutors. He already has a snitch jacket that followed him from the Harker case. As for anything else, you have to ask him, but I believe that he wasn't telling the truth when he said Rick Harker was the one who killed Lisa Farrow."

Jamison picked up his legal tablet and stood up. "You're not giving me anything, Mr. Gifford."

"Oh, but I am. I'm giving you Christine Farrow. Isn't she the victim here?"

"The victim here is Lisa Farrow, who's been dead for almost thirty years, years that were taken away from her by Rick Harker. I guess I'll see you in court."

Gifford stood up and extended his hand across the table. "I've been doing this a long time, Mr. Jamison. Over time I hope you learn that justice isn't always found in law books. Sometimes it's just up to the people who work in the system—either those like you who are inside and looking out or people like me who are outside looking in."

Chapter 14

They were a block away from Gifford's office before O'Hara said anything. "Well, that seemed to go well." O'Hara didn't add to his observation. The tone of his voice said everything.

"You have a point?" Jamison responded. "I thought you were worried that your presence might create a problem."

"He got under your skin as soon as he mentioned your father. It's none of my business—"

"Don't worry, it won't work twice. But you're right. It got to me. That was a mistake." Jamison didn't want to talk about his father. O'Hara was aware that they had not had a good relationship, but Jamison had never sat down with O'Hara and had a personal conversation about it. Neither man was inclined to let anybody get too far into their personal feelings. He changed the subject. "Anyway, Bill, what problem did you and Gifford have in the past?"

"The usual. Gifford defended a murder case—maybe you remember the Caro prosecution? It happened before you got into Major Crimes. Anyway, Gifford claimed that I did an illegal search that turned up a pistol—just happened to be the murder weapon. The judge found otherwise and Gifford's client is now sitting at San Quentin on death row. Gifford made a lot of allegations about me—usual type of stuff. We also had another case and Gifford argued that I'd taken a coerced confession. Typical defense attorney crap."

Jamison was well aware of O'Hara's effectiveness in interrogation and that he pushed cases to the edge. "The gun search?"

"It was a consent search. You know Gifford just didn't believe his client was stupid enough to consent to a search when the murder weapon was right where I needed to look. Anyway, that's what I testified to—he consented. Search and seizure rules that you lawyers dream up are bullshit anyway. That was the murder weapon and Caro was the murderer. Case closed." O'Hara glanced sideways as they drove back to the office. "Isn't that what we're supposed to do, catch murderers?"

"I appreciate, Bill, that you reject interpretations of the Constitution by the supreme court that slow down your investigations." Jamison was laughing. "But those are the rules."

"Yeah, well the judges who made up those rules don't seem to understand that crooks don't play by any rules."

Jamison decided to let the line of conversation die. He wasn't going to win a debate with O'Hara, who was outspoken in his contempt for anything that tied his hands in finding and arresting a suspect. There were no better investigators than O'Hara and Ernie Garcia, but O'Hara could be a bull in a china shop if he wasn't monitored. Jamison knew that, and he also knew that O'Hara had a tendency to rationalize the means used to get to the result that he believed was justified. From personal experience that was a road they had been down in the past. Neither of them ever talked about it because it was better not to know the answers.

O'Hara reached toward the ashtray in the car and retrieved a half-chewed cigar, sticking it into his mouth and rolling it around without lighting it. "So, you want to go talk to Christine Farrow? You aren't asking but I think maybe we need to start with Clarence Foster."

~

Like a gray monolith, Corcoran State Prison thrust up from the parched alkaline dust of the Central Valley, separated from the outside world by a barrier of high-wire fencing that surrounded it. Its cement walls were a forty-minute drive for O'Hara and Jamison but it may as well have been at the end of the Earth for the over four thousand inmates inside. Over the years it held Sirhan Sirhan, who assassinated Senator Robert Kennedy, Juan Corona, who was convicted of murdering twenty-five people, and it still held Charles Manson, whose reputation seemed to fascinate generations born long after his grisly crimes.

The guard at the gate reviewed the list notifying him of official visitors before waving them through. Clarence Foster was supposed to be waiting for them in a private area. Nobody asked too many questions when they asked for him. To the prison officials it was routine. A lot of people in prison were subjects of ongoing investigations.

Even though he had been inside several prisons before, Jamison was aware that Corcoran was a maximum-security facility and like all such facilities, it had a policy that was made very clear to all who came inside—you entered at your own risk. But it also had a minimum-security housing area separated from the heavily guarded inmates in maximum security. That was where Clarence Foster was. He hadn't achieved the distinction of being regarded as a major threat.

Jamison had gone through the transcripts of Foster's statements given to Jensen and Gage, as well as his testimony at trial. Foster had made a show of resistance but eventually his role had been pulled out of him. Some men were like that, they played the game of trying to make it look like they were forced to give up what they had, but at the very beginning they knew that eventually they would give it up. Others made no game of it at all, and then there were the few, the very few, who would just look at their interrogators with dead eyes.

It was obvious from the interrogation statements that he made that Foster hadn't yet turned into one of those. By the time of the trial, Foster pointed his finger at the accused and said Harker was the one. Harker's lawyer, Alton Grady, was no Clarence Darrow even in his prime, and he wasn't in his prime when he defended Harker. Grady didn't manage to leave a mark with his cross-examination. Foster walked out of court a free man, or at least free until the next time he had been arrested, which hadn't taken long.

Clarence Foster was sitting in a metal chair when Jamison and O'Hara walked into a steel-doored room inside the administration offices of Corcoran. The grizzled African-American man wore the years heavily. His head was shaved and the facial hair that clung to his face was a mixture of gray and white stubble sticking to skin that hung loosely around his mouth. A loosely coiled snake tattoo slithered across his right hand and he consciously or unconsciously flexed it, giving the snake movement. Right away Jamison knew this wasn't the same man that Gage broke. Foster had the dead stare that was often described as the look of a man who has been in combat—or prison—for a long period. Obviously, time had changed Foster and so had the gray walls of Corcoran.

Foster shifted his eyes up without moving his head and took in Jamison and O'Hara. Other than the slight gesture, Foster didn't acknowledge them at all. He was used to waiting to be told what was going to happen to him next. Clarence Foster was an institutionalized man and for an institutionalized man, waiting was simply the routine of life.

Before Jamison said anything, O'Hara stuck his hand out and said, "Mr. Foster, how are you? I'm Bill O'Hara, an investigator with the Tenaya County District Attorney's Office and this is Matt Jamison, a prosecutor in that office."

"I know who you are." Foster's lips barely moved as he responded. He didn't take O'Hara's hand. He spoke with a quiet, almost conspiratorial voice. "Word gets around pretty quick inside. Guards said you wanted to talk about Harker. Is that it? Nothing to say to you. I told the lawyer what I had to say, the one with the ponytail. Long trip for nothing." The abruptness of his words left no doubt that whatever cooperation he had provided to authorities in the past, it was over now.

Jamison put a copy of Harker's declaration on the steel table. Foster's eyes shifted down and then back up, waiting, saying nothing. Finally, Jamison broke the silence. "Did you make this statement to Harker?"

"It says I did, don't it?"

"I asked you whether you made that statement to Richard Harker."

Foster moved his head up, coal-black eyes staring directly at Jamison. "And I told you what I had to say."

"Before you came to Corcoran you were at San Quentin, where Harker was?"

"You got my jacket," Foster said, referring to the file kept on inmates. "You know where I been." Foster smiled. "I've stayed at all the best places, including Q."

"Did you talk to Harker while you were at Quentin?"

"Man, why you keep asking questions? I told you that I got nothing to say to you."

He looked Jamison up and down. "Your name's Jamison, that right? Your daddy Roger Jamison, right? The big-shot lawyer? You look like him. He's your daddy, right? Heard he was dead."

"That's right, Roger Jamison was my father. Yes, he passed away several years ago." Jamison didn't intend to answer more than those questions from Foster. It was never a good idea to get friendly with witnesses or criminal suspects and he was not inclined to discuss his father with Foster.

"You thinking I didn't know your daddy, right?" Foster squinted, focusing on Jamison's face. "You don't know, do you?" Foster started laughing as he got up and began turning toward the door where a guard was watching through the window. "Like I keep tellin' you, I got nothing to say to you. I got to live in here now. Different rules. You can't do nothin' to me. Nobody can. Worst some judge can do is put me in jail and I'm already here." As he reached the door he stopped. "I'll tell you this 'cause you'll find out soon enough anyway. Nobody told you how I got my deal, did they?"

Jamison didn't answer.

"Your daddy was my lawyer." Foster caught the raised eyebrow from Jamison. "That's right. Big-shot lawyer Roger Jamison liked to get down in the mud once in a while, I guess. Made him feel better to get his hands dirty from someone like me instead of from all that dirty money he made defendin' rich folks and drug dealers. He's the one that made my deal to testify against Harker. Got me immunity too. He was a real good lawyer, your daddy." Foster started laughing again. "That's funny. Your daddy made my deal and now here we are. Old times, huh?" Foster was still laughing as he asked the guard to let him through the door.

～

"Well that trip wasn't worth shit." O'Hara's teeth clinched his unlit cigar tightly as he wheeled the county car past the Corcoran prison gate. He kept glancing over at Jamison, who had not said a word while they walked out of the prison and got into the car. He seemed to have an idea of what Jamison was thinking. Eventually it would come out.

"Gage never told me that my father was the one who made the deal for Foster to testify against Harker."

"Maybe he forgot?"

"He didn't forget. He didn't want to hear me start making excuses about why I shouldn't handle the case."

"Does it make a real difference?" O'Hara was familiar with the sometimes arcane rules of ethics that lawyers used, although he was of the opinion that most lawyer's ethics depended on the downside if they interpreted them too strictly. Jamison was an exception as far as he was concerned but he maintained his cynicism for the rest of the breed.

His question to Jamison was met with a silence that lingered for several miles through the flat farmland bordering the road. Finally, Jamison spoke. "It doesn't really make a difference, I guess. It just makes me uncomfortable, but that's my problem. Our problem is that if Foster isn't going to talk to us, he's going to have to talk at the hearing because Gifford isn't going to be able to use Harker's declaration to prove what Foster said was true. Foster will have to testify. We just don't know what exactly he's going to say and he's right about one thing: we can't make him talk to us."

"What if the judge orders him to testify?"

"The only thing a judge can do is put him in jail if he refuses to talk and since Foster's already there I don't think that's much of a threat. We'll just have to wait and see if he's going to talk or not."

"Doesn't make any difference." O'Hara kept his eyes on the road. "Whatever Foster says is going to be jailhouse bullshit. Just because twenty-six years later a guy who's in the joint decides to change his testimony isn't going to persuade a judge, is it? Even judges got to see through that."

"I don't think a judge is going to be persuaded by a jailhouse conversion at this point." Jamison was looking out the side window as he spoke. "But it might make a difference when it gets packaged together with Christine Farrow. I'm going to call Ernie and have him see if she's available." He pulled out his cell phone and punched in a number on speed dial.

The rest of the ride was silent. O'Hara kept looking over at Jamison, who was staring out the passenger window, lost in thought. All O'Hara knew were bits and pieces about Jamison, that his father had been a famous criminal defense lawyer and that he and his son had a distant and contentious relationship that somehow related to the father's treatment of Jamison's mother. O'Hara was fully aware that he was in no position to offer fatherly advice. He had utterly failed as a father himself. All he knew was that it wasn't easy to be a good father, but he sensed that now wasn't the time to offer that thought. He kept his eyes on the road as his mind pushed forward memories of the daughter that he had lost because of his own shortcomings, a realization that had begun to sharpen with age and the clarity of hindsight.

As the flat country passed in the blur of high speed at which O'Hara was traveling, Jamison's mind tried to wrap itself around the fact that the man from whom he had tried so hard to distance himself was, in fact and in memory, now right in front of him again. As much as he tried to ignore it, resentment was clouding his mind—dead and buried and still his father's hand was moving across Jamison's life. He had spent most of his life trying to separate himself from what he was and what his father was, and now once again his father would have to be confronted.

Chapter 15

Christine Farrow wasn't available that afternoon, but she was off from work the next day. She was a waitress at a coffee shop that Jamison was familiar with, a late-night hangout for cops that had drawn shifts in the part of the city that time and economics had left to decay. He had been there many times himself, meeting with his investigators and detectives as they dealt with whatever crime demanded their attention in the middle of the night.

Jamison spent the time going over her testimony at the trial as well as listening again to the tapes she made. He had twice gone down to see Gage to ask why he hadn't told him about his father making the deal for Foster's testimony, but Gage's door stayed closed and his secretary said he wouldn't be available. Jamison wasn't sure if Gage's lack of availability was deliberate or not. In the end, he decided that there wasn't much he could say anyway other than Gage should have told him.

He debated about taking O'Hara with him when he went to see Christine Farrow. While he had deep respect for O'Hara's ability as an investigator, there was a practical aspect—O'Hara scared most people. While he didn't intend to, O'Hara was an intimidating presence. It was remarkably effective with interrogation but with victims it simply depended on the person. It wasn't only his rumbling voice; his already coffee-colored complexion seemed to grow visibly darker as he focused intently. The exception was women. O'Hara was always good with women. For some reason that Jamison was unable to fathom, O'Hara would look at a woman and she had his undivided attention. Unfortunately, his charm wasn't long-lasting as evidenced by two disastrous marriages. Ernie Garcia, on the other hand, was completely different.

Ernie had an affable personality that naturally set people at ease, even those he interrogated. He used it effectively. With his copper complexion and square face, he would smile and call somebody amigo, throwing them off with his combinations of Spanish and English. Built like a brick, Garcia lulled his suspects into letting their guard down, drawn in by what they perceived as his empathy or, at least, lack of rejection of them as human beings. O'Hara, however, simply beat down the barriers set up by his suspects.

After thinking carefully about it, Jamison decided he would take Ernie to meet with Christine Farrow. Even though O'Hara had an ability to connect with women, Jamison had a sense that she was going to be fragile and he wanted somebody who would work his way in slowly. Ernie was that man. He told O'Hara to devote his attention to gathering all the reports at the sheriff's office.

The county car moved to the edge of the street where Christine Farrow lived. There was no curb, only an end to the pitted asphalt where it slowly merged into beaten earth. Jamison imagined that all cities had their share of what some people called "the mean streets." The term never held much meaning to Jamison before he had become a prosecutor.

Set back from the street, a collection of single-story apartments stretched out, simple stucco boxes that filled the space available, cheap housing built on cheap land. Jamison knew what was in those apartments without ever going inside. He had walked through the broken doors of such places in the past, serving search warrants or arrest warrants or, more frequently, surveying the carnage of a moment of mindless anger as he looked at a body on the floor.

In every community, including his, places like this were where violence churned in the city's belly. As he and Ernie walked to the door, he couldn't help thinking that Christine Farrow had not climbed more than a rung of the ladder from where she had lived as a child—maybe not even climbed that one rung.

Wires stuck out where a doorbell had once been. Someone had taped the ends of the exposed wire as an accommodation to their notion of safety. The door showed the grime of countless hands. Jamison waited as Ernie knocked. He didn't say anything about who they were. Neither man had any illusions that people looking through slits in their curtains wouldn't know immediately that they were "the man," a collective reference to authority figures to be avoided. But in places like this, it was never wise to be seen as cooperating with authority.

When the door opened, a woman's wary face peered out. Ernie showed his badge and quietly asked if they could come in. She nodded and backed away from the open door, taking a seat on a couch that had a pile of unfolded clothes at one end. There was one other chair near the edge of the couch.

"Ms. Farrow? I'm Ernie Garcia, an investigator with the district attorney's office, and this is Matt Jamison, a prosecutor who has been assigned to the Harker case. We spoke on the phone?"

The woman looked back at both of them. "Yes, that lawyer, Gifford, said you would probably come to see me. It's about what I said in that paper I signed, right?" Her voice held a soft drawl common to people whose families had migrated to the Valley during the Dust Bowl era of the 1930s, seeking better lives, many only finding a different meager way to exist.

"Yes, I've read your declaration. That's what we'd like to talk about." Jamison took the single chair and set a notebook on his knee. "Like Ernie—Investigator Garcia—said, I'm a prosecutor, a lawyer with the district attorney, who's been assigned to look at the Harker case."

The face of Christine Farrow told a whole story of her life without saying a word. Jamison could see that she had been pretty once, in the way that some women are who have their glory days in high school, when slender bodies and high cheek bones have the luxury of young skin and soft complexions. But time is often not kind to those women unless life is kind to them. And life had not been kind to Christine Farrow.

What could be imagined as once defined bone structure now only supported the tightly drawn canvas of a too-soon-aged face. What beauty she retained was provided by cheap makeup and the confidence she projected that came from the attention of men who shared the same luck she had drawn in life.

But it was her eyes that spoke to Jamison. Deep set and hidden below arched brows darkened by eyebrow pencil until what had been real was now only painted slashes from cheap makeup, the blue eyes betrayed the memories of a woman who had seen images of life that were best left unimagined. It was the vestige of the face of the child Jamison had seen in the photographs, and the eyes still reflected the absence of innocence, only now they also held a hardness shaped by the reality of life.

"I've read the declaration you've signed, and I've gone over the reports from this case, Ms. Farrow. I would like to talk to you if I could about your statement." Jamison wanted to probe carefully.

"Call me Christine. That's what everybody calls me." She waited quietly before asking, "I guess this causes a problem, my saying that Rick Harker didn't do it?" She didn't seem to comprehend the magnitude of the understatement. "I feel bad, him spending all those years in prison but . . ." Her voice trailed off.

"It's been a long time, Christine. Memories fade and sometimes things seem different when we think about events that happened long ago." Jamison wanted to avoid any kind of confrontation that implied he didn't believe her or might make her defensive. "What caused you to think you'd made a mistake in your testimony? It was a long time ago, twenty-six years."

"I was only three when it happened, Mr. Jamison. People asked me a lot of questions. By the time I testified, everyone seemed so sure. It's hard for me to explain. Even now, I can close my eyes and see it clearly. The memory of all of it, my mother, the trial, it's like a movie in my mind. I can still remember sitting in that chair looking at all those people and the judge. Hardly a day in my life has gone by without me thinking about it. Then there were the dreams."

"The dreams?" Jamison had a feeling this was coming. He had dealt with children who had been through traumatic experiences and often dreams would be part of it. But he also knew that dreams could confuse a child, could confuse even an adult, and there was a real risk that dreams could become part of what a child thought of as reality.

"Growing up, I dreamed sometimes about my mother. I try to remember her but all I have are a few pictures of her and me." Christine pointed to the table at the end of the couch. It held two framed photographs, one of a woman who looked a lot like the woman sitting in front of Jamison, including carrying hard years on her face. Jamison hadn't noticed the resemblance at first because all he had seen were pictures of Lisa Farrow on an autopsy table, and nobody looks their best laid out on a steel slab. The other photograph was of the same woman and a little girl, sitting on a porch. The little girl whose face Jamison had stared at from the file in her mother's murder case. These were the images that Christine had of a woman who could only be a distant memory. Photographs that were a constant reminder of the best of her life and the worst.

"The last few years it seemed like the dreams started to come at night more and more often, and then it started to be dreams of the fire and of my mother— finding her. They were so real, you know? And they just got worse and worse, the images clearer and clearer. It was like watching a television show over and over again when at first you could only see blurry images and hear sounds, and then slowly each time it became more and more real. And I could see a man over and over. I don't know how to explain it. But there was this fear that was overwhelming. I would wake up sweating so much the sheets were wet. It was all I could think about—just the images over and over again. And this feeling of guilt that I couldn't understand. That's when I was able to see Dr. Vinson. He's the one who helped me."

"Tell me about Dr. Vinson. How did he help you?"

"They told me I didn't have to talk to you about that." Christine wasn't defensive. It was more of a question.

"Who told you that?" Jamison suspected that Gifford or maybe this Vinson had told her that she didn't have to talk about sessions with a psychiatrist or a psychologist.

"That attorney, Mr. Gifford. He said that what Dr. Vinson and I talked about was between us and that I didn't have to tell anybody. Is that right?"

"There are things called privileges, Christine. You may be talking about what we call the psychologist privilege, but all we want to know is the truth. Is that a problem?"

She looked down at her hands and began twisting at the T-shirt she was wearing. "Maybe I should talk to Dr. Vinson? It's hard for me to talk about this, you know? I just want to do the right thing. I made a mistake. I shouldn't have said that Rick Harker did it. I know that now."

Jamison didn't want to press the issue, but he needed to know. "Okay, for now, let's just talk about what you remember. Is that all right?"

She nodded. "I want to help. All I can tell you is what I know happened."

"So, tell us about that."

She closed her eyes. Jamison felt both guilty and ashamed that he was making this woman relive a horror that most people could not even imagine. And now she was going to have to not only relive it in a courtroom, he was concealing the fact that he was going to be tearing her story apart. Jamison pushed down the guilt. He had to do what he had to do. As he watched her, he could see the pain pulling at the corners of her mouth as her lips trembled.

"A lot of it isn't that clear in my mind. I heard voices in the kitchen, and then I heard my mama screaming and I could tell there was fighting. Then it was quiet. Then I smelled the smoke, you know? I didn't know then exactly what it was but I somehow knew it wasn't good. I waited a long time and then climbed out of bed. My mama was on the floor. I remember that. There was smoke under Mama. I remember pushing on her, but she didn't wake up. Then I stayed there waiting for her to wake up. I remember the neighbors and the police when they came."

Jamison waited for more, but Christine was silent. Tears were sliding down her cheeks. He felt guilty at even asking her to relive the memory, but this was something that he had to do and it would take time to build trust that he knew he would have to use as a tool to pry at every crack he could find. There was one more question he needed to ask, however. "Christine, you heard fighting. Did you hear voices?"

"I heard my mama saying, 'Rick, no.' I remember that. She just kept saying it over and over again. And I remember a man's voice."

"Did you recognize the voice?"

"No, they were yelling in the kitchen and when I try to remember all I can say is that when I think about it now, it didn't sound human. At the time it was just so angry and mean, like an animal, you know? That's how I remember it when I hear it in my dreams—like an animal. There was a lot of yelling. All I can say is that I heard Mama's voice and the other voice. It was a man. I can remember that."

"Christine." Jamison tried to keep his voice as comforting as he could. "Was there only one man or more than one?"

Tears were now streaming down Christine's face as both Jamison and Ernie could see her reliving the moment in her mind before she answered. "I only remember one man. After the sounds stopped of my mother screaming, he came into my room. That's what I kept seeing in my dreams. He was standing over my bed looking at me. Then I would wake up terrified. That's what Dr. Vinson helped me to remember. If there was more than one man, I don't know."

She stopped talking for a moment. "When I close my eyes, I can still see him standing over my bed, leaning down close to my face and telling me to go to sleep. I remember his breath, the way he smelled. He was so close to me. Then he left me, and then later that's when I saw light flickering and smelled the smoke. Then I found my mama, but he was gone."

He hesitated before asking, knowing that this was the answer that he had to have. "Did you know who he was, that man?"

"It was Rick Sample. It was Tommy's daddy. It was him. He's the one who killed my mother."

Chapter 16

The heat trapped in Ernie's county car from the late morning sun warmed the cold sweat built up under Jamison's shirt. He'd carefully watched Christine Farrow as she accused another man of the crime for which Rick Harker had spent over twenty-six years in prison. He could already tell what was coming. Harker's lawyer would put Foster on the stand to say that Harker was innocent and figure out some way to explain why he lied at the original trial and wasn't lying now.

Jamison wasn't worried about that. Foster simply coming in and claiming that he hadn't told the truth and had decided in jail to come out wasn't going to be enough to persuade a judge, not without hard evidence that didn't depend on Foster's credibility. Convicts did that all the time, rarely because of jailhouse conversions and usually because it bought them a way to avoid the stigma of a rat jacket. Honor among thieves was a value system alien to the rest of the world.

But Christine Farrow was another thing. She wasn't a criminal. And she had no motive to free the man convicted of killing her mother, no motive at all—except some deeply repressed misguided sense of guilt—or the truth—or both.

Jamison had seen it before, children who began to doubt the reality they had created for themselves as shards of the past battered them in unsuspecting moments. It was one of the things that he hated the most about crimes against children. Their immature minds would suppress the horror, pushing it back into dark recesses where it would lie, a slowly growing infection until years later it would rise up in the mind like stones buried in the soil. And when those memories pushed themselves out for whatever reason, there was just pain.

Jamison knew that some people could handle it, the memories of the past, but a lot of people couldn't. In one of his last cases he had seen the way a woman's molestation as a child had irreparably warped her ability to function as an adult. The worst part was that she knew it and she kept it hidden, struggling to present stability to the world, not allowing the world to see the turmoil in her mind until she could no longer hold it in.

But the memories were always there, like night monsters clawing for attention. Jamison understood that some people had better coping mechanisms and were able to get past it. He didn't have contempt or lack sympathy for those who couldn't cope. He only had empathy. It was one of the reasons he was a prosecutor. And he felt empathy for Christine, for the child she was and for the woman she had become. He felt empathy because he himself had learned to live with memories of the past that haunted him. All he really knew was that it wasn't easy.

What he also felt was his own guilt at what he would have to do to her on the witness stand. There was no real choice. Twenty-six years later, after the horrible trauma of her mother's murder, finding her, sitting in that kitchen next to her—Jamison shuddered at the thought. And now she would have to relive it again along with the guilt that she had sent an innocent man to prison, whether the guilt was justified or not. What had happened to her before had made her a victim her entire life and now he was going to tear open that scab once more.

That was the worst part, the destructive acid of memory and lack of closure, slowly eroding the ability to cope. And that was the lot of Christine Farrow, whether she had made a mistake or not. Either way she would never have the simple luxury of freedom from the impact of the past. Any way you looked at it, she was three years old and what happened to her had swept her up and pulled her down into a whirlpool of emotional destruction. For Christine, the best part of her life was over at three and what remained was simply the perseverance to make it through each new day and each new night of what was left.

As they drove back to the DA's office, Ernie let Jamison stare out the car window without saying anything. He seldom spoke unless he had something he wanted to say and right now he could sense that Jamison needed his own space. That was Ernie's ability, to sense when a person had withdrawn to the inside of their mind and to know when the moment was right to pull them back. It made him a skilled interrogator, but it also made him a man others instinctively trusted, and that allowed him to take advantage when people let down their guard to him, if they were a suspect, and to help people he cared about when they needed it. Right now, he wasn't sure exactly what Jamison needed, but Ernie understood that he needed to be left alone.

Finally, as they pulled into the parking garage at the county office building where the district attorney was located, Jamison spoke. "I want every piece of evidence in the Harker case gone over with a fine-tooth comb—nothing left to assumption. And I want you and Bill to find Rick Sample. I want to know where he is. I want to know everything there is to know about him."

"You're not thinking that Harker didn't do it, are you?"

"No, I'm not thinking he didn't do it. But I am thinking that Harker's come back into that woman's mind and screwed with it one more time, and I intend to make sure that this time we will rip him a second asshole. When we get through with Harker I intend to bury him and bury him so deep that he's done for good. I'm thinking that at the end of this we have to be able to help that woman believe she did the right thing. If I'm going to have to tear Christine Farrow's story apart, I want to make sure I'm right. I owe her that. We owe her that."

Chapter 17

O'Hara was waiting for them when Jamison and Ernie walked into the office. The first thing Jamison said was, "I want you to find Rick Sample and bring him in."

"Well, Boss, that's going to be hard to do because he got himself dead. Got killed in a bar fight almost nine years ago. I figured you'd want to know something about him so I checked. That's a dead end, really dead end, I guess." O'Hara sucked the bottom of his mustache into his mouth as he rubbed his upper lip. "I checked all the sheriff's reports in the case and had copies made so we could compare to what you got in that stack of boxes. There's also some tapes. I didn't play them. And the evidence from the scene is still boxed up. I had them pull it down. Figured you'd want to look at it."

"Tell me how it happened."

"I told you," O'Hara said with irritation in his voice that he hadn't sufficiently answered the question. "It was a bar fight. Sample got into it with some guy in a bar. They went into an alley. Nobody followed. When somebody took the trash out they found extra trash in the dumpster—it was Sample. I did a quick scan of the reports. You want more, I'll pull it all."

Before Jamison asked the next question, O'Hara finished the thought. "No, they didn't make an arrest. All they had was that the argument was with some guy. The bartender said he thought it was a white guy but he had on a hood, coulda been Mexican or maybe even black. Look, this was a bar over on G Street. You know what that part of town is like. It was Saturday night. Two men arguing, probably over some woman holding up a bar stool. Nobody looked, nobody heard, nobody saw nothin'. Case closed. One less asshole in the world."

"Real sensitive, Bill." Jamison's exasperation was not directed at O'Hara. It was the whole case. O'Hara smiled, although to some people it might look like he was in pain.

"Yeah, I get that a lot. I'm working on my sensitivity but so far not much progress. How'd it go with Christine?"

"Not much there. Apparently, she worked with this Dr. Vinson. We'll need to get more background on him. Ernie's working on that. Right now, I want to see the evidence."

⤵

The evidence room clerk took them to a table inside the evidence cage. He explained that everything the sheriff's office had in the Harker case was sitting in the boxes on the table. They were reminded not to open anything that was sealed unless they initialed it. Then he went back to the counter. They could call him when they were finished.

Jamison looked at the pile of boxes. "Bill, you already look at this stuff?"

"Yeah, I went through it and the inventory list. It all matches. Everything that was tagged and bagged at the crime scene is in here." He pulled off the lid of the first box and began removing plastic bags with evidence tags attached and court exhibit numbers. The first thing that caught Jamison's eye was bags with charred and partially melted beer cans.

Jamison picked up the bag of cans, feeling them through the clear plastic, charred bits flaked off the cans, joining other pieces of ash at the bottom of the bag. O'Hara was watching. "Those are the beer cans that were used to set the fire. Harker put gas in them according to the forensic report and then poured it on the victim. He didn't have much gas but what he had did the job. He put the empty cans on magazines under her legs, heavy paper, trying to make a big fire. The flash from the gas burned the victim real bad and then when the flame went out the thick magazines just slowly smoldered and burned and then went out. Where the gas got on the body, the flesh was charred, but other than destroying evidence of any kind of sexual assault, that was it. The thing is, the son of a bitch started that fire and left that little girl in the house." The anger in O'Hara's voice was evident.

There was a knife with a broken blade tip and another bag with the charred magazines. Jamison had seen the crime scene photographs and he knew that they had been lying under the body. Other bags had additional unburned beer cans that still bore remnants of fingerprint powder.

Jamison pulled the lid off of the other boxes, shoving aside the contents, looking to see if there was anything else he needed to see. One bag held clothing that was partially burned. Another held a child's T-shirt and underwear. Jamison surmised that it had been worn by three-year-old Christine Farrow. It still bore smudges from ash. Jamison flashed back on the photographs of the child and what the grimy clothes represented. That was it. "Not much for a capital murder, is it?" He pushed the various bags around on the table and then indicated to Bill that he should put them back into the boxes. "Was there any biological evidence taken at all? Any blood or other physical evidence? Maybe we could do DNA testing?"

O'Hara shook his head. "There was blood on the victim, but nobody took any blood samples from her face that I can find. There were some fingernail scrapings but as far as I know they didn't come up with any blood. I'm not sure where they are or if they even still exist. All I know is that according to the reports they didn't show anything. I know that Harker didn't have any scratches on him when they arrested him. He did have some abrasions, but he also resisted so how they happened isn't clear."

"Track down the fingernail scrapings and anything else that might be worth testing again."

There wasn't much else to do prior to the hearing with the exception of seeing if Alton Grady, Harker's trial counsel, was still alive and if he was, if he had anything he was willing to say. Jamison didn't hold out much hope. He had heard about Alton Grady when older lawyers told war stories. But Grady's prime was when Jamison had been a child. What he was now was anybody's guess and that assumed he was still alive and age hadn't withered his brain to the point where the synapses just kept his bodily functions going and stopped paying attention to anything else.

⌒

Jamison didn't have long to guess about Alton Grady. He was now in an assisted living center and had been for almost ten years. Jamison walked into the foyer of the center with O'Hara following him. It was bright and sunny but there was a faint odor that reminded Jamison of his grandparents' house. What he used to call "old people's smell" when he was little. It hadn't changed.

The attendant walked them to a solarium and pointed. "There's Alton, the one in the wheelchair staring out of the window. He's pretty alert, at least for this time of day. Some of them have good times of the day and bad. He'll talk to you. He was a lawyer—likes to tell stories. At least he used to. He doesn't talk much anymore that you can follow."

"Mr. Grady?" Jamison stood next to the wheelchair and leaned down to its occupant. Alton Grady looked ancient even by the standards of the other occupants in the solarium. What hair he had was tufted wisps of white that stuck out at odd angles. But when he looked up to see who was asking, his rheumy eyes seemed to get brighter. He nodded but didn't say anything.

"Mr. Grady, my name is Matt Jamison from the district attorney's office and this man with me is Bill O'Hara, an investigator with us. I'd like to talk to you about the Harker case if you have some time."

Grady slowly nodded and flicked one hand. "Time? I have time." He waited without saying more.

"You were the trial lawyer defending Rick Harker?"

"Maybe. Tell me about the case. That helps." Jamison had the sense that Grady understood far more than he was letting on, but he went along with the old man's question.

"It was a death penalty case. The victim was a woman, Lisa Farrow, and Harker set the house on fire, tried to burn the body. The jury returned a death verdict but the judge gave him a life sentence. You remember it? You were his lawyer." Jamison had a sinking feeling that this wasn't going anywhere. He added helpfully, "You saved him from the death penalty."

"Always said he was innocent." Grady smiled. "They all say that, you know? But he said he was innocent." The words came out of Grady's mouth in a mumble. "Jamison? You Roger's boy? You look like him. Good lawyer, Roger. Good lawyer. He still around?"

"Roger Jamison was my father. He's gone now. Thank you, he was a good lawyer. Everybody says so. I never really saw that side of him. Anyway, about Rick Harker?"

"Yes, he was innocent, you know? That was a bad case—that little girl. I remember her. And your daddy, he was in it too. I remember that. It was a big case. Harker never had a chance. I did my best. Sorry about your daddy. I guess I've outlived most everyone I knew . . ." Grady's voice trailed off and he resumed staring out the window. "Can't remember much anymore, just bits and pieces."

"Can you tell me why you say Harker was innocent? Did you have some reason to believe he really didn't do it?"

"Told me he was innocent. They all say that, you know? But you get a feeling over the years. I believed him. I did my best. I do remember that judge. What was his name?"

"Judge Stevenson." Jamison looked over at O'Hara, who shook his head.

"Yes, Walker Stevenson. Good judge. Good man. He made a tough call—the right call. Is he still alive?"

"Yes, sir. But was there anything else that made you think Harker was innocent? Anything at all that you can tell us?

"That young DA. What was his name?"

"Are you talking about Gage?"

"No, the other one. The one that became a judge."

"Jonathon Cleary?"

"Yes, him. I kept asking him for his files, but I didn't trust him. Never did. You can tell, you know?"

"Why—why didn't you trust him?"

"What?"

Jamison stood up. There was no point. He had one last thought. "Did you keep your files?"

"Ask my daughter. She knows. Ask her. She comes to visit me. Only one that still knows I'm alive I guess. Lorie's a good girl. Wife's gone now—long time. Lorie takes care of my house. I'm sorry. I don't remember much anymore. Just bits and pieces. All Harker ever said was that he was innocent. He had no alibi." Grady lifted his head. "I was a good lawyer. I was. Won a lot of cases. I remember Harker. He was innocent. Ask your father. I should have won. He knew. Ask him." Grady's eyes were losing their focus, the brightness fading.

O'Hara broke the silence when they walked out of the assisted living center. "I think I'd rather be dead than like that."

"Maybe. I'll remember that when I visit you in the home." O'Hara's only response was with a middle finger.

"Tomorrow we have to make an appearance in this case. Take me back to the office. I need to get ready."

"Ready? We got nothing." O'Hara chewed on the unlit cigar in his mouth.

"That's not true exactly. We got a conviction. Let's see what Harker's lawyer's got. He's the one who has to prove there's something there. We don't."

Chapter 18

Jamison felt his throat tighten as he entered the swinging gate leading into the well of the courtroom. The press had been outside taking his picture as he walked down the hall with O'Hara. The Harker case was still big news. He moved carefully past the television camera shoved in his face and smiled but offered no comment. He knew that this would be the file film the press would use over and over again on the evening news. He had learned to smile. If you made any kind of face or looked angry, that was the picture they would use.

O'Hara took a seat next to Jamison at the counsel table. Gifford was already seated. He looked rumpled, but Jamison suspected that Gifford always looked rumpled, clothes not quite matching, tie carelessly knotted. It was passive defiance of the lawyer's dress code. Jamison, on the other hand, had dressed carefully in a black suit and red silk tie. He nodded a greeting at Gifford and waited for the two other main participants to come into the courtroom—Judge Herman Wallace and Richard Harker. They would not come through the same door.

It didn't take long for the door to open from the holding cell area. A burly bailiff walked through first. Behind him shuffled Richard Harker, dressed in an orange jailhouse jumpsuit, followed by another bailiff. His hands were manacled in front of him and attached to a belly chain that ran around his waist and then down to another set of manacles that went around both ankles. He didn't walk with the awkward steps of someone unfamiliar with such chains. It was evident that Harker had learned how to adapt to the restrictions of his place in the world. After all, Jamison thought, he's had twenty-six years to learn.

Harker looked around the courtroom with a quick bird-like movement, a man trying to rapidly take everything in to understand his surroundings. It was a common reaction of men who had spent a great deal of time in prison. When you lived in an environment where you never knew if the others in the room were your friends or your enemies, you needed to have a rodent's awareness of your situation. Survival was the daily lot of the Richard Harkers of the world. His face showed the pasty complexion of a man who didn't see the sun very often. Harker had spent much of the last few years of his existence in what was commonly called "the SHU," the secured housing unit. Twenty-three hours a day in lockdown with one hour to exercise in a narrow-walled area. Some men were kept there for discipline. Others did their time there for protection from other prisoners. Harker had apparently managed to get there for both reasons. His time in the SHU was an intermittent interruption of his time in the mainline, except for the time in the local jail, which some people who had done hard time claimed was worse than the joint.

Jamison had gotten as much information as he could from Harker's prison jacket, his file. At first, he had spent time in a segregated housing area at San Quentin for high profile prisoners. Jamison had seen that facility before, a cold concrete edifice that was a constant cacophony of noise, clanging steel doors, and words reverberating off of hard walls that kept such prisoners separate from the mainline, the hard-core prisoners. The floor was usually slick with water dripping from men leaving the showers, which added to the mélange of odors that permeated the walls of such closed facilities. It was not a pleasant place in a warren of unpleasant places but it was reasonably safe from the alternative.

If you acted up or were difficult, then you went to the mainline, and if you went there, it was often the end of the line for men like Harker. Even hard-time prisoners had standards, a pecking order. Rapists and child molesters were always at the bottom and Harker had managed, with his crime, to slide even below the bottom-dwellers in the prison cesspool. For such people, there were constant assaults and you either fought or died or you ended up in the SHU. And if you ended up dead, nobody expressed outrage except at the additional paperwork, not when you were a man whose life was confined by a six-by-ten room to keep you away from everyone else.

Harker nodded at Gifford. He didn't say anything. His face showed the onset of the lines of middle age. He carried no extra weight, the orange jumpsuit hanging loosely on him. But his eyes were hard, glinting through a squint as he swung his head around the room. As with many such men, his reputation and his crime were far more threatening than the way the man actually looked.

"He doesn't look like a vicious murderer, does he?" Jamison nudged O'Hara.

"They never do—except when they admit it." O'Hara spoke from years of experience. He often observed that for most people, murderers looked no different than the person who sat next to them on the bus.

The bailiffs pushed Harker into the seat next to his lawyer while one of them knelt down and attached the leg irons to a bolt in the floor. They then released the handcuffs and slid off the belly chain. To the world Harker would look like he was just sitting at the counsel table but beneath the table he would be leashed by chrome-colored steel restraints. As he made himself comfortable, the chains rattled. He had just enough room to stand when the bailiff called the court to order.

Judge Herman Wallace didn't walk through the door that led to his chambers; he burst through the door without waiting for ceremony. His massive bulk was draped in a black robe that was large enough that the running courthouse joke was that it could also be used as a small car cover. The robe was only slightly darker than Wallace's complexion, and his eyes seemed to burn when he looked at you. Wallace's raspy voice asked everyone to be seated. He took the file from his clerk and read the name for the record. "In the matter of Richard Harker, case number F 36842."

Wallace peered over the reading glasses perched on his nose and acknowledged Gifford and Jamison before addressing the focus of the hearing. "You are Mr. Richard Harker, I presume?"

Gifford responded, standing quickly. "Yes, Your Honor, Mr. Harker is present in court."

"Thank you, Mr. Gifford. My question is addressed to the prisoner."

"Yes, sir, Your Honor. Richard Harker, that's me."

Wallace shuffled paper in the thick file and then flipped through what Jamison assumed was the order returned from the supreme court. "Well, Mr. Gifford, it seems you got somebody's attention in San Francisco." Most people assumed the supreme court was in the state capitol of Sacramento, but it had been in San Francisco since the turn of the last century. Wallace coughed. "So what are your intentions, Mr. Gifford—a full-blown hearing?"

Gifford rose from his seat. "Yes, Your Honor. As the court is aware, my client has been granted a right to a full hearing, which we would like as soon as possible. He *has* been in prison for twenty-six years."

"When will you be ready to proceed, Mr. Gifford?" Wallace ignored the thinly veiled sarcasm from Gifford. He was used to Gifford's opinions of the justice system.

"I can be ready in a week, Your Honor, the court's calendar and Mr. Jamison's schedule permitting."

Jamison had been waiting for his moment. "Your Honor, the People can be ready to proceed quickly but first there are some preliminary matters to clear up. What witnesses does Mr. Gifford intend to present?"

Gifford turned sideways and spoke to Jamison rather than the court. "That depends, Mr. Jamison, what witnesses do *you* plan to present?"

Wallace's hand slammed against the surface of the bench. "Mr. Gifford, Mr. Jamison, you will address the court, not each other."

Gifford made a desultory effort to be contrite, as Jamison directed a response to Wallace. "Your Honor, my answer to Mr. Gifford's question is we don't intend to present any witnesses at this time since we don't know what evidence or who Mr. Gifford plans to present. The ball is in his court. He's the one who has to show that there is some reason to overturn the conviction, not me."

The judge turned to Gifford. "Mr. Jamison is correct. At this point it's unclear what the evidence is that you plan to present. Until that's known, there is no basis for him to present evidence. Let me suggest this. Let Mr. Jamison know who your witnesses will be, and then he will be in a position to investigate and respond. Your client is obviously in custody and he has no speedy trial rights under the circumstances so we will do the hearing in parts. I will allow you,

Mr. Gifford, to present your case. Mr. Jamison can cross-examine, and then he can put his witnesses together and respond if he has any rebuttal. We will do this over several weeks. I have a busy trial calendar and I can't interrupt it with this case because the other cases have been set for a considerable period of time, but I will give you Fridays, and if there is a break in my trial schedule I will give you those days. We will work around my schedule and yours. That's the best I can do unless you want me to set this case at least three months from now."

"Your Honor," Gifford said in a measured tone, "my client has been in custody a long time. We understand the court's trial schedule. I have trials also as, I imagine, Mr. Jamison does. Mr. Harker accepts the schedule of the hearing."

Jamison considered the proposal. The hearing would be stretched out over several weeks, but what Wallace was proposing would give him time to investigate and to react instead of scrambling trying to put together a case when he didn't know what Gifford had. "Acceptable to the People, Your Honor," he said.

"Anything else?" Wallace said, as he flipped through the file.

"On behalf of Mr. Harker, we would like access to the evidence in the case and a copy of all the reports. I believe we have everything, but I just want to be sure."

Jamison thought about the bulging boxes of reports. There was no point in arguing. Gifford was entitled to them as well as access to the evidence. "I will begin the process of copying as soon as I return to my office. And just so we don't waste a lot of time, if the court pleases, what is the answer to my question? What witnesses does the defense plan to present?"

"On behalf of Mr. Harker, we plan to call Clarence Foster, Christine Farrow, and Detective Mike Jensen. And possibly—Mr. Harker." Gifford paused, glancing over at Jamison. "And we will be calling the district attorney, William Gage, and Justice Jonathon Cleary."

Jamison reacted immediately. "What is it that Mr. Gage and Justice Cleary will be asked about? They were the prosecutors in this case. I see no relevance to their testimony. Everything is in the reports and in the trial record."

"I suggest you ask them, Mr. Jamison." Gifford closed his briefcase. "I suggest you ask them."

Chapter 19

O'Hara and Ernie followed Jamison into his office, waiting to discuss what had happened in court. O'Hara spoke up first. "Okay, Boss, so where do we start? We know what Christine Farrow's going to say. Why he wants Gage and Judge Cleary, I haven't figured out."

"What I want to do is prepare for cross-examination of Gifford's witnesses." Jamison scanned his notes from the hearing. "That means I'll need all the background on Foster and Christine. I think we can pretty much guess that Foster's going to claim that Sample did it or something like that, or that he lied. Whatever. It doesn't make any difference. We need to be ready for him. I want to look at the file on the killing of Sample also. Probably nothing there but you never know. Ernie, get me the background on Christine's shrink, Vinson. I'll talk to Gage one more time. Then we talk to Judge Cleary. Probably nothing there but we need to close the door."

"What about the files from Harker's first lawyer, Grady?" Ernie asked.

"And what about your old man's files? He's the one that represented Foster. Maybe there's something there?" O'Hara said it quietly because he realized it would touch a nerve with Jamison, but it seemed like a logical place to start.

Jamison shook his head. "We can't do either one. Grady was Harker's lawyer and attorney-client privilege applies. Same with my father's files on Foster."

"Do you still have your father's files?" Ernie asked.

"Yeah, I think they're in storage. My mother wouldn't have thrown them out. Still pays the storage bill for his stuff. I don't know why."

"Well, maybe you could look? Who's going to know?" O'Hara had the look on his face that he got when he was sliding by what he considered a legal technicality.

"I would know. Under the law, anything Foster said to my father was privileged and Foster has to give us permission. Maybe he will and maybe he won't. I'm guessing no. Same with Harker. For right now, Bill, I want you to get me the background on the Sample case. Maybe there's a connection, probably not. Ernie, I want you to get me the background on Vinson and poke around and see if there's anything on Christine Farrow, but take it real easy with her, nothing direct. I'm going to see Gage and then I'll go see Judge Cleary."

⌐

As usual, Gage's secretary was the ferocious gatekeeper. "Mr. Gage isn't available, Matt. I can call you when he breaks free but he's been on the phone constantly." Jamison knew Sheila well enough to know that she wasn't being entirely candid. Gage didn't want to see him, but he needed to see Gage.

"Tell him that he's going to be subpoenaed in the Harker case, him and Judge Cleary. I'll wait."

Ten minutes later the phone buzzed on Sheila's intercom line. She answered and then nodded at Jamison. "Mr. Gage will see you now."

Gage was sitting at his desk, drumming his fingers on an open space between piles of papers and reports that looked like polling statistics and fundraising records. "Sheila says I'm going to get a subpoena in the Harker case? Okay, so you move to quash it. I don't have time to testify and I would prefer for that to all end without a lot more attention." To quash the subpoena meant to ask the court to refuse to force the witness to respond to the subpoena because there was no showing of good cause or necessity.

"I'm not going to be able to quash the subpoena, Bill, and you know it. If Gifford wants to call you, he's going to call you. And besides, refusing to testify will be taken the wrong way by the press. What I need to know is what do you think he's going to ask? The other thing I need to know is"—Jamison's voice rose more than he intended—"why the hell didn't you tell me that my father represented Clarence Foster? I had to find that out from Foster."

There was no shred of contrition in Gage's answer. "I didn't say anything about your old man because you would've just argued with me. It doesn't make any difference about you handling the hearing. So your father represented Foster and got him immunity. Your dad just did what defense lawyers do. So what? I know you, Matt. You would've spent wasted hours trying to figure out if there was some technical ethical bullshit. There isn't. Besides, you're into the case and you're my guy. That's it. Move on. What else?" The tone of Gage's response made it clear the subject was closed as far as Gage was concerned. It wasn't closed as far as Jamison was concerned but at this point he was astute enough to realize that further argument wouldn't do any good.

"Okay, Bill. Foster's going to testify and so will Christine Farrow and Jensen. I have to talk to Judge Cleary. Is there anything, anything at all that you think Gifford is going to bore in on?"

Gage's expression hardened. "Gifford has a guilty client. I put Harker in the gas chamber where he belonged, and that weak-ass judge let him out. Gifford doesn't have shit. He just wants to parade me in court and ask a lot of questions with a lot of innuendo and implications with nothing behind them. I can handle myself. You handle Gifford." The vehemence in Gage's voice startled Jamison but it also told him the conversation was over.

Jamison rose from his chair and started toward the office door before turning again to Gage. "You should've told me about my father. Maybe it doesn't make any difference, but you should've told me."

Gage's voice softened. "Maybe so—but it doesn't make any difference. I need you on this, Matt. I need my best man. Take care of it. I know you had issues with your dad. A lot of sons have issues with their dads. Your dad was a great lawyer. You're a great lawyer. Just take care of it. Okay?"

That afternoon O'Hara walked into Jamison's office. "It took me a while to dig all the reports out on the Sample killing. The evidence is in storage and I've asked them to pull it."

"So give me the short version." Jamison was eyeing the thick file.

"It looks like Sample was in Jack's Place. You've been there before, remember? That's the place where that biker shooting went down last year?" Jamison nodded. He remembered. Jack's was a rough place even by the standards of a rough place, a redneck, honky-tonk bar where the only person inside who wasn't armed was a guy who walked in by mistake.

"Anyway, the Sample killing," O'Hara continued. "It was October 1998. There were only a few people in the bar and, as usual, nobody saw nothin'. According to the reports the bartender gave a statement. Said that Sample wasn't a regular, but he came in once in a while. But that night there was a guy that came in and sat next to him. He didn't pay any attention to his face and the guy had the hood up on a sweatshirt. You know the drill. Jack's isn't the kind of place that you stare at anybody very long unless you're looking for a fight. The bartender thought the guy had a ball cap on because he thought he remembered the bill of the hat sticking out. Seemed to the bartender like they knew each other because he remembered Sample nodding to him when the guy sat down next to him. Something made him think the guy was out of place but he said it was just a gut feeling, had something to do with the way the guy moved, like he wasn't comfortable being there. I'll bet he remembered that because Jack's is a place folks stay away from if they don't fit the crowd, 'specially if it was a black dude. A lot of assholes."

O'Hara grinned. He liked nothing better than walking into redneck beer joints where everyone turned when he came through the door. "Anyway, according to the report the bartender heard the two of them getting loud and told them to take it outside. He said he didn't pay any more attention until his cleanup guy came in at the end of the night and said there was a dead guy out by the trash cans. Well, to be more accurate, I guess he was in the trash can— the dumpster anyway. He went and looked, then called the police. Said it was the guy who had been on the stool that got into an argument."

"No identification of the suspect?"

"The usual. Bartender said they all looked alike to him. That's a quote, by the way. Said he couldn't ID. Basic description, male, maybe white, maybe Hispanic, maybe black. Not a whole lot there. One sixty-five to one seventy, ball cap, older, maybe fifty or so but could have been younger or older. Thought he remembered a mustache and goatee with a little gray in it but he also said he might be thinking of somebody else. Didn't remember any tattoos but made some smartass remark about not being able to see them anyway, 'specially if he was black. That's it. Obviously, the bartender knew more than he was willing to share but you expect that in a place like that. I'm sure the detective who wrote the case up figured the same, but you squeeze an asshole and you know what you get."

Jamison grimaced. "That's disgusting."

"Yeah, I know. It's a skill set. Some people play golf." O'Hara gave a little grin.

Jamison ignored O'Hara's game. "Any follow-up? Photo spread for identification? Anything?"

"There wasn't anything to go on. They backtracked but couldn't find anybody that had seen Sample with someone fitting the description, which could have been anybody. It was a dead end. Typical Saturday night bar killing. No prints that they could find. Bartender said he wiped the whole bar down before he knew anybody was dead. My bet is that he hadn't wiped that bar down since the place first opened but it was clean when the forensic boys went over it. The bartender did say one thing, though. He said that when he asked the guy what he wanted he could tell by the way he looked at him that he'd been around."

"Been around?"

"The joint. Been around the joint. Said he could tell by the look. Said that his regular crowd probably averaged at least one felony conviction just to get a seat at the bar. That's it. Seems to me if the dude was black that the bartender could have told that when the guy looked at him, but you know the routine. The detective was going through the motions because he knew he wasn't going to close the file the minute he walked into the place. It was Saturday night, business as usual on that side of town."

"So, the bartender said he could tell all of that from the look he got but he couldn't tell if the guy was black or white?"

O'Hara shrugged. "Whatever he knew he wasn't giving anything up. Only other thing is Mike Jensen was the supervising detective and his report said no identification because of the lack of description."

"What was the cause of death?" Jamison was already sensing that this was going to be a waste of time.

"Knife. Right in the diaphragm—two quick hits. Whoever it was, he knew how to drop a guy real quick—right under the breastbone. Funny thing was, he didn't take any money. Sample still had his wallet. Anyway, Rick Sample's dead so he isn't available for questioning." O'Hara's mouth pulled back into a wolfish smile. "The case is old and cold."

"Yeah, I know—one less asshole as far as you're concerned."

"That's right, Boss. So, what you want me to do next?"

"Get me everything on Clarence Foster. I want to know where he did time, what he did time for, and when he did time and who he did time with. Go through the files and find out everyone who had contact with him."

"What about Christine?"

"Ernie's working on Christine and her shrink, Dr. Vinson. You and I need to go see Judge Cleary. I've made an appointment."

⌒

Jamison, like most prosecutors, avoided the Court of Appeal. As far as he was concerned, the real work was done in the trial court and the justices at the Court of Appeal were like color commentators for a football game or the talking heads at ESPN. They got to take their time and got to criticize with the benefit of hindsight while trial lawyers and trial judges had to make fast decisions with everything on the line. But Jamison recognized that appellate courts guided the law and the real power in the judiciary was concentrated in the very small group of men and women in the Courts of Appeal and the Supreme Court. He looked at the massive stone steps leading up to the doors of the court of appeal. It was intended to intimidate. It certainly had that effect on him.

The security officer put both Jamison and O'Hara through the screening procedure and O'Hara was required to turn over his service weapon, a nine-millimeter automatic, as well as his extra ammo clip and handcuffs. The security officer kept his hand out, watching him until O'Hara reluctantly reached down and produced a Walther PPK from an ankle holster. Then they were allowed inside the main lobby where another security officer waited to escort them to the office of Justice Cleary. Two things immediately struck Jamison: the amount of security and the smell. There was no pungent odor that flooded the senses like an arraignment court full of prisoners, or a courtroom full of spectators. It smelled crisp and clean and was remarkably quiet, like a church.

The security officer left them at the outer office to Justice Cleary's chambers, where his judicial assistant sat as gatekeeper. Jamison introduced himself as she nodded efficiently. "The justice is expecting you." She picked up the phone and said they were now here, then indicated that they could go through the heavy dark wood door that had a brass plate outside with Justice Cleary's name on it.

Justice Jonathon Cleary was an imposing figure. If central casting had been asked to find someone who looked like a judge, Cleary would be the man they would put in front of the camera. He was at least six feet one or two inches tall with dark hair sprinkled with gray and completely silver at the temples. His face was austere, but his eyes seemed warm and receptive. Jamison had no illusions. He had heard about Cleary's notorious ability to look at lawyers with a coldness that could turn a lawyer's blood to ice. For the moment, however, Cleary radiated warmth and extended his hand. "So you're Matthew Jamison? I've read about you and seen you on the news. I knew your dad well. Great lawyer." Unlike his abrupt response when Gifford mentioned his father, Jamison just nodded and smiled. Cleary seemed to sense the reserved reaction and changed the subject. "Rumor has it that you're the man who drew the Harker case?" Jamison assumed that the district attorney had called Cleary as soon as he had walked out of Gage's office. Cleary turned toward O'Hara. "I'm guessing you're Bill O'Hara?" The fact that Cleary knew who O'Hara was confirmed Jamison's suspicions about communications between Gage and Cleary.

"What can I do for you, Mr. Jamison?" Cleary sat quietly behind a highly polished mahogany desk that didn't have a scrap of paper on it while Jamison explained that he wanted to talk about the Harker case and if he had any idea why Gifford might be calling him as a witness.

"The Harker case was a long time ago, Mr. Jamison. But like most trial lawyers, I remember it very well. At least I remember my part in it, which"— Cleary laughed—"like most lawyers, has become more prominent in the retelling. It was a horrible murder. Harker's defense attorney, Alton Grady, did the best he could, but Grady didn't have a lot to work with—an alibi that only Harker could confirm. Is Grady still alive? He'd have to be at least ninety by now."

"He's alive. We spoke to him, but it was obvious that his mind has slipped quite a bit."

Cleary sighed. "That's too bad. In his day he was formidable but when he defended Harker I think he had given up a step or two. I don't think there's much I can say. It's all in the trial record. Has Harker's lawyer made any contentions that I might be able to respond to?"

"He has a declaration from Richard Harker that Clarence Foster lied when he identified Harker as the killer and that the detectives were aware of it." Jamison waited to see if there was any reaction.

Justice Cleary's expression was bemused. "That's it? What does Foster say? I was there when we took his statements." Cleary paused. "You do know that your father was Foster's lawyer, don't you?"

"Well, I found that out after I was given the case. Anyway, Foster's not talking, at least not to us. I'm not sure what he'll testify to but I need to make sure there's nothing I'm missing."

"You're not missing anything, Mr. Jamison. Foster wouldn't tell us anything at first, and then he lied about Harker killing Lisa Farrow, and then he admitted it was Harker. It's all in the reports. And, if I recall correctly, it's all on tape. That can't be all the supreme court based its order of a hearing on, is it?"

"No, there's a declaration from Christine Farrow. She says that she wrongfully identified Harker. She says the real killer was a Rick Sample."

Other than a slight twitch at the corner of his mouth there was no reaction. "Christine signed a declaration that says exactly what?" Jamison handed over a copy and watched Cleary's face while he read it.

Cleary scanned the declaration carefully. "Christine was only three years old, five when she testified. It was horrible having her go through that, but she was the only witness we had besides Foster. And she was the nail in Harker's coffin when she identified him. I remember that Grady tried to shake her on the identification because Sample and Harker looked a lot alike, and there was some confusion at the beginning of the investigation about whether it was Sample or Harker. But most of the confusion was created by Christine's grandmother. I remember that Sample had a solid alibi. And then there was Foster who put Harker at the scene. Harker's prints were also inside the house. And he had no alibi that was supported by anyone but him."

Cleary's eyes iced over. "Richard Harker is a murderer, Mr. Jamison. He deserved to be executed. Mr. Harker's lawyer can ask me whatever he wants. I've got nothing to say that will help him. His lawyer is Samuel Gifford, correct?" Cleary waited for confirmation from Jamison before continuing. "I've heard Mr. Gifford argue cases before. It's always the same, some great injustice that the system has imposed on his clients. Well, he'll have to do better than that if he wants to get anywhere with the Harker case. I feel sorry for that little girl. She went through so much and now this. Have you talked to her? Did she say anything about what happened?"

"We talked to her. All she says is that she began having dreams and went to a psychologist, a Dr. Vinson, and that she realized she had made a mistake and it wasn't Harker who killed her mother. That's it."

Cleary stood up, signaling the interview was over. "Mr. Jamison, if Sam Gifford is looking for something from me that will help his client, he won't get it. Call me if you have any more questions."

"Thank you, Justice Cleary." Jamison stuck his hand out and shook Cleary's. "Rumor has it that you are going to be moving back East. We all wish you luck. It would be nice to know that somebody back there actually has been in the trenches."

Cleary's smile was circumspect. "We will see. You never know about rumors from Washington. I'm just as much in the dark as everyone else." Jamison doubted that but it was a standard line. He'd heard it before. Right now, his concern was that he didn't know much more than he knew at the beginning.

Chapter 20

Jamison sat at his desk, looking at Christine Farrow's declaration. It kept going through his mind that why after all these years had she suddenly decided that Harker wasn't the man who killed her mother? It didn't make sense. Jamison knew that sometimes children lied and then later recanted, but something had to have caused Christine to decide she was wrong. It didn't just come to her. She'd been only three years old when it happened and five when she testified. Based on the police reports and the transcripts she hadn't wavered in her identification until Dr. Vinson came along. He needed to see Vinson. Jamison doubted Vinson would cooperate, but one way or the other he would find out what happened.

⟿

Vinson's office was precisely what Jamison expected: deep carpet that muffled any sound, subdued lighting, and the ubiquitous *People* and health magazines that seem to clutter every doctor's office Jamison had ever been in. The decor wasn't that of some social services psychologist. This was a man whose services were hundreds of dollars an hour. A receptionist stared at him with a questioning expression. "May I help you? Do you have an appointment?"

Jamison flipped out his identification with the gold district attorney badge next to his picture. O'Hara slid his jacket to the side, exposing the badge attached to his belt and a glimpse of the butt of his gun. O'Hara's attempt at subtlety carried the same finesse as a hammer. "I'm Matt Jamison with the district attorney's office. My investigator and I would like to speak to Dr. Vinson."

The receptionist seemed flustered, which wasn't an uncommon reaction. The sight of badges and guns caused most people to be nervous, whether they had any reason to be or not. "Is Dr. Vinson in trouble?"

"No." Jamison smiled. "We need to talk to him about a patient. Is he here?"

"He's with a patient now. I'll let him know you're here, but he doesn't like to interrupt patient sessions. I'm sure you understand?"

A few minutes later she returned to her desk. "Dr. Vinson said you'll have to wait. He will be with you when he's finished." O'Hara's expression of impatience caused the receptionist to shrink as she tried to find something to distract herself from Jamison and O'Hara—primarily from O'Hara as he squeezed his bulk into a low-slung office chair, muttering.

"Dr. Vinson will see you now." Jamison asked where the patient had gone, not seeing anyone exit through the reception area. "They go out a different door when they leave."

Dr. Arnold Vinson sat behind a desk with nothing on it except a tablet and a pen. He stood up as Jamison and O'Hara crossed the room. Jamison extended his hand and reflected that Vinson looked exactly like what most people expected a psychologist to look like and very few did. He was balding, having left a fringe of hair circling his head and hair a fraction too long in the back. In Jamison's mind, it was a weakness some men had when their hair left the front of their head and they let it grow out in the back. He tucked his observation away for future reference. Vanity was always a weakness.

Vinson's voice was soft and controlled. If his receptionist had been intimidated, he didn't appear to be. "I understand you gentlemen are with the district attorney's office?"

Moving past any small talk, Jamison got right to the point. "Matt Jamison. I'm a prosecutor. This is Mr. O'Hara, my investigator. We would like to talk to you about Christine Farrow. I'm sure you're aware that she's going to testify with respect to a murder case where she has now alleged that she made a wrongful identification. She said that you helped her realize that she had made a mistake. Is that correct?"

Vinson sat back down, quietly measuring the two men before him with the gaze of a clinician. He placed his fingertips together, touching the index fingers to his nose before responding. "You are evidently already aware that Ms. Farrow is a patient of mine and since you are with the district attorney's office I assume you are also aware that my discussions with Ms. Farrow are privileged. I can't discuss our therapeutic sessions with you."

O'Hara interrupted. "Can't or won't?"

Vinson smiled. "Either answer would be correct."

Jamison tried to soften O'Hara's blunt edge. "Dr. Vinson, I really need to know how Christine Farrow decided she had made a mistake. We've talked to her. She's been through a lot, I realize that. I don't want to make her life more difficult. It would help if I could get a sense of how she decided this."

Vinson appraised the two men. "I understand, but my position remains the same. I will tell you that Christine is confident she has made the right decision and it has brought her some peace. Given the trauma that she's carried with her I'm sure understand."

Jamison looked around the office. "You will excuse me for asking, but I'm guessing Christine is not your usual patient and would not be able to afford your normal hourly fee?"

"What do you lawyers call it, pro bono? I help people if I can. It isn't all about money. I was asked to talk to her."

"Who asked?"

"That is another matter I'm not going to discuss with you, Mr. Jamison."

"Are you going to testify in the Harker case?"

"I've been asked to testify. Whether I do will depend on what I am asked to testify about." The tone of Vinson's answer politely made it clear that he was through answering questions.

On the drive back to the office O'Hara expressed his opinion about "head-shrinkers" and psychologists in general, before asking Jamison, "So, Boss, what're you going to do?"

"There's not much I can do." Jamison pursed his lips and blew out a burst of air. "You do a background check on Vinson. Find out everything you can. Maybe somebody in the office has had experience with him, maybe not, but I'm guessing Dr. Vinson has been involved in cases like this before."

Chapter 21

Jamison threaded his way through the reporters standing outside the courtroom, brushing aside questions. Harker's hearing was front page news and the centerpiece was Christine Farrow's declaration and the intimation floated by Gifford that Harker might testify. He had been over the entire trial transcript and the physical evidence. There just didn't seem to be any doubt that Harker was guilty. But there was no question that Christine's declaration and his interview with her nagged at him.

He had read numerous articles about recantation by witnesses years after they had given their testimony, particularly children. There were all kinds of reasons for it but usually it involved sexual molestation. The accused was frequently a family member. Not only that, much of the time the recantation simply wasn't true. But sometimes it was. He'd decided that whatever the reason was for Christine's disavowal of her childhood testimony, he was not going to overreact to the contentions of Harker's lawyer. He would make Gifford prove his case and then he would react to whatever Gifford had that might raise an issue.

It was to his advantage that it wasn't easy to set aside a conviction based on new evidence, unless that evidence was more than somebody just saying they were wrong. DNA sometimes provided that kind of exonerating evidence, but there was no DNA in this case. It was just Christine and Foster and Harker's fingerprint, and Jamison knew the fingerprint didn't lie. He looked forward to getting started. He could feel the buildup of adrenaline. It was that way every time he walked up to the counsel table and said, "Ready for the People, Your Honor." Today was no different.

Judge Wallace carried his massive bulk into the courtroom with surprising agility. He looked out at the packed room as everyone stood. "Be seated please." Wallace wasn't much for formality, but he recognized that sometimes it had its uses and today was one of those days. The timber of his rumbling voice added to his authority. "In the matter of Richard Harker versus the State of California, County of Tenaya, are the parties ready to proceed?"

Samuel Gifford stood to address the court. "Samuel Gifford for Mr. Harker, Your Honor, and Mr. Harker is present." There was a slight sound of chains jangling as Harker acknowledged his presence. He had been brought in earlier and had his leg chains locked to the steel O ring under the counsel table, but his hands were free, as ordered by Wallace. He had been allowed to "dress out" for the hearing. Instead of the usual orange jumpsuit, he was wearing a rumpled blue shirt and tan slacks that, Jamison surmised, came out of Gifford's wardrobe closet for his clients. Despite the chains, two armed bailiffs sat near the jury rail with their eyes fixed on the prisoner.

"Matthew Jamison for the People, Your Honor. Mr. Bill O'Hara will be at the counsel table with me as my investigator." Normally only attorneys and clients were permitted at the counsel tables, but if there was a primary investigator the prosecutor was usually permitted to have him or her seated at the table.

Wallace peered over the bench at Harker's counsel. "Mr. Gifford, it's your show. I've read the petition and the attached declarations. Why don't you explain to me what you plan to present. I know this hearing is going to be interrupted by my regular calendar of cases, so I would like to have a handle on what it is you want me to focus on."

Gifford nodded. "Your Honor, thank you. This hearing has been a long time coming for Mr. Harker, twenty-six years in fact. I know the court hears the argument all the time about insufficient evidence and what might have happened if the defense attorney had only brought in evidence that he failed to put before the jury. This isn't one of those cases."

Wallace's head was tilted slightly as he listened. The usual argument was that the jury might have found reasonable doubt if it heard the new evidence the most recent lawyer had found that disputed the prosecution's case in some way. The other argument was more common: that the trial lawyer had simply over-looked crucial evidence because of incompetence. It didn't change the argument. It was always that hearing the omitted evidence might have affected the jury concluding the defendant was guilty. It was still different than concluding that the defendant was in fact innocent. Lawyers carefully rationalized as they walked the line on the legal distinction between innocent in the eyes of the law and actually innocent, the thin barrier between the ethics of legal argument and the subtext of society's morality.

Gifford continued. "The reality is that Mr. Harker *is* in fact innocent." The defense lawyer put added emphasis on his assertion of innocence before continuing. "He was convicted of a horrible crime, a murder that *he* didn't commit. And I'm going to prove it. I expect the prosecutor is going to say if Mr. Harker didn't do it, then who did? But I don't have to show that. All I have to show is that there is substantial evidence that Mr. Harker was the victim of wrongful identification, perjury by a petty criminal, Clarence Foster, and a mistake by a little girl, Christine Farrow, who has come forward after all these years to try and make this right. Why did it happen? Well, I think I know why it happened, and I believe that Mr. William Gage and the man who was his associate, now a judge, Jonathon Cleary, not only let it happen, they made it happen." He spit the last comment out with a force of conviction that insured everyone understood the nature of the accusation.

Jamison was on his feet trying to speak over the murmuring in the audience reacting to Gifford's allegations about the district attorney and Justice Cleary. "Your Honor, I object to Mr. Gifford's inflammatory rhetoric. If he has evidence, then I haven't seen it, and if this is just an attempt to disparage the reputations of two highly regarded members of the legal community, then it is inappropriate and defense counsel knows that. What Mr. Gifford may or may not believe in his fevered web of conspiracy theories about the justice system is not proof and I request he be admonished right now."

Jamison didn't expect much to happen. He knew that the damage was done and that the headline on the news would repeat Gifford's allegations without the benefit of scrutiny. He could hear the reporters rustling around in the audience, anxious to get the inflammatory claims on the next broadcast or news ribbon on the bottom of whatever game show was on television.

Wallace slammed his gavel down on the bench harder than he realized, the crack of wood against wood silencing the courtroom. "Mr. Gifford, I'm not here to listen to speculation and innuendo. If you have credible evidence relevant to Mr. Harker's trial, then I'll hear it. If you are going to posture, then you're wasting my time. I remind you that I haven't cultivated a reputation for patience with irrelevant nonsense. I also remind you that Mr. Gage and Justice Cleary are very distinguished members of the legal community and I will not look kindly on splattering them with mud just to further your client's interests."

Jamison could sense what was coming. Gifford was going to try to show that Harker was an innocent man railroaded by the system. It was basically what he believed happened to most of his clients—not that they were all innocent in fact, but that the system rolled over them like a freight train. Jamison sat back down, shaking his head.

Gifford persisted. "Your Honor, Mr. Gage and Mr. Cleary were the prosecutors. They had the responsibility—"

Wallace slammed his gavel down again. "Enough, Mr. Gifford. Present your case."

"We call Michael Jensen."

Jensen walked through the swinging gate separating the counsel tables from the audience and raised his right hand. He glanced over at Jamison, slightly nodding his head. Wallace's clerk swore him in and Jensen settled himself in the witness chair, stating his name at the direction of the judge, and waiting for Gifford to begin.

Gifford didn't waste time on pleasantries. "Detective Jensen, am I correct that you are now retired as a detective with the Tenaya County Sheriff's Department?"

"Yes."

"While you were employed as a detective, were you assigned to investigate the murder of Lisa Farrow?"

"Yes."

"Do you recognize my client, Mr. Harker?"

"Yes."

"Did you arrest him for the murder of Lisa Farrow?"

"Yes." Jensen looked around the courtroom and shrugged, implying he didn't understand what the point was of Gifford's questions. Anyone who had watched cops testify understood that what he was really signaling with his terse responses was his disgust at being there. It wasn't lost on Gifford.

"Detective Jensen, you don't like my client, do you?"

"No, I don't like murderers and I have no use for men who beat up women or leave children to burn to death. Am I supposed to?"

"No, Detective, I suppose not, but you are assuming Mr. Harker did that, aren't you?" Jamison shifted uncomfortably in his chair. Gifford was baiting Jensen and Jensen was biting.

"It isn't an assumption, counselor. I know he did it."

"And how do you know that, Detective Jensen?" Jamison looked down at his legal tablet. Jensen had walked right into it.

"His fingerprints were at the scene. He was identified by the neighbors as going into the house with another man. The other man identified him and testified that your client started hitting Ms. Farrow. And Christine Farrow identified him." Jensen leaned back in the witness chair, satisfied that he had made his point.

"There were also other people's fingerprints at the scene, weren't there, specifically Richard Sample's, correct?"

"Yes, but he wasn't the one who did it."

"And you know that because Clarence Foster and Christine Farrow identified Mr. Harker, correct?"

"That and the fact that Sample had an alibi."

"But you initially put out and all-points bulletin, an APB, for Mr. Sample, didn't you?"

"Yes, but like I said, he didn't do it."

"You keep saying that, Detective Jensen."

"So did twelve jurors, so I'm not alone in my opinion."

"Isn't it true that Richard Sample was initially identified by Christine as the one who was in the house, the man who killed her mother?"

"She was confused. That little girl was three years old and they found her next to her mother's body. What she said was, 'Rick did it.' At the time I didn't know that there were two men named Rick who her mother had been with. The grandmother said it was Rick Sample that the little girl was talking about, so our initial reaction was to go after Rick Sample. Later we realized that it was your client. They look a lot alike, Sample and your client."

"In fact, you arrested Sample, didn't you?'

"Yes, but he had an alibi and it put him out of the county when Lisa Farrow was murdered."

"And in your mind that meant Mr. Harker did it, isn't that right?"

"That and the fact that he was identified as the murderer."

"Right. Let's talk about that, shall we? The neighbor, a Mrs. Nancy Slaven, she identified Mr. Sample, didn't she?"

"And so did the other neighbor, Maria Castillo. They were the ones that saw the two men go into the victim's house and they were the ones who found the little girl, Christine, sitting next to her mother."

"And according to you, they were wrong in their identification also, correct?"

"Like I said, Sample and your client looked a lot alike. But when they testified in court they pointed straight at your client, Counselor."

"What made you decide it was Mr. Harker?"

"Like I keep saying, Mr. Gifford, your client's fingerprints were in the house and Clarence Foster admitted it was him and the little girl said so too."

"Let's talk about Clarence Foster. Did you question him?"

"I did at first and then the DA Mr. Gage, well he wasn't the DA then, he was there and so was Mr. Cleary."

"Did you tape record your interview?"

"Yes, I tape recorded all my interviews. Best evidence of what happened is a confession and a jury gets to hear the person say it himself. Not the way we used to do it but it's better, I think."

"Not the way you used to do it?"

"No, we used to just write it all down in our report, and then guys like you would say we were making it up. So now it's all recorded."

"And isn't it true that Clarence Foster denied knowing anything about the murder; in fact, denied that he remembered anything?"

"Yeah, but after he realized what was involved, a vicious murder, he cooperated."

"After you gave him immunity. Isn't that right?"

"We didn't give him immunity until the trial. That was the deal."

"And that deal was made with Foster's lawyer, who just happened to be Roger Jamison, the father of the prosecutor in this case, Mr. Matthew Jamison. Isn't that true?"

Jamison came to his feet. "Your Honor, is there a point to this?"

Wallace held up his hand, stopping Jamison from further comment. "Mr. Gifford, are you trying to imply something here about Mr. Jamison's father defending Mr. Foster and the fact his son is the prosecutor in this case?"

"No, Your Honor. Just connecting the dots."

"Then unless you have a point to make, I suggest you move on."

"I didn't make the deal. Mr. Gage and Mr. Cleary did," interrupted Jensen.

"Isn't it true, Detective Jensen, that you put my client and Clarence Foster in a patrol car together?"

"Yeah, I did. Wanted to see if your boy would talk."

"You just wanted to see if they would talk?"

"That's right, Counselor. Sometimes when criminals think no cops are around they talk to one another and sometimes they talk about why they're in the back seat of a patrol car. Given that they knew one another, I thought maybe your client would talk to Foster about why they were both there." Jensen paused before adding, "Especially since they were both there for the same murder."

"And Clarence Foster admitted to my client that he had lied when he identified him, didn't he?"

"Not that I'm aware of, no."

"Well you were taping the conversation, weren't you?"

"Yeah, but we got nothing. Harker kept threatening Foster and Foster kept saying he had to do what was right, or words to that effect."

"And where is that tape?"

"I don't know, Counselor. I turned over the tapes and the evidence. Besides, there was nothing on it."

"Nothing on it? You mean it didn't record?"

"Sometimes it happened with those old wire transmissions. They didn't record. I don't know why. Anyway, I turned it into evidence, but I listened to it when they were talking because Foster had a wire on so I could hear it, and that's all I heard. But there was nothing on the tape, just some hissing and static."

"Well, that's convenient, isn't it? All we have is your word about what was said?"

Jensen leaned forward. "All we have is your client's word that he's innocent, but I have witnesses. So what's your point?"

"My client told you that Foster admitted that he had lied, didn't he?"

"No. All he ever said about Foster was that he was lying. Same thing his lawyer said at his trial."

"So, Clarence Foster was supposedly in that house when he said my client attacked Lisa Farrow?"

"That's what he said, Counselor. But it was Christine who said your client stood over her bed before setting the victim on fire. What's your point? Do you have a point? Your client killed that woman. You know it and I know it. Everyone knows it."

Gifford turned his back on Jensen and walked back to the counsel table. He stood, staring at Jensen for a minute, and then sat down. "I have nothing further of Detective Jensen."

It was difficult to keep the surprise out of his voice because Jamison expected something more because there *had* to be something more. Gifford hadn't made a dent. He momentarily debated with himself about asking any questions before saying, "No questions, Your Honor. Detective Jensen may be excused."

Wallace leaned back in his chair, dominating the courtroom with his silence before he leaned back. "Call your next witness, Mr. Gifford."

"Your Honor, we call William Gage."

Chapter 22

Gage dominated every room he was in. It wasn't much different in a courtroom, despite the presence of someone like Judge Wallace. As Gage walked through the swinging gate into the well of the courtroom, his eyes moved around like he was a general surveying a battlefield. Then he raised his right hand and walked to the witness chair. Gage stared first at Gifford and then at Harker, the expression on his face impassive as granite but his eyes telegraphing cold contempt.

Gifford walked around the counsel table and approached the witness stand. "Mr. Gage, you are presently the district attorney of this county, correct?"

"Yes, for over twenty years."

"And you recognize my client, Richard Harker?"

"Yes."

"In fact, you prosecuted Mr. Harker for the murder of Lisa Farrow, which is why we're here, correct?"

Gage sat silently, staring at Gifford who finally asked, "Did you understand my question?"

"What I don't understand, Mr. Gifford, is why I'm here. Yes, I recognize your client. Yes, I questioned him. Yes, I prosecuted him for the murder of Lisa Farrow. Yes, I asked the jury for the death penalty and I got it. Let's not drag this out, shall we? Your client murdered Lisa Farrow and I was the prosecutor. Just ask what you want to ask instead of dancing around." Gifford looked over at Judge Wallace, waiting for him to admonish Gage to simply answer the questions. But Wallace sat in Buddha-like silence.

"All right, Mr. Gage, we'll do it your way. You interrogated my client after his arrest, correct?"

"I said that I did."

"My client consistently denied that he killed Lisa Farrow, didn't he? In fact, he cried during that interrogation when you went into the details of how she died, didn't he?"

"A lot of men cry during interrogations, Counselor. And there are a lot of reasons why they cry, not the least of which is that they are sitting there in handcuffs. Yes, your client denied killing Lisa Farrow."

"And you didn't believe him, did you?"

"No."

"But you had already arrested Rick Sample for the same murder, so why are you so sure that my client killed that woman?"

"That woman? You mean Lisa Farrow? Counselor, since you seem hell-bent on asking, my answer is this. I've interrogated a lot of men and women over the years. I've watched them as they sat in an interrogation room and sweated and squirmed and twisted their hands, claiming they didn't do what they were arrested for. Some of them only looked at the floor and lied and some of them looked me straight in the eyes and lied. But you get a sense of guilt. You can smell it. The stink comes off of them like a sour rag. You look at the facts and the evidence and, in your heart, you know they did it—and your client did it."

Gage's voice began to take on an edge of barely controlled anger. "I had a witness who was in that house with your client when he began to beat Lisa. I had a witness who saw your client walk into that house. I had his fingerprints, and most of all, I had a little girl sitting in a chair just like this, pointing her finger at your client when I asked who stood over her bed that night. You asked. That's my answer. There hasn't been a single night since I prosecuted Rick Harker for murder that I have lost a moment's sleep wondering if I did the right thing. Do you have any other questions?"

Gifford stepped back, the intimidation of Gage pushing out like a force field. "Mr. Gage, isn't it true that Clarence Foster admitted to you that he lied when he said my client was the one who beat Lisa Farrow? You questioned Foster repeatedly, didn't you? Why? Wasn't it because he kept saying that he didn't know?"

"Clarence Foster said a lot of things, Mr. Gifford, and they are all in the reports that have been given to you. But he never said your client didn't kill Lisa. I pushed him hard. I admit that. It was an interrogation in the worst murder I've ever seen. I wasn't nice. I did my job. He finally broke and when he did he pointed the finger at your client. End of story. I don't prosecute innocent men, Mr. Gifford." Gage started to get up. "Are we through here?"

Gifford held up his hand, putting some steel into his own voice. "No, Mr. Gage, I'll tell you when we're through. I have one more question. Isn't it true that before Clarence Foster told you that my client killed Lisa Farrow, that he told you that he was so loaded on drugs and alcohol that he didn't know what happened? And that you threatened him with the gas chamber if he didn't tell you who was with him? And you then shoved a picture of my client in front of him? Isn't that what really happened?"

Gage smiled thinly, pausing before answering. "That did not happen, Mr. Gifford, and you have absolutely no evidence that it did."

"That's not what Clarence Foster says."

Gage stood up. "Counselor, Clarence Foster is a criminal. He's always been a criminal. I never thought he was a murderer. You can tell. Some men don't have it in them and there are a lot of reasons for that, but in Foster's case it's because he has no backbone and I could see it. I knew he would break and I put the pressure on him until he did. Put Foster on the stand, and then we'll see what he says. Until then, don't try to smear me or anybody else. We're not the ones with Lisa Farrow's blood on our hands." Gage didn't wait to be excused. He stepped down, turning to look at Judge Wallace. "Am I through here, Your Honor?"

Wallace directed his question at Gifford. "Is Mr. Gage done, Mr. Gifford?"

"Mr. Gage is done for now, Your Honor. But I want him excused subject to recall because I will be back."

Jamison stood up. "Just for the record, Your Honor, I have no questions of Mr. Gage."

Gifford sat at the counsel table while Gage walked through the swinging gate of the courtroom like a battleship leaving the harbor. "We call Jonathon Cleary, Your Honor."

Jonathon Cleary walked across the well of the courtroom with all the assurance of a man in complete control of his surroundings. He nodded to Judge Wallace as he took the witness stand and waited quietly before Wallace deferred to him. "Justice Cleary, I appreciate you taking the time out of your busy schedule to do this." Cleary nodded in acknowledgment but remained quiet.

Gifford began deliberately. "Mr. Cleary, you were one of the prosecutors of my client, Richard Harker, correct?"

Cleary ignored the slight with respect to his title. "Yes, that was some twenty-five years ago, but that is correct, although I was the second chair lawyer, assisting Mr. William Gage, who was the primary prosecutor."

"That was a big opportunity for you, wasn't it, a young lawyer sitting as second chair in one of the most notorious cases in the state at that time?"

"Yes, it was," Cleary answered quietly, looking directly at the defendant.

"Were you present with William Gage and Detective Jensen when Clarence Foster was interrogated?"

"Yes."

"Did you participate in that interrogation?"

"If by participate do you mean did I ask any questions? Not that I recall. I wasn't there to ask questions. I hadn't seen many interrogations and nothing like that. Mr. Gage was in charge and I wasn't there to do anything except what I was told."

Gifford smiled. "Things have changed since then, haven't they?"

Cleary laughed. "Well, I've been married for twenty-five years. I'm not sure they've changed all that much."

Nodding, Gifford answered, "I think we all understand that reality. Did you ever have a private conversation with Clarence Foster during the interrogation?"

"If you mean outside of the presence of Mr. Gage or Detective Jensen, no I did not."

"Did you ever have a conversation with Clarence Foster before he identified my client as the killer of Lisa Farrow?"

Cleary pursed his lips, pausing momentarily like he was considering his answer before giving it. "I believe I just stated that I did not have such a conversation, so the answer remains, no."

Gifford stared for a moment at Cleary, measuring what to ask next. "If I were to tell you that Clarence Foster says you did, are you saying he's lying?"

Cleary's calm expression momentarily hardened before Jamison leapt to his feet. "Objection. The question is argumentative. First of all, the witness already said it didn't happen and now he's being asked to dispute what some convict says. I object."

Wallace visibly sighed. "The objection is sustained. Mr. Gifford, ask your next question."

"Were you aware of any conversation between my client, Mr. Harker, and Clarence Foster in the back of a patrol car?" The tone of Gifford's question had lost any deference to Cleary's status as a judge.

"I was aware later that the two of them were put in a patrol car together, but I was not present when it happened. I just recall reading the report of the conversation."

"Did you ever listen to any tape of that conversation?"

Cleary's face took on a quizzical expression. "As I recall, there was no tape."

Abruptly switching subjects, Gifford asked, "Were you present when Christine Farrow was questioned?"

"Yes, I was there when she identified your client as the man who stood over her bed the night her mother was murdered."

"Isn't it true that she originally identified Rick Sample as the man who murdered her mother?"

"I was only present when she identified your client. I am not sure precisely what you are asking."

Gifford's voice rose with barely concealed irritation. "She was three years old when you questioned her. I am asking whether she picked Richard Sample and either you or William Gage told her that she picked the wrong man."

Cleary straightened up, forcefully pushing his answer out. "Mr. Gifford, if you are asking whether either I or Bill Gage influenced that poor little girl to give an answer because we wanted it, that did not happen, and I resent the implication."

Undeterred, Gifford persisted. "But that is what happened, isn't it?"

As Jamison rose to object, Cleary said, "I've answered your question, Mr. Gifford. My response isn't going to change simply because you throw out unsubstantiated innuendo."

Gifford returned to the counsel table and made a show of writing a note. "No further questions."

Jamison resisted the temptation to ask any questions. There was nothing really to ask. "No questions, Your Honor."

Wallace looked at the clock on the back of the courtroom wall. "Mr. Gifford, is your next witness here?"

"My next witness will be Clarence Foster and he will have to be transported from the jail. I had him brought in from Corcoran State Prison."

"Well, as I told you, I have another scheduled calendar to call. If Mr. Foster is in the jail, then he won't be unduly inconvenienced by staying there a few more days. We will resume next Thursday."

Chapter 23

Jamison sat behind the desk in his office, fiddling with a pen and drawing circles on a yellow legal pad. O'Hara and Ernie sat across from him waiting for Jamison to say something. Finally, O'Hara broke the silence. "Well, so far Gifford hasn't done anything but throw out some bullshit to see if anybody is going to step in it. I haven't heard anything." O'Hara approached most situations like a rock smashing a walnut; there wasn't much finesse.

Ernie shrugged. "Matt, I wasn't in there when Gage testified but the old man was madder than hell when he came out. His face was so red I thought he was going to have a stroke. I followed him up to the office, but he didn't do anything except swear. I hope you have this under control."

Jamison's pen dragged aimlessly across the paper in front of him. "Well, it's as under control as it can be when we don't know what's coming. Gifford hasn't gotten anywhere so far. But you don't ask questions unless you know answers or think you know answers. Gifford thinks he knows something. I'm guessing that either Foster told him something or maybe Harker says that's what Foster said. We won't know until they go on the stand. Either way his objective is to tar Bill Gage with whatever he can smear on him. This is personal with Gifford and now he has a chance in a courtroom to get away with whatever accusation he wants to make."

"So, you think Foster is going to get on the stand and say that he told Gage that he was lying?" O'Hara slit open the wrapper on a cigar and shoved it in his mouth. Jamison eyed the wrapper as O'Hara dropped it on his desk. O'Hara finally reached over and picked up the crumpled cellophane, grinning that he had provoked a small reaction.

"We won't know that until Clarence Foster takes the stand or Rick Harker. We'll just have to wait and see. Anyway, I want you and Ernie to go back to the files at the sheriff's office. Pull everything. Look everywhere. Make sure we have absolutely everything. If I don't have it, then I doubt that Gifford has it, but you never know. Go back and see Alton Grady and talk to his daughter. Chances are that Gifford has already been there, but you never know."

O'Hara pulled a speck of tobacco off his lip. "Boss, I think you need to be the one to talk to Grady and his daughter. I don't think Ernie or I will get very far. You're the lawyer. Don't you guys all swim in packs like sharks?"

⌐

It didn't taken long to find Alton Grady's daughter, Lorie. Jamison remembered that Grady had told him she took care of Grady's home, which was in an older section of the community where elegant, aging houses reflected the affluence of yesterday's social icons. Jamison heard the crunch of gravel and hard-packed dirt as he pulled up to the area in front of the house. It struck him that while most people who moved to new neighborhoods wanted sidewalks and gutters, in this section of the city the homeowners insisted that there be no sidewalks. Old money preserving old ways and new money ignoring the subtlety of restrained affluence. Towering evergreen trees and thick-trunked oaks lined the street and the yards of homes set back behind lawns larger than the average lot of a new home. Jamison knew the area well. It was where the old movers and shakers had lived and now it was where younger generations lived who wanted the same luster and were willing to accept it with a little patina of age.

The house was two stories with white painted brick and dark green shutters. Jamison waited on the uneven brick porch for the door to be answered. A young woman opened the door quietly, looking at him with questioning eyes before saying, "Matthew Jamison?" He was surprised that she knew who he was and it showed on his face. She answered his unspoken question. "I've seen you on the news and I've been reading about the Harker case. Isn't that why you're here? I heard you visited my father."

"You're Lorie?" Jamison inadvertently blurted. "I expected . . ."

She finished the sentence. "You expected someone older, right? My parents said I was their late-life surprise. But yes, I'm Lorie Grady." Jamison stood uncomfortably. Lorie Grady was beautiful in the way that some women can be whether they have on a T-shirt and jeans or a cocktail dress. Right now, she had on a T-shirt and jeans and her hands showed that she had been working in dirt. She stepped back from the door and waved him in, saying she would just be a minute while she washed her hands. The art on the walls wasn't what he expected. It was modern with slashes of color that jumped out, contrasting with the formality of the home.

Lorie walked back into the entry area again, answering his question before he asked. "I'm a painter. Those are mine." She smiled before offering, "I'm also a lawyer like my father, but I don't practice. Didn't like it. It didn't fit my artistic spirit." And then she laughed again. "The law is only about logic. Art is about emotion. Each one clashes with the other. I only went to law school because I admired my father so much I wanted to do it for him."

"So you make your living as an artist?"

She laughed. "Don't sound so surprised. Some people do, you know. I make part of my living as an artist. The rest I make from working with emotionally challenged children." She laughed again. "It helps that I had the experience of growing up around lawyers—and then there's the trust fund. So, what can I do for you, Mr. Jamison? You want to look at my father's old files, right?"

Jamison had tightened up as soon as he heard her say she was trained as a lawyer, and he tightened up more at her answering questions before he asked them. It was like she knew what he was thinking. He shifted uncomfortably, hoping she didn't know everything that was going on in his head, but he could see her bemused expression and the thought crossed his mind that she probably did.

"Did your father keep his old files?" It was a careful question because there were attorney-client privilege issues. He knew as a lawyer that she would be aware of it.

"If you're asking about the Harker file, it's down in the basement, but I will tell you right now that Gifford has already been here and gone through it. Before you ask, I watched him the entire time. He didn't take anything, but I did make some copies of papers that he asked for. As you know, the file belongs to the client and Gifford is Harker's lawyer. As far as I was concerned that meant Gifford could look at the file."

Jamison knew she was right and that debating the matter was pointless. He tried a different tack. "Look, this case is about whether Harker was wrongfully convicted. Your father defended him. If there's something there it might help me to know what to do." He could feel growing discomfort because he was dissembling, and he knew she knew it. Most of what was in those files was probably still subject to attorney-client privilege. But not all of it. He tried a different direction. "Certainly, the discussions your father had with Harker are privileged. I understand that, but witnesses he talked to, those aren't privileged."

"No, they're not, but they may be my father's work product and that is privileged. Anyway, I'm not going to hand it over without a court order. You know that the work a lawyer does on a case may not be privileged as an attorney-client communication, but it does have the protections of work product for a lawyer's ideas and strategy." She paused. "Mr. Jamison, I do understand the problem and I will tell you that I know what's in that file because I've read it. I figured how my father handled it would become an issue and I do handle my father's estate as his conservator, so as far as I'm concerned I have the legal authority to protect his interests. I will tell you that there's no smoking gun in there. My father was a good lawyer. If he had something he would have used it. I remember how stressed he was when he was defending Harker. I was, I think, in the third or fourth grade. He sat in his study and I could see the strain on his face. After Harker's conviction, he just sat at his desk and stared out the window for hours at a time. He cried with relief when the trial judge refused to impose the death penalty. And I can tell you the only other time I saw him cry was when my mother died." She walked over to a heavily cushioned chair and sat down. "I met your father, you know. He spent time in that study with my dad. Did you know that?"

"No, I didn't know. He's been gone for a number of years."

"Maybe you're looking in the wrong place." Her expression was thoughtful.

"What does that mean?"

She leaned forward in the chair. "I mean maybe it isn't the Harker file you should be looking at. I've already probably said too much from a lawyer's perspective, but as I said, I didn't like practicing law." She stood up and started walking back to the front door. Jamison understood that the discussion was over. As she opened the door to let him out she smiled. "Come back anytime. We don't have to talk about our fathers." After the door closed, Jamison stood in the walkway thinking about that. But he guessed that Lorie Grady already knew what he was thinking. He walked to his car and started driving back to the office. Then he made a quick turn and headed for his parents' home.

As soon as he walked through the door, Jamison's mother was trying to feed him. Then she began her relentless interrogation about his private life, which always centered around whether he had met "a nice girl." At first, he had tried to be flippant and acknowledged that he had met a few who "weren't so nice," but his mother wasn't amused. Now he just dodged and weaved, hoping she would give up. She never did.

After trying to get answers from him as to why he wanted to see the files, she told him that they had stayed at his old law office that he shared with a few other lawyers. She didn't have them and she had no idea where they might be. She suggested he call a few of the lawyers who worked with him. It didn't take long for her to get the one name he didn't want to hear, Samuel Gifford. "Try Sam. Don't you know him? Isn't he the one defending that awful Harker case that you're working on?"

Waiting for the answer to her question about Gifford, his mother started pulling leftovers from the refrigerator. "As long as you're here you should eat." Jamison didn't feel much like eating. The fact that his father's file was probably with Gifford had made him lose his appetite.

Chapter 24

Jamison sat in his office debating with himself about calling Gifford. Legally the file belonged to the client and the client was Clarence Foster. Jamison had no right to go through that file, even though Gifford might hand it over, which he doubted. But then again, neither did Gifford because he wasn't Foster's lawyer. But there was a possibility. Right now, Foster didn't have a lawyer but that could change quickly.

O'Hara sauntered into Jamison's office. "What you got? Anything?"

"Bill, go pull the file on Clarence Foster. There might be something there that isn't in the Harker file."

It didn't take long for O'Hara to walk back into Jamison's office. "Boss, I went to the dead files. I checked Foster's rap sheet. It shows that he was arrested for murder in this case but it didn't show anything else. I went through our files. He was charged so there should have been a file because it was a murder case, but I couldn't find it." Jamison nodded. Old files were routinely destroyed ten years after the case closed, but Foster's file was related to the Harker case and that should have red flagged the file.

"Did you check the file shelves? Sometimes files get put in out of sequence."

O'Hara sniffed, insulted that Jamison would imply that he didn't know his job. "I checked the entire shelf of files and boxes. It wasn't there. So, then I checked the records on files that have been destroyed. They keep a record of that." O'Hara sat down heavily and waited for Jamison to ask.

Jamison knew O'Hara was stringing it out. "Well? I know there's more from the expression on your face."

O'Hara slowly shook his head, acknowledging that he had something else. "The destruction record didn't show that Foster's file had been destroyed, so it was supposed to be there where I looked. I went back again because it would be a thick file, maybe even a box. It wasn't there, but there was something that *was* there. I could tell from the dust and the discoloration on the files next to where it should have been that a file had been removed. Boss, that file should have been there and I'm sure it was there, or at least some file was. I looked at the checkout file but there was nothing. It looks to me like somebody removed it and they didn't do it that long ago. Before you ask, there's so many people who have access to those dead files that there's no way I can tell you who took it or when. All I know is that it wasn't that long ago because of the dust pattern."

Jamison got up and walked toward the door of his office. "Well, there's only so many people in this office besides us that would look at that file. I'll check with Sheila." Jamison walked the short distance to the outer office of Bill Gage, smiling at his gatekeeper, Sheila Barrow. "Sheila, I'm looking for an old file that has to do with the Harker case. I thought maybe Bill might know something about it. The name on it is—"

Sheila interrupted. "Clarence Foster? Is that what you're looking for? Mr. Gage may still have it, I think. He asked for it the other day and I sent down for it."

"Did he happen to say why he wanted it?"

"He said that Judge Cleary wanted to look at it, so that's why I had it brought up. Should I tell him you're looking for it?"

"No. I'll talk to him later, thanks." Jamison walked back to his office, seeing O'Hara with his feet up on his desk. O'Hara didn't take them off until he saw Jamison raise his hand in a sweeping motion. He said, "Bill Gage has the file. Apparently Judge Cleary wanted to look at it. At least that's what Sheila said."

"So, what're you going to do?" O'Hara started rubbing his mustache, which meant he was spinning through the options in his mind.

"I think I'm going to go see Harker's lawyer. I suspect he has the Foster file put together by my father. Maybe not. But if he has it, whether he'll give it to me—I don't know."

"But you gotta ask?" O'Hara got up, preparing to drive Jamison over to Gifford's office.

Jamison grimaced. "No other way. The only claim I have to that file is my dad put it together. But it legally belongs to Clarence Foster."

"What do you mean it belongs to Foster? Your dad was the lawyer, right? And you're his son?"

"Technically, legal files belong to the client, not the lawyer. There are things in there that belong to the lawyer but I can't go rummaging through it without Foster's permission and neither can Gifford."

"But you think Gifford's already gone through it, right? I mean he's not going to pass up that chance." O'Hara's cynicism about the ethics of lawyers always took him in the most suspicious direction.

"Well, he shouldn't have, but that depends on Foster, and it depends on Gifford's ethics, and it all depends on whether he has the file. Even if he does, we don't know what's in it."

◡

Gifford walked out into the entry area of his office when Jamison walked in with O'Hara trailing behind. "Your phone call said you wanted to know if I have your father's old legal files?"

Jamison moved quickly to the point. "My understanding is that you used to work with my father in the office he shared with other lawyers."

Gifford shook his head. "I wouldn't say I worked with you father. It was more like I worked around him. I was young, and he was what I wanted to be."

"Do you have his files?"

"I ended up with a collection of files that built up over time. As the law office changed and more lawyers came in, the files just got bigger, and when lawyers left or retired or died, the files just stayed. Same as your father's files. Most of them went to storage and eventually there was just me. I pay the storage fees."

"So, you have them?" Jamison was trying unsuccessfully to contain his impatience, realizing that Gifford was playing with him.

"I have the files that were left behind, but I'm assuming what you want to know is if they include Clarence Foster's, right? I wondered how long it would take you."

"It took me this long," Jamison snapped back.

"And you want to know if I've looked at that file, don't you?" Gifford waited, his eyes narrowing as he measured Jamison's demeanor.

"Did you?"

"Well, I don't suppose my answer would satisfy you one way or the other, but I do know the rules. Just because I defend people accused of crimes—unjustly of course—doesn't mean I don't try to do what's right ethically. I'm sure you might question that, and I'm confident your attack dog"—he nodded at O'Hara—"doesn't believe that, but it's of no importance to me what you think. I thought about it and I decided that you can have the file." Gifford walked over to a closet and pulled out an accordion folder. "Here you go. It's been my problem, now it's your problem. What's the line? Choose wisely." Gifford smiled like a parent watching a child get ready to do something that he would be sorry about, knowing the experience would be a lesson learned rather than a lecture disregarded. "See you in court tomorrow. I assume you'll be there." Judge Wallace had notified them that his calendar was open and they were on.

As Jamison walked out the door with O'Hara carrying the file, he heard Gifford say in a quiet voice, "Do what you think is right, Mr. Jamison."

Chapter 25

O'Hara slid into the driver's seat, putting the legal file on the console between him and Jamison. "So what do you think's in there? You going to look now?" He stared at the file like a kid looking at a present under the tree two days before Christmas.

Jamison moved the file to the back, not answering. His father had made this file, touched it, written in it. And now that file was going to taunt him as he thought about what he wanted to do and what he knew he was supposed to do. It was almost like Roger Jamison was physically present in the car watching him. Jamison considered the irony of it. His father placing an ethical choice in front of him, a choice he doubted his father would have hesitated at.

O'Hara glanced over again at Jamison. "You going to open it or not?"

"I can't open that file and Gifford knows it."

"Whether he knows it or not, he figures you will."

"Maybe so, but if there's something in there one way or the other I can't use it, and if I try I'll be up before the state bar on charges for violating Foster's attorney-client privilege. Let's go back to the office." Jamison didn't say another word. Gifford hadn't done him any favor.

O'Hara knew when to keep quiet.

‿

Ernie was waiting for both of them when they walked back into the office. He had retrieved Foster's DA file from Gage's secretary. Jamison walked in and set the accordion file from Gifford down on the corner of his desk. He then opened another accordion file with Clarence Foster's name on it and an old district attorney case number. Written in thick black flow pen on the front of the file were the words *HARKER 187*, the penal code for murder. Jamison turned to Ernie. "You gone through it yet?"

Garcia shook his head. "I waited for you."

Jamison looked at the papers in the file and started pulling out stapled reports. It became quickly apparent that there was nothing in there that he hadn't seen before in terms of reports, but there were notes in the precise handwriting he had seen in the main Harker file, the handwriting of then deputy district attorney Jonathon Cleary.

Slowly, Jamison read through the notes carefully scribed on a yellow lined legal pad. There wasn't much. The notes had general trial strategy, a comment about the arrest of Foster, and comments about Farrow's autopsy, at which

Cleary had apparently been present. It was unusual that Cleary would be at the autopsy but not uncommon. He stopped when he came to a reference to Roger Jamison, his father. The notes roughly outlined a proposed agreement for Foster's testimony. He read to the bottom of the page and flipped to the next page, but it was blank. If there was more it wasn't in the legal tablet. The agreement for Foster's testimony had to be memorialized somewhere because no defense attorney, particularly his father, would allow his client to testify without a very specific agreement in writing. He flipped through a few more pages in the legal tablet but that was it. The rest of the papers were evidence receipts and carbon paper copies of jail custody slips when Foster had been moved out of the jail for interrogation. Why he had suspected there might be something else he didn't know. He handed the file over to O'Hara and Ernie. "Here, maybe you guys can find something."\

⌒

Judge Wallace tapped his fingers impatiently, waiting for Gifford to finish shuffling papers while Harker squirmed around in his seat, his leg irons jangling indiscreetly. Jamison simply waited patiently. He didn't know who was going to be Gifford's next witness. Just because Gifford had indicated Foster the last time, that was then, and this was now. It wouldn't surprise him if Gifford tried to catch him off guard. He was guessing it would still be Foster.

Jamison focused on where he was going to go with Foster. He had an objective and he had thought it through. He knew better than to go into cross-examination without having a focus and discipline. O'Hara had made another effort to talk to Foster in the jail but he had refused to cooperate, telling O'Hara to "fuck off." Jamison considered that Foster had no idea how big a mistake that was to get on O'Hara's bad side. In addition, Foster said he wanted a lawyer. Jamison had passed the word on to the public defender and left it at that.

He glanced at the back of the room and saw Paul Carter, a seasoned homicide lawyer from the public defender's office. Carter shrugged when Jamison caught his eye. Carter had called and given him a heads-up that he had been assigned Foster, but he also hinted that Foster hadn't been cooperative with him either.

Jamison felt sorry for public defense lawyers, who didn't get to pick who to defend. Most of the time the defendants didn't respect their public defenders. They didn't consider them to be "real lawyers" because they didn't charge five hundred dollars an hour. It never made any sense to Jamison. Most public defenders had far more experience than private lawyers. What they didn't have was time. What they did have in abundance was too many cases and limited resources. All they really had was dedication and commitment, which, in Jamison's experience, they gave to their ungrateful clients without reservation.

Doing the right thing was a vastly different obligation for a public defender and a district attorney. A public defender made sure a usually guilty client got their constitutional right to a fair trial, even though he or she might want to take a bath after sitting next to an accused child molester or rapist as defense counsel. Jamison recognized that he didn't have to rationalize what he did, at least most of the time. He had long come to realize that even what he did had its own shades of gray in it.

Jamison's reverie was broken up by the rumble of Wallace's voice. "Mr. Gifford, are you planning to put on any more evidence?"

Gifford seemed very tense, nodding to the court. "Yes, Your Honor. We call Clarence Foster." Background noise disturbed the usually quiet courtroom as reporters and court watchers anticipated that this was going to be interesting.

Paul Carter walked forward, asking for the judge's attention. "Your Honor, Paul Carter, public defender's office. I'm here because it's my understanding Mr. Foster has requested legal counsel in this matter."

Wallace pursed his lips. "Has Mr. Foster made that request?"

"Well, Your Honor, it is a somewhat unusual situation. My office received a call from the district attorney's office saying they wanted to talk to Mr. Foster, but he said he wanted a lawyer. So, they called us. Mr. Foster wasn't very cooperative when I went to see him, but he did indicate—in his words, 'I don't care'—that he didn't mind us being here. So I wanted the court to understand I will stand by in case the court needs me."

"Thank you, Mr. Carter. I appreciate it. I suspect we'll need your services today, but it remains to be seen." Wallace turned his head toward a bailiff. "Get the witness from the holding cell, please."

Foster was led into the courtroom by a bailiff who guided him into the well of the courtroom in front of the judge's bench. He wasn't wearing leg irons or handcuffs. Jamison surmised that Wallace hadn't deemed him much of a threat, but that didn't mean a bailiff wouldn't be standing next to him. In the prisoner jumpsuit from the county jail, Foster looked like what he was, an aging man whose clothing had begun to bag on him as the years took their toll. The clerk swore him in as a witness and asked him to state his name. He took a seat on the witness stand without further direction.

Foster scanned the courtroom, his eyes momentarily locking on Harker. Nobody had to stand between them to feel the chill. Foster's eyes moved slightly to his left as Gifford approached him. "Mr. Foster, you are currently an inmate at Corcoran State Prison, correct?"

"You're the one what brought me here so you already know that. I want to go back. I told you, I got nothin' to say." The words were spoken quickly and without emotion. Gifford ignored the answer and persisted. "You know my client, Richard Harker, correct?"

Foster nodded before answering yes. He again gazed around the courtroom, avoiding Harker and looking at Jamison and O'Hara.

"In fact, you testified against Mr. Harker when he was accused of the murder of Lisa Farrow, correct?"

"I already testified. I got nothin' more to say."

"You served time at San Quentin State Prison at the same time as Mr. Harker, isn't that true?"

"You already know or you wouldn't have asked." Foster's tone remained flat even though his words themselves had an edge.

Gifford moved closer to Foster. "While you were at San Quentin did you have a conversation with my client, Richard Harker, in which you admitted that you lied when you testified he was the one who killed Lisa Farrow?" The question hung in the space between Gifford and Foster.

Jamison had anticipated this line of questioning and how he was going to handle it. Before Foster answered, Jamison was on his feet. "Your Honor, I object on the grounds of hearsay." Jamison had thought about the legal problem that Gifford had. Hearsay was simply statements made outside of the proceeding that were offered to prove the truth of the content of the statement. Gifford had phrased his question carefully to avoid the objection, but he was still trying to get in the statement indirectly when he couldn't do it directly. Jamison had speculated that Foster would be uncooperative. So far, he was right. If Foster didn't testify the statement shouldn't come in.

Wallace looked at Gifford. "The objection is sustained, Mr. Gifford. You can ask the witness whether he lied when he testified before, and if he says no, then you can impeach him or you can ask him what happened before. And if he says something different, then you can impeach him. But I want to caution you that before you do that I think we have to figure out whether Mr. Foster wants a lawyer or not since you are essentially contending he perjured himself."

Jamison sat back down. Gifford was in a legal box, exactly where Jamison had hoped he could put him. The next move was appointment of the public defender, and no lawyer was going to let Foster testify without protecting his client's Fifth Amendment right not to incriminate himself. Jamison had antici-pated that also.

Gifford stepped back to the counsel table and then spoke with barely controlled anger. "Mr. Foster, you lied when you testified that my client killed Lisa Farrow. Isn't that true?"

This time, before Foster could answer and before Jamison said anything, Judge Wallace held up his hand, stopping the proceedings. "Mr. Foster, do you want a lawyer before answering any more questions?"

The expression on Foster's face looked almost reptilian as he answered. "I'll take a lawyer if you'll give me one. Don't got no money. They don't pay me much at Corcoran Prison."

Wallace ignored the sarcasm and motioned toward the public defender. "The court will appoint Mr. Paul Carter of the public defender's office to represent the witness. Mr. Carter do you accept?"

Carter walked past the counsel table and stood in front of the judge's bench. "Yes, Your Honor, the public defender accepts and as the court might expect, I need some time to talk to my client before there are any more questions."

Wallace inhaled with a rasping sound. "We will recess while Mr. Carter talks to Mr. Foster." He looked over at Gifford. "Mr. Gifford, is there some reason you didn't anticipate this is what was going to happen, so we wouldn't have to stop everything?"

Gifford stood up before answering, glaring at Jamison. "What I didn't anticipate is that the district attorney would be less interested in the truth than playing games to keep out the truth."

Wallace leaned forward across the bench. "The objection was sustained because it was a proper objection. The motives of the district attorney are not the issue and you know it. We are in recess for an hour."

After Wallace left the bench, Gifford walked over to Jamison and leaned in close to his face. "I would have thought you would want to know the truth." The vehemence with which he spoke caused O'Hara to tense up and stand.

Jamison remained controlled. "Mr. Gifford, you bring me something solid and credible and I'll listen to it. But I'm not going to let you bring in a bunch of hearsay and innuendo. You're going to have to do a whole lot more to get where you think you are going, and I have no intention of making it easy. Now please step away from me."

O'Hara followed Jamison into an attorney conference room, waiting until the door was closed before speaking. "You knew this was going to happen? Why didn't you say anything? You know Foster isn't going to talk, especially now that he has a lawyer." O'Hara made the observation while smiling. He looked like a proud father whose son just scored a touchdown.

"I expected this might happen. Unless Foster wants to cooperate, which I doubt, there's no way he's going to give up what Gifford claims. Besides, I want Gifford to put Harker on the stand. If Gifford wants to get all that crap in, then he's going to have to expose his client. There's a lot of risk in that and Gifford knows it. Since I don't know what he has, I'm going to make him pull teeth to get it out. And he's not going to be able to get in what Harker says that Foster told him unless Foster testifies."

"What about the Clarence Foster file you got from Gifford?" O'Hara asked. "You *have* looked at it, right?"

Jamison gave him a sour smile. O'Hara seldom allowed rules to interfere with objectives. "No, I did *not* look at the file. I told you that it was privileged and only Foster's lawyer could look at it." He waited expectantly for O'Hara. It only took a few seconds.

"So now Foster has a lawyer and . . ."

"That's right, Bill. Now I'm going to give that file to Paul Carter and if there's anything in it, he will come to me and want to deal. I won't do anything unless I know exactly what he's got, and that's assuming he's got anything."

O'Hara sat down heavily. "You know, for a lawyer, you're a lot smarter than you look."

"Same goes for you, Detective O'Hara."

⟿

Everyone was seated when Wallace came back in. This time Foster was in the witness box with his newly appointed lawyer standing next to him. Wallace went on the record. "Mr. Carter, have you had a chance to confer with your client?"

"Yes, Your Honor. Mr. Foster asserts his Fifth Amendment right under the United States Constitution. He declines to testify without immunity from prosecution."

Wallace tilted his head. "I thought Mr. Foster already had immunity in this case?"

Carter moved over by the jury box, so he was in the direct line of sight of Judge Wallace as well as Jamison and Gifford. "Your Honor, my client *may* have immunity as I understand it, but I haven't seen the immunity order and my client is asserting his Fifth Amendment rights based on my advice. I am not allowing Mr. Foster to testify further without adequate assurances that he has immunity."

Wallace's voice showed his exasperation. "Why wasn't this resolved before today, Mr. Jamison, Mr. Gifford?"

Jamison stood shrugging his shoulders and looking sideways at Gifford. "Your Honor, I'm happy to provide anything to Mr. Gifford that he wants. I've given a full copy of our file."

"It doesn't include any immunity order," Gifford snapped.

"Your Honor," Jamison responded, "as the court is well aware, an immunity agreement requires the court to sign off. It should be in the court's file. It isn't in our file but as the court is also well aware, that file is over twenty-five years old. I gave him what I had that was subject to disclosure. I will acknowledge that I haven't seen an immunity order, but I wasn't the one calling Mr. Foster."

Gifford snapped at him again. "What does that mean, 'subject to disclosure'? You're supposed to give me everything."

Jamison responded calmly and precisely. "I'm supposed to give you all our reports. I don't have to give you our notes of strategic plans or attorney notes, and you know that. All our reports, including witness statements of which I am aware, have been turned over to you."

Wallace stood up and started walking off the bench. "Straighten it out, gentlemen, and call my clerk when you have something to tell me."

Chapter 26

Within an hour of the court recess, Jamison had received two phone calls, one from Samuel Gifford demanding that he produce the immunity agreement and one from Paul Carter asking that he produce the immunity agreement. Jamison told them both the same thing, although he didn't use the same tone of voice with Carter as he had with Gifford. He didn't have any written immunity agreement and if there was one it should have been in the court's file. He added something to the conversation with Public Defender Carter, telling him that he had something for him. Then he sent Ernie down to go through the court file with a fine-tooth comb and bring back a copy of the immunity agreement if it was there.

Jamison wasn't expecting Ernie to find anything because he suspected that there was no written agreement. It wasn't uncommon. Prosecutors and defense lawyers made deals all the time in exchange for witness testimony. Chances were that the actual deal was that if Foster agreed to testify, truthfully of course, that he wouldn't be prosecuted for any part he had in the Farrow murder. Usually such deals were put on the record at some intermediate proceeding and weren't in the form of immunity agreements, but it would also be likely that it would be brought up during cross-examination of the witness to impeach their credibility. That meant that Alton Grady would have asked about it, should have asked about it, and it would be in the cross-examination by Grady of Foster. Prosecutors liked witnesses to say that they weren't testifying under a grant of immunity from prosecution but had only been told that as long as they told the truth they wouldn't be prosecuted. It wasn't much of a difference, but it did make the witness sound a little more sincere.

Jamison had gone through the testimony of Foster in the Harker trial, but he didn't remember seeing any reference to a deal. That didn't mean it wasn't there. It only meant that he wasn't focusing on it and he needed to go back. He made a mental note to do that, also flashing on the expectation that there should have been something in the notes in the DA file, when the phone rang. It was Paul Carter wanting to talk.

⤸

Carter looked around Jamison's office with barely concealed envy. "Your offices are a lot nicer than ours." Both men had fought it out in court a number of times. Aside from mutual respect, Jamison genuinely liked Carter and after most of their trials they had gone out and shared a beer or two—or three—and told war stories. It wasn't a real social relationship. Carter had a wife and three kids and Jamison was single, but it was a solid professional relationship.

Jamison laughed. "Well, what public defenders do doesn't make them the most favored people by the county board of supervisors. Besides," he said, remembering the fraying carpet in the DA's hallways, "if our offices are that much better than yours, then you really have a problem."

Carter laid the ubiquitous yellow legal pad on the table. It was covered with scribbled notes. "I'm not going to let him testify without immunity."

Jamison had expected this. "What's Foster got to say?"

Carter leaned in. "Matt, I can't tell you now. All I can say is I'm not sure what I need to do. I have to think about it. And my client isn't doing anything to help me. But he did tell me enough that I'm not going to let him testify without immunity. He also told me that your father was the one who defended him. Is that right?"

"That's right."

Jamison shoved over the Clarence Foster file that he had received from Gifford, explaining, "I got this from Sam Gifford. You can ask him how he got it. Before you ask, I haven't looked at it. I'm not going to say I wasn't tempted but I don't know what's in it. I also know that it was my father's file. He defended Clarence Foster and any deals that were made he made them. You're now Foster's lawyer. You have a right to that file because it belongs to your client. I don't know if Gifford looked in it. You'll have to ask him."

Carter ran his hand across the brown accordion file and the flap with a string tie. "So this is from the famous Roger Jamison?" Jamison nodded but didn't say anything. Carter looked at Jamison with a quizzical expression. "You know there's a possibility what's in this might hurt your case, don't you?"

"Whatever's in that file, it is what it is."

Carter measured his words. "So what are you willing to give in exchange for what's in this file? Like I said, I'm not going to let Foster testify unless we have some kind of a deal for immunity."

Jamison had expected the question. "I'm not going to give you anything. I haven't seen it but it's pretty obvious Foster's deal was for him not to be prosecuted in exchange for his testimony against Harker. Foster got his end of the deal. It still stands. Assuming the deal is what I think it was, then the DA's office will honor it. Foster won't be prosecuted as long as he testifies truthfully. If he doesn't, then the deal's off."

"But if my client lied during the Harker trial like Gifford says he did?" Carter's eyes narrowed as he considered the implications of Jamison's carefully framed comment.

"Well, if Foster lied, then that wasn't part of the deal, was it?" Jamison kept his eyes directly focused on Carter, wanting to make sure there was no misunderstanding of the implication. "Paul, you look at that file. Maybe it has answers for you that I don't."

Carter stood up, taking the file off of Jamison's desk. "What if the file says that Harker's innocent?"

"Twelve people said he isn't beyond a reasonable doubt. Now the shoe's on the other foot. It's Sam Gifford's job to prove otherwise and it's my job to make sure he does. It isn't my job to make it easy for him."

Carter rocked his head back and stared at the ceiling. "You don't really believe that do you? You have a job to make sure justice is done."

Jamison stood and extended his hand across his desk. "Paul, my job *is* to make sure justice is done but it is *also* my job to make sure justice isn't undone. Take the file. I'll be here when and if you want to talk."

Carter walked as far as the door. "You know I can't let Foster talk without a deal."

"Like I said, Paul. Foster had a deal. It hasn't changed."

"Your dad was a legendary lawyer. I used to watch him, you know, when I was in law school. You're a lot like him."

"You probably saw him more than I did. Look at the file, Paul, and talk to your client." Jamison sat back down as Carter walked out the door. He could feel his stomach knot. For some lawyers, the comment comparing him to his father would be a compliment. Jamison didn't think it was and he knew Carter hadn't meant it as one.

Chapter 27

Jamison was scanning Foster's testimony in the Harker trial when Ernie walked in. He didn't have any papers in his hand. Ernie sat down. "Nothing there, Matt. I looked through the court file. There's stuff about Foster but it's just records saying he appeared in court. Nothing about what he said or any deal."

"I didn't think there would be. I've been going over the testimony of Foster and the cross-examination of Foster by Alton Grady. Actually, even though some people said Grady was past his prime, he did a very thorough job of going after Foster. He just didn't hit an artery."

Ernie furrowed the eyebrows on his usually placid face. "Nothing? Grady must have asked about whether Foster had a deal. That's kind of law school 101 isn't it?"

"I didn't say he didn't ask. I said he didn't hit an artery. What the transcript says is that Grady asked if Foster had a deal to testify and Foster said that as long as he told the truth he wouldn't be prosecuted. According to Foster that was the total deal. There was no immunity in exchange for cooperation."

Ernie persisted. "That doesn't seem quite right. All you lawyers want assurances and tie deals up in bullshit written agreements. You're telling me there's nothing there except a promise not to prosecute as long as he told the truth? I can't believe your dad would agree to that. He was supposed to be some kind of big deal criminal defense attorney, right?"

"He was a big deal defense attorney and you're right. He wouldn't have let Foster testify unless he had a deal that guaranteed his client wouldn't be prosecuted. Even if Foster did tell the truth that still put him at the scene of a murder and it still exposed him to possible prosecution. And criminal defense lawyers don't depend on their clients to be entirely truthful. What the DA wants to hear and what actually happened can be two very different things and you can't afford to take any chances. So, any third-rate criminal defense attorney would have demanded an agreement for immunity from prosecution, and my dad wasn't a third-rate defense attorney."

"So, where's the agreement?"

"That's a good question. All I know is I don't have it. If it exists, it should be in Foster's DA file, or Harker's, but it isn't. I went to see District Attorney Gage but he's in Sacramento gearing up for his political future. The other person is Judge Cleary, and before I go to him I'd rather have more information. The only other place is Foster's file that I gave his new lawyer. But if there was a written agreement, then Alton Grady should have had it and that means that Gifford would have it because it should have been in Grady's file. And I do know from Grady's daughter that Gifford went through that file, and in court he claimed he didn't have it."

"You want to go see Alton Grady?"

⤸

Within a half hour, Jamison and Ernie were back at the convalescent facility where Grady now finished his days. Grady was in the same spot he'd been before, warm sunlight highlighting motes of dust hanging in the air around him. Grady was dozing when Jamison touched his shoulder. If the elderly man was startled, he didn't move abruptly, but Jamison suspected he never moved abruptly anymore. Grady looked up with rheumy eyes. Jamison hadn't noticed before that one eye was clouded by what appeared to be a long-present cataract.

He crouched down to directly face the elderly man. "Mr. Grady, you remember me? I'm Matt Jamison with the district attorney's office. I'm handling the Richard Harker case. Remember me? We talked before?" Grady didn't seem to show any spark of recognition. "I'm Roger Jamison's son, remember?"

Grady reacted to Jamison's mention of Roger Jamison. "Roger, yes, good lawyer. Is he still alive? Thought he was dead."

"No, my father was Roger Jamison. He passed away a number of years ago."

"They're all gone, you know. Not many left. You look like him." Grady squinted with his good eye, although Jamison doubted he could see anything through his thick, smudged glasses.

"Mr. Grady, you defended Richard Harker, remember? We talked before."

Grady nodded slowly. "Yes. He was innocent, you know. Did my best."

Jamison nodded. "I'm sure you did your best, sir. But there was a witness, Clarence Foster—do you remember him? He was a black man who testified he was at the scene with Richard Harker. Remember?"

"He lied." Grady's words came out emphatically. "That man lied. I tried. Couldn't shake him. Didn't have anything to use. Ask your father. He knows."

Jamison put his hand on Grady's shoulder, feeling the bone and not much else through Grady's thin robe. "Was there an immunity agreement for Foster? Do you remember?"

For a moment Grady's eyes seemed to focus and clear. "No—no agreement that I saw. Gage, he was the prosecutor, you know. Him and that other one, they said there wasn't anything. All I had was Foster's testimony. Did my best. Gage—son of a bitch. Didn't trust him or that other one." The strain of talking seemed to sap whatever strength Grady had. His head dropped down and Jamison thought about calling the orderly before he heard Grady begin to breathe heavily. The old man was asleep.

Ernie and Jamison got back in Ernie's county car. Ernie looked over before starting the car. "Well, that went well. My plan is to die in my sleep after getting laid."

"Yeah, that's the problem with plans. They don't always work out."

Chapter 28

Jamison and Gifford waited outside Judge Wallace's chambers. His clerk had called and told both of them that Judge Wallace wanted to see them at three o'clock. Neither man spoke to the other.

Judge Wallace opened his door and asked them to come inside. The walls of the dark wood-paneled office were covered with awards, plaques, and photographs. Even though there was hardly any room on the walls for more, there was even less on the edges of the office. Piles of files covered the floor and Wallace's desk.

"Did you two find any immunity agreement?" Wallace's tone registered his impatience with the delay in proceedings.

Gifford spoke first. "I don't have one and the DA hasn't given me one."

Wallace looked over at Jamison who stared straight back. "There's nothing in our file. What I have, I turned over."

Wallace's eyes narrowed as he took in Jamison's statement. "There must have been something—you're telling me that there's no record of any immunity agreement?"

"Judge, all I can say is that it isn't in our files, if there ever was one, and it isn't in the court's file. This case is over twenty-five years old."

"Have you talked to Bill Gage or Justice Cleary? They would know." Jamison felt Wallace's eyes boring in on him.

"Your Honor, Bill Gage is in Sacramento and, no, I haven't talked to Justice Cleary." Jamison hesitated. "But then again, it is Mr. Gifford's burden of proof, not mine. I'm not going to do his investigation for him."

Gifford interrupted the two-way conversation between Wallace and Jamison. "Your Honor, the DA is obligated to turn everything over."

Wallace leaned back in his chair, reaching for the single mug of coffee that his doctor permitted him and that he nursed all day, warm or cold. "He isn't obligated to help you prove your case. If he says he doesn't have it, then maybe it doesn't exist. But nothing is stopping you from calling Gage or Judge Cleary, either."

Wallace shuffled papers around on his desk as he reflected on the appropriate course of action. "I suggest you go talk to Foster's lawyer and then talk to Mr. Jamison. You and I both know I can't do much about it if Foster refuses to answer. First of all, without some indication of the immunity agreement, I can't make him answer because he has a Fifth Amendment right to refuse. And, more obviously, even if I order him to answer and he refuses I can only put him in jail, which is where he already is. So, I'm not much of a threat to Foster, am I?" Jamison kept silent. The judge had thrown the ball back to Gifford. "For right now, I suggest you move forward and call your next witness, so we can get through this. I will see you in court tomorrow. Thank you, gentlemen." Wallace began pulling papers off the pile in the corner of his desk. The meeting was over.

⌒

Jamison suspected that Gifford had spent a sleepless night. That wasn't his problem, but he hadn't slept much either for, he suspected, different reasons. He looked back over his shoulder at the filled seats in the courtroom. The Harker case still drew in the media. They were like dogs waiting to see if there was still meat on a bone. Jamison knew that Gifford's options were limited. He could call Christine Farrow, or he could call Richard Harker. There was no way he was going to get anything out of Foster until the immunity issue was resolved. He was betting on Harker and his decision as to how to cross-examine Harker was what had kept him sleepless most of the night.

"Your Honor, I call Richard Harker to the stand." Gifford stepped to the side as the bailiff unlocked the leg irons tethering Harker to the steel eye bolt under the counsel table. The courtroom filled with murmuring from the reporters present, only silenced when Judge Wallace's dark expression fell on them. Harker stood and waited, moving his head from side to side, stretching his neck. Wallace's clerk told him to raise his right hand. Harker pulled up on his handcuffs attached to a chain around his belly to emphasize that he couldn't raise his right hand to be sworn. Wallace waived off the ensuing confusion by the clerk, had Harker acknowledge the oath, and directed him to take the stand.

It was really the first time that Jamison had actually looked carefully at Harker. He was only fifty-two years old but the years rode hard on him. Prison could do that to a man, sapping him of the smile lines and wrinkles around his eyes from the sun and replacing them with the lines of a man always watching, waiting for predators. Jamison had learned early on that the lines on a man's face often told his story. In prison if you aren't a predator, you are prey. Harker didn't have the look of a victim. His face was hard and drawn, his skin showed little color, and his eyes were shrouded by lids that he kept narrow as if squinting from the sun. But there was no sun and the squinting came from measuring everyone around him for the threat they might pose. Whatever he had been when he walked into prison, he was now a predator. Jamison imagined that Harker rarely opened his eyes wide. Today was no different.

Gifford circled around the counsel table asking Harker to state his name. He then went through the preliminaries of Harker being in San Quentin prison and how long he had been there before moving to the reason for his imprisonment. "You were convicted of the first-degree murder of Lisa Farrow, isn't that correct?"

"That's what a jury said."

"And the jury said you should be sentenced to death, isn't that also correct?"

"Yes, I don't forget that. I never forget that, thinking that I would be executed for something I didn't do." Harker spoke quietly, although his voice was edged with projected resentment. "The judge refused to impose the death penalty. At the time, I thought he did me a favor. After all this time in Quentin, I'm not so sure. Twenty-six years of my life are gone."

"When you were sent to San Quentin, what schooling did you have?"

"I hadn't finished high school."

"And now?"

"I have my high school diploma and a college degree." Harker turned toward Judge Wallace with an ironic smile on his face. "In criminal justice, Your Honor."

"Did you testify in your trial?"

"Yes, and I told the truth. Nobody believed me. Nobody ever believed me."

"Did you kill Lisa Farrow?" Jamison considered the strategy of Gifford moving straight to the point, rather than going through the details. The implication being that if Hacker hadn't murdered Lisa Farrow, then how would he know any of the details?

"No, I did not. I always loved her. I didn't do anything to her. I wouldn't hurt her or her little girl. I'm not perfect but I wasn't no murderer." Jamison caught the tense that Harker used, he wasn't a murderer then. He suspected that Harker was skirting what he might have done to stay alive for the last twenty-six years.

"You said you loved Lisa Farrow. Describe your relationship." Jamison started to object and stopped short. The more Harker said, the more Jamison had to ask about.

"I knew her when we were in high school. I never went out with her but we knew each other, you know?" Harker described how he had done a short stint in the Army but ended up being discharged for bad behavior. When he got out he went to work at different labor jobs in construction, eventually finding work as a mechanic. One night he met Lisa in a convenience store. One thing led to another and they lived together for a short period of time when Christine was around three, and then he moved on.

"Why did you and Lisa break up?"

Harker remained silent, slowly turning to look at Jamison before answering. "We began to argue a lot because of my drinking. We had a fight and I hit her. It wasn't the only time. Anyway, I left. We saw one another once in a while. I would go by and give her some money if I had any to spare."

"Did you know Rick Sample?"

"I knew him. Saw him around anyway. I heard he was livin' with Lisa but I had no hold on her. I wasn't the one who killed her. I wouldn't have done that. She was the best thing that happened to me, but I wasn't the best man for her. Maybe too young. I don't know. But that little girl. I cared about her. I would never hurt her or her mother."

"Do you know Clarence Foster? Did you know him back then?"

"Yeah, pretty much everyone in the neighborhood knew Clarence. He didn't live that far from Lisa's house. That's how I met him. On weekends there was a bunch of us and we would sit in the park or on somebody's porch and drink. There was a lot of us. When somebody had beer money we shared."

"How did Clarence Foster make a living? Do you know?"

Harker barked out a laugh. "Same way I did when I didn't have no money. We took it. Stole it mostly unless I was working. Sold some weed, things like that. I didn't sell hard drugs. Clarence did the same thing but mostly he was a thief, and I guess you could say so was I. But we didn't hurt nobody. I wasn't no robber or nothin'."

"Where were you when Lisa Farrow was murdered?"

"I was home drinking. I was passed out, I guess. When I came outside it was all over the neighborhood. That kind of news travels fast. I went over there but cops was everywhere so I stayed away. Next thing I know, cops came after me and I was in jail. I kept tellin' 'em I didn't hurt her but nobody believed me and that lyin' son of a bitch Foster, he told 'em I did it."

Gifford paused, clearly contemplating his next question. "Did you ever sit in the back of a patrol car with Clarence Foster?"

Harker leaned forward. "Yeah, I did, and he admitted he lied about me." The words came out quickly and it was evident that Gifford had coached him.

Jamison was immediately on his feet raising a multitude of objections, including hearsay. Wallace tilted his head to the side, shaking it a little before sustaining the hearsay objection and granting Jamison's motion to strike the answer. The effort to strike the answer ensured that it was not part of the record for purposes of evidence. It didn't go away but it did render it meaningless, at least meaningless as far as lawyers were concerned. When a jury was present it was like telling them to forget hearing the bell ring. No juror really did, but for the purposes of the hearing with Wallace, it meant that Jamison had kept Harker from talking about what Foster said unless Foster testified. Jamison had calculated that he would cross that bridge when he came to it.

Gifford began arguing the point with Wallace, pointing out that if Harker wasn't allowed to testify to what Foster said, that his admissions of lying wouldn't be before the court. Wallace made it clear he wasn't going to argue the point. His ruling would stand, pointing out that the rules of evidence didn't change just because of the nature of the hearing.

"Did the prosecutor interrogate you?"

"You mean Gage, the guy who tried to get me executed? Yeah, he asked me questions. So did the detective."

"Did you tell them that Foster had admitted he lied?"

Jamison again rose to his feet, but Wallace cut him off. "I'll allow it because my understanding from Mr. Gage and Detective Jensen was that they never heard anything like that."

Harker turned to Wallace. "It wasn't them, Your Honor. It was that young prosecutor."

Gifford interrupted. "You mean Judge Cleary, the man who testified?"

"Yeah, him. He's the one I told. He talked to me and I told him."

Gifford looked over at Jamison. "Did you ever see Clarence Foster at San Quentin Prison? Was he also doing time there?"

"Yeah, Foster was there for a while, but he stayed away from me. He stuck with the brothers, you know."

"The brothers?"

"Yeah, the black guys. In the Q everybody sticks with their own kind. I stayed with my kind and Foster stayed with his. But if you're asking did he tell me he lied, yeah, he did."

Jamison immediately objected on the grounds of hearsay and the answer being nonresponsive to the question, which was only asking about what Harker meant by "brothers." Wallace leaned back in his chair, holding up his hand for silence. "Why should I let this in, Mr. Gifford? Mr. Foster hasn't testified, and it is clearly hearsay."

"Your Honor, Foster hasn't testified because the prosecutor won't give him immunity. He's keeping Foster off the stand and arguing technical objections to keep out evidence of my client's innocence. This isn't right."

"You still haven't answered my question, Mr. Gifford. I'm sorry, you are going to have to do more for me to consider your client's statement as to what somebody allegedly said who refuses to testify. This hearing is about new evidence, evidence that couldn't be produced at your client's trial. "

Gifford exploded. "This hearing is about justice. Foster lied."

All of a sudden Harker stood up, shouting, "I'm innocent, goddammit. You're supposed to listen to me." Harker's voice broke and he began to cry. "I'm innocent. I can't go back. I didn't do it."

Wallace sat silently until Harker calmed down. "Objection sustained. Anything more, Mr. Gifford?"

"What's the point?"

Wallace leaned forward, leveling his gaze on Gifford. "Mr. Gifford, don't cross the line with me. You knew walking in here that if you were going to be effective with your writ, you were going to have to get in evidence that wasn't available at your client's trial, and you weren't going to get to bend the rules of evidence. I'm not here to allow you to bring in inadmissible evidence and I'm not going to be flexible on that. Mr. Jamison, unless Mr. Gifford has something more you may cross-examine."

Jamison sat, tapping his pencil on the counsel table. As much as he would like to cross-examine Harker about the crime, he hadn't said anything. The witnesses who were important were Foster and Christine Farrow. Foster hadn't testified to anything. The more he questioned Harker, the more Harker would talk about his innocence while reporters furiously scribbled in their notebooks, and the greater chance he would ask a question that would allow Harker to get in what Foster allegedly said. This hearing was all about new evidence, and Harker testifying to self-serving statements about what somebody said wasn't going to help him. "No questions, Your Honor."

∽

At lunch, O'Hara and Ernie sat in Jamison's office chewing on sandwiches from the courthouse cafeteria. As far as Jamison was concerned it was like eating mystery meat wrapped in cardboard, but his investigators didn't seem to mind. However, Jamison had learned early on that the diet of cops was somewhat similar to goats; they weren't very discriminating. Finally, O'Hara spoke up about Jamison's refusal to ask Harker questions. Jamison put his sandwich down and explained that for Gifford to prevail he was going to have to bring in new evidence that wasn't available at the trial. Evidence from Foster that he lied when he identified Harker would be such evidence, but Foster hadn't testified and Gifford wasn't going to be allowed to get in statements he said Foster made without getting them in through Foster. What Gifford had been counting on was that Foster would testify or that Judge Wallace would give him some slack in the rules. Jamison had been counting on the fact that Wallace was a stickler for the rules. As far as Foster was concerned, it wasn't the prosecutor's job to allow in evidence that wasn't otherwise admissible. Gifford was on his own, and if it took Jamison objecting to exculpatory evidence, that was his job.

Ernie listened quietly before asking, "But what if Foster really did tell Harker that he lied? Shouldn't Judge Wallace consider that?"

O'Hara offered his opinion before Jamison could answer. "Harker's a convicted murderer and now he's just trying any bullshit he can think of to get out of the joint. It's not Matt's job to help him."

Jamison didn't make any excuses for his objections. "Gifford knew that what he was trying to get in shouldn't be admitted. What he was counting on is the seriousness of the case and that Wallace would cut him some slack. Wallace would do the same thing to me if the shoe was on the other foot. I knew if

Foster didn't testify then Gifford should not be allowed to get in those statements. Wallace was right. The rules don't change depending on consequences."

Ernie persisted. "Well, what if Foster testifies?"

"Then Gifford will be able to ask what he wants and impeach Foster. But first he has to get Foster to testify. That's his job, not mine. Look, Ernie. No judge is going to grant a new trial simply because a defendant comes in and says that a witness lied. The judge is going to have to have clear proof or hear it from that witness, and even then the judge may not believe it. Foster is in the joint. He isn't going to win any friends by cooperating. It is all about newly discovered evidence. They had their chance to cross-examine Foster at Harker's trial. I'm not doing anything to Gifford that he wouldn't do to me if our roles were reversed. Gifford is the one who has to prove his case. So far he hasn't and I'm not going to help him."

Ernie asked, "Are you going to give Foster immunity from prosecution? His lawyer isn't going to let him testify unless he has immunity."

Jamison shook his head. "Hell no, I'm not going to agree to immunity. First of all, I have no idea what Foster might say and whether we could believe it even if he testified. Second, if I give Foster immunity, then Foster becomes Harker's witness. I'm not going to do that. There's no downside for Foster to come in now and start testifying that he lied. What can we do to him? I'm not going to help his lawyer do that. My job is to make sure the conviction is upheld unless I have real evidence that shows it was wrong. This is Sam Gifford's show, not mine."

Ernie persisted. "So no matter what Foster has to say, you aren't going to allow him to say it?"

"It's not a case of me not allowing Foster to say it. Foster can get up and testify if he wants. I'm not stopping him. But I'm not going to let Gifford get in evidence without Foster testifying."

"And Foster isn't going to testify without immunity." Ernie was obviously disturbed by the strategy.

O'Hara stood up, tired of the discussion. "What difference does it make? Nobody's going to believe Foster's statements. It's all lawyer bullshit, anyway. Harker did it. Matt's job is to keep him from trying to get out of it. This happens all the time. Twenty, thirty years after the trial, somebody comes in and starts questioning what was long ago decided. It's done and we need to stick him back in his hole where he belongs."

After the two investigators left, Jamison sat at his desk, turning to stare out the window. What he had said to Ernie and O'Hara had been legally correct. But there was a difference between legal and moral. The law satisfied itself that legally right was a moral result. What Jamison reflected on as he sat there was not whether he was legally wrong.

Chapter 29

"Your Honor, we call Christine Farrow." Jamison kept his eyes focused on Judge Wallace, knowing that all other eyes were fixating on the young woman being led into the courtroom. She was Gifford's silver bullet and it was now clear he was not going to keep everyone in suspense. It was also clear that Gifford intended to feed the press so it would draw them in. His goal was to arouse the sympathy of the news media for his client and to create a narrative that District Attorney Bill Gage and his chosen warrior, Matt Jamison, were perpetuating injustice to an innocent man.

Jamison allowed himself a sideways glance as she was sworn. Not much had changed since his interview with her. Perhaps she was a bit thinner. She had more makeup on but it only emphasized her age-sharpened features. She had on a simple blue dress, belted at the waist, and shoes that were probably her only good pair other than work shoes. But one thing came through all of that. Her defense had been her anonymity and her face showed that she was clutching at the prison bars built by her life. This was a woman to whom life had given little measure of kindness and mercy, a very small victim in a very large world. When she took her seat on the witness stand she seemed to shrink even smaller. Jamison felt queasy about what he had to do, knowing the system was going to damage her again. And she was simply an innocent.

"Please state your name."

"Christine Farrow." Her voice was so low that it came out as a whisper. Judge Wallace quietly asked her to speak louder and she nodded her understanding, repeating her name. "Christine Farrow."

Gifford's demeanor noticeably changed as he began methodically taking Christine back in time.

"Christine, do you recognize the man sitting next to me?" he asked, pointing to Richard Harker.

"No."

"You don't know who he is?"

"I know who he is because of his picture on the news but other than that I don't know who he is—I mean I don't recognize him."

Gifford circled around the counsel table and stood well away from Christine. "You've never seen Richard Harker before?"

"No—I mean I don't know. I don't remember . . ." Her voice trailed off and Wallace again reminded her that she had to speak louder. "I'm sorry. All of this is hard for me. I'm not used to this." Wallace nodded sympathetically and told

Christine that she should try to stay calm and he would make sure that if she needed a break she would have it.

Jamison sat watching this and focusing on the witness. What he noticed was that Gifford didn't seem surprised when Christine said she didn't recognize Harker. That told him that he had expected that answer. Why he expected it was a question that he jotted down for further examination.

"Christine, do you recall ever knowing a man named Richard Harker?"

"It was a long time ago. What I remember is jumbled up with what people have told me. I've looked at his picture and I've looked at other pictures, but it was a long time ago. I was only three. What I remember is not clear and he looks different than what I remember. Faces change over the years. He could be the man I remember but I can't be sure. I only remember the face as I saw it then, and even that I don't remember clearly."

"I'm sure this is very difficult for you." Gifford pulled out the declaration that Christine had signed and showed it to her. "Do you remember signing this declaration?"

"Yes." Her voice was almost a whisper as she nodded but in the stone silence of the courtroom it resonated like a footfall in the night. "I said it wasn't Rick—Rick Harker—who was there that night when my mother was killed."

"And was that the truth?"

"Yes, because I remember the face of the man who stood over me in my room. I knew who he was. That's what I remember now. I knew who he was."

Gifford paused, holding the moment before asking the next question. "And whose face was that, Christine?

"It was the face of the man I knew as Rick Sample."

"And is there some reason that you know that?"

"Rick was Tommy's daddy. He had a little boy named Tommy. Rick lived at our house for a while and sometimes he would bring Tommy over and I played with him. I knew that. The man who stood over me when my mom was killed was Rick Sample. That's what I remember. And when I realized that, I had to make it right. Rick Harker didn't murder my mother. I know that now. I'm real sorry that he's been in prison for that. I was a little girl. I tried to make it right. I signed that paper." Her mouth contorted as she tried to hold in her emotions.

Gifford wasn't going to let the moment go. The rustling in the courtroom and the murmuring from reporters and onlookers caused Wallace to tap his pen on the bench for silence. The glowering expression on his face made his point without saying anything further. "And you know now that is the truth? My client didn't murder your mother?"

"Yes." Christine's head tilted forward. Her hair fell across her face, but it didn't hide her soft whimpering.

"Christine, do you remember testifying in court when you were little, testifying in this case?"

"No, at least not in a way that I can explain it. I know that I said Rick Harker was there that night because that's what people have told me, but I know now that wasn't right. I can't explain. It's like my memory has a big hole in it. That part is just not there. I . . . I was so little. My memory of it—I just need it all to go away. I'm sorry."

Gifford probed gently. "Christine, can you tell us what you remember of that night, the night your mother was murdered?" Gifford glanced back at Jamison, daring him to object at the open-ended question. Jamison kept his impassive expression. He had no intention of objecting. His focus was on letting Gifford draw out as much of Christine's memory as possible so he could cross-examine.

Christine looked up at the courtroom ceiling and then at a spot on the back wall of the courtroom. Everyone in the courtroom could see her face take on a vacant expression. She looked like a lost child as she began to wander through the minefield of her memory in front of strangers. She talked about her mother, who she called Mama, and she spoke about Tommy, the little boy she remembered, and the man she knew as Tommy's daddy. And she talked about the other man that she also knew as Rick. She spoke in fragments of images that she tried to relate, explaining that she only remembered bits and pieces. Finally, she said that most of what happened that night and in the courtroom was gone, like it had been wiped clean from her memory. What she remembered was the sound of her mother crying and the man standing over her bed. She had struggled with nightmares, and her agitation and nervousness had gotten worse and worse over time. Images flashed through her head as she slept. And the older she got the worse they were, waking her up to the clamminess of cold sweat and tremors as she grappled with slivers of horrifying images that she couldn't see clearly. And finally, she had sought help. That was when she met Dr. Vinson. He helped her. And then she remembered and understood what she had kept in the darkness of her memory. What she described as changing from a jumbled blur of violence into images she could at least understand. And all the time Christine talked, not a sound was made in the courtroom as everyone watched her relive the night that had ruined her life. Finally, she stopped and looked around as if she was startled to see everyone present, looking at her. Then she began to weep, the sound erupting from her in convulsive sobs.

Gifford looked up at Wallace, who had reached over and handed Christine a box of tissues, the expression on his face thoughtful as he leaned back in his chair. Gifford said, "I have no further questions at this time, Your Honor. I think we need to take a recess."

"I agree, but perhaps we should give the witness some time. Should we start in the morning?" Wallace responded.

Gifford shook his head. "Your Honor, I'm sure Ms. Farrow would like to get this over with as soon as possible. Maybe we could just take a longer break than usual?"

"Mr. Jamison?" Wallace looked over at Jamison, waiting for his comment.

Jamison understood why Gifford wanted to force him quickly into cross-examination, and while he wasn't so cynical that he thought Gifford didn't care about the emotional state of Christine Farrow, he was cynical enough to believe that part of the defense attorney's motivation to go forward was to place him at more of a disadvantage. "Your Honor, a couple of points. This is the first time I've heard all of this from Ms. Farrow. She hasn't talked to me or my investigators about this, although we did try. Second, and more importantly, I think she needs time to compose herself, because her cross-examination will probably go on for quite a while."

Wallace held up his hand blocking further comment from both attorneys. "Tomorrow morning, gentlemen, nine a.m." Wallace turned to Christine Farrow. "I certainly appreciate that you would like to be done with this. Please try to rest. We will start again tomorrow."

Jamison looked at his watch. The rest of the day wasn't much time. He turned to O'Hara. "Tell Ernie to pull up everything on Richard Sample."

O'Hara snorted. "I told you he was dead."

Jamison said, "He's dead now but he wasn't dead then. We need to know why everyone decided that Sample wasn't the killer and we need to look at the alibi he had that apparently convinced Jensen, Gage, and Cleary that he was a cold trail."

"Boss, you do understand that was over twenty-six years ago?"

"That's why you and Ernie are detectives. If I can show that Sample couldn't have been the one standing over her, then her whole story comes apart at the seams. Tell Ernie I need it yesterday. And call Dr. Levy. Tell him I need to talk to him."

Chapter 30

D r. Aaron Levy and Jamison had a long history going back to when Matt was a young man. He had met Levy through his father, or, perhaps more accurately, because of his father. For reasons Matt had never been able to fathom, his father and Aaron Levy had been friends, but Levy's insights also caused him to reach out to Matt. Levy became a secret confidant and a provider of fatherly guidance and more. Over the years, and when Matt became a prosecutor, Levy had also become a source of professional advice who Matt went to when he needed to understand the psychological motivations of the people he dealt with. Levy maintained a clinical practice as well as a professorship at Tenaya State University.

O'Hara spun the wheel of the county car into an open space near Levy's campus office. Jamison looked over, but O'Hara anticipated the reason. "I'll stay here while you talk to the shrink, okay?"

O'Hara was way too impatient to sit quietly and listen. He regarded most of what psychologists had to say as babble that only provided excuses. What he never realized, and Jamison did, was that Levy regarded O'Hara with amusement as a walking bundle of psychological stereotypes. He frequently privately referred to him as Matt's "junkyard dog." But he also saw and respected the loyalty that flowed from the older investigator. They both shared a form of paternal affection for the young prosecutor.

With his carefully trimmed silver beard and metal-rimmed glasses, Levy was almost as much of a stereotype of a psychologist as Vinson. The aging psychologist listened intently as Jamison explained Christine's recantation and the circumstances of the murder. It didn't take Levy long to make an observation. "I know of Dr. Vinson's work. He deals a lot with people with a history of child abuse, repressed memory. He has theories that I've heard. They aren't widely accepted but there is some measure of accepted credibility in repressed memory. It's not unusual for witnesses to recant their testimony or identification. Interestingly, the most common cases are murder and sexual abuse. But the key question is why? Usually there is some triggering reason. Something has caused Christine to change her testimony. However, she could be telling the truth and suppressed it all these years. How a child is questioned can affect what they say, but you have recordings and other records of her questioning. Then there is simply lying. The child lies for whatever reason and feels great guilt, which they have suppressed and now it has bubbled to the surface. But people who do this, especially adults struggling with childhood memories, are particularly susceptible to what we call confabulation. It simply means that retrieval of long-term memory has been disrupted. It's very complex but basically what happens is that a person who is having difficulty with memories has allowed suggestions to simply become the memory. In other words, what they think they remember or what someone suggests to them becomes the memory. And this new memory becomes their truth. They are not lying, at least in the intentional sense. They are telling something untrue that they are convinced is true.

"The process of confabulation is particularly dangerous with hypnosis, which is sometimes used to relax the patient and help them with memory retrieval. Sometimes it is referred to as the misinformation effect.

"My surmise is that Dr. Vinson used hypnosis. It's a common tool in controlled settings. Recantation cases frequently have hypnosis as a vehicle to pull out allegedly repressed memories. Used carefully it's useful. Used carelessly it can create memories that the patient believes are true, even though they never occurred. That would be my first guess. Do you have any knowledge as to whether Christine was hypnotized?"

"No, not yet at least. I haven't cross-examined. Gifford didn't bring it up. What about all of this lack of memory?"

"Given what this woman lived through, I don't find that particularly surprising. Besides, do you remember everything that happened to you as a child? A lot of what we see is useless information, clutter that the brain puts away because it's unnecessary. Sometimes the mind decides what it needs to put away, other kinds of memories that hurt. It's not gone but it's like the brain tries to suppress it because it knows that the memory is too painful. This can particularly be true with post-traumatic stress disorder, which this sounds like. Of course, I haven't talked to Christine but that's what I suspect."

"You're talking about what soldiers sometimes have because of combat?"

Levy walked over to a shelf and pulled down a book that Jamison immediately recognized as the *Diagnostic and Statistical Manual* used by psychiatrists and psychologists to diagnose and evaluate psychological disorders. They called it the *DSM*. Levy flipped through the pages. "Recurrent and intrusive distressing recollections of the trauma, including images, distressing dreams, flashbacks. All of these things can be part of post-traumatic stress. I would be shocked if Christine didn't have psychological scars. She probably has spent a good portion of her life simply trying to function, and now the underlying reason for her trauma has erupted to the surface after years of being suppressed."

"Well, does that mean she's telling the truth?"

Levy was thoughtful. "It means that it is likely she *believes* she's telling the truth. It may be the truth. But what is the truth is often far from certain. That's your job, isn't it? But I suspect you have more empathy for her than you want, isn't that perhaps also true?" Levy knew Jamison well enough to understand that he sometimes struggled with what he did. One of the reasons he had become a prosecutor was because his father wasn't, but he had his own demons that he dealt with.

"I have to cross-examine her."

"Just remember that she's very fragile and she's being asked about things that she probably doesn't even understand."

"The evidence says Harker's guilty of murder."

Levy slid the *DSM* back onto the shelf. "But evidence is often based on memory, isn't it?"

Chapter 31

While Jamison and O'Hara met with Dr. Levy, Ernie drove over to Detective Jensen's house. He didn't call first. He expected that Jensen didn't have many places to go. He wasn't wrong, Jensen yelled through the window looking out onto the front yard for him to come in. Ernie had seen Jensen at various sheriff's functions, which were attended by a lot of the retired deputies. Most of the time the old guys sat around together and told lies about their glory days, but they were always treated with respect by the younger deputies, as long as they didn't have to sit and listen too long.

"What brings you here, Detective Garcia? Still working on that asshole Harker?"

"Still trying to get it sorted out." Ernie had been warned about Jensen's drinking and noticed a number of beer bottles on the table next to the chair Jensen sat in. Several still had beads of condensation on them, and it was early in the afternoon.

Jensen caught him looking. "Not much else to do these days. You'll find out soon enough. Want one?"

Ernie shook his head. "On duty. You understand. Anyway, Jamison wants to know more about the alibi for Rick Sample."

"Why? Harker did it. I told Jamison that. Didn't O'Hara tell you?"

"Yeah, he did, but there's a new wrinkle."

"What's that?"

"Christine Farrow just testified that the killer was Rick Sample."

"Well, that's bullshit. She identified Harker and she testified in court that he was the one."

"All true, Mike, but Jamison says we need to look at the reason Sample was ruled out, and if we can prove that then Christine's whole story gets blown apart. So, I figured I'd start with you."

Jensen sat back in his recliner. "Have you looked at my reports on this?"

"Better to start with you and get the whole story if you can remember all of it. Then I'll go pull all the reports and begin backtracking."

Nodding at Garcia's logic, Jensen leaned forward and got up, relishing the opportunity to relive the past with somebody new. "Gonna get another beer. Sure you don't want one?"

Jensen settled back in and started talking. Ernie didn't interrupt. He would save his questions for the end. Jensen was nothing if not thorough, and since he was the central figure in the story, he began with his opinion of the case being reopened. That took five minutes, mostly filled with barnyard expletives that Jensen had apparently managed to store like a thesaurus. Ernie began to wonder how many words for *shit* that Jensen had. But he knew he had to be patient.

Jensen recounted that Christine Farrow's grandmother, Barbara, had led them down the wrong path when she said that Christine's ID of Rick was Rick Sample. It was true that later they determined that Sample and Harker looked a lot alike. But Jensen also added that in his experience, white trash looked like all other white trash so he wasn't surprised. Ernie remained silent. There was no point in disagreeing because it would just result in diverting the conversation while he got an earful of Jensen's old cop philosophy, much of which would include what was now called inappropriate profiling. Ernie knew that nothing much had changed except cops now came up with more sophisticated explanations for why they could look at somebody and spot trouble.

First Jensen had put out an all-points bulletin, an APB, on Sample and then went to his last known address, which he pulled from Sample's contact cards that were available to him. Even though now almost everything had been put into some kind of computer file, back then the various law enforcement agencies kept alphabetized card files with contacts on them, so they could backtrack on the activities of troublemakers. But given the expansion of the criminal population, technology had likewise evolved. Now card files were a thing of the past. But back then they showed Sample lived with his mother, or at least slept there according to his files.

Jensen contacted the mother at her home, which was in a newer residential area of tract houses. Jensen recalled being a little surprised because it didn't fit his expectations. Sample's mother had answered the door. "I remember that her name was Dolores, but she told me to call her Dori. She was good-looking. I remember that. Looked younger than I expected too. Good figure, kinda busting out, you know?" The look on Jensen's face told Ernie that Jensen had probably revisited that image a number of times. "Anyway, she told me that her son wasn't at home. She said he had been at a baseball game in LA, a Dodger game during the time when the murder occurred. There was a Dodger game with the Giants in LA the day Lisa was killed. It didn't take us long to bag Sample up, but he had ticket stubs for the game and he had a buddy with him. He couldn't have been there and here at the same time. I questioned him, and he had everything down as far as the game was concerned."

Ernie didn't ask whether Jensen had checked the seats to see if anybody remembered Sample. He would wait on that. It would just have pissed Jensen off being questioned about how thoroughly he did his job. Jensen did say that Sample had given him the ticket stubs and a program. He thought it had been booked into evidence at the time but once they got Foster's ID of Harker, and Christine identified Harker, that had been the end of it.

Ernie's next stop was the sheriff's office file room. He stared at the banker boxes occupying an entire shelf and began pulling them down. Unlike the DA file, which was mixed with crime reports and DA investigative files, the sheriff's file was sequential by date. It didn't take long to pull Jensen's reports from the crime scene as well as his report on Sample.

Jensen's memory had been surprisingly accurate given the passage of time. He had picked Sample up and taken him to the station. Sample said that he and a friend, Jimmy Stack, had gone to the Dodger game with the Giants. His friend Stack confirmed the alibi, even producing a game program that he gave to Jensen. Sample gave him the ticket stubs and a parking receipt. They both claimed that the game had run late because it went into extra innings. They drove as far as Gorman, which was at the top of the State Route 99 from LA to the Central Valley, and slept in the car. Then they came home the next day, and that was when his mother told him about Lisa Farrow being murdered.

Ernie went back to the evidence room and asked for all the evidence in the Harker case. It didn't take him long to locate the program from the game. The ticket stubs were paper-clipped to the brochure. It was enough to show that Sample couldn't have been the one that killed Lisa Farrow. But Sample was dead and that meant he needed to talk to Sample's mother if she was still alive and Jimmy Stack if he was still around. That would close the loop.

It didn't take long to run a motor vehicle license check on Dolores Sample. Unsurprisingly, there was more than one in the state of California but only one in Tenaya. The same address on Jensen's original report. Ernie pulled up in front of the house, instinctively surveying the yard and neighborhood for hidden threats. It was a well-kept area of nice tract homes and neatly kept yards. He walked up to the door, then waited for someone to answer the doorbell. A woman opened the door enough that she could see Ernie holding his badge in front of him.

With the exception of the effect of twenty-six years, Dolores Sample looked a lot like what Ernie expected from Jensen's description. She was a full-figured woman, taller than he expected, almost five-seven with blonde hair. For a woman who had to be in her sixties at the very least, she managed to take advantage of what she had. Ernie could tell that she had once been striking in a way that would attract attention. She still carried herself with a sense of assurance. There was something about her that immediately told Ernie that Dolores Sample knew her way around men and men knew their way around her. She didn't seem the least intimidated by his badge or his identifying himself as from the DA's office, and, Ernie noticed, she didn't seem surprised when he said he was there about the Harker case.

She stood at the open door staring at him. She didn't invite him in. Before Ernie got much out of his mouth other than why he was there, she interrupted with a torrent of words. "I can't help you. My son's dead. He didn't have anything to do with Lisa's murder. He loved that girl. He was murdered, and you people didn't do anything about it. You people made his life hell. His name was in the papers. People knew the cops accused him. I don't blame that little girl, Christine. She was just a baby, didn't know any better, but I blame Lisa's mother, Barbara. She was always a bitch. My son wasn't here when it happened. That's it. Now unless you've got something else to talk about I want you to leave me alone." She slammed the door. Ernie stood there for a moment thinking, *That went well*, and then walked back to his county car.

☙

Jimmy Stack wasn't very difficult to find. He was in jail.

As soon as Ernie ran the background check on Stack, he learned that he was doing a year for multiple petty theft convictions. His rap sheet was a litany of low-grade crimes and alcohol-related offenses with a few minor drug offenses mixed in, the poetic lines of a wasted life. His primary achievement appeared to be that he hadn't done anything serious enough to earn straight prison time.

Jimmy Stack was a bottom-feeder, fairly harmless but a constant irritant to the law enforcement community. Like a lot of his ilk, he accumulated a number of minor offenses and when a judge decided that he needed to clear the file and consolidate the sentences to run concurrent, Jimmy would pull a year or so in jail, then be out for a year only to earn his way back in again. He was a familiar jail resident and wasn't a problem prisoner, which garnered him almost immediate trustee status and put him on work crews or other menial jobs necessary to the business of a jail.

For a person doing county jail time that was as good as it got. It was symbiotic in many respects. The jail got a reasonably good worker and Jimmy got to spend the winter in the relative comfort of the jail with extra privileges as opposed to the street, dried out for a while, giving his liver a chance to revive, and got three meals a day. Or as he would call it, "three hots and a cot."

Ernie was waiting in a sheriff's interview room when Jimmy was brought in. From the information in his file, Jimmy Stack was in his early fifties. He wore those years hard, because from his appearance he looked like he was seeing the back end of his sixties. Time, cheap booze, and life on the street aged a man. Years of sleeping in the rough and sitting in the sun had made his skin look like tanned leather. Ernie had seen it too many times to be shocked or even sympathetic. Many people chose that life, despite the best efforts of social services and well-meaning citizens to provide alternatives.

Stack's expression was one of resignation. No one had told him why a detective wanted to see him, and he couldn't think of anything he had done that merited a detective. Experience likely told him that whatever it was it probably wasn't good and that he should just sit down and wait. There was no reason to hurry bad news. Eventually someone would tell him what was going on or what to do or what was going to happen to him. That was the story of his life.

"You want to sit down?" Jimmy Stack slumped in the only other chair. Ernie didn't try to be friendly or unfriendly. He knew that street people like Jimmy would be suspicious and would view an overt effort to be friendly as weakness to be exploited. Treating him with respect was the best approach. "What do they call you?"

"Jimmy, everybody calls me Jimmy." His voice had the gravelly sound of a longtime smoker. A coughing fit reinforced the reason for his voice. He shuffled around in his chair until he was comfortable.

"Jimmy, my name is Detective Ernie Garcia. I'm an investigator with the district attorney's office." Jimmy's eyebrows went up a fraction. It had been a long time since anyone from the district attorney had even acknowledged his existence other than to call his name at a misdemeanor arraignment. He wasn't going to ask what Ernie wanted.

"I've been told that you used to run with Rick Sample. Is that correct?"

"Long time ago. Why?" Jimmy's eyes narrowed, and Ernie caught the guarded reflex telling him that there was a nerve close to the surface.

"I'm not here because you're charged with anything. I need to ask about whether you know anything about Rick Sample and a murder that happened twenty-six years ago, Lisa Farrow. You remember that?"

Jimmy's posture stiffened. "I didn't have anything to do with that. I've never been into anything really bad. Violence isn't my thing—booze, drugs, and an occasional desperate woman." Stack shrugged with a forced smile, unembarrassed by the admission.

Ernie nodded. "Do you remember being questioned by sheriff's detectives regarding you being with Rick Sample the night of Lisa Farrow's murder?"

"I told you I didn't have nothin' to do with that."

"I didn't say you did. You told detectives that you were with Rick Sample the day of the murder and you both were at a baseball game in LA. I want to talk to you about that."

"Sample's dead. Why are you askin' now?"

"Because I need to know if he really was at that baseball game."

Jimmy sucked in his lower lip, chewing on it. "I told those cops that he was. Why you askin' me again?"

"Because somebody says he wasn't."

"That was a long time ago. I said what I said."

Ernie's patience was growing thin with Stack's dancing around the question. "I need you to testify in court."

"No. Rick's dead and none of it makes no difference. I'm not gonna go to court."

"You will if you get a subpoena and a judge orders you to. All I'm asking is whether you and Rick Sample went to that ball game. If you did, then that's that."

"Well, I did so that's that. I told you, I ain't gonna go to no court." Ernie could see the ember of defiance beginning to glow in Jimmy Stack's eyes. Now wasn't the time to push. He had very little leverage.

"Suppose I got your sentence reduced and you could be out on the street?"

"I got nothin' on the street that's better than what I got here. I gotta live here and people that live here don't help cops, not if they want to sleep through the night." Jimmy Stack looked at Ernie with tired eyes. "No cop never did anything good for me. Look, I'm too old to jail fight and I don't want to. I talk to you, it gets around. Everything in here gets around. Someone will start rumors and next thing I'll get the shit kicked out of me by some punk with nothin' better to do. You do what you have to do, and I'll do what I have to do, but you got nothin' that does anything for me." Stack stood up. "Are we through?"

Ernie stood up and rapped on the table, summoning the guard. "Maybe—maybe not. Jimmy, if we need you, you *will* testify. Don't make me show you what will happen if you don't. You have privileges inside that make life easier. They can also disappear and make life inside a lot harder for a man your age. I'm not asking you to lie. I'm asking you to tell the truth."

"You're asking me to say what you want me to say. That's what cops always want. The truth? I been down this road before." Jimmy turned when the guard entered and walked out.

⤴

Ernie walked back from the sheriff's office to find O'Hara and Jamison talking about their contact with Dr. Levy. As usual, O'Hara didn't waste any breath on greetings. "You got anything?"

Ernie deposited himself in a chair next to O'Hara. "Well, it didn't take me long to do what you wanted," he replied, addressing Jamison. "I talked to Jensen. He was relatively sober, I guess. He told me he checked out Sample's alibi. Sample was at a Dodger baseball game in LA and didn't come home until the next day. Jensen got the ticket stubs from him and they were still in evidence. I looked. They're there. He put me onto Sample's mother, Dolores. She basically told me to put a stick up my ass but she did confirm that her son wasn't in town. According to the information, Sample was with a friend named Jimmy Stack. I talked to Stack. Wasn't hard to find. He's in the county jail. He wasn't very cooperative, but he did tell me that he told Jensen that he was at the ball game with Sample. That's it."

O'Hara leaned in. "Okay, so we bring in Jensen and this Stack guy and they close the door on the girl's testimony. That's it."

"Maybe." Jamison was shaking his head. "Just like I stopped Gifford from getting in the prior statements of Foster, I can't get in what Sample told Jensen about being at a baseball game. But I can use this Stack. What do you think, Ernie? You talked to him."

"I think we're going to have to give him some incentive to testify. He wasn't straightforward about anything. The only thing he would say is that he told Jensen that he and Sample were at the game. Other than that, he wouldn't say much of anything."

"Why not? There's no downside for him."

"That's from your perspective, Boss. From his perspective, he thinks he'll get a snitch jacket for talking to cops, and then he'll have a rough time. He has a point. I mean, I get it. If you want him to testify you're probably going to have to try to force the issue. But I wouldn't be sure exactly what he'll say or even if he'll say anything."

Jamison was thoughtful, considering his options. "Dr. Levy says he thinks Christine Farrow was hypnotized. For now, we go with making Gifford put on his case. The only thing he has so far is her and we'll see how that plays out." He swiveled in his chair and looked in Ernie's direction. "You say there were baseball tickets?"

"Yeah, two ticket stubs, a program, and a parking receipt."

"The tickets have the times on them? How about the parking receipt?"

"Yeah. There's no doubt they're from the game."

"That may be enough with Jensen's testimony that he got them from Sample. We'll play it by ear."

O'Hara looked puzzled. "I thought you said you couldn't get in what Sample told Jensen?"

This was one of the problems with trying to rebuild twenty-five-year-old cases. It was fine for appellate judges self-righteously sending cases back years after the fact, but the reality was that it meant trying to find witnesses and facts that were almost impossible to rebuild. "I can't unless Gifford is asleep at the switch. But I can get in the tickets and they have dates and times on them, right?" Ernie nodded. "Okay, so that's just maybe enough to show Sample couldn't have been there. We bring in Jensen to say he got the tickets from Sample, and we bring in the tickets themselves. We'll show that Sample *was* investigated, and nobody ignored him or just relied on the testimony of a three-year-old and Foster. It will certainly undermine Christine's story. I feel bad about her, but I think she's been screwed up even more by that psychiatrist, Vinson. I'm not going to let Harker get off the hook because of some psychological bullshit." Jamison felt bad for Christine Farrow, confident that she was just being victimized one more time.

Chapter 32

Judge Wallace asked Christine to retake the witness stand, reminding her that she was still under oath. She had on the same blue dress from the day before and the same tired eyes looked out on the courtroom full of spectators. On the way into the courtroom a reporter asked her how she felt. She thought to herself, How do I feel? She felt drained, exhausted by the questions and the stress of reliving the worst moment of her life in front of strangers. But she had relived that moment a hundred times in her dreams, waking drenched in cold sweat.

Dr. Vinson had told her that doing this would help bring an end to those nightmares. Christine couldn't help but wonder whether what would be left of her life would be better. It had to be better. God help her, it couldn't be worse. Her life had been spent on her feet, shoving plates in front of people barely better off than her, and on her back, trying to find moments where she could hope that the man she had met only hours before could be the one that would give her a better life. So far that hadn't happened.

She looked at the man sitting at the counsel table with Sam Gifford. It wasn't the face that she remembered, but those faces from her past were simply blurred images. She thought she remembered what her mother looked like but even that memory was nothing more than fogged images. What she did remember was the terror. Now as she looked at the prosecutor sitting and staring at her, she could feel the terror rising again.

Wallace's voice rumbled. "Ms. Farrow, you are reminded you are still under oath. Mr. Jamison, you may cross-examine."

⟿

Jamison walked around the counsel table, finally standing about ten feet from Farrow, enough for him to be her primary focus but not so close that he would intimidate her by closing in on her. "Ms. Farrow, may I call you Christine? It might be a little easier." She nodded but didn't answer. "I'm sorry, the court reporter has to take down what you say so we need an answer."

"Yes, call me Christine. That's okay." She kept watching him with a wary expression on her face, like watching a dog that you weren't sure was friendly.

"Christine, I don't want to go back over what happened the night your mother died. I understand how painful that memory is. What I want to talk about is when and why you came to the conclusion that the man standing over your bed was Rick Sample." Christine nodded understanding. "You testified that for a long time, years in fact, you didn't remember who was standing over your bed. But you did testify very close to the time this happened that it was the defendant, Rick Harker. Did anyone help you remember now that it was Rick Sample?"

"Dr. Vinson, he's the one who helped me. I went to see him because the nightmares were happening all the time. I kept seeing it in my head, faces staring at me but they were like blurs, you know? I'd wake up screaming and sweating. It was like I did something bad but I didn't know what it was. I can't explain better than that. There was a man who came into the diner where I work and I found out he was like a social worker or something and I told him that I needed to talk to somebody. He's the one who told me to go to Dr. Vinson and that maybe he wouldn't charge anything. I don't have any extra money."

"And you did do that? You went to see Dr. Vinson?"

"Yes, I called his office and explained. He saw me and said he thought he could help me, that he studied these kinds of cases."

"You say Dr. Vinson helped you. How did he help you?" Jamison waited for the objection to come from Gifford regarding a privileged communication between a psychologist and a patient, but nothing came. He knew the law. Farrow wasn't Gifford's client but still she had a right to assert a privilege. He wasn't going to push that issue, deciding that it was better to hear what she had to say and deal with the issue if the court or Gifford raised it. He pressed forward, waiting for an answer.

"I told him about the dreams and about what happened that night. I kept getting ..." She hesitated, searching for a word. "You know, when you see something from the past?"

"Flashbacks? Is that what you're referring to?"

"Yes, flashbacks. I would see things in dreams and I would wake up scared and shaking. It got so bad I didn't get any sleep."

"Did these flashbacks just start all of a sudden?"

"They started coming a couple of years ago. At first, I would think I smelled smoke and I'd wake up, you know? And then I started seeing someone standing over my bed but nobody was there. Then it started happening all the time and I kept seeing the man over my bed but I didn't know who it was 'cause I couldn't see his face. I thought it had to be Harker because he was the one I always thought killed my mother, but I couldn't see the face. Just a feeling. It got so bad I was afraid to go to bed at night."

The objective of cross-examination is to undermine credibility. Tearing witnesses apart or dramatic courtroom recantations or confessions may happen on television or movies, but they weren't the stuff of reality. Careful cross-examination is like pulling a thread on a sweater, tugging gently until the sweater slowly unravels. That was Jamison's intent. He wanted Christine to focus on Dr. Vinson as the reason she remembered. He had a reason.

"Christine, how many times did you see Dr. Vinson before you remembered that the man standing over your bed was Richard Sample?"

Christine testified that at first, she just told Dr. Vinson what she remembered, and he began to separate it from what she'd been told. She explained that she had an intense feeling that something wasn't right, something made her feel like she had done something that was wrong, and the feeling was getting worse almost day by day. The dreams were coming more and more frequently. If she smelled smoke it would cause such anxiety that she would get intense headaches. She had begun to forget things and had started writing down even basic things like which days when she was supposed to be at work. She was struggling at her job and impatient with customers who she had helped many times. Her boss had told her that the only reason she kept her job was because she had been there so long, and he was sympathetic. Then Dr. Vinson told her she had a form of what he called post-traumatic stress disorder that needed to be treated. That was when he gave her medications to help her, anti-anxiety drugs. The drugs helped but didn't stop the dreams.

Jamison decided to interrupt Christine's narrative with what he wanted to focus on. "Did Dr. Vinson ever suggest hypnosis to you?"

"Yes, and that's when I began to remember what happened."

In a low and conversational voice, Jamison asked, "And how did that happen?" Slowly pulling the thread of hypnosis, Jamison didn't want Christine to feel that he was going to use it as a weapon.

She began to simply talk to Jamison, losing awareness of the others in the courtroom as she explained that Dr. Vinson said that hypnosis would allow her to relax and that it wouldn't hurt. The first time they focused on the sounds of that night and she seemed to hear the voices in her head and her mother begging Rick to leave her alone. She remembered starting to cry afterward as the fog of memory cleared. Then in another session they focused on who the voice of the men belonged to, but she couldn't put them together with anyone. All she knew was that she heard the voices of two different men, but one was loud, screaming at her mother. That was the voice she remembered.

"Did Dr. Vinson ever show you any photographs, pictures of men who might have been involved?"

"No, I never saw any pictures of anyone. But he did ask me to focus on the face of the man who stood over my bed and if there was anything about that face that I could tie to some other memory. That's when I realized it was Tommy's father. I put the face together with Tommy and that's when I knew. That's when the face became clear and I knew that it was Tommy's daddy who stood over me that night. It was Rick Sample."

Jamison moved slowly backward as he let her words hang in the stillness of the courtroom before he asked his next question. "And now, because of the hypnosis you believe that the defendant, Richard Harker, was not the man who killed your mother. Isn't that true?"

"Yes, the hypnosis helped me to remember, but it's the truth. I don't remember much about what happened in court when I was a little girl. I know I testified that Mr. Harker killed my mother and all I can say is that I know now that wasn't true. I don't know why I did that. I wasn't very old."

Jamison took his seat at the counsel table, deciding whether to push further. He drew a random line on his legal pad as he considered his next move. "I have no further questions of Ms. Farrow at this time, Your Honor." He stood up as Judge Wallace looked at him with a measure of expectancy. "Your Honor, I move to strike all of Ms. Farrow's testimony as inherently unreliable and the product of improper suggestion." He hardly heard the murmuring behind him in the spectator section.

Gifford was immediately on his feet, leaning over the counsel table, but before he could get much more out of his mouth than exasperated noise, Judge Wallace held up his hand. "Ms. Farrow, you may step down. I would like someone to escort Ms. Farrow back to the witness waiting room. We'll take a short recess. I will see counsel in my chambers." Wallace abruptly stood and walked out of the courtroom.

In his office, Wallace cradled his mug of coffee, obviously cold, sipping it before saying anything to the two lawyers seated in front of him. He pursed his lips and exhaled loudly through his nose before directing his first question to Jamison. "So, Matt, let's hear it."

Jamison started to stand until Wallace told him to stay seated. He slumped back in the heavily padded leather chair. "Your Honor, you know the rules better than I do. Testimony that is the product of hypnosis is inherently unreliable. There is a procedure that has to be followed if hypnotically refreshed recollection is admissible and it wasn't used here. At least there's been no foundation. What we have here is this poor woman now believing that she sent an innocent man to prison years ago. She testified close in time to her mother's murder that Harker was the one. She told that to the detectives who talked to her. You and I both know that memories of children can get very confused with the passage of time. She was cross-examined at the time. Even if the court were to seize on this testimony as a basis of a new trial, the consequence would be the same; it wouldn't be admissible. The US Supreme Court has made it clear that hypnosis creates inherent unreliability. So have the high courts of this state. There's even a statute which says that the testimony of such a witness is not admissible unless very specific procedures are followed. And even then, this court has to conclude by clear and convincing evidence that the hypnosis did not impair the witness's prehypnosis recollection. Christine Farrow was very clear that her ability to say that she was wrong about her mother's murderer being Richard Harker is totally due to hypnosis. It should be stricken and disregarded. Defense counsel obviously knew about the hypnosis. He didn't bring it up and he didn't even try to lay a proper foundation."

Wallace swiveled his chair to directly face Sam Gifford. "Sam, did you know about the hypnosis?"

"Yes." Gifford's voice was firm and unapologetic. "Your Honor, these cases are very difficult. I had nothing to do with Christine Farrow being hypnotized. When I got the call about her, this was already done. But you can't ignore it. We're talking about a man's life here. I'm not going to apologize for putting her on the stand. I'm asking the court to deny the prosecution's motion. His office bullied Christine as a child and they railroaded Richard Harker. Somebody has to stop this."

Gifford's voice had risen so much that Wallace's bailiff knocked on the door and stuck his head in. Wallace waived him off. "Sam, there's big problems with hypnotically refreshed testimony. You *know* that." Wallace put his head down on his chest, accentuating the growing rolls of his neck. Jamison started to respond but Wallace lifted his massive hand and stared him down. "All right, I will not grant Mr. Jamison's motion at this time. I'm not saying what I may ultimately do. But I will allow you, Sam, to put Dr. Vinson on the stand so we can get a better picture of what happened and if there is some proper foundation." He swung his chair back to face Jamison. "And, Matt, I will take your objection under submission but, gentlemen, and I damn well mean this, that young woman has been through enough. I am not going to be a party to both of you tearing at her like rampaging dogs. Do I make myself clear? She's suffered enough. Now let's get on with it."

Before they left Wallace's chambers, Jamison stood at the door, directly confronting Gifford. "Who called you and told you about Christine Farrow? You said you knew nothing about this? Who called you?"

"Dr. Arnold Vinson called me."

Back in the courtroom, Gifford remained standing. "Your Honor, I will excuse Ms. Farrow at this time subject to recall. Based on the discussions in the court's chambers I will need some time to get my next witness here."

Chapter 33

By midafternoon, Vinson was available. Gifford looked over his left shoulder as the bailiff escorted Vinson in the courtroom. It was evident from his expression that he didn't want to be there. As he raised his right hand to be sworn he interrupted the clerk. "Your Honor, I wish it to be known that I will be asserting the psychotherapist-patient privilege. I do not intend to testify to matters discussed between me and my patient."

Wallace waved Vinson up to the witness stand. "One thing at a time, Dr. Vinson. We'll cross that bridge when and if we come to it." Wallace looked questioningly at Gifford. "Your witness."

Gifford went through Vinson's educational background, including his medical degree and board certification as a psychiatrist as well as his many articles and speeches on recovered memory. He avoided asking a direct question about his discussions with Christine Farrow. Given the center stage to elaborate on his studies, Vinson talked at length about the issue, initially explaining that it wasn't a recovered memory as opposed to a repressed memory of a traumatic event involving something extremely stressful. His work, which he maintained had been corroborated by other studies, showed that the brain blocked the memory so that the person could function without the memory continuing to cause stress. He referred to this as dissociative amnesia. In his experience, people who had been exposed to severe trauma frequently began to experience memory flashes and other physical symptoms as the memory struggled to get out. The repression of the memory was the method by which the person maintained the ability to function.

Jamison listened intently, occasionally objecting and being overruled by Wallace as the judge focused on Vinson's explanations. Finally, Gifford moved to Christine Farrow, asking how she came to his attention. Vinson explained that he taught at the graduate school of psychology, and one of his former students had met Christine and referred her to him based on his initial reaction that she might be a person who would fit into his area of study.

He asked whether Vinson had done any independent study into the events surrounding Lisa Farrow's murder. Vinson explained that he had read the articles about the murder before talking to Christine and that was how he found out about the fact that there were several suspects, including both Harker and Sample. The newspaper articles about the trial had gone into great detail about Harker's defense attorney, Alton Grady, cross-examining both Christine and Foster about Sample.

Then he was asked about his conversations with Christine Farrow. Vinson was very explicit that without her express approval or an order from the court he had no intention of discussing what she had told him based on the privilege of a psychotherapist to refuse to disclose communications between himself and a patient. Gifford argued that Christine had already disclosed what had happened and that was an exception to the privilege. It would mean the conversations were no longer confidential. Wallace shook his head. "Why don't you just bring her in and we will see if she has any objection? If she does, then I will make a ruling on the privilege and if she doesn't, then we don't need to go there, do we?" Like most judges, Wallace wasn't going to make a ruling unless he had to, having learned early on that it was better not to create an issue by ruling on it than seeing if the whole thing could be avoided.

Fifteen minutes later, Vinson informed the court that Christine Farrow had permitted him to discuss her sessions with him.

"Dr. Vinson," asked Gifford, "when Christine Farrow came to see you, did she discuss with you why she was there?"

"Yes. She was experiencing what she described as nightmares with glimpses of a man standing over her bed the night her mother was murdered. She said she kept waking in a cold sweat and could see the image of a man, but he was unclear. She was experiencing increasing anxiety and the feeling that she had done something bad, as she described it. She told me she had no clear memory of the night her mother was murdered and that she wasn't able to recall it, except that she had become afraid if she smelled smoke. She felt like she was, in her words, going crazy."

"And have you seen this type of thing before?"

"Yes, I've done many studies of adults who experienced severe trauma as children, including sexual abuse and violent events. These people often become increasingly anxious as the memory forces its way to the surface. It is my conclusion that the memory never actually disappears, and the brain is in a constant battle to control the memory. Much depends on the individual. Some people are better able to handle the anxiety than others. In Christine's case, it was simply tearing her apart."

"And did you have an opinion as to why she felt this increasing anxiety? Was it only the memory of that night coming back?"

"No, Christine seemed to feel great guilt about that night and what happened, even though it didn't appear that she remembered it in detail. Obviously, she was a small child. There was nothing she could have done to stop it. She clearly had nothing to do with the crime itself. But the intensity of her feelings of guilt made me suspect that those feelings related to something that deep in her mind she believed was wrong or had been done wrong related to the murder."

"And did you attempt to find out what that was, that she thought was wrong?"

"Yes, I read a great deal about the crime itself. The horrific nature of it was such that it didn't surprise me that it had a life-shattering effect on Christine, but what was very disturbing to me was that she had testified as a child. That can be a traumatic event for an adult, but for a child it had to be frightening. I concluded that her anxiety stemmed from that testimony."

"And did you make any determination of the best way to deal with that?"

"I decided on hypnosis therapy to help Christine unlock her memories of what happened that night, so we could deal with them. Hypnosis is a recognized and accepted method to help people remember things that they saw but can't clearly remember. It's used all the time to help police sketch artists get more accurate descriptions or to recall license plate numbers. While it is very complicated, the mind records what the person sees but it doesn't record it all the same way. Some things are trivial and register only as short-term memory if they register at all. Other things make a long-term memory. We're not sure how it all works but we do know that if we can unlock the mind, sometimes people can retrieve repressed memories. Then we can treat the real problem."

"And did you do hypnosis on Christine?"

"I did over several sessions. Ultimately it became clear that she had identified the wrong man as murdering her mother. She told me it was Tommy's father standing over her bed, and it became immediately apparent that Tommy's daddy was Richard Sample and not Richard Harker. She had identified the wrong man as her mother's murderer. While she had not consciously remembered that it was Richard Sample, she had recognized him, and that conflict was still operating in her subconscious—that she had said it was one man but knew it was another. Why she knew it was Sample but identified Harker in court is not fully defined for me, but I suspect suggestibility."

"What does that mean?"

"It means that young children, and even older children, can be very susceptible to suggestion. They trust or defer to authority figures who intend to, or unintentionally, influence their memory of events. Ultimately the suggestion becomes the memory even though it isn't what actually happened. There are many reports in the publications on this subject and experiments that bear it out." Gifford slowly took Vinson through various studies and experiments that had demonstrated that a child could have something repeated to them or suggested to them to the extent that they would begin to repeat the suggestion until they simply accepted it as their own story, and would then relate it to other people when asked about the experience, even though it had never happened.

Satisfied that he had made his point, Gifford abruptly changed course. "Did you contact me when you concluded that the wrong man had been identified?"

"Yes."

"And why me and not the district attorney?"

"Because I had heard you speak at a conference on eyewitness identification that I attended, and it seemed logical to ask you what should be done. So, I did."

Turning to Jamison, Gifford said, "Your witness."

Jamison sat silently for a moment, staring at Vinson with a thoughtful expression on his face before standing and carrying his legal pad to the well of the courtroom in front of the counsel table. He made a show of flipping through the pages, holding the tablet in a way that would show the witness pages of notes before abruptly flipping the tablet, causing the pages to flatten out again. He laid the tablet on the counsel table.

"Dr. Vinson, are you aware of how Mr. Gifford became aware of Christine Farrow's statements that Richard Sample was her mother's murder?"

"Yes, I called him."

"Isn't it correct that Christine's statements to you were protected by the psychotherapist-patient privilege?"

"Yes, depending on the circumstances."

"Circumstances? Isn't it true that when you called Mr. Gifford, you in fact violated the patient privilege of Christine Farrow?"

"I didn't look at it that way."

"I didn't ask you how you looked at it, Dr. Vinson, I asked you whether you violated the most sacred relationship of psychotherapist and patient. You did, didn't you?"

"I felt a responsibility to ensure a man wasn't wrongfully imprisoned."

"But that wasn't your responsibility, was it, Dr. Vinson? Your conduct was unprofessional and a violation of your oath as a psychotherapist, wasn't it?"

Vinson inhaled deeply, looking up at the ceiling before looking at Wallace. "In retrospect, it was something I should not have done."

"And you did not ask Christine Farrow for permission to do that before you did it, did you?"

"No."

"But you did refuse to talk to me and my investigators, didn't you, based on claiming that same privilege—isn't that correct?"

"I felt I had a responsibility."

"You felt you had a responsibility to a defense attorney for a man convicted of murder but not to public prosecutors? You don't need to answer. I withdraw the question. I think the answer is clear. Let's move on. Have you testified before on the subject of repressed memory?"

"It has been several years but yes, I have. Not here in Tenaya County but in New York and Florida because of my published body of work on the subject. And I've given many lectures on the subject."

"Are you familiar with the concept of false memory syndrome?"

"Yes."

"And what is that, Dr. Vinson—what is false memory syndrome?"

"It is basically when an individual has memories which are in fact incorrect but which they strongly believe."

"And that means they could believe what they are saying is true even though it is in fact false, correct?"

"Yes, that is correct."

"And isn't it correct that there is significant acceptance in the community of psychotherapists that recovered memory techniques such as hypnosis can result in false memories?"

"There is some thinking supporting that, if the memory recovery is done incorrectly or by a person who does not have proper training."

"Isn't it correct that the American Psychiatric Association has expressed serious concern about the techniques of memory recovery having a high likelihood of creating false memories?"

"I do not accept that. My experience is, if done properly, the repressed memory is an accurate reflection of what actually occurred."

"In this case did you discuss with Christine Farrow the events surrounding her mother's murder before you engaged in your repressed memory techniques?"

"Yes, I needed to focus on what might be the primary issue."

"You would agree that human memory is highly suggestible, wouldn't you?"

"I would agree that depending on the individual and the circumstances, human memory can be affected by suggestion, particularly with young children. But I would also state that in my view much of the controversy about supposed false memories has been created by defense attorneys trying to defend clients being charged with child molestation."

"So, you discussed with her that in her dreams she could not see the face of the man who stood over her bed? In fact, you discussed that Richard Sample was also a person who had been mentioned as a suspect, didn't you?"

Vinson bristled at the attack on his techniques, firing back that he had been very careful and had great success over the years with his research and treatment.

Jamison walked closer to the witness box before asking his next question. "But you did not record any of your discussions prior to the hypnosis, did you?"

"No, I didn't believe it was necessary."

"Did you record your sessions under hypnosis?"

"Yes."

Jamison made a calculated decision to have the tape recordings played. He knew he wasn't going to be able to stop it if Gifford tried to use it to lay the foundation for Christine's testimony, even though she had been hypnotized. It was a risk, but he preferred to control it if he couldn't stop it.

The recording of Vinson's sessions with Christine Farrow were difficult to hear. Vinson had used a small handheld recorder with mini-tapes. It was evident no effort had been made to ensure that either was speaking clearly so that every word was recorded. It was done primarily to reinforce notes and impressions. But still, the sound of the words created an eerie image in the otherwise silent courtroom.

Vinson's voice came through as soothing, almost monotone, as he slowly guided Christine into a hypnotic state. She began to recount the night that upended her entire life. It was like listening to a child's description in the voice of an adult. The first tape simply took her through the outlines of what happened. Vinson clearly avoided spending time on any specific details. The second tape was done a few days later and began to focus on the man in the room.

Christine remembered being in her bed, her legs pulled up tightly against her chest, and she remembered the feeling of summer heat in the room, the still air lying over the bed like a heavy blanket. Slowly bits and pieces emerged. Her mother's voice and the sounds of violence came to life in her description. The third tape recorded Vinson probing deeper into Christine's memory of that night and the smoke. Christine's voice was tremulous as it described her fear and the image of a man standing over her bed. Slowly Vinson asked her to describe the man. All she said was "Tommy's daddy, it was Tommy's daddy."

Vinson sat on the witness stand, arms folded across his chest, a smug expression on his face as he explained that based on the sessions under hypnosis Christine had explained that Tommy's daddy was Richard Sample. She now knew Richard Harker was not the man who killed her mother.

Jamison could feel the tension in the courtroom as he deliberated about what to ask next. "Before you did these sessions under hypnosis, you discussed with Christine that there were two men who were suspected of Lisa Farrow's murder, correct?"

"Yes, as I testified to earlier."

"And you had gone into detail with Christine as to those men, correct?"

"I wouldn't say 'detail,' but I did go into the relationships between her mother and each man as best she could remember."

"And you went into detail about the fact that she had originally said the man who killed her mother was Tommy's daddy, didn't you?" Jamison's tone was well modulated but carried an edge as he pressed in.

"I needed the background, but if you are implying I suggested it was Richard Sample—Tommy's daddy—you are mistaken."

"But if subconsciously Christine Farrow thought she had made a mistake in her identification over twenty years before, that would itself cause great anxiety, wouldn't it?"

"Possibly."

"In fact, probably, isn't that correct?"

Vinson remained silent, staring at Jamison as he contemplated his answer. "Possibly."

"And in fact, you suspected that her anxiety was about the indistinct image of the face of the man standing over her bed, didn't you?"

"Yes, I did suspect that could be the issue."

"And you discussed that with Christine Farrow prior to the hypnosis, isn't that correct?" Jamison's tone had now risen a level as he placed his body directly in front of the witness, dominating Vinson's field of vision.

"I was very careful."

"Your answer is yes?"

"My answer is we talked about it."

Jamison turned his back on Vinson and walked to the counsel table before addressing the court. "Your Honor, it is evident that Christine Farrow's testimony has been improperly influenced by the use of hypnosis. The reason it must be utilized with careful safeguards is precisely because once the memory of the hypnotized person is influenced, they cannot distinguish between what actually happened and what they believe happened because of the suggestion left in their mind. I mean no disrespect to Dr. Vinson, but his sessions with Christine Farrow completely undermine her credibility on this issue. I'm asking the court to strike it and reject it."

Gifford did not allow any gap between Jamison's argument and his own. "Your Honor, the court can't seriously be considering Mr. Jamison's motion. If the court is thinking of doing this, then I would like the opportunity to-to . . ."

Wallace pushed his bulk over the top of the bench. "To do what, Mr. Gifford? If you want to do further examination of Dr. Vinson I'll allow it but I'm going to make it clear right now. I am not going to strike the testimony of Christine Farrow. Mr. Jamison's motion will be denied. That's final. Do you have any more witnesses?"

Gifford's color slowly returned to his face as he lost the flush of argument. "No, Your Honor."

"Then, Mr. Jamison, you may present your case in response, if you have one you wish to present."

Jamison drew a line across his legal pad as he allowed himself time to regain his composure and considered his response. "Your Honor, I would like some time to think about this. Would the court consider resuming in the morning?"

Wallace tapped his gavel, something Jamison had seldom seen him do. "Nine a.m. tomorrow."

Chapter 34

O'Hara was fuming, pacing back and forth while Jamison watched from behind his desk. "Wallace let in all that psychobabble bullshit. He's actually thinking of letting Harker out."

"I don't know about that," Jamison responded. "Wallace isn't stupid. But there's no question we have to think about the direction we want to take." Jamison at first had felt his blood pressure skyrocket after Wallace's ruling, but now had moved into the zone of damage control. Letting in the evidence didn't mean the issue was over. It simply meant the judge would think about it and Jamison's job was to make sure that he placed it in perspective as much as possible in order to diminish any impact. "We already decided to bring back Mike Jensen, and I'm not going to fool around with Jimmy Stack. I see real risk there."

"What about Dr. Levy?" Ernie asked. "Wouldn't he take a bite out of Vinson's testimony? And what about Foster?" Ernie hesitated, obviously wanting to ask another question. Jamison looked at him, waiting. "Boss, why don't we just bring in Gage and Cleary?"

"You think that hasn't crossed my mind?" Jamison immediately regretted the sharpness of his response, even though it was driven by stress. "The simple answer is because it isn't going to do any good. What are they going to say that they haven't already said, and it would just give Gifford another crack at them. Gifford has to show that there is enough credible evidence to undermine the conviction. So far all he has is Christine's statement coupled with Vinson. Wallace could do it, but I think if we close the door with Jensen that's going to be the end of it. Remember, even if Wallace granted a new trial based on the identification, I don't think any of Christine's testimony would be admissible in a new trial because Vinson didn't comply with the rules of evidence. Admitting that evidence in a writ is one thing but admitting it in a trial is something else. That's a judge up there making the decision, not a jury. He's already heard that evidence to rule on it. You think he's going to forget it? Wallace certainly isn't going to decide that Harker is in fact innocent. All he'd do is set the case for retrial. I need to think about whether to come back at Vinson with Levy."

Jamison rubbed his face, feeling the tension spreading across his forehead. "I'm going to meet Foster's lawyer for a drink later on. We'll see. Get Jensen ready for tomorrow to meet with me before court. I'm going to go see what Clarence Foster's new lawyer has to say.

﹌

The Cosmo had been around a long time as had some of the regulars, including a few lawyers who had staked out possession of their own personal bar stools. Like most bars it was dark, and it took Jamison's eyes a few moments to adjust before he saw Paul Carter waving from a corner booth and nursing a beer. As he walked over, Jamison caught the eye of the bartender, indicating he would have what Carter had; beer was all he could handle at the moment. Jamison nodded greetings to a few lawyers grabbing a drink before going home or, more likely, taking a break before going back to their offices. He could hear the dice cups rattling as the lawyers decided who would pay for drinks by playing liar's dice. He always appreciated the irony of the name.

Carter tilted his head to the side. "Heard you had a rough day."

"I've had better and I've had worse. Like they say, it doesn't matter what happens today or tomorrow, the wheels of the bus will keep going round and round. Anyway, you wanted to talk? You got something for me. Is Foster ready to cooperate?"

"I need immunity. I can't let him talk without immunity, but I think you should hear what he has to say."

"You think I should hear what he's got to say?" Jamison had been down this road before. "So what's he got to say?"

Carter eyed him apologetically. "I need immunity first. You need to trust me on this, Matt."

"You're serious? Look, no taste first, no immunity. He's already testified in this case and I'm not giving anybody immunity unless I know what they're going to say *and* unless they say it to me first. I'll go off the record, Paul, but that's it."

Carter took a sip of his beer and looked at Jamison with what appeared to be a measure of sympathy, which Jamison immediately discounted. Carter said, "Your father's fingerprints are all over this, Matt. I need immunity."

"My father's fingerprints are all over a lot of shit. Give me what you got and we can talk. Otherwise, I can't make a deal. Give me what you got off the record. I'll listen and then we can talk. Besides, Foster already has immunity. That was established when he testified before."

Carter said, "Did you find the immunity order?'

Jamison sat back, scrutinizing Carter. "No. Did you? But I'm guessing that there was something and it was in my father's file on Foster. Was it?"

Carter looked uncomfortable. "There are notes and a handwritten memorialization regarding a deal for Foster to testify." Carter didn't say any more.

"Who wrote it?"

"If I read it correctly your father wrote it and it was signed by then deputy district attorney Jonathon Cleary on behalf of the district attorney's office. Your father initialed it."

"Is Foster's signature on it?"

"No, so I'm guessing Foster did what your father told him to do and that handwritten deal was the agreement."

"You're guessing? Okay, so Foster *has* immunity. He's supposed to cooperate. Are you going to give it to the court or to Gifford?"

"I plan to give a copy to Gifford, but I'll also give the original to the court."

"And to me?"

"Yes, and a copy to you."

"So, there you go, your client has immunity because that's the original deal. He doesn't need anything else." Jamison smiled. "You aren't going to let him testify without *another* immunity order, are you? You want to cover his ass." As he made his last comment Jamison's eyes narrowed. "You're worried that there's more." Jamison paused as he considered the implications before saying, "He's not talking to you, is he? Otherwise, you'd know what he was told about the deal. So, you don't know what he's going to say, do you? And I'm going to guess that the notes in the file don't necessarily jibe with what he's said before—do they?"

"You need to hear this, Matt. You have to trust me on this."

Jamison finished his beer. "Uh-uh. Give me something. I'm not putting Foster on the stand without knowing what the hell's going on. Right now, this is Gifford's problem, not mine."

"I think maybe there were serious issues about the trial."

"I knew that when I sat down. Otherwise, you wouldn't want to talk. I need more than that and you know it. But you're going to have to give it up. Your decision. No information, no immunity, and I'm not accepting anything that can't be corroborated. So just Foster giving me some new bullshit isn't going to do it. I want evidence to support it. Besides I already know my father would have protected his client's ass, so implying the file may be a little different than what was testified to doesn't mean anything to me." Jamison threw a five on the table. "I know you're trying to do the right thing, Paul. So am I. We just have different jobs. But you have no idea what your client's going to say because I'm betting he's not talking to you. Is he?"

Carter finished his beer and threw another five on the table. "What is it Jack Nicholson said in that movie? 'You can't handle the truth'?"

"I can handle the truth, Paul. You just don't know what it is."

"And you do?"

"I have the guilty verdict of twelve jurors, and to a prosecutor and the justice system that's the truth beyond a reasonable doubt. That's the way it works. If you have something different, then serve it up. But no immunity without corroborated testimony and that *is* the truth as far as Foster's concerned."

Chapter 35

Jamison examined the copy of a handwritten agreement he had received that morning from Paul Carter. It was his father's handwriting. He was sure of that. Cleary and his father had agreed that if Foster testified truthfully, he would not be prosecuted for his actions related to the murder of Lisa Farrow. It was an enforceable agreement and guaranteed that the DA's office couldn't charge Foster. He'd been thinking most of the night about Carter's demand for immunity for his client. Foster didn't need immunity. He had immunity. Therefore, Carter was concerned about exposing his client to something that might void the immunity agreement.

Jamison had carefully considered his course of action. There was no way he was going to extend a blanket immunity to Foster when Carter wouldn't tell him what Foster was going to say. Not only would it be naive, it would be irresponsible. As far as he was concerned, Gifford could put Foster on the stand and Wallace would order Foster to answer. If he did, he did. If he didn't, then there was nothing Jamison could do about it unless he was willing to act blindly. He wasn't. He walked over to the sheriff's office to meet with Jensen.

Mike Jensen clearly relished his return to the sheriff's office. As O'Hara brought him down the hall, older detectives came out to greet him with younger ones following to get the opportunity to shake his hand. Whether he had achieved legendary status or not, he was treated like he had and he was going to enjoy every minute of his day in the sun, even though he likely had a throbbing headache from his excesses the night before.

Ernie had earlier taken Jensen to the evidence room to go through the items still maintained in the Harker case. The tickets to Dodger stadium were still in a plastic bag along with the program from the game. A faded parking receipt was clipped to the game program. Ernie had checked it out of evidence and carried it over to a detective office where Jamison waited to go over everything before Jensen testified. Then they walked to court.

⤵

Jensen fidgeted in the witness chair, pulling at his collar and tie. He wasn't used to wearing a tie anymore and he hadn't noticed how tight his shirts had become around the collar because he never buttoned the top button. He scanned the courtroom and rested his eyes on Harker, who glared at him. Jensen allowed himself a faint smile in response.

"Detective Jensen," said Jamison, "you have previously testified in this matter. You were the primary investigating officer in the murder of Lisa Farrow, correct?"

"Yeah—yes, I was in charge of the case."

"And during your investigation did you initially focus on anyone as a suspect besides Richard Harker?"

"Yes, as I testified to before, we looked at a guy named Richard Sample. That was because of the victim's mother giving us that name based on a misunderstanding of who the little girl was talking about as the person who murdered her mother."

"Did you contact Richard Sample?"

"Yes, myself and several uniformed deputies found him at his mother's house. We bagged him up and took him in for interrogation."

"As a result of that interrogation, did you receive anything from Richard Sample?"

"Yeah, he gave me two tickets to a baseball game, at Chavez Ravine in LA."

Jamison held up a plastic bag that had an exhibit tag on it. "Do you recognize People's Exhibit One?"

Jensen took the bag and examined it, then handed it back. "Yes, those are the tickets I got from Sample. You can see my initials on the plastic bag and I made a very small pen mark on the back of the tickets. I got those from Sample."

"Did he have them on his person when you arrested him?"

"No, we didn't get him until late the next day after the murder. If I recall correctly, we had to go back to his house where the tickets were. The game program we got from his buddy, a guy by the name of Jimmy Stack. Sample claimed he had been at the baseball game until late the night before and didn't get home until the middle of the next day. I got the same story from Jimmy Stack."

"Did you check out the tickets?"

"Yeah, I went down to LA and they confirmed these were tickets for that day. The Dodgers played the Giants the day of Lisa Farrow's murder. The game didn't finish until late and the parking receipt matched up. It's about a four-hour drive from Dodger Stadium back here. Sample would not have been here to have killed Lisa Farrow. Jimmy Stack backed him up."

"Now do you know what happened to Richard Sample?"

"Yeah, he's dead. And I know that because he was killed in a bar fight. It happened right before I retired. I was the supervising detective and sent our guys out to the scene. I came out later and he was still on the floor. Well, actually he was in an alley behind the bar—in a dumpster."

"So, you did a complete investigation of Richard Sample's alibi for the night of Lisa Farrow's murder?"

"Yes. Initially I thought he was the perpetrator based on what the little girl and her grandmother said. I followed up with Sample's mother, and him and Stack, and I checked out the tickets and the times. He wasn't here when she was killed so his alibi checked out. Then we got information that led us to the defendant, Richard Harker. Our investigation caused us to conclude he was the one."

Jamison looked at the tickets in the clear evidence bag. Something in the back of his brain was nagging at him like he was missing something. He pushed it aside. He had so far carefully avoided asking Jensen what Sample had told him, knowing it was inadmissible hearsay, but he decided to take a chance. "Did what Richard Sample told you about his activities the evening of the murder all check out?"

"Yes, from the very beginning Sample's story was consistent with the physical evidence and backed up by his mother and Jimmy Stack."

Gifford wasn't asleep. He immediately objected that the question and answer had to be based on inadmissible hearsay. Wallace blew out a long sigh. "I'll allow it. It's evident that Sample is dead and we are plowing over a case that is almost thirty years old. I'm going to let it in but I am also going to give Mr. Gifford a great deal of latitude in cross-examination."

Gifford picked up the bag containing the tickets. "You say you checked these tickets out. What did you do?"

"I went to LA to Dodger Stadium. We called it Chavez Ravine back then but I guess nobody calls it that now. Anyway, I went to the ticket office and they showed me where they were on a seating chart. They confirmed that the tickets were legitimate. The parking receipt checked out too. The game ran late, like I said, and they wouldn't have gotten out until maybe after eight thirty or nine that night. Sample said that he and Stack ended up driving partway and sleeping in the car. But even if they drove home right after the game, they wouldn't have been back here until well after midnight, maybe two in the morning. None of that matched with the time of the murder."

"And how did you know the time of the murder?"

"The autopsy was consistent with time of death being prior to midnight, and Clarence Foster said that it was around nine. Plus, the neighbors saw Foster and Harker go into the house around that time. If they were all correct, then Sample was still in LA. He couldn't have been in two places at the same time, Counselor."

"Did you check out who was sitting next to Sample at the game?"

"I tried to find that out. This was a long time ago, Mr. Gifford. Back then most people didn't use credit cards like they do now. Most people paid cash. All I knew was the seats were sold. After all the investigation I did and the interrogation of Foster and the identification by the little girl, it was obvious who committed the murder—your client. I don't waste time going down rabbit holes. This was a brutal case. I wanted the man who did it."

"What if Sample left early from the game—could he have gotten back during the time you say the murder was committed?"

Jensen shook his head. "Anything's possible I guess, but there was no evidence of that and Stack backed him up on the alibi. I asked them some details from the game based on the news accounts and they were able to tell me enough to convince me they were there—although it was pretty obvious both of them, especially Stack, drank a lot of beer while they were there so Stack wasn't much help." The frustration reflected itself on Gifford's face and the tone of his questioning. He wasn't getting anywhere and Jensen was only going to help him dig his hole deeper. "Nothing further, Your Honor."

Jamison stood. "Your Honor, I don't intend to present any further evidence. The People rest."

"Mr. Gifford?" Wallace was looking over the top of reading glasses with his eyebrows slightly raised, waiting to see what Gifford was going to do.

"Your Honor, I want to talk to this Jimmy Stack myself. I also intend to recall Clarence Foster." Gifford approached the bench and handed Wallace his copy of the immunity agreement. "I received this early this morning from Mr. Carter, who the court appointed to represent Mr. Foster. My understanding is that Mr. Jamison also received a copy. I would ask the court if we can reconvene early tomorrow?"

Wallace tapped his pen on the bench, his lips scrunched together before answering. "All right, but be prepared to argue this tomorrow unless you have more evidence. Is that clear?"

Chapter 36

As soon as court reconvened and Wallace settled himself on the bench, Gifford stood up and called Clarence Foster to the stand. It didn't take long for Carter to tell the court that without a further immunity order his client wasn't going to testify. He turned to Jamison, who stood to respond to the court's inquiry.

"Your Honor, Mr. Foster has an immunity agreement, which is in the hands of the court. I have no intention of extending another immunity agreement to Clarence Foster. I have no legal obligation to do so and I certainly won't do it without knowing what is going on." Jamison knew that Foster could say anything he wanted and there was nothing he could do about it. He could never put together a case on Foster with respect to the murder based on the evidence he had, and if there was something else he wouldn't get it from Foster.

Wallace directed his question at Foster. "Mr. Foster, this is an immunity agreement between a deputy district attorney and your lawyer, Roger Jamison. It means that you agreed to testify in this case. Do you understand that? Do you understand that under that agreement you can't be prosecuted?"

Foster looked over at his attorney and then back at Judge Wallace. "My attorney says not to say nothin' until I get another immunity order so I'm not saying nothin' until he says okay. So, I guess you can put me in jail, Judge. Wait, I am in jail, so I guess I got no more to say."

There was very little Wallace could do. He could order Foster to testify based on the agreement he had been given and his previous testimony. But if Foster refused to testify, all he could really do was put him in jail for contempt. Foster already was in jail so that was an empty threat. The smirk on Foster's face didn't improve Wallace's mood.

Gifford held his hands out. "Your Honor, I'm asking the court to grant immunity. We need to hear the whole truth here." Gifford's voice was barely controlled as he tried to keep his emotions in check.

Wallace leaned back before speaking. "Mr. Gifford, the court has no authority to grant immunity without the concurrence of the district attorney. You know that. It's evident that isn't going to happen. I understand your frustration but move forward. Do you have another witness?"

"Jimmy Stack, Your Honor. We call Jimmy Stack."

Jimmy was brought from the holding cell area, dressed in a jail jumpsuit, his hands cuffed. Wallace ordered the cuffs removed before Stack was sworn as a witness. He looked around the courtroom, waiting for something to happen. It didn't take long

Gifford positioned himself in front of Stack. "Do you know my client, Richard Harker?"

Jimmy peered over at Harker. "Seen him at the jail but don't know him."

"Did you know Richard Sample?"

"Yeah, never said I didn't. But like I told the DA investigator, Sample's dead and I already told what happened." Jimmy looked over at Wallace. "How come I don't have a lawyer? I'm supposed to have a lawyer, right?"

Wallace's eyebrows raised noticeably before he answered. "You want a lawyer? Are you refusing to testify?"

Jimmy shook his head. "Nah, I been around. I don't need no lawyer. I got nothin' to say I ain't said before. Okay, go on."

Gifford didn't hesitate. "You refused to talk to me, didn't you?"

"Yeah. I don't like lawyers and I don't want to talk about this. Like I told you, I said all I got to say about this. It was a long time ago."

Gifford persisted. "You remember being questioned by detectives when Lisa Farrow was murdered?"

"Yeah, told them Sample and me was at a baseball game."

"Were you at a baseball game? Tell us about that."

"I just did. We was at a ball game and watched the Dodgers play the Giants. Don Sutton pitched. I remember that. After that I was drinkin' a lot of beer and the rest of it I don't remember much. We left late and slept in the car. Came home the next day. I didn't know nothin' about the murder until a detective came to see me and I told him. It was a long time ago. My memory isn't that good anymore. That's it."

Gifford stood silently in front of the witness box; his shoulders showed growing resignation. "So, you're saying that Richard Sample was with you until early the day after Lisa Farrow was murdered."

"That's what I said and that's what I been saying." Stack's head jerked around with quick bird-like movements before turning to Wallace. "I want to go back. I don't want to talk no more."

Wallace directed his question to Gifford. "Any more?"

"No, Your Honor. No more."

Wallace turned toward Jamison, who didn't wait for a question. "The People are ready to argue, Your Honor."

"Mr. Gifford, I'll hear your arguments now."

Gifford began to breathe heavily as the stress of the moment weighed on him. "Your Honor, what we have is a grave miscarriage of justice. My client, Richard Harker, has been imprisoned for the better part of his life for a crime he didn't commit. Finally, someone came forward, and that person is Christine Farrow. This is the daughter of the victim and she was plagued most of her life by the growing realization that she had made a mistake. There can be no more compelling exoneration than comes from the voice of the victim of a crime. She was only a child when this happened. And it is understandable that a child could be misled and frightened by this whole process. My client is just grateful that she came forward.

"Now I know Mr. Jamison is going to argue about hypnosis and disparage Dr. Vinson, but let me ask this question. Shouldn't it shake this court's confidence in the verdict that this case rested on the testimony of two people: one of a five-year-old child and the other someone who had to have immunity? Shouldn't it shake this court's confidence in the verdict that the one innocent witness in this entire tragedy has now said it wasn't my client? Mr. Jamison will say that isn't enough. What I say is, what if it's true?

"How confident can this court be that Christine Farrow isn't telling the truth? Just because she was hypnotized doesn't mean what she said isn't true. And if it is true, then this man, Richard Harker, has been sent to hell by the system and his only hope is that the system will want to make sure a mistake hasn't been made. Let a new jury decide. Give this man a chance to show he is innocent.

"I can't make my point any more clearly, Your Honor. Christine Farrow's testimony should cause this court to be unsure. Certainly, it would raise a reasonable doubt if a jury heard it. This whole case rested on the tiny shoulders of a five-year-old. This court knows that is an age when many children aren't even allowed to testify.

"This man's condemnation depended on a five-year-old who now says she was wrong and she's had almost three decades to know that. If you say no, then you are saying you have enough confidence in this case that you are willing to send Richard Harker back to prison for the rest of his natural life. If he's guilty, then that's a just sentence. But justice requires confidence in the certainty of its verdict. There can be no certainty here.

"The district attorney has refused to allow a full hearing because he wouldn't agree to let Mr. Foster testify. He is the only other witness who pointed an accusing finger at my client. That isn't right, and it isn't fair. Mr. Jamison has the power to grant immunity and he won't do it because he doesn't want me to expose the truth in this case. You are Mr. Harker's last hope.

"Christine Farrow is the voice of an unburdened conscience and you, Your Honor, are the voice of justice. I am asking you to give this man the chance to have a jury hear Christine Farrow and let them decide. You don't have to decide that Richard Sample committed this crime. All you have to do is decide that there is sufficient doubt that my client committed this crime, that you are unwilling to allow this case not to be retried. Let the district attorney prove it *now*—with all the evidence that exists *now*. Isn't a man's entire life worth making absolutely sure an injustice hasn't been done? It's in your hands, Your Honor. Do the right thing."

Wallace remained impassive, but his skin showed a slightly gray pallor. Jamison could see that he was absorbing the weight of the decision. Jamison waited a moment before he rose to speak. He had thought about what he was going to say. He didn't need his notes.

"Your Honor, I appreciate the passion of Mr. Gifford's argument, but what it lacks is admissible evidence or a viable justification for the relief he's demanding. This court is well aware that Christine Farrow's testimony is not only undermined by the use of hypnosis, it should not be admissible in any retrial because it failed to comply with the rules of evidence. There is a reason why this type of testimony requires recording and evidence of what was said before hypnosis. The credibility of this type of testimony depends on the assurance the court has that it wasn't influenced by the person doing the hypnosis. This court has no such assurance here. This court heard what Dr. Vinson did. I asked him if he brought up Richard Sample being a suspect before the hypnosis. He planted the seed. I'm not saying Dr. Vinson did it intentionally. I am saying it was irresponsible given what is at stake here both for Christine Farrow's peace of mind and the public's right to have finality.

"What Mr. Gifford is really asking is for this court to grant a new trial when he knows that we have an almost thirty-year-old case and we won't be able to use Christine Farrow's testimony without somehow getting into testimony that is inadmissible. Her testimony has been irretrievably corrupted. There is no way that poor young woman knows what is or is not the truth, or even has any real memory of what happened back then. She was just a small child forced to go through something no child should have to go through and now she has been forced to go through it all again.

"If this court does what Mr. Gifford is asking it to do, the consequence is that Richard Harker may eventually walk out the prison door, having escaped responsibility for a crime that is beyond moral comprehension because of the outrage of the system not respecting its own finality. There is a reason that to overturn a verdict in a case like this that a court has to have serious concerns about the integrity of the conviction, and those concerns have to be based on new evidence, credible evidence. A jury's verdict is entitled to be honored and not constantly attacked without some showing there is a reasonable likelihood that a jury would have reached a different verdict. This isn't new evidence, Your Honor. This is a carnival stunt cruelly distorting the mind of a tortured woman and this court can have no confidence in its integrity under the law of this state.

"What Mr. Gifford is asking you to do is to take evidence that has no legal value and trump a verdict rendered years ago after a jury heard all the evidence and all the testimony. Mr. Foster's testimony alone was sufficient to uphold the verdict of guilt. We know Richard Sample didn't do this so what's left? There should be justice for Lisa Farrow. There was justice for Lisa Farrow.

"I feel great compassion for her daughter but at this point she is being asked to go over what she saw when she was three years old. What adult even remembers what they did at five years of age, let alone three? Now she is being asked to revisit that time of her life and she is being made insecure about what she did and said then.

"I remind the court that a jury heard her testify. A jury understood that she was a small child. The defense attorney argued that because of her age a jury should be very concerned about relying on her. All of that was considered at a time when these events were unfortunately fresh in her memory. She was examined by a very capable lawyer for Mr. Harker. That is the way our system works. That young woman is again being made a victim here because of the guilt that she is being forced to carry. This court should do the right thing and rely on the law, not emotion and pleas of uncertainty. This court has the confidence of the verdict of twelve people who decided guilt in this case beyond a reasonable doubt. It should have been over almost thirty years ago. It should definitely be over now. Deny the writ of habeas corpus that asks the court to grant a new trial, Your Honor. That is the right thing to do under the law."

Judge Wallace rocked back and forth in his high-backed black leather chair, the creaking under the weight of his bulk resonating in the courtroom as he looked over both counsels at the back wall of his courtroom. He had been a young lawyer when this case happened and now this same case was in his hands. He could feel his chin resting on his chest as he moved his gaze over the cluttered top of his bench. The sounds of the courtroom, the presence of other people, all was lost to him as he considered the moment. He knew he could recess and be given time to think about it. But like most judges, he had let the issues and the facts slowly resolve in his mind as he waited for the end of the case. There were cases where he had to reflect in the quiet of his office and in his study at home. But those cases generally involved issues of policy or complex factual or legal issues. And then there were sentencing cases where he had to carefully consider what was right with the full weight of his discretion bearing down on him as his responsibility. The issue here wasn't so much the right thing to do, it was the consequence of doing the right thing. The law and conscience were not always pushing in the same direction.

Wallace pulled off his reading glasses and let them drop on the bench, the sound much louder in the silent courtroom where everyone's eyes were on him. He rubbed his face, thinking about the fact people often forgot that in the justice system, not even the United States Supreme Court could overrule the reasoned discretion of a single trial judge. And now that discretion rested with him. He could hear himself breathing. It was always easy for the public or the press to decide what the right decision was. They didn't have to make it. As he considered what he was about to say he realized only another judge would know how he felt at a moment like this. It was far more difficult being a judge than people understood. People didn't stand up for you when you walked into court, they stood up to acknowledge the responsibility you had. You internalized decisions that other people couldn't make. You had to be decisive. The worst sin for a person in a black robe was indecision. The second worst sin was showing it. He had already spent his time lying awake listening to his wife's steady breathing beside him as he considered this case, his thoughts moving back and forth as he looked to find the thread of logic that would guide him, allowing him to do the best he could and always praying he was right.

The silence waiting for the judge's decision seemed to fill the courtroom with its own sound, shuffling feet and rustling paper, but Wallace heard none of it. He had closed his ears to everything except the sound of his own thoughts. Finally, he raised his head, his rumbling voice sounding even more gravelly than usual as emotion tinged it. "The law of this state is clearly expressed by our supreme court where new evidence or arguments are raised involving the guilt or innocence of a person who stands convicted of a crime. It isn't sufficient that the evidence raised in a habeas petition might weaken the prosecution case in a new trial or make the decision more difficult for a judge or a jury. The law is that a criminal conviction can only be successfully attacked if there is new evidence and that new evidence casts fundamental doubt on the accuracy and reliability of the proceedings. Our high court has said that the new evidence, if it has credibility, must undermine the entire prosecution case and point unerringly to innocence or reduced culpability.

"Mr. Gifford has claimed that Clarence Foster was lying. If that was so, it is reasonably probable that it might have affected the outcome of the defendant's trial. However, neither Mr. Foster nor any witness produced by the defense has established that Foster was lying. Yes, there is innuendo and implication, but all of that was before the jury when this case was tried.

"As for the testimony of Christine Farrow, I'm very troubled by this. Any caring person should have compassion for this young woman and the destruction this crime caused to her life. And now she is back in court with no end to her understandable anguish. The law of this state with respect to hypnosis is clear and it wasn't followed. Yes, I let it come in because of the gravity of the consequences in this case and because I personally needed to have confidence that I had considered everything. But beyond that, admissible or not, I have no confidence in her change of testimony as to identity. Her original statements were near the time of the crime. She knew the difference between Harker and Sample even then. There is no evidence she was lying as a child and no evidence that her testimony then was the consequence of inappropriate influence. Even now as an adult the reason for her recanted identification undermines it. It is the product of an understandably troubled mind, rendering it far from reliable. If I were to grant a new trial based on the recantation by Christine Farrow, I don't believe it would be admissible in a new trial. And even if it was admitted, I don't think it is credible. Even if Christine had not testified in the original trial, there would still be Foster and the neighbors who identified Harker. And even though Harker and Sample look very similar to one another and Sample could have been mistaken for Harker, the weight of the evidence is that Sample wasn't there and Christine could not have identified Sample because he wasn't there. Therefore, that further undermines the validity of her statements under hypnosis and her recantation of her identification of Richard Harker."

Wallace's voice grew stronger. "These are always difficult decisions and this one is especially so, but I have carefully weighed the evidence presented. The law requires finality unless it is clear that finality creates an injustice. I find no reasonable basis to conclude under the law that injustice was done. The writ is denied. The defendant, Richard Harker, is remanded to the custody of the sheriff for transport back to the state prison facility at San Quentin." Without waiting for any further comment, Wallace slammed his gavel on the bench and walked out of the courtroom.

That was when all hell broke loose. Harker stood up and started screaming he was innocent. He was flailing his arms and pulling on the chain that bound his legs to the eye bolt under the table. He hit Gifford, but it was unclear if it was intentional or simply an accident. Two bailiffs grabbed Harker and pulled him down while other bailiffs came in from adjoining courtrooms and tried to control him. Finally, a deputy fired a Taser, which hit him squarely in the chest, disabling him with a significant electric shock until they could get him restrained. But the physical reaction was not what would long remain in people's minds. It was Harker screaming that he was innocent, crying and sobbing. Nobody would soon forget that sound as bailiffs hurried everyone out of the courtroom except the lawyers.

Jamison and O'Hara watched as Harker was taken from the courtroom, his feet dragging on the floor as he continued to thrash as much as he could in the chains wrapped around his stomach and attached to his wrists and legs. O'Hara was muttering, "Son of a bitch, son of a bitch," over and over. It wasn't because of the scene. It was because that's what he thought of Harker.

Chapter 37

As Jamison walked down the hall of the district attorney's office, deputy DAs came out of their offices to congratulate him. Apparently, Helen the receptionist, had announced the decision before he had walked out of the courtroom. After being totally unavailable for the last several weeks, the district attorney himself was standing in the doorway of his office waiting as Jamison came down the long hallway. Bill Gage extended his hand. "I knew you'd get that bastard. Maybe now we can put it all behind us. Good job." Jamison nodded in response and shook Gage's hand before going into his own office and surveying the pile of paper that had accumulated. O'Hara wasn't far behind.

Jamison slumped in his chair, the courtroom image fresh in his mind. He'd seen this before, when guilty men made one last desperate wail as the reality of their situation settled on them, claiming innocence to all who would listen. No matter what he thought of the defendant, it was always unsettling. Jamison was sure that Judge Wallace was legally right. In the back of his mind, however, he knew that the right result under the law wasn't always the right result in the eyes of men.

O'Hara plopped in a chair in front of Jamison's desk, an unlit cigar firmly clinched between his teeth. His eyes seemed to bore right though Jamison. It was the same look he gave a man as he decided how to interrogate him. O'Hara had an almost unerring instinct for what a man was thinking. "Okay, Harker made a lot of noise. It's never easy to watch but he got what he deserved. It's always the same way. Twenty years after the fact they never look like the dirtbag they were when they committed whatever brutal goddamn act they did. You know how many men I've sent to prison who claim they're innocent, who still claim they're innocent, and every one of those sons of bitches were guilty as sin. So is Harker. Your problem is you think too much. I told you that before. So, get your head out of your ass, Matt. You just put one of the worst criminals I've ever seen back in his hole and slammed the door shut for a final time. Don't sit here thinking about whether you did the right thing. I know you. I know what you're thinking. Fuck him. Walk away. You're a hero."

It was always easier for O'Hara, Matt thought. He saw the world in black-and-white, right and wrong. There were no shades of gray clouding his judgment or his confidence in his judgment. Jamison nodded. It was a process. He had followed the law. Jamison looked toward the door when Ernie tapped on the edge of the doorway. "You better hear this." From the look on his face, it was obvious that whatever it was, it wasn't good.

"Hear what?"

"Harker's dead."

Jamison came halfway out of his chair. "What do you mean dead? We just saw him less than thirty minutes ago." Jamison stopped talking, waiting for Ernie to explain.

"I guess when he got hit with that Taser nobody knew he had some kind of heart problem. At least that's what they're saying they think happened. The jail sergeant called me. Harker started gasping for breath as they took him back to his cell. I guess he was dead before he hit the floor. The bailiffs worked on him, but his eyes just rolled back in his head. Figured you needed to know as soon as possible. Press is going to be all over this."

"Well, shit." O'Hara threw his head back, rocking his chair. "Son of a bitch will finally be getting what he deserves. All we could do is sentence him to life. Couldn't send him to hell. Now he's there."

Jamison took a deep breath. "Does Gage know?"

Ernie shook his head. "I don't think so. If he does, I didn't tell him, but I guess the sheriff could've called him."

Jamison didn't wait for Gage's secretary to buzz him into Gage's office. He walked through the door as he knocked. Gage was sitting behind his desk, leaning back in his chair and talking on the phone. He glanced at Jamison with momentary irritation and then smiled, hanging up the phone. "For a man who's just won a major victory in court you don't look very happy. I heard about Harker's outburst but you and I both know that shit happens. You shouldn't let it get to you." He waved Jamison over to a chair.

As he sat down, Jamison said abruptly, "I just got word that Harker's dead. Apparently, he collapsed as they put him back in his cell. I thought you should know." Gage buzzed his secretary to get the sheriff and found out that the sheriff had left a message to call while he was on the phone.

Gage blew out a stream of air, stood up, and walked to the large window in his office. He didn't ask any questions requesting more information about what happened. "You know he was a rotten bastard. What he did to that poor woman was the worst thing I ever saw. He deserved to be executed and the judge let him live. As far as I'm concerned, he's been on borrowed time ever since. I can't feel sorry for him. I feel sorry for that girl." Gage seemed to be searching for a word.

Jamison filled it in. "Christine."

"Right, Christine. She didn't deserve what happened to her. Harker destroyed her life too." Gage turned his back to the window and faced Jamison. "It's almost like a generational case, your father, me, you. Well now it's finally over. You can let it go and so can I." Gage moved around his desk and sat back down, appearing to consider his words before he spoke again, the news of Harker's death passing from him like a momentary cloudburst. "That was the state party chairman on the phone. Looks like I'll be the Democratic nominee for attorney general. Everybody else is getting pushed out. That means two things. First, I'll be the next attorney general of this state, and second, this chair is going to be vacant." Gage let the implication hang in the air. "You're not still pissed about me not telling you about your old man, are you?"

"No, but you should have told me, Bill."

"Maybe. But it seemed like the right move at the time. You need to learn that if you sit in this chair you don't just make policy decisions, you also make political decisions—do what's best to get done what needs to be done. You *are* going to piss people off." Gage's eyes narrowed, squinting at Jamison. "That is if you plan on sitting in this chair." He kept his hands resting on the desk and raised his index finger, pointing at Jamison. "Of course, the next man sitting in this chair will be here because I put him here." Gage didn't say anything else for a few seconds, although the silence seemed interminable. "You did a good job. Take it for what it is. All these things add up in your career. Forget about Harker. I already have." Gage reached for his phone. The conversation was over. "Remember what I said, *if* you want to sit in this chair."

Chapter 38

The next morning Paul Carter was waiting in the reception area when Jamison walked through the front door of the office. "I want to talk to you—in your office."

They walked the hallway to Jamison's office. Jamison closed the door as Carter settled in a chair. The file he had received from Jamison, his father's file, was in Carter's hands. Jamison moved behind his desk and waited.

Carter was definitely uncomfortable. He kept fidgeting in his chair while Jamison stared at him. Finally. Jamison said, "Well? You obviously have something to say that you don't want to tell me. What is it?"

"I heard about what happened yesterday with Harker in court and then what happened at the jail. Look, Matt, I'm just trying to do my job. It doesn't mean I always like the decisions I have to make."

"I understand that. Being a public defender is a tough job. You don't get to pick your clients. I know that."

Carter's face showed indecision. "I need your word that you'll never tell anyone what I'm going to say. I need your word." Jamison nodded. Carter said, "I want you to say it."

"Okay, you have my word. What is it?"

"I don't think Harker was guilty."

"That's it? You going to tell me why?"

"You going to give Foster immunity?"

"I told you before, not without knowing what he's going to say. You're holding that file. Is that supposed to be the answer? Does that file contain material that shows Harker wasn't guilty?" Jamison's voice grew louder. "You come in here waving my father's file around. Are you telling me my father's file shows that Harker wasn't guilty?"

"Not exactly."

"Then what, *exactly*?"

"I don't think Harker got a fair trial."

"Is that because you have evidence he didn't do it or because you think maybe there's evidence that would affect his trial? Paul, I'm not going to run around reacting to this when you're giving me nothing."

"I'm giving you all I can give you."

"Then you're not giving me anything. I can't do a damn thing with 'you don't think Harker got a fair trial' and you know it. First you say you don't think Harker was guilty and then you say you don't think he got a fair trial. That isn't the same thing. He got a fair trial as far as I'm concerned. Do you know if he's not guilty? Give me what you have, or I can't do anything."

"I gave you what I can. I don't think he got a fair trial. Look, I have an attorney-client privilege responsibility with Foster. I'm already stepping over the line. I wouldn't be here if I didn't have a good reason and if this ever gets back to me I won't be able to explain it. I'm counting on your word."

"You got *my* word but *you* didn't give me shit in return. All you did was come in here and tell me you don't think Harker's guilty because you don't think he got a fair trial. Harker's dead. Case over."

Carter got up to leave. "Some cases are never over, Matt. I'm sorry about coming here. It was the best I could do. I only came here because I consider us friends. But you need to read between the lines. I wouldn't be here if I didn't have a good reason. You and I have different jobs. I'm trying to help you do yours." He tapped the file with Foster's name on it. "The case isn't over."

Jamison stood up behind his desk. "Yes, Paul, it is."

Carter stood silent for a few seconds, a pained expression on his face as he appeared to debate with himself about saying anything else. "I'm probably going to regret this, but I can't sleep at night. Frankly I don't know what the hell to do. I get told the worst shit by people and I sit next to them and defend them and never share anything because that's my job. And if I get them acquitted I walk out the door, have a drink, and then pick up the next file." Carter hesitated, indecision still written on his face, and then spoke emphatically. "I'm not going to do you any favor, Matt. The investigation reports in this case show there were multiple Foster interviews before he gave up Harker, right?"

"That's right."

Carter took a deep breath. "There was another interview that's not in the file."

Jamison sat back down. "What do you mean there's another one? Have you seen one? Is that what's in Foster's file?"

"No, I haven't seen one but you'll have to trust me. I know there was another one and it isn't in the reports. And I know what should be in it."

"What's in it?"

"Matt, I've already crossed the line. I'm telling you, I don't know if Harker did it but I do know he didn't get a fair trial. If he did it, then I'm not going to lose any more sleep over it. He got what he deserved. But if he didn't, then I can't make it right. Only you can."

Chapter 39

It was a long night. Jamison kept thinking about what Paul Carter told him. If there was another interview there was no report about it in the file. At first, he'd pushed Carter's statement out of his mind, but he knew there was only one place he could have gotten information about an additional interview. It was either in his father's notes about what Foster told him or Foster had told Carter that there was another interview. Either way it was privileged information that Carter couldn't disclose. Jamison felt some guilt for his sharpness with Carter. It wasn't simply because Carter didn't give him anything. It was because he was still uneasy about what had happened in court with Harker screaming he was innocent. Carter's words had only fed that uneasiness. Maybe O'Hara was right and he should ignore it, but there was something about the whole scene that nagged at him. After tossing and turning he finally fell into fitful sleep. He left his apartment the next morning having made a decision.

As he walked into the district attorney office, Jamison headed directly for O'Hara's office. As usual, O'Hara's feet were up on his desk as he read a police report. The stale smell of cigar smoke permeated the office. The first thing O'Hara said when he saw Jamison was, "You look like hell. You didn't get any sleep, did you? I hope it was because of a woman and not because of Harker. He doesn't deserve you losing sleep over him." As usual, O'Hara's lack of sympathy was unvarnished and direct.

Jamison ignored the comment. "Where's Clarence Foster? Is he still at the jail?"

"Why?"

"Because I want to talk to him. That's why." Jamison's tone wasn't deferential, but O'Hara didn't react to that. O'Hara's lower lip pulled in the bottom of his mustache, a tendency the investigator had when he was thinking. He repeated his question. "Why?" Jamison didn't answer.

O'Hara took his feet down from his desk and swiveled his chair to face Jamison. Unlike his usual gruffness, O'Hara's voice took on a serious, paternalistic tone. "Matt, you need to listen to me. Nothing good can come of this. Rumors are all over the place that Gage is going to name you the heir apparent when he moves up the ladder. Asking questions is just going to set everyone on edge. The case is over. Let it go."

"Paul Carter came to see me yesterday. He told me there was another interview with Foster that isn't in the file or the reports. I need to know."

O'Hara lurched forward in his chair, moving his face close to Jamison. "No, you don't need to know. What the hell good is it now? Harker's dead. He killed that woman and now you're going to kill your career over that piece of shit?" O'Hara stared at Jamison, disgust written on his face. "You're going to do this with me or without me, aren't you?"

"If you won't do it, then I'll get Ernie and if he won't do it, then I'll do it myself. Now where's Foster?"

"He's back at Corcoran Prison. As soon as the case was over he was screaming to be sent back." Most people who were pulled out of prison and brought to local jails wanted to go back as soon as possible, preferring the prison to jail facilities.

⌒

The ride to Corcoran was mostly silent. O'Hara occasionally glanced over at Jamison and shook his head just enough so that Jamison would notice the disapproval. Jamison ignored it and kept scribbling notes on his legal pad. He only looked up when they stopped at the gate and were waved through after O'Hara flashed his badge.

Foster was already sitting in the visitors' room when Jamison and O'Hara walked in. His sullen expression telegraphed that he wasn't happy to see either man. Foster clench and unclenched his handcuffed hands, stretching the snake tattoo on the back of his right hand. The way he did it made the snake look like it was moving. He waited until one of them spoke first. It was Jamison. He didn't mince any words. "How many interviews did you give to Gage, Jensen, and Cleary?"

"Where's my lawyer? I don't have to talk to you and I already know about Harker so why are you here?"

Jamison slammed his hand on the metal table separating him from Foster. "I'm here because I have a question and I want an answer. Your lawyer isn't here and nothing you say to me is usable in court. There's no tape recorder going. I need you to do the right thing. Just answer my question."

Foster tilted his head to the side, making a sucking sound with his teeth, his eyes never leaving Jamison. "I already did the right thing."

"What's that supposed to mean?"

Foster started standing. "It means what I said. Why are you really here? I may be in the joint but I'm not stupid. Why do you give a shit about any of this? It's over."

"Because I think there was an interview with you I haven't seen and I want to know if that's true."

"What do I get if I talk to you?" The expression on Foster's face was unreadable.

O'Hara reached in, grabbed the front of Foster's shirt and pulled, smashing Foster's chest so hard into the edge of the steel table that it moved. "You'll get your reward in heaven, asshole. Now answer the man's questions. I know people in here too. Do you feel me? Now quit fucking around. Answer the man's question."

Foster no longer looked at Jamison, his eyes never wavering from O'Hara, but they didn't show either hatred or fear, just recognition of who he was really dealing with. "There were lots of interviews."

Jamison leaned in closer to Foster's face. "Before you identified Harker did you ever say anything about Sample or anyone else?" It was a shot in the dark.

"I told that DA Gage and the dickhead Cleary, the one that's now a judge, that I was so fucked up I didn't remember any of it. I told them that. They told me if I didn't cooperate that I would get the gas. They kept shoving Harker's picture in my face, so I told them it was him. I didn't know what happened, but I was sure I was there. They had my fingerprints and told me the neighbors said I was the one. I was loaded. They asked me so many questions I figured out what happened from what they asked about, so I just laid it out like I figured they wanted to hear. I just knew it wasn't me. I may not be much but drunk or sober I never hurt no woman. I just wanted them off my ass, man."

Jamison sat back in his chair. "You're telling us that you told them you didn't know who did it?"

"Yeah, I told them that."

"Was the tape recorder running?"

"The man had that thing runnin' all the time. Then they shut it off when I kept tellin' 'em I didn't know, and they put me back in a cell and told me to think about it. They did that to me two times and that guy Cleary came to my holding cell each time and told me to think about it *real* hard. He's the one that said I'd be sniffin' gas with Harker unless I remembered what happened. Said we'd be sittin' next to each other in the greenroom so we could both hear the gas hiss. So, I remembered what happened the way they wanted it. Big shot judge now but he's a real prick."

O'Hara asked, "Did you ever sit in the back of a patrol car with Harker while you were wearing a wire?"

"What difference does that make now?"

"Because I asked." O'Hara's voice was edged with menace that wasn't lost on Foster.

"Yeah, he asked me why I lied about him and I told him that I just said what they wanted to hear. Dog-eat-dog. I'm not proud of it, man, but Harker's dead. Nothin' you can do about that. Dead is dead. Why you keep askin' me about this?"

All of a sudden Foster leaned back in his chair, a sly smile of satisfaction crept across his face. He looked like a vulture that just discovered something dead. He turned toward Jamison. "You want to know if I told your daddy that, don't you?" Foster let out a harsh laugh. "Well yes, I did. I'll throw that in for free seein' as how you and I have kind of a father-son relationship and all, your daddy and me and now you and me."

Foster stood up and banged on the door for the guard. "Now, I got nothin' else to say. I told you I did the right thing." As the guard opened the door and waved Foster back inside, Foster turned again to Jamison. "Your daddy did what he had to do. So did I. You remember that."

Chapter 40

O'Hara drove about ten minutes before either man talked about Foster's allegations. The reasons for each man's silence were different but the bottom line was the same. Finally, Jamison broke the quiet. "If Foster's telling the truth, then Gage, Cleary, and Jensen all knew that Foster's statements weren't worth a rat's ass in court if it came out that he had told them over and over that he was loaded and couldn't identify anybody." There was a gap before he finished his thought. "And my father knew it. He let Foster testify anyway. Why would he do that?"

O'Hara took one hand off the wheel and rubbed his mustache, giving a guttural sigh. "Maybe your old man knew it and maybe he didn't. But why Jensen and Gage might do it isn't hard to figure out. They were convinced they had the right guy. When you're a cop you focus on proving that a specific person is the crook. Sometimes you're so convinced you're right that you over-look things that should be a red light. You don't want the bad guy to get away and you just pile on. Without Foster, all they had was that little girl. They knew Sample didn't do it and they didn't want Harker to get away with it. If it ever came out in court that Foster had told them repeatedly that he didn't know who did it, then there's no way a jury would have just relied on the testimony of someone who was three when this happened."

O'Hara took his eyes off the road momentarily and glanced at Jamison. "We don't know if Foster's telling the truth. He's a con. Those guys lie about whether the sun is up at lunchtime. He could just be screwing with us. Maybe it's true and maybe it isn't. But you need to make a decision."

"What decision?"

"Whether you want to risk your whole career on the word of that asshole Foster, because that's what you'll be doing. You better think about that." O'Hara spit out each of his next words. "It. Isn't. Going. To. Make. Any. Difference. Don't you get it? Even if you're right it won't accomplish anything except destroying your career. Harker's dead. You can't make this kind of allegation without proof and you sure as hell can't rely on Foster's word."

"Unless there's a tape."

O'Hara's voice thundered. "Unless there's a tape? Are you fuckin' crazy? Even if Gage, Jensen, and Cleary did what Foster said, there isn't any recording now, if there ever was. It would disappear like the eighteen-minute gap on the Nixon tape. Those guys would have destroyed it."

"Why?" Seeing O'Hara's expression of incredulity, Jamison uttered what he was thinking. "I mean, they could have just not made a report or gotten rid of the transcript."

O'Hara finished the thought. "And then left the tape lying around in the evidence file? Well, I'm betting it isn't in the evidence file."

"We don't know that. We didn't listen to it. We just looked at the transcripts of Foster's statements. The only tape I listened to was Christine's." Neither man spoke as they sped by dusty fields on either side of the road. Finally, as they neared the city Jamison said, "Look, Bill. I get what you're saying. But I also know that I kept a lot of evidence out with objections because it was not in my interests to let it come in. I wouldn't give Foster immunity not just because I didn't know what he was going to say, but also because I figured he would just come in with some bullshit that he lied because he had nothing to lose. And I did the same thing with Christine's testimony to undermine it. I didn't believe any of it. But what if it's true? I have to know if I did the right thing—and I need to know if my father did the right thing."

Neither man spoke the rest of the way to the office.

⌐

O'Hara walked down the aisles of the sheriff's records room until he reached the right case number, then rummaged through the boxes of evidence in the Harker case. There were tapes with Christine's name on them and tapes with Foster's name. He pulled Foster's out and logged them on the sheet attached to the box used to keep track of any evidence checked out. He spent the afternoon listening to the tape while he read the transcripts. There was no tape like Foster described and no report. If it ever existed it wasn't there and he doubted that it ever existed. He walked over to Jamison's office.

"No tape like Foster described, Boss."

"That doesn't mean there wasn't a tape."

O'Hara was exasperated. "Maybe, but it does mean that there's nothing but Foster's word and all the tapes are consistent with the transcripts. You need to let this go."

"There's something in my father's case file on Foster that makes Paul Carter think there was another interview."

"It could just be a note he made of the same crap Foster told us. We're at the end of the line on this and you need to let it drop or you're going to get buried in some con's bullshit."

Jamison nodded absently. O'Hara was right. He needed to push it out of his mind. There was nothing there.

⌐

O'Hara walked back to his office. Regardless of what he'd said to Jamison, Foster's story troubled him more than he let on. He wasn't easy to con and he had an almost uncanny ability to read when he was being lied to. That thought was still burrowing in the back of his mind. If Foster was lying, he hadn't seen it. There was one more thing he could check. He doubted it would do any good but if it came back to bite him in the ass at least he could say Jamison had nothing to do with it.

⌒

It had been years since he had been to Margaret Campos's home, but it didn't look any different. The yard was neat and tidy with rows of flowers planted at the edge of the lawn. He knocked on the door and pushed the doorbell.

Margaret answered the door and her face lit up with recognition. The years hadn't lined her face much. She still looked much younger than her almost eighty years but she'd let her hair go white, and that was a change. "Willie, I haven't seen you for years. Come in and tell me why you're here." She held the door open and waited for O'Hara to come inside. It smelled like cookies. "You don't look any different, Willie." O'Hara smiled. Most people didn't even know that his given name was Willie. Only old timers knew that and only old timers called him that. But Margaret was an old-timer, long retired from the sheriff's office where she had worked as a secretary in the detective division. She was there when O'Hara became a detective and he'd been warned his first day to stay on her good side because he wouldn't like the consequences if he didn't. Not only did she keep the office supplied with her fresh-baked cookies, she kept the schedules and transcribed the reports and the tapes of interrogations. It was a long shot but that was why he was here.

O'Hara made himself comfortable on the couch in her living room and reached for a still-warm cookie from the plate she had immediately put on the cocktail table. "Margaret, I need a favor and I'm not sure you can help me. I've been working on the Harker case. You remember that case?"

Immediately Margaret launched into a detailed recollection of what she had read in the reports before asking O'Hara why he would visit her to ask about it. He saw no point in being vague. "You transcribed the tapes of the interrogations in that case. Your initials are on the transcriptions. I thought maybe you might remember them. I know you did a lot of tapes."

She looked at him with a quizzical expression. "I'll never forget that case but the tapes should be in the files. Why are you asking me?"

"Because there's been some information I've received that there was a tape that I can't find in the file. I thought maybe you might remember enough of that case to tell me what you heard or didn't hear. I need to know if maybe you transcribed a tape. Probably you didn't because I can't find any record of it but I thought I'd take a shot."

"If there's no tape in the file, then there wasn't a tape that had anything on it worth hearing." Margaret said it quietly, but it was clear that there was a darker meaning behind the statement. She waited for O'Hara to be more explicit, before continuing. "It was a long time ago, Willie. I remember listening to those tapes, but I couldn't be sure how well I remember. A lot of years have passed. Besides, you and I both know that sometimes things didn't get recorded."

O'Hara understood. Detectives recorded statements and sometimes they waited until they were sure that there would be no ambiguities on the tape, especially ambiguities about reluctance to make a statement. Margaret's face didn't conceal that she intuited there was a reason O'Hara was there that he wasn't revealing. "I read in the paper that Harker's dead. He was an evil man. I remember listening to that little girl's tape, Mr. Gage asking her questions before she identified Harker. But she was just a little girl. I felt so bad listening to those tapes." Margaret smoothed out her dress and looked intently at O'Hara. "Willie, why're you really here? What is it you really want to know?"

The question made O'Hara uncomfortable because he didn't like people seeing through him and it was obvious that she did. She always had opinions for the detectives after she transcribed the tapes, little details that revealed lies the detective didn't pick up in the questioning. Most of the time her insights were right, almost like a mother who could read her child like a book. He debated with himself and decided to be honest. "Margaret, I need to know if maybe there was a transcription that was removed from the file. There was a witness, a Clarence Foster, who was interrogated by Mike Jensen and Bill Gage. I have information that there was another tape, a tape in which Foster claimed he didn't know who killed that woman. I also believe there's maybe other tapes of the little girl. There's no record of tapes like that."

"Maybe there were no tapes like that." The way she framed her words telegraphed that she was guarded.

O'Hara looked directly at her. "Maybe there wasn't—and maybe there was. I have to know."

Margaret stood up and slowly walked toward the kitchen, motioning for O'Hara to follow her. They walked into the garage where she unlocked a door opening onto a storage area covering the back wall, and pulled on a chain that went to an overhead light. "Sometimes I pick one and listen." She seemed embarrassed.

O'Hara looked at the shelves lined with plastic boxes holding tape cassettes. It was impossible to count them all but O'Hara could see that the front of the boxes had numbers neatly typed onto a card taped to the front of each box— case numbers—hundreds of case numbers. She waved her hand around the room. "I made copies of the tapes I transcribed so I could go home and type. I only kept the important ones, the ones that interested me. We didn't have a lot of the fancy computers they use now, at least not then. I couldn't finish them at work and I didn't want to remove the original tapes, so I would make a copy and take it home. That way I wouldn't lose the original. And I kept them. I didn't at first but sometimes something would get lost or there was a question about the transcription and I always knew I had a copy. I know copies of the tapes in the Harker case are here."

O'Hara stared in amazement. "How do you know they're here?"

"Because when the case was in the paper I went back and listened. I don't have much to do anymore." She laughed. "Except to make cookies and tend to my yard. Nobody's visited me in a long time." O'Hara felt a twinge of guilt. She went straight to a box sitting near a tape recorder. "These are the tapes. I don't know if what you want is there but this is everything I was given. If it's on there, then I transcribed it." She wrapped a rubber band around a collection of tapes and handed them to him. "He was a bad man, Willie. Don't do anything that you'll be sorry for. He wasn't worth it." O'Hara took the tapes. Margaret had always seen right through him.

Chapter 41

The smoldering cigar nested in the ashtray on O'Hara's coffee table. For a bachelor, the home was surprisingly neat except for the heavy smell of cigar smoke that clung to the walls like a layer of paint. It didn't bother him, and he didn't care if it bothered his few guests. The occasional woman who spent time with him either accepted his lifestyle at face value or didn't return. And he'd grown resigned to the fact that eventually none of them returned. He wasn't going to be changed by any woman, at least any he'd met so far. Two wives had tried and failed. Maybe they had high hopes but it didn't take them long to realize O'Hara was what he was.

He knew women regarded his unwillingness to change as a flaw, but he'd long ago accepted it and rejected that it was a defect in his character. He did have one regret, the daughter who wasn't part of his life. With her he had tried—and failed. She ignored all of his overtures, and she didn't know he kept tabs on her from a distance.

Condensation dripped from a glass of bourbon with a single large melting cube of ice. O'Hara was basically old-school in his approach to drinking, no soda or juice in his drinks, only water from the slow melt of a single cube to soften the edge. He only drank single-barrel sour mash bourbon, and one of O'Hara's measures of a man was whether he knew the difference between whiskey and bourbon. He picked up the heavy glass and took a sip while he listened to the tape again.

It hadn't taken long for O'Hara to find what he hoped he wouldn't find. He'd listened several times to Foster's voice over the tape, a tape that wasn't in the reports, for reasons that when he heard it needed no explanation. Put in sequence, it didn't take years wearing a badge to understand that Foster had given Jensen and Gage what they wanted only after repeatedly telling them he was high on drugs and alcohol and didn't remember any of it.

O'Hara punched the Play button again. The whining voice of a younger Foster was cut through with interruptions by Detective Jensen and Bill Gage squeezing him like a boil. They clearly didn't like what they were hearing, and they were pushing him relentlessly to identify Harker. When he was ready to do what they wanted, that's where the other tapes came in. If the listener didn't know there was a tape that warmed Foster up the others simply sounded like good interrogation that broke a reluctant suspect. But O'Hara knew what broke Foster was fear that he would be charged with a murder he didn't even remember, that and the fear of the gas chamber, even though they actually used lethal injection. But the mopes didn't know that. O'Hara recognized the mind game. He had played it himself many times.

And then there were the tapes of Christine in which it was clear she was confused about which Rick had hurt her mother. Gage had kept pushing Rick Harker's picture in front of her and asking her if that was the man. Finally, she said yes. Children liked to please adults and once they told them something, the more they repeated it, the more they believed it. The tape of Christine revealed that her identification of Harker was not reliable. Both the damning tapes of Foster and Christine had been removed from the file. The tapes that were left presented a much different picture.

Last but not least, there was the tape in the back of the patrol car of Harker demanding Foster tell him why he lied and Foster telling Harker that he did what he had to do.

Now the question burrowed into his mind. What was he going to say to Jamison? If he told him that there really were tapes, he knew exactly what Jamison would do. It had taken a while to file the sharp edges off of Jamison's black-and-white view of the world, but O'Hara knew the younger man was hardwired in his basic notions of right and wrong. If he told Jamison about the tapes, he would start digging and slowly but surely he would dig a hole for himself too deep to climb out of.

Besides, even if Foster was telling the truth that he didn't know if Harker did it, that didn't mean Harker didn't do it. It just meant that there would be a complete obliteration of Foster's credibility, which would only leave the child and the fingerprints. And the tape of Christine being pushed to identify Harker would completely undermine her identification at the trial. Harker would get a new trial. At least he would have if he wasn't dead. And Gage's and Cleary's careers would be destroyed for concealing evidence. Mike Jensen would be charged with perjury. Jamison's career would be trashed even though he was just the messenger. Doing the right thing as far as O'Hara was concerned generally had better be its own reward because it wasn't appreciated that much or remembered that long. And in the end, it would all be for nothing. Harker was dead and there wasn't a lot of logic, as far as O'Hara was concerned, in burying everyone else with him.

O'Hara thought about the young prosecutor. He had allowed Jamison inside the hard shell he carefully cultivated. It wasn't quite like the younger man was the son he never had. He wasn't even sure what that bond would feel like, but he did feel an emotional connection that went deeper than mere friendship and loyalty. And he also owed Jamison, though they never talked about it or why. Even if Jamison did what he thought was the right thing it wouldn't change a damn thing except destroy lives, including Jamison's.

O'Hara relit the cigar that had gone cold. All that bullshit about never inhaling was lost on him as he drew the warm taste deep into his lungs and exhaled a stream of blue smoke. O'Hara sipped on his glass of bourbon and felt the liquid amber slide down his throat. Sometimes what was past was better left to the past. If doing the right thing wasn't going to accomplish anything but create wreckage, then what was the point?

He finished the bourbon and snuffed the cigar. He wasn't a philosopher. There was nothing philosophical about it. He popped the tape out of the recorder and slid it into a manila folder with the rest of the tapes. He would save Jamison from himself. What was past would best remain past.

Chapter 42

One Week Later

Jamison watched his mother move rapidly around the kitchen, gathering food that seemed to flow endlessly from whatever nook and cranny she reached into. At the same time, she asked a stream of not so subtle questions about his personal life in order to expand on the limited direct answers he'd already given. No, he didn't have a girlfriend. No, he wasn't dating anyone special or otherwise. No, he didn't have anyone in mind to ask for a date. He didn't mention that he had been thinking more and more about asking Alton Grady's daughter, Lorie, for a date, but that was all he had done—thinking. He didn't have any problem standing in front of a jury or asking a female lawyer to plead her client guilty, but he seemed to wilt if he was asking a woman for a date. All things considered, it took him a while to get moving in the dating department and it helped if he got a signal, preferably not subtle. Lorie seemed to send that signal.

Drifting back from thoughts of Lorie Grady to his mother's endless flow of questions, he sometimes wondered if his skill at cross-examination had been inherited from his mother instead of his father. Finally, the questions stopped for a minute before she brightened and mentioned a young lady she had seen at church that she thought would be perfect for him. That was when he stopped listening again and just nodded. He jumped slightly when he heard the name Harker.

"What?"

"I said, I read in the paper that you won the Harker case. I remember when that case was tried. It was a long time ago. You were a little boy when that happened. It seems like these murder cases never end."

Jamison took the opportunity to find out if his mother might know something. "Did you know that dad was involved in that case?"

His mother became uncharacteristically quiet and turned away, speaking with her back to him. "He didn't talk much about his cases. What did he have to do with it?" Jamison had the odd feeling that his mother already knew the answer to her question and was being deliberately oblique.

"Apparently, he represented one of the witnesses in the case. It seemed kind of weird hearing his name come up in a case I was now trying."

"What was the name of the witness?" The question seemed to be more than idle curiosity. She was probing in a subtler way. Jamison recognized it from the number of times she had pulled information out of him as a teenager.

"Clarence Foster, a small-time criminal who apparently was in the wrong place with the wrong person at the wrong time. Why?"

"Was anybody else mentioned?

Jamison sensed that he had stepped into something he didn't understand. "Like who?"

She hesitated before answering. "Did the name Sample come up?"

He was startled that from so many years past his mother would dredge up the name of someone who wasn't a central figure in the case. "Yeah, there was a Richard Sample who was a suspect at first, but he had an alibi, and then Foster and the victim's daughter identified Harker as the murderer." Jamison now realized that whatever the reason was that she was asking questions, it involved more than the Harker case. "You said Dad didn't talk much about his cases but you seem to remember a lot about that case."

"It was a big case at the time and I didn't like your father's involvement. He said it was his job but I didn't like it." From her expression, Jamison could tell she was cutting off the conversation.

"Mom, is there something about that case that bothers you? There were a lot of unanswered questions that didn't make any sense. But it was a long time ago. I finally let it go. Harker's dead and my investigator convinced me that it didn't make any difference at this point."

"That would be your Mr. O'Hara? Maybe you should listen to him." The way his mother said it raised Jamison's antenna.

"Did Dad tell you something about that case?" He knew there was more to his father's involvement than he'd been able to discover, particularly with Foster's statement to him that he had supposedly told his father about the additional interrogations. Husbands and wives told each other a lot of things that were supposed to be secret, and that included privileged information.

"Your father didn't talk about his cases and he didn't ask me for my opinions. He did what he did and I spent my time raising you." His mother was using the same voice now that she used on him as a child when the conversations was over as far as she was concerned.

"That's not an answer."

"Well it's my answer." His mother's voice was unusually sharp.

"Why did you ask about Sample?" Jamison could see his mother twisting her apron and he could also see the tears at the edges of her eyes.

Finally, she said, "Dolores."

"Dolores? Who's Dolores?"

"Richard Sample's mother. Your father knew his mother, Dolores."

"I don't understand what that means."

"Yes, you do. Leave it be. I did."

A silence lingered, filling the gap before Jamison said goodbye. There was nothing more either was willing to say. Both retreated to their private explanations. They were entitled to that and each dealt in their own way with the personal rationalizations that alter the truth so that life can go forward.

⌒

Jamison left his mother's home and drove with the aimlessness of subconscious direction. The reality of his father's involvement in the Harker case was clawing at him. O'Hara was wrong. He couldn't let it go but at the same time he was unable to undo the tangle of threads that seemed to dangle limitlessly. He thought he was driving toward his apartment when he passed the street that led to Lorie Grady's home.

All of a sudden, he made a quick right and found himself parked in front of her house. He wasn't sure why he was there. Well, he was sure why he was there, but it reminded him of something he might have done in high school. It also reminded him that now that Harker was dead Lorie might let him look at Harker's file. Another thread. What was there to protect?

She answered the door before he had a chance to ring the doorbell. He was immediately struck by how vividly the reality of her appearance and his memory of her appearance matched. Somehow, she had etched herself in his mind and he acknowledged to himself that he'd been thinking about her more frequently than he'd admitted consciously to himself. She didn't wait for him to say anything. "I saw you coming up the walkway. You lost or found?" She seemed amused by her question.

"Found, I guess. May I come in?"

Lorie gestured for him to follow her into a sun porch where she had her easel set up. A large canvas balanced on the wooden structure, paint smears decorating it as well as the floor around it. She noticed him looking at the drops on the tile floor and shrugged. "It adds something, don't you think?" She pulled a few empty canvases off a couch that had seen better days, the cushions holding the permanent impression of years of use. "Have a seat." She still hadn't asked why he was there and he was still trying to think of the answer to that question if she asked. He had the feeling she already knew the answer even if he didn't.

"Ms. Grady—Lorie—last time I was here you said your father's files were in the basement, including the Harker file. Is that still there?"

Lorie looked at him with the same amused expression she wore when she answered the door. "I wondered how long it would take you to ask. I read that Harker's dead. That right? So, you think there's no need to maintain the attorney-client privilege. That right?"

Jamison took a long time with his explanation that now that Harker was dead he didn't see any need to keep the file secret. She waited patiently for him to finish before quietly asking, "And why does that make any difference to you now? Harker's dead. The case is over. But you want something else, don't you? Maybe a glass of wine?"

Jamison could tell she was laughing at him. She just didn't do it out loud. "Sure, wine would be fine." Actually, he would prefer a drink at the moment. Instead he added, "But I need to know something."

"You need to know whether there's something in that file that will tell you whether Harker really did it?" The fact that she asked and answered his questions before he asked them put him off-balance, reminding him of the same thing she had done before.

"I need to know if your father had any notes, anything that might tell me whether he was looking at other possibilities."

She pulled a bottle of wine down from a rack on a credenza in the corner of the room and expertly slipped the cork out, pouring two glasses. "You mean like whether he knew who else might have done it instead of his client? I recall telling you before that it wasn't in my father's file but I also told you maybe you were looking in the wrong place."

"And is there a right place?"

"Tell me what you're looking for and, of more interest to me, tell me why."

"I'm not really sure. I think maybe one of the witnesses lied—but I can't prove it. That doesn't mean Harker didn't do it, but if he didn't, then somebody else did, and I need to be sure. Maybe your father's notes on a witness?"

"Like Jimmy Stack?" She saw the startled expression on his face. "After you left I went through my father's files again. I told you Sam Gifford also looked through them. But my father didn't always keep everything in one spot. That was fine if you knew where everything was but it didn't help if you just went to the place where you thought everything would be. I looked at all the witnesses and his notes and then I checked to see if there were any other files involving those witnesses. Richard Sample refused to talk to my father or his investigators for obvious reasons. But my father's notes on Jimmy Stack don't say much either except they have notations that my dad talked to your father. There was something about a woman named Dolores. It didn't make a lot of sense. Maybe it might to you but for some reason my father thought your father knew something about Dolores or that there was a connection because he underlined the names. Is this Stack guy still alive? My father's notes are just snatches of thoughts but he seemed to think that there was a connection between your father and Dolores and Stack. There were a lot of question marks and a note that he was going to talk to Roger. That was your dad, Roger?"

She told him to wait while she retrieved the file. The manila folder was limp from being kept in a damp place and there were mildew stains on the legal pad paper stuffed inside. The writing on the edge of the folder read "Jimmy Stack." Jamison flipped carefully through the paper, which was as flaccid as the folder.

It was typical of trial lawyer notes, snatches of phrases and lines and arrows to other snatches of phrases, decipherable only to the writer. But it was there, his father's name heavily underlined and an arrow to Dolores Sample, Tommy Sample, and Jimmy Stack. But underneath there was another arrow to Detective Jensen and DDA Jonathon Cleary.

Obviously, Alton Grady thought there was a connection, but he hadn't written down what it was and there was no way it was going to now creep out of the recesses of Grady's clouded mind. Before Jamison could ask she pulled a copy out and handed it to him. "I thought you'd ask. Now you'd like to go to dinner, right?" She laughed as his face turned red. "You were going to ask, right?" She decided to let him off the hook. "I was hoping you'd be back and ask."

Jamison waited for her to change, but unlike most women he had known it seemed almost instantaneous. She came back into the room in a dress that she only accentuated with a slash of lipstick. Unlike most women he had known, it was all she needed. He knew right there that not only had she known he would be back, she also knew it would be a beginning.

The next morning Jamison walked down to Ernie Garcia's office. The investigator was hunched over his desk reading reports. Ernie looked up when he heard Jamison knock on the door jamb as he walked in. "What's up, Boss?" Ernie had adopted O'Hara's penchant for calling Jamison "Boss," but he did it out of respect as opposed to O'Hara's slightly acerbic inflection. Jamison had long ago given up on O'Hara's private sense of humor. It wasn't personal. He was worse with other people.

"Ernie, you interviewed Richard Sample's mother, didn't you?"

"Yeah, Dolores. Why?"

"What can you tell me about her?"

"Not much to tell. She wasn't cooperative with me, I can tell you that. I think I told you that she basically slammed the door in my face when I tried to interview her."

"What did she look like?"

Ernie frowned at the question, his expression questioning what difference that made. "Look like? She's late sixties, still keeps her hair blonde. Still looks to be in pretty good shape for a woman that age." Ernie furrowed his eyebrows. "I'm not sure what you're asking. She had that look—you know—some women have it? My guess is she was a looker when she was younger but maybe a little harder edged. I mean she didn't spend any time talking to me. Why're you asking?"

"I want you to find out everything you can about her."

"What case is this relating to?"

"Just put it down to general investigation." Ernie gave him a sour look. "And Ernie, don't do a report for the file."

"Anything else?"

"Yeah, do a background check on Tommy Sample also."

"Rick Sample's kid? Why?"

"I don't know why. Just do it."

⌐⌐

Late in the afternoon Ernie came by Jamison's office and poked his head in. "Matt, you still want that information on Dolores Sample and her grandson?"

Jamison waved Ernie in, aware that the investigator was looking at him like he not only wasn't sure what the reason was that he was doing this for Jamison, but also like he suspected he wasn't going to get the answer either. At this point he was right on both counts. Jamison waited for the information without saying anything.

Ernie flipped open his notebook. "Okay, I did a quick Department of Motor Vehicle and criminal record check, plus there was background material in the reports. As for Tommy Sample, he wasn't hard to dig up. Believe it or not, he's a lawyer, works in Sacramento, public defender. Not married as far as I can tell. I did a little background check with some of my contacts in Sacramento. Apparently, he's well regarded. Looks like he's beginning to handle bigger cases. I didn't push that. As for Grandma, Dolores Sample. Maiden name Ryan, sixty-six years old, divorced from a Michael Sample, at least that's what the docs say that I was able to access. Anyway, Michael Sample is no longer in the picture—walked out on the family—died about ten years ago. She worked as a cocktail waitress. House paid for. I did find one interesting thing; the house was bought for cash. Kind of odd on a waitress salary but maybe she got an inheritance. No record except for an old speeding ticket. You want more? I didn't dig down into her personal life because I'd have to start talking to people. Wasn't sure you wanted me to do that. It might help if I knew why you wanted the information." Ernie waited.

"I'm pretty sure my father was involved with her."

Ernie mentally measured his words before carefully asking, "By involved, you mean having an affair?" Jamison stared at him without reaction, which, given the question, was a reaction. "Matt, that was a long time ago, man. There's nothing good you're going to find out by going there. Trust me on this. You know I'll do what you want but you should drop this right now. Nobody is going to like the secrets they find out about their parents. That's why parents keep some things secret. What difference does it make now?"

Jamison pulled his mouth into a straight line, biting his lower lip before answering. "Look, Ernie, this isn't personal. And the only surprise here for me isn't that my father was having an affair, it's who it was with. Doesn't it seem like an odd coincidence that my dad represented Clarence Foster and maybe at the same time was involved with the mother of Richard Sample, the other suspect?

"You're a cop. Bill and I interviewed Foster out at Corcoran and he said my dad knew that Jensen and Gage were told by Foster that he couldn't identify anybody because he was drunk—loaded according to him. He said there was a tape but there's no tape. Bill looked."

"I don't know whether to believe Foster or not but my dad would've known what happened. He would've talked to Foster and those notes would have been in his file. He would have protected Foster in the murder case, but if he thought Foster was lying I don't think he would've let him get on the stand and do it. A man's life was at stake. My old man may not have taken his marriage seriously, but he took his job seriously."

Ernie snorted derisively. "Come on, Matt. Lawyers do a lot of things to protect their clients. Your dad would have taken an immunity deal if he had any suspicion Foster was involved in that murder. He would've done it to save his client. He didn't owe anything to Harker." Ernie's opinion of lawyers was only slightly higher than O'Hara's, and that wasn't a very high bar.

Jamison had done nothing but think about this after returning to Lorie's house after dinner. Her incisive speculation as he explained the facts had started to pull the tangle of threads apart. His father wasn't just any lawyer; he was a lawyer with a national reputation. He wouldn't have jeopardized all that for a small-time piece of garbage like Foster. While Jamison hadn't given it a lot of thought before, he had been surprised that his father would even be involved in representing somebody like Foster. There wouldn't be any money in it and his father wasn't known for doing a lot of pro bono work unless a judge personally requested it.

However, if Roger Jamison thought Foster was involved and was vulnerable to a murder charge he would have demanded an immunity deal before letting Foster testify. There was nothing unusual about that. It was the right move to save his client. He had to know how badly the prosecution needed Foster's testimony. But if he knew the truth that Foster had no idea who committed the crime, then that would mean his father was willing to let a man go to the death chamber on perjured testimony.

Jamison had long ago abandoned any naive idol worship of his father, but he couldn't believe that. His father had to either not believe Foster was lying or there was another reason. He hadn't understood what other reason there could be until he saw the connection with Dolores Sample, and even then his mind set up reality roadblocks. It wasn't until 2:00 a.m. in the middle of a sleepless night that he accepted the possibility that his dad may have been protecting Richard Sample because of who his mother was. That thought had kept him tossing and turning until morning.

Jamison shook his head. "I've been thinking about this all night. The reason Jensen and Gage cut Sample loose was because he had an alibi that seemed rock-solid. What if that alibi was ginned up to protect Sample?"

Ernie looked at him like he was crazy. "You want to try and crack a twenty-six-year-old alibi? Matt, almost everybody's going to be dead and Sample's mother isn't going to help us."

"Maybe not but there are two people who can, Foster and Jimmy Stack."

"Well, don't forget about Jensen, Gage, and Cleary. I'm sure they'll be happy to step up to the plate." The sarcasm fairly dripped from Ernie's mouth.

"I haven't forgotten about them but before I go to them we need to figure out what we have. Go bag up Jimmy Stack."

"You have any idea where I'll find him?"

"If he isn't in jail, then he's probably laid out on some sidewalk. We start there."

Ernie stood up and flipped his notepad closed. "You talked to O'Hara about this?"

"We've done nothing but talk. O'Hara thinks we should drop it."

Ernie had a thoughtful expression on his face. "Maybe you should listen."

Chapter 43

O'Hara was sitting in Jamison's office when he returned from lunch. From the look on his face it didn't take much for Jamison to figure out that Ernie had talked to him about bringing in Stack, as well as his speculation about his father. O'Hara's first words confirmed that. "I thought you were going to drop this whole Harker thing? I'm telling you for your own good that you're just putting yourself in a bad position with no upside. Even if your old man was screwing this Dolores woman, what's it going to accomplish now to dig that up?"

"I see you've been talking to Ernie."

"Hell yes, I've been talking to Ernie. He thinks the same thing I do. You're going to shoot yourself in the head and nobody—and I mean nobody—is going to give a shit except me and Ernie, and maybe not even me since I told you not to do it."

"Thanks for caring, Bill. The sensitivity means a lot. There's something wrong here. I can smell it."

"What you can smell is the shitstorm that's going to come out of you messing with this case. I hope this isn't about your father doing the hokeypokey. That happens. It's over. Even if he was involved with Dolores Sample, where's that going to take you? Let it go."

"What if Harker isn't the one who committed that murder? What if he spent twenty-six years in prison for something he didn't do?"

"Matt, I'm not a total prick but he's dead and you can't give those years back. Besides, even if Foster lied and he didn't know who did it, that doesn't mean that Harker didn't do it. And if you're saying that maybe Richard Sample did it, then you still got nothin' because he's dead too and you aren't going to break an alibi that's almost thirty years old. If Gage finds out what you're doing he's going to bust your ass. I'm telling you please let this thing die." O'Hara was pleading, and he didn't do that.

"Bill, you're right about one thing. If that alibi sticks, there's nowhere to go. I need your help on this. I need you and Ernie to work over Jimmy Stack. I just think he's lying. If you and Ernie can't break him, then it's done. Okay?"

"And you think he's lying why?"

"Because I saw part of Harker's lawyer's file and there was something there that showed that his original lawyer, Alton Grady, thought there was a connection."

"And you saw that because his daughter let you see it? Is that an issue here?"

"It isn't an issue and yes, she let me see it. My gut says that we need to do it and I'm going to do it either with you or without you."

O'Hara nodded with resignation. "Yeah, all right. When Ernie brings him in we'll take him apart. But if he doesn't give us anything I want your word this is done." He stared at Jamison until he acknowledged that he agreed.

⤚

Ernie had checked at several charity food kitchens. The street community was its own little society with its own rules and one of its rules was that you didn't give information to cops. It had taken a while, but he had a few street connections he occasionally used as snitches in exchange for a few bucks or a pack of cigarettes. Finally, he found one of them and got a location. It cost him a pack of Marlboros. With the price of cigarettes, information was getting more expensive.

Ernie picked his way through a homeless encampment under a freeway overpass. The smell was overpowering: too many unwashed people, too much garbage and human waste. The bathroom facilities were usually a hole and the hole was whatever shallow depression was conveniently close.

He found Stack sitting on a well-used lounge chair next to a grocery cart full of empty bottles and cans, the currency of the homeless. Stack looked up. "What do you want? I ain't done nothin'. I only been out a week." He laughed. "This is my vacation time. I winter at the county."

Ernie wasn't smiling. "I need you to come with me." Ernie looked over at the grocery cart, recognizing that Jimmy wouldn't want to leave it unattended. "Get your stuff and we'll put it in the trunk of my car until I bring you back."

"If you're bringin' me back, why are you taking me? I didn't do nothin', and I certainly didn't do nothin' that the DA would care about. I'm not going anywhere." A few of Jimmy's neighbors had shuffled over, closing around the scene. Ernie didn't want backup and he wasn't in the mood for trouble.

Ernie slipped his shirt up over his paddle holster so that everyone could see that if they interfered they were making a bad choice and reached down, taking Stack by the arm. "I'll decide what you did. Now get your shit and let's go."

⤚

Jamison watched through the one-way glass window in the interrogation room while Stack sat fidgeting and pulling at the handcuffs tightly encircling his wrists. Both the cuffs and the isolation of the interrogation room were intended to remind Stack that what would happen to him was under the control of men who were not in the room. It was all about breaking the will of the person being questioned. Sometimes it happened quickly and sometimes it happened slowly but it only happened when will was lost and control was gained—and the man being questioned accepted that there was only one end that he could not change.

O'Hara and Garcia waited for some direction. Jamison knew what they wanted to know—what the rules were. Jamison kept it simple. "No Miranda rights. I need information. I want you satisfied that you got everything there is to get. You know what to do." Jamison fully realized that O'Hara might hear something different in the rules than Garcia.

The two investigators had done this many times, and they both knew one another's tactics and personality well enough that they could play off the lead of the other one and move back and forth as the scene played out. Interrogation wasn't like television. Nobody cracked between commercials. It could take a long time or a short time but it definitely took time. Good interrogators were part psychologist and part ruthless inquisitors. Their job was to get information and they only played as fair as they could get away with, bending the rules to the breaking point but only to the breaking point. The old days of nightstick confessions were long past.

Both men were masters at their craft and they had learned from other masters. If there was anything there, Jamison was confident they could squeeze it out. He knew that by taking Miranda rights out of the process he wasn't going to be able to use anything Stack said against him—but he didn't care. He needed information and he would deal with the fallout later. It was one less impediment in the way of his investigators. The droning of Miranda rights—that the person interrogated did not need to speak to them, that he had a right to a lawyer—simply gave the quarry choices. Jamison did not want choices. He wanted results.

There was really no question who was going to be the good cop and who was going to be the bad cop. O'Hara stepped back and glowered at Stack, who quickly figured out that O'Hara was not a man to fool with. Ernie kept his voice friendly. "Jimmy, Detective O'Hara and I want to talk to you about Richard Sample. Now before you say anything I want you to know that we know you had nothing to do with the murder of that woman."

Stack interrupted. "Harker did that. I told you before I didn't do nothin' with that."

Ernie didn't react by raising his voice. He simply said, "I didn't say you did." Sweat was steaming from Stack. Ernie recognized the distinctive stink of fear. Interrogators could latch on to it like a bloodhound in heat. There was something there, something buried but he could still smell it. Now he began the slow process of digging. "Jimmy, tell me about the baseball game you say you went to with Sample." Both he and O'Hara had spent some time with a baseball almanac before meeting Jamison.

"I already told you about that. He had the tickets and we went. That's all. Then the cops were asking about that murder and where we was. I told 'em. That's it."

O'Hara edged closer to the table separating Stack and Garcia. Stack's eyes began to flick back and forth between the two detectives and he noticeably shifted in his seat away from O'Hara. Ernie sensed a loose thread unraveling and began to pull. "Who played in that game?"

"Dodgers and Giants."

"Who played first base for the Dodgers?" The smell coming off of Stack grew stronger and Ernie could hear Stack's shoes scraping against the floor as he moved them nervously. Ernie pushed a little harder. "Anybody who was a Dodger fan would know. Who?"

"I don't remember. I had a lot to drink."

"When you were in court you testified that Don Sutton pitched. Is that right?"

"Yeah, that's right. That's what I said. Sutton."

O'Hara leaned in until his face was within inches of Stack. His voice sounded like a bag of grinding gravel. "There's one thing about baseball, Jimmy. They keep statistics on everything. I looked it up. Sutton didn't pitch that day. It was Bob Welch."

"Maybe Sutton pitched later. I remember Sutton. I'm a Giants fan anyway."

"Really? So, you remember Willie McCovey pitching that day for the Giants?"

"Yeah, I remember that."

O'Hara's voice took on an even harsher edge. "Don't screw with me Jimmy. Sutton didn't play that day and McCovey was a first baseman. You don't know shit about baseball."

"Okay, so I was drunk and don't remember who pitched. So what?"

"Give me the name of one player who played that day."

"Look, I ain't a baseball fan. I just went 'cause Sample wanted to go and the tickets were free."

O'Hara reached out and squeezed Stack's arm until Jimmy winced. "Cut the bullshit, Jimmy. You didn't go to any game that day, did you? Sample's dead. You don't owe him anything, but I want the goddamn truth." O'Hara's voice came out a rasping hiss. "And. I. Want. It. Now."

Ernie reached over and pulled O'Hara's hand off Stack's arm. "Jimmy, all we want is the truth. I promise you right now that you tell us the truth and nothing's going to happen to you. But if you keep lying, then I'm leaving right now and you can finish this discussion with Detective O'Hara. You understand?"

O'Hara grinned like a wolf who saw an easy meal. He put both hands on the steel table and curled his fingers loosely. "What's it going to be, Jimmy? We can make this easy or hard. I don't mind hard but I guarantee you won't like it."

Jimmy's hands were streaking sweat onto the table as he smeared them around, scraping the steel handcuffs against the metal table, adding to the scars left by men who had set there before. "I want a lawyer. I got a right."

Ernie stood up. "Wrong answer, Jimmy. I'm going to get some fresh air."

O'Hara slid onto the chair vacated by Garcia as Ernie moved toward the door, where he paused. Stack's eyes flashed toward Ernie and then back toward O'Hara, whose face was now directly in front of him. "Your choice, Jimmy. You got ten seconds to make it. Tell me the truth or I let you spend the night in the jail with the Bulldog Boys and I'll make sure the guard thanks you for your cooperation when he shuts the cell door." Jimmy's gaze darted over again toward Ernie as he opened the door to the interrogation room. The Bulldog Boys were a notorious gang of criminals who always managed to have a number of their members in jail and had very simple rules about snitches. O'Hara started counting. "Five seconds, Jimmy. Three. All right, you made your choice."

"Okay."

"Okay, what?" O'Hara's voice carried the hard edge of a meat cleaver.

Stack deflated like a week-old Halloween pumpkin. "Okay, I wasn't at the game. That's what you want to know, right?"

"I already know that, Jimmy. What I want is the truth."

"I didn't hurt that woman. I had nothin' to do with that."

"I know that too, Jimmy." O'Hara tried to soften his tone but his next words were about as soft as a lead-lined glove. "Otherwise, I would have reached across this table and you and I would have had a much different discussion. What I want to know is why did you say you were at the game and where did Sample get the tickets?"

"Sample called me. He said he needed me to cover for him. I didn't know it was for no murder. He just said he might be in trouble and needed somebody to back him up. He said he'd pay me. We met up and he had the tickets and a game program. I don't know who gave them to him, just what he said."

"And what was that?"

"He said he got them from somebody who'd been at the game. I didn't care." Jimmy's voice was a torrent of words. "He gave me a wad of cash and told me what to say but I figured it was his mom because later she told me stuff about the game 'cause she was there. So, I could make it sound good for the cops, you know? I tried to remember all of it but we just decided to say I was drunk most of the time. Pretty close to the truth anyway. The important thing was to say I was with Rick. It wasn't until the cops talked to me that I found out it was 'cause of a murder." Stack began wiping his nose with his sleeve. "But I didn't think Rick did that so I went along."

"Why'd you think Sample wouldn't do that?"

"I don't know, man. I known him a long time and he really liked that girl. I don't know. Anyway, he said Harker did it. So that was enough for me. He really hated Harker."

"Why?"

"I don't know. Dude didn't confide in me."

"Jimmy, do you remember if Rick had any cuts on him, scratches, things like that?"

"He had like a cut or a scrape on his finger. I remember that 'cause I grabbed his hand when I saw him, and he pulled away. Said he got it sliced on a beer can."

"Did Rick carry a knife?"

"Yeah, sometimes. He had a Buck knife. You know, one of them knives with a wood handle, folds up. A lot of guys carried 'em that worked construction or odd jobs. I had one too."

"How much cash did Sample give you?"

"It was a lot—maybe twelve hundred or fifteen hundred dollars."

"You don't remember?"

"Nah, like I said I was drunk most of the time. There's whole parts of my life I don't remember."

"Do you know where he got that kind of cash?"

"I'm guessin' his mom. She was doin' some rich lawyer. That's all I know. I mean she was workin' as a cocktail waitress. She didn't have that kind of money. So, I figured it was from the lawyer. She was a real looker back then. She must of gone to the game with him 'cause she couldn't afford to pay for no baseball tickets."

"Did you ever meet the lawyer or see him?"

"I saw him once. He drove a big Lincoln—real shiny black Lincoln, you know. Guy just looked rich but guys like that don't have nothin' to do with guys like me."

Watching through the one-way glass, Jamison felt his blood run cold. His father had driven a black Lincoln back then. Now it all was in front of him separated by a wall of mirrored glass—what his father had done. He could feel the bile rising up in his throat. It amazed him how many years separated these events in his life and how all of that separation collapsed in a microsecond.

"So, you lied to the police about Sample being with you?"

"Yeah, but I didn't have nothin' to do with killin' that girl. I don't do shit like that. I heard they charged Harker with it and he got convicted so I figured it was all okay. He must of done it, right? I mean they found him guilty. So, I figured what was the harm."

"Do you know Clarence Foster?"

Stack's gaze shifted to the left. He hesitated almost imperceptibly before answering. "Nah, maybe I seen him around, but I don't know him. I know Rick hung around with him sometimes. They drank together but I wasn't with them. Anyway, Sample's dead and word on the street is some cop hit Harker with one of them electric guns and fried him. So, what difference does it make now? All I know is I didn't do it."

For a seasoned interrogator, every movement, every gesture of the person being questioned is like an electronic bit of code. Some of it is meaningless and some of it is a silent alarm. O'Hara had years of experience watching men and women evade and obscure. He had seen people look him straight in the eye and lie and he had seen people mumble and look away as they told the unvarnished truth. What he had just heard was not the truth. How to extract that truth was what set men like him apart. He glanced over at the mirrored glass. The next move would determine whether he could open Stack up to reveal what he was hiding down deep where even Stack was afraid to look.

O'Hara waited until Stack finally looked at him, then locked his gaze on Stack like a hawk circling his prey. "You're lying to me, Jimmy."

"I'm not lying. I'm telling you the truth. I didn't do nothin' to that girl."

The reaction blew out of O'Hara like a shotgun blast. "Cut the bullshit, Jimmy. I already told you that I didn't think you killed that girl. But you know who did, don't you? You know because you swim in the same piss stream as Harker and Sample." O'Hara's hand was pushed down on the table so hard that his fingertips blanched almost white. There was no mistaking the tone of his voice as he put his face within inches of Stack's. "I'm going to ask you again and I want you to think real hard before you answer me. Now you should have already figured out that I am not the man you want to fuck with. Do you understand that, Jimmy?"

The answer came out in a mumble. "Sample did it. He killed that girl." Stack's eyes were staring straight down at O'Hara's hand.

O'Hara reached across and grabbed the short chain separating the two wrist cuffs, twisting as he pulled. "Look at me, Jimmy. I want to hear you. Who killed that girl? How do you know who killed that girl?"

"Sample did. Later after the trial, we was drinking and I wanted more money. Sample hit me. He said he did it and he would do me too."

"Is that what he said, Jimmy?" Ernie's voice was tense. "Tell me exactly what he said."

"He said what happened to her could happen to me too. He said he'd do me just like her. That's what he said. I didn't ask him to explain. I got it."

Ernie moved forward, holding his hand out signaling O'Hara to back off. O'Hara slightly loosened his grip. "Why didn't you go to the police. Why didn't you tell the truth?"

Stack looked up at both men through rheumy red eyes. "And say what? I been a drunk most of my life. I didn't owe Harker nothin'. I took money. There was people involved like that lawyer—rich people. Who was gonna believe me? All that would happen is Sample would kill me too. I mean I heard that girl got cut up bad. You think I was gonna fuck with him?"

Ernie's voice was quiet. "Well why lie now? Sample's been dead for years. Why not tell the truth?"

"Who's gonna believe me? I may not know much but I was in it, man. I was in it and there was no way out."

Ernie put his hand on Stack's arm. "Jimmy, did you ever tell anyone what you just told us?"

"I told Foster."

"You told Clarence Foster? Why? I thought you said you didn't know Foster."

Stack squirmed in his chair, confusion spreading across his face as he tried to remember what he'd said, the stress of the interrogation leaving him no time to think clearly. Resignation sank his body farther down into his chair. It was always like that, the slow extraction piece by piece, each bit pulling a chunk out of what was left of the last vestiges of defiance. Stack squeezed out a smirk. "Well, I lied about that. We was in jail. What else we got to talk about? Besides, I figured he should know. He said he just told the cops Harker did it because they were going to make him go down on it and he was scared too. He was gonna do a dime in the joint. I just figured, you know? Sample was still alive. Harker was in the joint too."

Both interrogators could smell it. There was still something buried, something left. "Did you tell anyone else?"

"No. Nobody."

O'Hara reached in between them and grabbed Stack's cuffs again, pulling him forward, slamming Stack's chest into the metal table. "You're fuckin' lying again, Jimmy. I told you I want the truth. Who else did you tell? I know you're lying."

The sour smell of fear filled the room like tear gas. "I told you I didn't ..." O'Hara twisted the cuffs.

The fury in O'Hara's voice even clearly shook Ernie. "Bill, take it easy."

Jamison watched through the glass and couldn't constrain himself. He banged on the window before it got completely out of control. Then Jimmy Stack began to wilt. It happened that way sometimes. All of a sudden, a man just broke and when he did all his resistance drained from him. Jimmy Stack was about to become an empty grave.

"I told that prick Jensen. I told him." O'Hara let go of Jimmy's cuffs and stood up, glancing over at the one-way glass. While O'Hara seldom had a moment of indecision he could feel it creeping over him. Ernie was looking up at him with the same question on his face. This was now going down the rabbit hole and where it was going to come out was anybody's guess. The only question was whether to ask the next question and the answer to that was there was no choice.

Ernie kept himself under control. "Are you talking about Detective Jensen from the Sheriff's Department?"

"That's right. I'm talking about that prick Detective Jensen. He came after me right after Sample got killed. He told me Sample was dead; that he got what he deserved. I remember just what he said. 'Sample got what all assholes deserve.' He said he knew I knew the truth and that's why he was there.

"He scared the livin' shit out of me. I was sleeping in a little place I built over by that recycling plant on the South Side, cardboard and some tarps I found. Next thing I knew Jensen was draggin' me out. I had no idea what was happenin'. He hit me and kicked me. I told him. That's it. Man, I was scared. I don't know how he knew but he kicked the livin' shit out of me. Yeah, I told him what Rick said—that he killed that girl. And he said he already knew that and then he told me that if I said a fuckin' word I was dead too."

"And you didn't say anything?"

"Say anything? Shit, are you crazy? Jensen told me that I could crawl into whatever fuckin' cardboard box I called home and he would find me and set it on fire if I ever breathed a word. You guys got to protect me now. And I ain't saying nothin' till you cover my ass. Right before you made me go to court he sent me a kite in jail." Both detectives knew that a kite was a jailhouse message. "All it said was, 'Remember what I said.' I knew who sent it. And I remembered what he said."

Chapter 44

O'Hara and Ernie walked through the door to the observation room where Jamison waited, watching through the one-way glass. Jimmy Stack was still sitting at the steel table looking back and forth at the graffiti scratched into the metal surface by other handcuffed men intent on leaving a mark for their legacy.

Jamison was lost in thought until the sound of the door startled him. Ernie broke Jamison's contemplation. "Well, this is turning into a real clusterfuck. What now, Boss? Where are we going to go with this?"

O'Hara was uncharacteristically quiet. Jamison stared at him for a moment. "What? I know you want to say something, so say it."

"Not here."

Ernie had a young deputy put Stack in a holding cell and get him something to eat. Then the three men walked back in silence to Jamison's office. O'Hara separated from them for a few minutes and came back to Jamison's office with a manila envelope. He laid it on Jamison's desk. "The tapes."

Jamison pulled the envelope across his desk and looked inside. "What tapes?"

O'Hara explained his visit to the retired sheriff's department secretary, his listening to the tapes, and his decision not to give them to Jamison. He was unusually subdued. "Look, Matt, I knew those tapes weren't going to do anything but keep you asking more and more questions that I didn't think there were going to be any answers to. All I could see was you pissing off a whole lot of people and screwing yourself. But now . . ."

"But now what?" Jamison wasn't sure whether to be angry or irritated or appreciative. He decided to move forward for the time being. "What's on them?"

"Foster told us the truth. Jensen and Gage and Cleary knew that Foster said over and over that he was so drunk he didn't remember who was involved. When you listen to them and wrap Foster's explanation around them, it's clear that somebody took Foster out and convinced him what story he needed to give. Foster says that was Cleary. I don't know about that but there's no question in my mind that they knew about the tapes and they made them disappear. And then there's the tape of the conversation in the car, the one Jensen said wasn't recorded and the one Cleary said he thought didn't exist. On that tape Foster admits to Harker that he lied. If a jury ever heard that tape . . ." O'Hara didn't need to finish the sentence in order to explain the consequences.

"Anything else?" Jamison was subdued.

"Yeah, there's something else. The other tape is of Christine being pushed by Gage on the identification of Harker. There's no question it would be used to argue that Gage tainted her identification.

"There's no way that Gage and Cleary wouldn't have known what Harker's lawyer would do with those tapes if he got his hands on them. So, they buried them. I've thought about this a lot, Matt. I'm not saying they thought Harker was innocent and they let him go down. I think they were convinced he was guilty. They had Sample's alibi. They had Christine's identification. They didn't want Harker to get away with it so they made their case stronger by getting rid of the tapes. Why the hell they let Margaret Campos transcribe them is beyond me. I'm not saying it was right.

"I knew you'd just go storming into Gage's office and he'd take a big dump on your career and nothing would happen. Now we got Jimmy Stack and we got the tapes."

Ernie finished O'Hara's thought. "And now we have a real pile of shit to deal with."

Jamison nodded to O'Hara. He understood why O'Hara did it. O'Hara was right about what he would have done, and O'Hara was right that he would have gone to Gage and buried his career right then and there with nothing to show for it. He thought about all of it. Some of it made sense and yet *none* of it made sense. He got that there was a cover-up of Foster's interrogation, but that wasn't going to prove that Harker didn't do it. If he was going to take the investigation to the end then there was only one way to do it and Jamison knew it. If you attack the king you have to kill the king. If you don't kill the king, then he will kill you. Bill Gage would surely crush him like a bug. Gage would be fighting for survival and he was surrounded by people who not only would protect him, they would also protect themselves. And then there was Justice Jonathon Cleary, a judicial rocket. Gage and Cleary would both say he was protecting a vicious killer. They were protecting the community. What was he going to do, drag out Jimmy Stack?

"Bill, you have the file on Sample's murder, right?"

"You want me to talk to the deputy that was first on the scene? He's retired now but I don't think he's still local. I'm not even sure he's still alive."

"No. You talk to him and he'll call Jensen. You guys all stick together. He'll want to know why you're fishing around on a second-rate murder case and wonder why you haven't talked to Jensen. I want you to find the bartender. See what he has to say. I have a feeling."

"A feeling about what?"

"A feeling about Clarence Foster and Mike Jensen."

It wasn't as hard as O'Hara had anticipated. The only thing that changed about Jack's place was that now it was called Mikey's. When O'Hara walked in there were a few customers sitting at the bar who looked like they were already dead and nobody told them, at least until they swiveled their heads to look at the black man who walked through the door. That was new. It wasn't often that any black men even stuck their head in the door. Mikey's was that kind of place and it didn't need a sign out front to advertise who was welcome and who wasn't.

O'Hara wrinkled his nose at the sour smell and then shifted his coat so that the gold badge on his belt glinted in the dim light. He walked over to the bartender who was making a desultory effort at wiping glasses and watching television. "I'm looking for Mike Rickman. Used to work here. You know where I might find him?"

The bartender began wiping the bar top with the same towel he'd been using to wipe glasses. "I'm Rickman." O'Hara refrained from making a remark about health regulations and made a mental note not to order a drink.

"You also the owner?"

"Mikey, yeah that's me. Place used to be Jack's. That was my father. What can I do for you?"

"There was a murder in this place about eight years ago—"

Rickman interrupted. "You'll have to be more specific than that."

O'Hara pulled out a cigar and made a show of holding it while he heated the end slowly with a gold butane lighter before jamming it into his mouth.

Rickman shoved an ashtray across the bar. "Smoking isn't allowed, Deputy. I'd think you knew that."

O'Hara coughed. "Yeah, I guessed that from the cigarette butts on the floor." Rickman shrugged and waited for O'Hara to tell him what he wanted.

O'Hara blew out a cloud of blue smoke, watching it slowly settle between him and Rickman before continuing. "About eight years ago, early December. Reports say you found a customer, Rick Sample, out in the alley. Somebody knifed him. Remember that?"

Rickman looked back at the customers sitting at the bar and raised his voice. "Like I said, you'll have to be more specific. That was a busy month, holiday season and all." The customers at the bar laughed.

O'Hara leaned in until his face was close to Rickman's. "Cut the shit, Mikey. We can talk here on your turf or we can talk downtown on mine or we can just go outside and talk. Your choice."

Rickman tapped the countertop and lowered his voice. "I remember. What about it? Don't tell me you guys are just following up on that now?" His tone wasn't belligerent, but it was edged with a show of defiance.

O'Hara deliberately reached toward his back and made a point of adjusting his gun. Rickman's eyes shifted with the movement as O'Hara responded. "Not exactly. The reports say that he was in the bar earlier and that there was another man with him. According to the reports, you weren't sure of the description. I was wondering if you'd had enough time to think about that to give me a better description."

Rickman leaned over, resting a heavily tattooed arm on the bar top. "I'm not telling you how to do your job, but I gave a description to the cop that came in."

"My report says you told the officer the guy was one hundred sixty to one hundred seventy pounds, maybe white, maybe Hispanic, maybe black. Not much of a description unless I'm looking for a zebra."

Rickman dropped his voice even further. "Look, the officer that was out here first was askin' questions in front of my customers. Everybody's got standards, you know? I wasn't going to say anything in front of them. Most of my customers have done time. I don't judge but I also know the rules. Anyway, later I told the detective what the guy looked like, gave him a full description."

"The detective?"

"Yeah, the detective that followed up. He was a supervisor or something."

O'Hara hesitated. "Do you remember the detective's name?"

"Hell no."

"Could it have been Jensen. Does that sound right?"

"Yeah, Jensen, maybe. Sounds right, but I'm not sure. I remember that he looked like he'd spent a lot of time himself in bars. You get to know the look, you know. Don't you guys have reports? Should be there. Check the reports. But I gave him a description."

"And that was?"

"It was a black guy, maybe late forties, early fifties. We don't get many black dudes in here." Rickman shrugged again. "Nothing personal. Everybody has their own crowd, you know?" O'Hara nodded, tapping the ash off his cigar, missing the ashtray, his face impassive.

Rickman stared back, tensing slightly before relaxing his shoulders and continuing tersely. "Guy had a scruffy goatee getting' gray. But he had the look, like he'd done time. He and the other guy knew each other, that's for sure. They didn't talk loud, but in this place it doesn't take you long to see when things are getting intense and most of the time nobody gets loud before somebody gets hurt. I told them to take it outside and the guy gave me a real hard look. Then I guess they really took it outside.

"I didn't hear nothin' but when I took out the garbage there the guy was, spread out in the dumpster. I didn't bother to check whether he was alive. I seen lots of dead guys and he was definitely dead. So, I called the cops. That's it. It wasn't the first time somebody walked out of here and settled a fight in the alley. Better than inside."

O'Hara sucked his mustache into his mouth and thought about his next question. "You say you gave a description to the detective?"

"Yeah, just what I said, and he came back later and showed me some pictures. All black guys. But none of them were the guy. Hell, I told the detective that he had a tattoo on his right hand of a snake. I could tell it was a joint tattoo. Seen plenty of 'em. His was actually pretty good. When I told them to take it outside he turned his hand so I could see the snake; kind of flexed his hand to make the snake move. Trying to scare me, I guess. Showing me your prison tats doesn't mean shit to me. Everybody in here knows I keep a shotgun under the bar. Guess they never caught him 'cause nobody ever came back or showed me any more pictures. Anyway, you should ask the detective."

O'Hara didn't need to ask the detective. He'd seen that snake move before,

Chapter 45

Ernie yawned. He hated going to LA, driving in LA, and being in LA. And he hated the drive back too because it didn't make any difference what time he left, there was still traffic moving like the 5 Freeway was a school zone. The 405 was worse. It was a parking lot. How people handled it was beyond him. He guessed they turned their radios up and just tuned out. Finally, he was approaching the 5 and 405 merge at the start of the highway over the Tehachapi Mountains—what everybody called the Grapevine.

Dodger Stadium had still been basically how he remembered it. His dad had taken him there a few times as a kid. Visiting it brought back those memories. Baseball was always better when you were a kid. He was old enough that he remembered when ball players actually signed a kid's baseball and you took it home and treasured it instead of selling it on the internet.

It hadn't been a productive day, at least not in the sense of getting anything that would help much. He'd taken the tickets that Jensen said he got from Sample and showed them to people in the Dodger office at the stadium. They were real. But that was about it. There were no records as to who bought them. But there was no doubt in his mind that Sample hadn't bought them. They were expensive seats and guys like Rick Sample would have been in the nose-bleed sections at best. He hoped that O'Hara had something better.

⌒

Jamison walked into his father's home office. He hadn't been in there in a long time. In fact, he couldn't remember when he'd last been in it. When he was a kid, if his father was home his time in that office generally meant he was in trouble. The leather recliner was still where it had always been. The walls were covered with awards that reflected his father's accomplishments as a lawyer, and the triple-arch bookcase held at least five crystal award clocks that had long ago stopped ticking but still sat as silent mementoes of some achievement that meant something at the time. That wasn't what he was looking for.

There was a locked glass-enclosed display case behind his father's desk. He'd never been allowed to do more than put his fingerprints on the glass. The shelves on one side held autographs of famous lawyers and judges. The other side held a sports memorabilia collection that meant more to a little boy who couldn't have cared less who Oliver Wendell Holmes was. There was a 49ers football signed by Joe Montana, a Green Bay Packers helmet signed by Bart Starr, a photograph of his father standing with Johnny Unitas, signed photos of his father with golf greats from Arnold Palmer to Jack Nicholas, and what Jamison was really interested in, his baseball mementoes—all sitting prominently in front of signed photographs of baseball stars.

Jamison reached to the top of the case and felt around for the key. Something had clicked in the back of his brain when he'd been cross-examining Jimmy Stack but it didn't register clearly at the time. Slowly but surely it had wormed its way to the front, a childhood memory sprung from the recesses where such things are kept. He stared at the mounted baseballs before picking up several of them, searching the autographs on them. He hadn't been sure that any of them might be what he was looking for as he picked up one after another and set them back down, until he turned one of the baseballs over in his hand and stared at it for seconds that seemed to suspend time. He slipped the ball back into the case.

⌒

Jamison drove over to Lorie Grady's house. This time he called ahead. He needed to know whether her father kept anything else related to what Jamison didn't want to face. Their dinner had been an experience that kept popping up in his mind. She was vibrant, committed to what she did, interested in what he did, funny, and incredibly attractive. And she knew it. And she knew he knew it. What she thought of him was something he was less sure of, but he was sure that he wanted to see her again and again and he was pretty sure she would say yes. But his reasons for seeing her today were because of her father, not her. She answered the door before the chime of the doorbell faded. "You've found what you were looking for." It wasn't a question. How she seemed to know what he wanted before he said it still put him off-balance.

Jamison walked in and quickly turned. "I'd like to look again at your father's files."

"And here I thought it was all about me."

She had a way of setting him back on his heels before she made him feel like he was completely in control, even though his rational mind told him he wasn't.

"You want to know if there's a file on Dolores Sample, don't you?" Again, it wasn't a question.

He was tempted to ask how she did that but all he said was, "Have you seen one?"

"I've looked at it."

The veiled answer caused him to hesitate. "What does that mean?"

"It means that some things are better left to the erosion of mildew and time. How's that for a poetic effort?" Lorie came close and put her hand on the side of his face. He could feel the heat. "There's no point to this, let it go."

"Everybody keeps telling me that, but nobody has convinced me, yet."

"That's because you aren't listening. And if they're telling you that it's because they think you should listen."

"And is that what you think too?"

"Is this more about your father or more about whether there was an injustice that you think you're supposed to right?"

"Are you going to show me the file?"

Lorie watched as Jamison slowly read and then flipped one by one the several pages in a file with Dolores Sample's name on it. Alton Grady may have been past his prime when he defended Rick Harker but that didn't mean that he hadn't tried. Apparently, Jamison's mother wasn't the only one who knew about Dolores and Roger Jamison. Grady's notes showed that he had talked to Roger about it, but it was because he had warned Roger that his information was that both Jensen and Cleary knew about the relationship. The page also had lines connecting a lot of the principal players, but that was all there was—lines without notes.

Jamison put the file down without saying anything. Lorie reached over and put her hand on his shoulder. "I'm sorry, Matt. I knew your father and mine were friends. I'm not sure why my father made a record of this. But it looks to me like he thought that Jensen or Cleary would have used that information to make sure your father got Foster to cooperate."

Jamison held her hand for a moment. "Your father was right but not for the reason he thought."

Jamison drove back to his office in silence. The radio was off, and he had no desire to hear the news or music. What he wanted was the absence of sound. He had no way of knowing that both O'Hara and Garcia were also driving back in the same frame of mind.

Chapter 46

All three men converged on Jamison's office at virtually the same time. It wasn't planned. The realities of the case had reached a level of subconscious interaction that put everyone on the same plane of thought, and even time seemed to match their actions. Jamison was taking a seat behind his desk when Ernie walked in followed seconds later by O'Hara.

O'Hara didn't wait for the others to speak. "Clarence Foster killed Rick Sample."

Ernie's head swiveled around. "Wait. What?"

"The bartender identified that snake tattoo on Foster's hand and the description was a perfect match."

"That wasn't in the reports."

O'Hara spit out a response. "No shit." He immediately regretted the way it sounded. Ernie didn't deserve that. He unloaded the rest of it. "Mike Jensen showed the bartender a photo spread but it didn't include Foster. But the bartender told me he described a black guy, scraggly goatee, with the tattoo of a snake on the back of his right hand. Does that sound familiar? Jensen had to know it was Foster."

Jamison hadn't said a word, waiting for O'Hara to finish before he put a period on O'Hara's explanation. "Jensen said he was the supervising detective when Sample was murdered. So, if he knew that Foster killed Sample why not bring him in?"

O'Hara exhaled heavily. "I'm going to guess that he did but I'm also going to guess that Foster told him that Sample had admitted to Stack that he killed Lisa Farrow."

"I'm not quite tracking this," Ernie said. "Why would Foster kill Sample?"

"Foster told us that 'he did the right thing.' My guess is that Foster decided to do a little jailhouse justice. He knew he'd screwed Harker," Jamison answered.

Ernie snorted. "Guys like him don't give a damn about that."

"Well, my question is whether Foster talked to Jensen before or after he killed Sample." O'Hara let his comment fall with a thud that momentarily stopped the conversation.

"What are you saying, Bill?" Jamison hadn't connected the dots.

"What I'm saying is who had the motive? There's always a motive. Sometimes it's real simple and sometimes its complex but you look to the motive and that usually tells you where to start digging. If Jensen knew that Sample did it, then he had a motive to want to see Sample dead. Think about it. Stack told Foster that Harker hadn't done it. And somebody told Jensen. My guess is it was Clarence Foster.

"Whether he intended it or not, Jensen would know that he let an innocent man go down and he'd pulled shit to do it. He'd buried the tapes; committed perjury. It was all going to go if anyone found out—his pension, his reputation. He could even go to the joint with all the rest of the assholes he'd sent there. So, Foster either went into that bar because he intended to see to it that Sample got what he deserved, or Jensen sent him into that bar to make sure Sample got what he deserved. Either way, Jensen covered it up and then he went looking for Stack to make sure the loose thread was taken care of."

"Well, we aren't going to know the answer to that until we talk to Jensen," said Jamison.

"Or until we talk again to Clarence Foster," O'Hara said in a low voice as he walked out the door.

⤸

O'Hara went into the interview at Corcoran Prison by himself. He hadn't brought Jamison with him because he didn't want to listen to the disapproval of how he was going to handle it—and with the way he intended to handle it he didn't want any of Jamison's fingerprints on this.

"You back again?" Foster sat, drumming his fingers on the metal table in the interview room. "I haven't had this many visitors since they wrote about me in *People* magazine, Sexiest Man Alive and all that." Foster gave O'Hara a smirk and leaned back in his chair. "Why don't you bring a woman and maybe I can work up some of those conjugals. Or maybe you and I can work something out? You know what I mean? You get more flexible about your choices with only men around you all the time. You're not bad lookin' for an old guy. I've done worse." Foster's eyelids shrouded his eyes like a hood, making them look like black slits in his face as he laughed at his own humor.

O'Hara didn't laugh in return. "Okay, Clarence, you've been fucking with us from the beginning. Now it's time to tell the truth. I know you killed Rick Sample." O'Hara had decided to get right to the point. He would deal with the fallout later. Right now, his need for answers took a priority over his concern about going after Foster. He knew he was rationalizing. O'Hara had never regarded his ability to justify his conduct as a character flaw.

"You don't know shit, man." Foster started to get up. "I want my lawyer. I got a right to my lawyer."

Experienced cops read a lot by the look in a man's eyes and O'Hara saw the look of a man that he wouldn't turn his back on in the prison yard. There was only one way to talk to him and only one way for him to understand. "Fuck your lawyer, Clarence. I want answers and I want them right now. I know that you were out of the joint when Sample was killed." O'Hara slammed his hand over Foster's right hand with the curled snake. "And just so you know, Clarence, the bartender remembered that tattoo that you like to show off so if you think I can't prove you did it you're wrong." O'Hara pushed down so hard on Foster's hand that he could feel Foster's pulse throb. O'Hara's voice came out in a razor-edged whisper. "I know you did it but that's not why I'm here. What I want to know is the rest of it."

"I already said you don't know shit. Fuck you." Foster tried to pull his hand out from under O'Hara's, but O'Hara was pressing down so hard the hand didn't move.

"You know I'm not the man you want to say that to so let's quit measuring one another's dicks."

O'Hara could see the side of Foster's mouth twitch with pain. He lifted his hand. "Clarence, you go down for murder and you're going to die in this place. You'll have no chance to see the light of day. I'm going to give you a chance not to be carried out of here in a used body bag. I already know what you did, and I know that Detective Jensen knew it too, didn't he? But nothing happened to you, no arrest, nothing. Now what did you do to buy your way out of a murder? You know what I want. Give it to me."

Foster raised his head and opened his eyes. They looked like two black holes, absorbing all light—dead eyes. O'Hara knew he was watching a man who had died a long time ago and already released his soul. There was something about him that emanated not a lack of fear but a lack of caring about fear or anything else for that matter. O'Hara had seen too many men just like Foster, a shell who was filling air space. All he had left was some code that justified him holding his head up when he walked back and forth to his cell.

The words that came out of Foster chilled the room like they'd been buried in ice. "I did the right thing. Your boy Jensen, he's no different than me. The only thing that keeps him from being in here just like me is that badge. And if you do your job maybe I'll get to tell him myself." Foster laid his hands flat on the table and flexed the snake until it took on its own life. "That little girl, Christine. She used to talk to me. She didn't care what I was. That's your answer. I told you I was too damn drunk to even know what was happening to her mama, let alone stop it. There's not enough time for me to make much of my life right. I did the right thing for that little girl—and for me." He stood up and banged on the door for the guard.

Chapter 47

As he rolled past the gate, O'Hara glanced at the side mirror. The walls of Corcoran Prison receded behind him, their massive size still filling the view. He wondered how many secrets that concrete carapace held and then shook off the thought. It wasn't what he had done that worried him. It was what was going to happen next. He already knew what Jamison was going to say. He was right.

"Bill, you went too far. Foster wanted a lawyer . . ."

Ernie slipped in the office just in time to hear O'Hara respond. "Fuck Foster and his lawyer too. You wanted answers. You and I both know you aren't interested in who killed Rick Sample. At this point it's really hard to care. He deserved dyin' the hard way. He just didn't get it from a clean needle. The world has one less asshole. That's a positive improvement.

"Besides, if this went down the way I think it did, not pulling out a Miranda card and reading Foster his rights isn't going to make a damn bit of difference. If you want answers we needed to talk to Foster and if you want to prosecute somebody for the murder of Rick Sample, then we still needed Foster because you and I both know that Foster isn't the guy in your gunsights. There are a whole lot of bigger fish than Foster. But now you crossed your own line, Matt. You know what happened and you're smart enough to know who's going to be in front of you. I told you not to do this. You going to take down Jensen? You going to take down Gage and Cleary too? You do and you know who's going to be coming after you. Sometimes you just need to let shit go, Matt. You can still control this. Let it go. There's no upside here for you. Let. It. Go."

Jamison stayed quiet. He knew O'Hara was right. He also knew that he was edging close to the line now in everything he was doing, and if he was wrong, then he wasn't going to be able to justify edging across that line, assuming that he could ever justify it. And if he was right he was still crossing a line and he couldn't go back. It was a choice and he had to make it.

O'Hara changed the subject. "Foster's last comment, about the little girl, Christine?"

"Yeah?"

"That's your answer. Even cons have their own morality code. You don't hurt kids. That was Foster's justification. The question is what was Jensen's? There's only one way to find the answer to that." O'Hara exhaled heavily. "Matt, if you think Bill Gage is going to let you pull the governor's chair out from under his ass or that Judge Cleary is going to let you steal his golden ring without a fight, then you are not just naive, you are stupid. Harker's dead. Sample's dead. And if this is still about your old man, well he's dead too. This is about *you* now. You keep this up, there's going to be blood on the floor and no matter what, a lot of it is going to be yours."

Ernie hadn't said a word. His face was an opaque brown mask. If O'Hara was in, then he was in. And if Matt was in then, they were all in. Jamison glanced over to read Ernie's face. His lack of reaction telegraphed that as far as he was concerned O'Hara was right.

"My dad—"

O'Hara interrupted. "You need to let that go too. Ernie and I both know you're a better man than he was. You don't have to prove that to the world."

Jamison gave an almost imperceptible nod of acknowledgment before finishing. "That isn't it. I went through my father's office. He kept a lot of stuff in his ego display case. It was right behind his desk, so you couldn't see him without seeing all that stuff. One thing he kept was sports mementos, including baseballs and pictures of baseball stars. When he went to a game he liked to get a baseball or something like that signed. I guess it let people know that he was important. One of those baseballs was signed by Steve Garvey. You remember him, played first base for the Dodgers? Garvey didn't just sign his name, he put a date on it—July 5, 1980—the day Lisa Farrow was murdered and the day that Sample said he was at the game. Those tickets that Sample had for an alibi? I'm pretty sure those were my dad's tickets. My father helped put an innocent man in prison for twenty-six years and almost put him in the greenroom at Quentin. I don't know why he would do that, but I have to make it right. I want to talk to Mike Jensen. I need to know why."

O'Hara's face registered his resignation about what was going to happen as he shook his head. He kept silent. He was in.

"Before we talk with Jensen, maybe we need to start with Dolores," Ernie said, "or go back to Alton Grady." Ernie was in.

Both men looked at Jamison. He stared back. They were all in.

Chapter 48

Jamison and Ernie picked up Lorie Grady on their way to see her father while O'Hara started pulling out the files surrounding Jensen's investigation of the murder of Sample. Jamison thought it might be easier to talk to Alton Grady with Lorie there and he asked her to bring the original file on Dolores Sample. That was Lorie's idea. She thought it might jog her father's memory, seeing his old notes.

Her father was right in his usual spot, sitting near the window with the sun streaming in. When he heard his daughter's voice there was a flicker of recognition, but he looked at Jamison and Ernie with confusion. Lorie reminded him that Matt was Roger Jamison's son. The old man sat up a little straighter. "Roger, good man. Good lawyer. I was a lawyer too, you know." He squinted at Jamison, his eyes slightly clouded by the encroachments of age. "You look like Roger."

Lorie took the file on Dolores Sample and put it in her father's lap, flipping it open to his notes with the lines drawing connections between Roger Jamison, Dolores Sample, and Detective Jensen. "Dad, this is part of your file on the Harker case. Do you remember this? Do you remember why you wrote this? Why were there lines between these people? Was there a connection between Roger Jamison and Dolores Sample? Why is there a line to Tommy Sample? Do you remember why you drew that line to Detective Jensen?"

Alton Grady's face lost its vacant expression as he passed his hands over the notes he wrote almost three decades before. What came out were disconnected pieces of memory. "Roger was my friend. There was a woman. I talked to him. Told him people would find out. Detective Jensen knew." There was a cloud of anger that crossed Grady's face and then passed.

"What did he know?" asked Jamison. "Are you saying the detective knew about the woman? What did he know?" The burst of questions seemed to cause Grady to withdraw.

Lorie touched her father's arm. "Dad, what did Jensen know? Did he know about Roger and the woman? That Roger was having an affair?"

"He knew. He was a bastard. I tried to warn Roger. Good man. Bad choices." Grady's eyes closed and his breathing shallowed as his mind moved to somewhere in the past where he was a trial lawyer who could command a courtroom.

Lorie shook her head. "That's it. I'm surprised we got that much. There are good days and bad days but now there are mostly bad days. It's happening so fast. I'm not sure what it all means but it sounds like my father was worried that

Detective Jensen knew about Dolores Sample and would use that to leverage your father. I'm not clear why, though. Maybe because it would get your father to cooperate on Foster? Maybe to get something else out of your dad? My guess is that Jensen was threatening your father for some reason."

Ernie flipped his notebook closed. "We need to go talk to Dolores. Not sure where that will get us. Last time she slammed the door in my face."

↬

They dropped Lorie off and drove past Dolores Sample's home. There was a car in the driveway. Ernie took the lead and rang the doorbell. He instinctively stepped back and adjusted the gun on his hip even though he didn't feel any threat.

For Jamison, it was an unnerving experience coming face-to-face with Dolores Sample. She didn't look much like a femme fatale, which was an image he had built in his mind. He wasn't sure what he expected. He was looking at the "other woman" but she looked more like somebody's mother or grandmother. She was in her late sixties, but she had a figure that insinuated what she must have looked like when she was much younger. Her face was still youthful, although the edges around her eyes hinted at a depth of worldly experience. What he could tell was that this was a woman who was used to men looking at her and could read their faces before they said a word.

She stared directly at Jamison, ignoring Ernie. "So you finally decided to come yourself." It wasn't a question and it wasn't a statement, more of an observation. Dolores opened the door and retreated into the entryway.

She arranged herself on the couch in the living room, moving a few too many decorator pillows aside, never removing her eyes from Jamison. "I met you once, you know. I'm sure you don't remember. You were only six or seven and your father took you to a baseball game. I sat nearby. Roger wanted me to see you. He was very proud of you." She intuited his reaction. "You find that strange that your father would want me to meet you?"

"Frankly, I find the whole thing hard for me to think about. My father, you, it's difficult to process."

"You look like him. In many respects Roger was the best thing that ever happened to me—and the worst."

"Can I ask?" Jamison's discomfort registered in the stiffness with which he sat on the chair across from her.

"Can you ask what? How we met? What was it like? How long were we together? Do you really need to know all of that? I doubt if that's why you're here."

"It's not, but I would like to know." Jamison couldn't restrain himself. Ernie watched with the unease of a person watching a personal moment between two people and knowing he wasn't supposed to be there.

"You didn't know your father very well, did you? I mean, you didn't know him deep down, what kind of man he was, did you?"

"He was my father. I knew him."

"Well, that's an answer, isn't it, Matt? I hope that doesn't bother you, me calling you Matt. When we talked about you that's what we called you. I feel like I know you. Everything you did in school, the difficulties with him that you had and the difficulties with you that he had. The short answer, and all the answer I'm going to give, is that your father and I were together until he died—well over twenty years. I'm guessing that surprises you. It wasn't an affair, Matt. Not for me and not for your father. I doubt if you can understand that. It happens. I worked in a restaurant when we met. He bought this house for me, sent me back to school, helped me become something different. But you should know that I always understood that he wasn't going to leave your mother—or you. Your father was a great man to many people. For me it was enough."

Jamison was surprised that he didn't feel more anger. Perhaps it was the surreal nature of the conversation. It wasn't why he was there, but it was also something that he couldn't ignore.

Ernie intervened. "Mrs. Sample, we need to ask about how your son Rick had baseball tickets that he gave to the police as an alibi for where he was when a murder happened."

It was evident from her lack of reaction that she knew exactly what Ernie was asking about. "Why is that important now? Rick's dead. You never found the man who murdered him. He had his own problems; there was too much of his father in him for it to turn out much different. But he didn't deserve to die in a filthy alley and be left there like trash."

This was why Ernie was doing this and not O'Hara. Ernie could talk to people without them feeling threatened. He drew people out by a combination of deflection and empathy. "Mrs. Sample, we're here because we're investigating who killed your son, but we need to ask about those tickets in order to help us prove it." It wasn't exactly the truth, but it was all the truth she needed to know at the moment. Omission and stretching the truth were also interrogation tools in the hands of a skilled detective. And Ernie was certainly skilled.

Ernie decided to treat his speculation as a fact in order to see the reaction. "We know that you gave those tickets to your son. What we want to know is where did you get them and did you ever meet or talk to a detective Mike Jensen?"

"Who killed my son?"

"We're narrowing it down, but we have new information that will help us."

"Whoever he is I hope he rots in hell. All this time and this never goes away. As for Detective Jensen, yes I met Detective Jensen." Dolores sat straighter on the couch and there was no mistaking her body language as her face flushed.

"He accused Rick of murdering that woman. My son wasn't a murderer. He didn't do that. I gave my son those tickets to make Jensen go away." Ernie kept his face impassive. His speculation had been right. Dolores kept talking. "Besides, the man who killed that woman was convicted and now he's dead too. I read all about it in the paper." She looked over at Jamison. "And I read about you too. I kept up with you and what you've done. It was like reading about Roger."

"Where did you get those tickets from?" Jamison interjected.

"You already know that, or you wouldn't be here. They came from your father. He and I went to that Dodger game, and I kept them. Your father loved the Dodgers. I guess you know that. I kept everything that had to do with your father. Is that what you wanted to hear?"

The raw tension in her voice told Ernie that she was about to end everything right now and they needed a lot more. He needed to put oil in the water before it boiled. "Mrs. Sample, we're not here because you gave those tickets to your son." It was a lie but none of that showed on Ernie's face as he slid around confrontation. "Do you know whether Detective Jensen ever talked to Roger about those tickets?"

Dolores Sample seemed to shrink, her face suddenly aging. "Roger didn't know I gave those tickets to Rick. I was afraid, and I did it but your father didn't know, at least until later. Rick told me that he heard the police were asking questions about him and that poor girl. He wanted me to tell the police I was with him, but I was afraid that would lead to Roger and besides, I was his mother. There had to be something that was solid proof. So, I gave him the ticket stubs if Rick needed something to make the police go away. Then Jensen came around and he started asking questions about those tickets. He knew Rick couldn't afford those tickets and it all just started to go wrong. I had to tell Roger, and then Jensen went to Roger. I don't know how he knew. But by then I knew Jensen wasn't interested in the tickets. *He didn't want my son to be a suspect.* He didn't want anything to raise questions about Harker's guilt. Don't you see? Harker killed that woman, but my son was involved with her too. He would be somebody that Harker's lawyer would try to blame. But those tickets meant he had an alibi. It was only to make sure that Harker couldn't find some way to worm out of it. And Cleary made Roger keep quiet."

"How?"

"Because Cleary knew about Roger and me. He told Roger that if he said anything about the tickets it would all come out about the two of us. Everything would come out. Jensen told him. Roger told me that Cleary was the one who got him to defend Foster, the one that was supposed to have been in the house with Harker. Roger was trying to protect all of us and your mother and you. It didn't hurt anybody. Harker killed that girl. There were two witnesses. Rick was my son. But my son wasn't a murderer."

"You have a grandson named Tommy," Jamison blurted out.

"Why would you ask that?" Dolores's face was ashen.

"We'll need to talk to him."

The sharpness with which she responded caused Ernie's antenna to go up. "I don't have anything more to say to you. I want you to leave now. I don't want Tommy dragged into this. He doesn't have anything he can tell you because he was just a little boy when this happened. He's made a different life for himself. Leave him alone. For your sake and your mother's sake you need to leave this all alone. Nothing is going to come out of this that won't hurt people who don't deserve it." Whether it was instinctive or just the situation, Ernie realized he needed to stop the conversation before Jamison dug himself a hole he couldn't climb out of. And he did.

Chapter 49

Jamison had been surprised that Ernie abruptly stood up when Dolores Sample objected to him talking to Tommy. Ernie thanked Dolores and walked to the front door with Jamison following him. He'd deferred to Ernie's decision because he trusted his judgment but as soon as they got in the car he wanted answers. When they got in the car, he asked one question. "Well?"

"Instinct. There could be a number of reasons why she didn't want us to talk to Rick Sample's kid but it was the way she reacted that told me we needed to know more before we asked more questions. She's feeding us bits and pieces, but if we want the whole truth out of Dolores Sample we will need to know a whole lot that we're only guessing at. We can always come back to her. It isn't like this has to be resolved today. Sometimes you have to pull the thread slowly.

"Whether Harker killed Lisa Farrow or Rick Sample did, they're both dead and Foster's in the joint. So, we're not chasing down a suspect." Ernie looked over at Jamison, who was staring at his notepad instead of Ernie. "Listen to me, Matt. Think about what we heard in there. She says that Cleary helped force cooperation from your father to get Foster to testify. I'm sorry, Matt, but she's saying your father knew that Sample's alibi was bullshit. What you're doing is going to destroy careers, including your father's, not to mention Cleary's, Jensen's, and Gage's and who knows who else's."

Ernie hesitated to carefully frame what he thought was necessary to say next. "It isn't going to be enough to just walk in and say we found out who really murdered Lisa Farrow. We have to prove it. And we have to prove how it happened or the ones who go down on this will be us. All we have right now is what Foster and Stack say but that doesn't prove Harker didn't do it. It just creates suspicion that Sample did it and that isn't going to cut it. And another thing, Matt. It isn't just our careers at risk here. It's your father's reputation also. If this becomes public, no matter what, you're going to have to live with the fallout and you'd better be prepared for it."

⤳

While Jamison was out with Ernie, O'Hara spent several hours at the sheriff's office looking through electronic records and then paper records. It hadn't taken him that long to find what he was looking for but only because he knew where to look. He had a very good idea how files were buried because he'd done it himself.

First, he looked up Foster's arrest record. Those records were kept on a state-wide data base. Foster's record showed an arrest for burglary a week before the bar killing of Rick Sample. With Foster's record, it wasn't hard to figure out that he would have been in custody when Sample was killed. But he wasn't. That meant that either he was simply arrested and then cut loose for lack of evidence or that some judge let him out. With Foster's record that wasn't likely. He pulled the records of the burglary. Foster's fingerprints had been found inside and he had been identified with stolen property. It was a clear-cut case and the only question was how much time Foster would get. And with Foster's record it would be time in the joint.

He dug deeper into the reports. One thing about law enforcement records, whether the records were there or they weren't gave you answers either way. Whether the answers were helpful depended on whether you knew what questions to ask. O'Hara knew what questions to ask and where to look for the answers.

O'Hara walked down to Jamison's office when Ernie let him know they were back. Ernie filled him in while Jamison sat, listening and drawing lines on his legal pad. He hadn't said much after Ernie talked to him in the car and he didn't add anything while Ernie related what Dolores said.

O'Hara took it all in and then explained what he'd found. "I looked up Foster's record. He'd done a burglary that he got arrested for about a week prior to Sample's murder. His prints were in the house he burgled, and they had a picture of him in a pawn shop trying to fence a diamond ring that was taken in the burglary. The case was dead bang. He was in the county jail looking at serious hard time. Stack was in there at the same time. So, I'm guessing that while they were in custody together that Stack told him Sample had threatened him and admitted he killed Lisa. And that gave that scumbag Foster the keys to the city because now he had something to trade. Two things happened. The case had a notation on it that the DA had refused to file it and Foster was released from custody because no more charges were pending. The name that was on the file showing no charges filed by the DA was Mike Jensen.

"Jensen simply made a notation on the file that the DA refused to charge Foster. Both of you know that cases go to the DA and if they get filed the case goes forward. If the DA refuses to charge, then it just goes in the dead records file unless investigation continues. Unless somebody actually looked at the case they would never have any reason to suspect. My guess is that Foster contacted Jensen because he had something to sell. Whatever it was it bought Foster out of ten years hard time for burglary and got him out of custody. But the next question is the murder.

"There isn't a lot in the records, but Jensen was the supervising detective and the records show he put a photo ID spread in front of the bartender at Jack's Place with no ID. But there's no mention of the suspect having a snake tattoo or being a black male. The murder of Rick Sample went into the cold case file along with all the other bar killings that nobody has time to follow up on unless they have a solid lead. Without reports showing that the bartender gave any kind of useful lead or ID, there was nothing there. No reports were ever made even though Jensen was the lead detective and he had to have known Foster's picture should have been in that photo spread. But it wasn't and there's only one reason for that—Mike Jensen. Bottom line: Jensen buried those files. Why is the big question."

Jamison had been listening intently. "And do you have an answer to that question?"

"We'll have to talk to Jensen about that."

Jamison's voice was calm. "And when we do, all hell's going to break loose, so everybody needs to decide right now where they want to be. Look, both of you don't have to stick with me on this. It's my decision. I like to think I'm doing the right thing but that doesn't make it the right thing. Besides, if I make a mistake on this the whole world is going to come down on me and whoever's standing next to me."

Ernie waited for O'Hara to respond. He did. "We both understood that before we started. I'm not going to walk away from you now. As much as I hate to admit it, you're as close to family as I got at the moment, both of you. I already told you that I thought you should drop this but I'm sticking with your call."

Jamison thought he detected a slight quiver of emotion. "Bill, is it possible your heart may actually be in the right place?"

O'Hara shoved an unlit cigar in his mouth before answering. "I prefer to believe that unlike you I don't think with it. Anyway, you're not going to find out for sure until I'm dead."

"I told you before," Ernie said. "I'm all in. Maybe not for the same reasons, but I need to know the answer if I want to sleep at night. I can handle any shit that comes at me. I've been with O'Hara long enough to know that."

"I'll just say that I told you two to do this and you didn't question it."

Ernie choked out a laugh. "Yeah, everyone will believe that."

Chapter 50

Ernie sat in O'Hara's office. Talking to Jamison was one thing but they both knew they needed a private cop discussion to keep things on track. "Okay, so how do we keep Matt from completely blowing his career to hell?" He kept eyeing O'Hara playing with his lighter while keeping his cigar unlit. Ernie couldn't stand O'Hara's cigars any more than Jamison, but he had accepted long ago that O'Hara didn't care and if he didn't smoke in front of you it was because he didn't feel like it.

"There's only one way and even that might not work," O'Hara said as he touched the butane flame of his lighter to the tip of his cigar to warm it evenly. "What I want to know is why did you pull back on Dolores?"

"You caught that, did you?"

"I've been stuck with you as a partner longer than I've been married to any woman. So, what is it?"

"Instinct, I guess. There was just something about the way she reacted that told me there was a raw nerve that had something to do with Tommy. I came back to the office and pulled up some records. It wasn't hard to do."

"And?"

"And Dolores Sample isn't Tommy Sample's grandmother."

O'Hara put his cigar in the ashtray and sat up. "Meaning?"

"Meaning she's his mother."

"His mother?" O'Hara inhaled deeply before asking his next question. "Who else is listed on the birth certificate?"

"You mean who's the father? According to the birth certificate it was Michael Sample, same as Rick Sample. The only problem is Michael Sample was long since gone. I looked that up too. So, unless Michael Sample paid a nocturnal visit, he isn't the father."

"Don't make me guess."

"I don't know the answer to that. I know what I think but there's only one way to find out."

"Does Matt know?"

"I didn't say anything. I guess it will come to the surface soon enough, but it didn't seem like something for casual conversation. For right now I figured I'd just say nothing."

Both men sensed somebody quietly standing at the door. There was no telling how long Jamison had been there. If he heard anything, he didn't react to the conversation. "I want to go talk to Christine Farrow."

⤷

Ernie and Jamison pulled to the curb in a no parking area. That was one advantage to driving the undercover car. There was a cardboard placard in the glove box that read "District Attorney Investigator." It was like parking a squad car in a tow-away zone. Nobody would touch it.

The coffee shop where Christine worked had seen better days, and that was assuming it ever had better days. They walked through the front door and were hit with air heavy with the smell of old grease and working men. A few tables held people talking and the sudden silence was noticeable as heads turned to look at them. In this neighborhood cops stood out like a match flaring in the dark. As far as the people at the tables were concerned, nothing good ever came from cops walking through the door. Heads turned away as if that would hide them from notice.

Christine Farrow was behind the counter pouring coffee. The expression on her face was louder than any words. She obviously didn't want to see them, and she didn't want to be seen with them. But her expression also carried the resignation that she knew it wasn't a choice. She tilted her head toward an area with empty tables and walked over holding a coffeepot. She didn't say anything, waiting for one of them to let her know what they wanted.

Jamison kept his voice subdued. "I need to talk to you."

"The last time you talked to me you said I was lying."

Jamison blanched. She wasn't going to make this easy. He hadn't expected her to. "I didn't say you were lying. I said that it was possible you had been influenced by the process you went through. Look, Christine, we need to talk to you."

While she kept her voice low, the tone was sharp. "Not here and not now. I get off at three o'clock. I don't want to talk to you at all, but I definitely don't want to talk to you here. You should have come to my house if you wanted to talk. All this will do is cause me more trouble."

⤷

At 4:00 p.m. Ernie and Jamison parked outside Christine's house. Little had changed, there were the same patches of dead grass like islands in the dirt, the same bunches of dried foliage that may or may not have once been flowers. Jamison felt a pang of guilt as he walked to the front door. This woman's life had been nothing but struggles that he couldn't even begin to relate to and nothing he was going to do would help her. Ernie knocked and waited.

Christine was still in her uniform from work, the splatters of coffee and various stains telling the story of the breakfasts and lunches she'd served. She left the door open and walked back to the couch that more or less filled the small living room. "I don't want to talk to you, either of you, anymore. I thought I was doing the right thing. All it did was bring it all back. What do you want now?"

"I want to talk to you about Rick Sample."

"Why? That bastard is dead. Harker's dead. I've got nothing left inside me that doesn't hurt. I tried to do what I thought was the right thing, something that would help me get beyond this. My whole life this has been on me." She began to cry and then to convulse as anguish overcame her.

"Christine, I'm sorry. We've kept working on this case and we want to make sure that we know who killed your mother. We've kept investigating and some things have turned up that have caused us to reopen the case. Your testimony is one of the reasons we're doing that. You need closure and we need to know. I want to go over what you remember. I need to do that and you're the only one who was there that can tell me."

Christine raised her head. Her sunken eyes were rimmed with cheap mascara running down in streaks, but all Jamison could see at that moment was the plea for help reflected back—and despair. It made his gut churn. All this case had done was sow destruction in its path, and all that was left now was more destruction reaped by the one left behind. Now he was asking her to go back to the day that began the ruination of her life. Jamison stood up. "I'm sorry, Christine. I shouldn't have come here. I won't put you through any more." He didn't know what else to say. Ernie followed him to the door, the sound of Christine weeping following them.

"If I do this will that be the end? I can't do it without help."

Jamison turned. He wasn't sure if what he felt was empathy or guilt or both. "Tell me what you want."

"If Dr. Vinson will help me, I'll do it."

⌒

Vinson sat behind his desk measuring Jamison and the man sitting next to him, Dr. Aaron Levy. Jamison wanted someone present who could help him decipher what was going on. Vinson finally spoke, addressing Levy. "So, Dr. Levy, how are you? I've been to some of your lectures. You don't think highly of my work."

Levy smiled. "And I've been to some of yours, Dr. Vinson. You don't think highly of my criticisms."

To Jamison it looked like both men were attempting to peer into the psyches of each other with little success. But who could tell. With the exception of Levy, his opinion of psychologists was they just stared at you, unblinking and impassive before they told you that it was your mother's fault or your father's fault or, occasionally, your fault. In Jamison's opinion, they had a pretty good chance of being right given that they'd covered most of the possible causes.

Right now, he wasn't concerned about his opinions of psychology. He needed to make sure that what was going to happen was watched by people he trusted, and Dr. Levy was definitely one of those, not because he was a psychologist, but because he used psychology as a tool for understanding.

Vinson finally addressed the issue of whether he would attempt to draw from Christine's memory in front of Jamison and Levy. In that respect, Dr. Levy understood the issue. He offered his office, which had an observation window that he used for teaching purposes. To the patient, it was a mirror. To those watching, it was a means of learning. Vinson agreed. He would do it. "Maybe, Aaron, you'll see that I'm not a witch doctor."

"And maybe you'll see that I don't hate witches." The smile from both men was forced as they struggled to avoid more personal barbs. Jamison kept his distance. All he cared about was that they agreed to cooperate. He was no longer concerned about whether Christine's statements could be used in court. No matter what she said, the only closure it would provide was whether Rick Harker or Rick Sample was a murderer. Jamison was satisfied that God could sort that out because there was nothing he could do now to either one of them.

↩

Christine sat quietly in an overstuffed chair. The process had taken much less time than Jamison expected. O'Hara and Garcia stood behind him. Vinson nodded toward the mirrored window. He'd taken her through what Levy described as levels of hypnosis necessary to allow what probing Vincent planned to do. Levy whispered that Christine appeared now to be in a deep state of hypnosis, nearing what he called "the third stage." What Vinson was doing was sometimes referred to as age regression. Levy explained that what Vinson claimed he could do was take a patient back to an earlier moment of the patient's life and then slowly draw out the memories that had been buried, taking the patient past the stage where they were watching the memory and put them in the stage where they relived it. It was controversial and criticized by many experts like Dr. Levy, but there was no doubt that it had a somewhat unstable place in accepted treatments.

Christine's eyes were closed and she appeared asleep, but they fluttered open as Vinson began taking her back. What startled Jamison was the way her voice became small and child-like. Levy had said that the literature described this phenomenon in regression therapy and he had seen it demonstrated. He was neither a believer nor an unbeliever. He was a skeptic with concerns about the danger of probing deeply suppressed trauma, but he also had concerns that whether the memory was accurate or not, it would become ingrained indelibly in the mind of the patient as accurate. It was the very concern that Jamison had when he listened to Christine testify and why hypnosis therapy was highly restricted if it was used as a forensic tool. Right now, that wasn't Jamison's concern. Christine was.

Jamison watched tensely as Christine was now removed from all of them as she responded to Dr. Vinson. His voice was subdued and gentle, reminding Christine that they had talked of this before. Vinson began asking about that night, pulling out shreds of memory leading up to what happened to her mother. It was like watching a human being sink into an abyss.

Christine pulled her body up in her chair, curling it into something resembling a fetal position while Vinson reached over and handed her what looked like a shapeless mass of gray fur. Jamison turned, the question written on his face. Levy answered. "Vinson told me he was going to give her a stuffed toy that she had that night. Apparently, she's kept it all these years. He said it helps her to maintain a level of comfort as she talks about what happened. It isn't uncommon to use different items associated with old memories as prompts. It's a stuffed rabbit, or at least that's what it used to be." It was hard to tell what the toy was at this point. Jamison recalled that Gage had talked about the toy and that it was inseparable from Christine when she had testified. It struck him how the most innocuous things could trigger not only the best memories but the worst.

"Bed shaking. Mama crying." Christine's voice became louder, the fear was evident in it. "Rick is yelling at her. He was mean. Mama crying. I'm scared, so scared." Tears were running down Christine's face. Jamison could feel his stomach wrenching with nausea. The psychologists might talk about violence, but they had never really seen it. He had seen it in all of its shades of red and brown and black. They were making Christine see it again, but she had seen it for real and smelled it all. For her the memory was a nightmare that was real.

"Christine, you have your bunny. Hold on to your bunny. Did a man come into your room?"

"Rick, it was Rick. He's breathing on me. He smells. He's breathing on me. I'm so scared. 'It will be all right Christine.' He's lying. I know he's lying. Where's my mama? Give me back Bunny."

Vinson hesitated. Christine was holding the toy so tightly Jamison could see pieces of stuffing sticking out of worn gaps in the fur. "Did Rick take your bunny?"

"He has it. He told me to stop crying. His hands are sticky."

"Why are his hands sticky, Christine?"

"I don't know. It's dark. I can't see. Give me back Bunny." Christine began to cry again.

Jamison nudged Levy. "Tell him to stop."

"It isn't that easy, Matt," Levy said. "He'll have to pull her back slowly." Levy tapped very lightly on the window, giving the signal he had discussed with Vinson, who nodded that he understood. Christine kept talking as Vinson slowly calmed her, but he did ask who Rick was. All Christine said was, "Tommy's daddy."

The process had taken more than an hour, but Levy had told Jamison it would seem like minutes to Christine. Minutes that revisited a ruined life. Slowly Vinson began to pull Christine back, taking her through the years until she was ready. He didn't ask her to remember what she had described. When it was over she looked like someone who had been ill for days.

Chapter 51

Jamison, O'Hara, Levy, and Vinson sat quietly in a small conference room arranged by Levy. Garcia had taken Christine home after she spent more time with Dr. Vinson. Jamison still wasn't sure about the validity of memory under hypnosis, but he was sure that Christine believed it and he hadn't seen anything indicating Vinson had influenced her answer. He asked the psychologist about the stuffed toy.

"She brought it with her after we first met. Apparently, she's kept it all these years and I thought it would help with the therapy. People hold on to all kinds of strange things that they were attached to as children." Vinson pulled it out of a paper bag that he had sitting next to his briefcase and laid it on the table. Closer examination drew out the features in what was an almost shapeless blob of stuffing. It was once a toy rabbit, that much could be made out, but it was so worn and dingy that it was hard to believe it hadn't completely disintegrated with the passage of time. It didn't look like it had ever been washed but it certainly looked like it wouldn't survive washing now.

O'Hara picked up the toy with surprising gentleness. "She said Rick's hands were sticky. My guess is they had blood on them. If he touched this toy, then there might be blood on it and maybe it's his."

Levy said, "That was almost thirty years ago."

"If they can find DNA from some three-thousand-year-old mummy, who knows? We'll have Andy look at it. If there's anything there, he'll find it." O'Hara put it back in the bag Vinson had kept it in. "Don't worry, he won't damage it. At least not in a way that anybody would notice."

⤚

The sheriff's lab was run by Andre Rhychkov. Andy, as he preferred to be called, was a first-generation Russian American. Other than his name, that was the only thing about him that would imply that he was anything other than an American wannabe surfer. His blond hair was cut in a sixties beach boy style that perpetually dropped over his forehead. He wore oversized Hawaiian shirts, jeans, and expensive sneakers with stains from whatever project he was working on. He loved his work and he loved telling people that he was a real forensic analyst, unlike what they saw on television. As soon as he saw O'Hara his eyes fixated on the brown paper bag that O'Hara sat on the disorganized pile of paper on his desk.

"Dude, what you got?" Andy knew O'Hara didn't like to be called "dude" but it entertained him that he could get away with irritating O'Hara, who scared the hell out of almost everyone else. O'Hara ignored the greeting, primarily because he needed Andy's help.

Andy peered into the bag, snapping on a pair of latex gloves. He pulled out the stuffed toy with barely concealed distaste. "Dude, did you find this? It looks like roadkill that's been run over by a truck." He turned the stuffed toy over in his palm. "Guess it's supposed to be a rabbit?"

"It belonged to a little girl whose mother was murdered. I have reason to suspect that it might have blood on it from the murderer."

Andy handled the stuffed toy with a little more reverence. "How long ago, man? I don't see anything on here that looks recent."

"Twenty-six, twenty-seven years ago."

Andy looked incredulous. "Dude, what do you think I am? I mean I hope you aren't looking for a miracle. This thing looks like it's been handled by everyone including Moses. And I know it wasn't kept in that bag all that time. It may be impossible to find anything." Andy saw the look of impatience on O'Hara's face. "I can look. You got blood samples for me to compare if I find anything?"

"First tell us if you can find blood and do anything with it. The killer is supposed to have picked it up after he murdered a woman. I'm pretty sure he had blood on his hands."

"Okay, it could be there but it's going to be way degraded so don't expect much and don't expect it quick." He examined it more closely. "How careful do I have to be with it? What's the crime number for my report?"

"Do your best to avoid damaging it any more than you have to. It means a lot to somebody." O'Hara hesitated. "Andy, this is a personal favor, understand? No crime number for right now. Just call me. I'll owe you."

"You already owe me, man. All you guys owe me but you never pay. I got Giants tickets I'm owed from last season." He could see O'Hara's jaw beginning to lock up. "Okay, I'll call if I find anything. Do you know if the killer was bleeding or is it just the vic's blood?"

"Don't know. If he bled and it's mixed with the victim's, can you do it?"

Andy grinned. "If it's there I'll figure it out. It won't be clean. I like challenges."

"Yeah, so do I. Just remember to keep it between us."

⌒

"So, now what?" Ernie asked O'Hara as they sat in a dark corner of Harrington's, a local hangout that catered to cops. The bar kept the food simple, the beer cold, and the place dark, and that was good enough to keep it full. The rattle of dice could be heard in the background as leather dice cups slammed against table tops to determine who was going to pay.

"Not a lot of options," O'Hara answered. "If Sample committed the murder, and it looks like he did, then we're going to have to prove it decisively. We need hard evidence linkage. Jimmy Stack's word isn't going to hold up just because he says Sample told him he killed Lisa Farrow. Foster's no help. Who knows whether he's telling the truth. Any way you look at it he's a lying asshole, but it seems pretty clear that he told Mike Jensen and Gage that he was so drunk he was blacked out. About all we can say is that he probably lied when he said Harker was the one—because those tapes show he was so drunk he can't remember anything—and that he kept telling Jensen and Gage that. I think it's pretty obvious that Foster killed Sample because he thought Sample killed that girl based on some weird convict code about Christine. If Sample killed that girl, then nobody is going to get too riled up about retribution, but if he didn't that's another story. It's also clear that Sample's alibi was phony and if Jamison's old man didn't help Dolores do it, he certainly knew it when the case went to trial. This is the worst kind of case."

"You mean doing the right thing even though it's not the result we want?" Ernie smiled with what could be confused for a grimace. "Yeah, that can get in the way of the result sometimes." He puffed out his cheeks and blew out a stream of air. "Well, it won't help you and me with career options but it will definitely crush Matt. Without something definite, Gage and Cleary will destroy him. He's hell bent on getting to the truth, but even if we get there, I agree it needs to be solid. Gage and Cleary hiding the tapes isn't going to prove Harker didn't do it and they'll just blame Jensen or say it was a mistake because there was so much evidence. Jamison will be out of a job and you and I will be working bad checks."

O'Hara continued. "Jensen knew that Foster killed Sample and he covered it up. We can prove that. And I'm guessing he may have told Foster to do it. If he didn't tell him to do it, he certainly didn't have a problem with it. And the only reason for that is because he was afraid it would all come out about the tapes and him lying in court. Unless Andy can come up with blood on that mangy rabbit we got nothin.'"

"We can wait to see what Andy finds or we can go talk to Mike Jensen," Ernie muttered. "I vote for talking to Mike. We're not going to stop Matt from pushing this so we may as well do our job and take it back to him"

O'Hara took a sip of beer. "Maybe if we give Matt the answers we find, he'll decide we'll never get the answers he needs. But if we talk to Jensen, you know Jensen's going to talk to Gage."

"Maybe," Ernie agreed. "But he also has reasons not to talk to Gage. First we have to ask."

⌒

O'Hara and Ernie sat in the car. The drive to Jensen's home had been mostly silent and they hadn't said much once they parked. They were waiting because both knew any way it turned out the discussion with Jensen was going to be bad. After all, he was one of them.

As O'Hara walked past the window on the way to the front door of the home he caught the image of Jensen sitting in his chair. They locked eyes through the glass. Jensen wasn't smiling, and neither was O'Hara. As he reached for the doorbell, they both heard Jensen yell, "It's open."

Jensen waved them over to the couch across from his chair. There was a glass filled with ice and from the color of the contents it was easy to guess it was straight bourbon. A newspaper was unfolded next to the drink. Jensen stayed silent, appraising the two men sitting across from him for a minute before speaking in a rasping voice grated raw by cigarettes. "I'm glad you came Willie, instead of bringing anybody else. I appreciate the courtesy."

"What do you mean, Mike?"

Jensen picked up his glass and took a sip. "Don't do that, Willie. Don't work me."

O'Hara didn't respond, letting Jensen talk. "Margaret called me. You stay in touch with the old group, you know? She knew you were looking for something involving me and she knew it wasn't good. You were always smooth with the ladies, Willie, but not that smooth. She still make those cookies? I haven't seen her in a long time. Should have visited but I stay pretty much to myself now days. I didn't tell you that I got lung cancer." He tapped his hand on a pack of cigarettes sitting near him. "I'm not sure which is worse, going this way or with the .357 option. So far, I'm willing to wait it out."

O'Hara let the last comment hang in the air for a moment. "I'm sorry to hear that, Mike. You getting treatment?"

"Nah. I've seen too many men end up just skin and bones fighting the inevitable. I got nothin' to keep me going, not even a dog. Now is just as good as later. Can't stop the reaper, you know?" He took another sip from his glass, coughed harshly, and tapped out another cigarette. "Margaret said you got the tapes?" He stared hard at O'Hara, letting O'Hara and Garcia know he knew why they were there and he was ready.

O'Hara didn't miss a beat. "Yeah, we've got the tapes. I'm surprised, Mike, that you didn't take care of that."

"You're right. It was a loose end. Got old I guess. Is that why you're here? You think that makes a difference now?"

"Well you did lie."

"Wasn't the first time. But it was always for a good cause—well, almost always. Why does anybody care?"

"The kid cares."

"Jamison? Why? Harker's dead. Sample's dead. The case is dead."

"Not the Sample case."

"Rick Sample was a scumbag. He ended up like a scumbag should—spread out in an oversize trash can. Nobody gave a shit then and nobody gives a shit now. Is that what this is all about? You here about some Saturday night bar killing?"

"I'm here because you knew about that bar killing and you knew Clarence Foster did it—you covered it up." O'Hara hesitated. "Or did you do more Mike?"

"Meaning what?"

"Meaning did you send Foster out to kill Rick Sample?"

"Now why would I do that?"

"You'd do it because you found out that Sample had admitted the killing to Jimmy Stack and if that came out, then everything you'd done would come out, the tapes, the perjury, everything. The capstone of your career, solving the Farrow murder, and it was all a lie. An innocent man sent to prison on perjured testimony and suppression of evidence. I know you covered up Sample's murder. I pulled all the reports. I talked to the bartender from that night. He gave you Foster's description. He remembered the snake tattoo on Foster's hand. And I know you kicked the shit out of Jimmy Stack and told him to keep his mouth shut about what Sample told him."

Jensen started laughing and then had a coughing fit. "I didn't send Foster to do that. I may not have given a shit that he did it but I didn't tell him to do it. That's not something I'd do, Willie. You should know that. I do have limits, although I didn't lose any sleep over Sample getting killed. What is it you always used to say? One less asshole in the world."

"But you did know that Foster did it, didn't you?"

"Yeah, I knew."

"Then tell me this, Mike. Why did you let Foster out of jail? I know you did because your signature is on the release papers. The case was a solid burglary. Why did you let him out if it wasn't because of what he told you about Stack?"

"It was because of what he told me about Stack. That and the fact that he was talking about telling people that he lied when he testified about Harker. So, I let him out. It was a two-bit burglary, Willie. It wasn't worth my whole career. I didn't know he'd kill Sample. But when he did, I was in the same boat so I let it go. Sample was a lowlife. If he killed Lisa, then he got what he deserved and if he didn't, then who was going to miss him? I couldn't change any of it. If Foster talked, all the shit was going to fall on me. It didn't make any sense for me to let that happen."

"You could have changed things for Harker. He was in prison."

"As far as I'm concerned Harker was a murdering son of a bitch and the rest of this is just garbage. Nothing I did would change any of that. Guilty is guilty. How you get there is just lawyer bullshit. Jamison won the case on that habeas corpus hearing. That should be the end of it. Why's Jamison still pushing this?"

"You know why."

"His father? Is that it?"

"Blood runs deep."

"Does Jamison have any idea how deep?"

"Meaning?"

"Meaning Tommy Sample—or don't you know about that, yet?"

Ernie interjected. "We know that Dolores Sample isn't his grandmother, she's his mother."

"You know who the father is?"

"Do you?"

Jensen choked out a laugh and began coughing again. "Roger Jamison tried to live with that secret, but after I looked at the birth certificate I put two and two together. He thought he was careful but there were rumors. It was a much smaller town then and you know how cops gossip, especially about defense lawyers. I heard about it and sniffed around. Besides, have you ever seen that kid? Looks just like Roger. He didn't deny it when I confronted him about it. I'll give him some credit. He didn't admit it either."

"And you used that to get what you wanted."

"Hell yes, I used it. We needed something from Roger and I had him by the balls. Hell yes, I used it."

"Who is 'we'?"

"You after them, Willie, or you after me?"

"We're not after anybody. We want the truth. We'll sort the rest of it out later."

"Well, I guess it doesn't make that much difference now. It was Cleary—now Justice Cleary. He needed Foster to testify and he needed him to be cooperative, so he needed a cooperative lawyer. He also needed to keep out that bullshit alibi of Sample's. That just made the water murky. We were convinced Harker did it and Cleary wanted to make sure that nothing interfered with convicting that son of a bitch. Foster said he did it and so did the victim's kid. All that would have happened with those tapes is create doubt, and Cleary didn't want that. Those tapes were just Foster sniveling and trying to avoid admitting what he did. So, Roger was perfect. Big-time lawyer represents Foster and makes the deal for his testimony. We keep our mouths shut about where those tickets came from and Roger Jamison's little mistake keeps running around on the QT. Everybody's happy. Cleary's a hero to his boss. Harker gets convicted and Roger gets to go on as Mr. family man. And now Cleary goes to Washington and Gage gets to be attorney general and then governor and I get this." Jensen held up his glass and drained it. "You going to pull the pin on me, Willie? It's a house of cards and nobody is going to come out a winner, but I guarantee Jamison is going to come out a loser for sure."

Jensen's hand slid down inside the cushion of his chair. It was a careful movement. O'Hara's eyes caught the subtle gesture, sensing his own nine-millimeter automatic nesting in his hip holster. He also felt the weight of the Walther that was against his ankle. "Don't be foolish, Mike."

"You going to arrest me?"

"No. At least I have no plan to."

"Who else does?"

"The kid possibly. After all, you did lie. But I'll talk him out of it."

Jensen pulled his hand back into open view. "Yeah, so did Clinton about the blue dress. Like I said, it wasn't the first time. But there's a lot of lying that went on in this case. You know how that works. If all you got is Jimmy Stack you don't have shit. I used to be a homicide detective. Willie. I helped train you. You didn't come in here because you had anything. You were fishing and you're still fishing. I get it. At least you treated me with some fucking respect and didn't try to mess with me like some perp. Wouldn't have worked anyway.

"Let it go, Willie. You and Ernie need to let this case die and so does Jamison or all the shit in the system is going to come down on his head—and yours. Let it go. It won't be the first time"—Jensen looked sharply at O'Hara—"and you and I both know it. The right result isn't all black-and-white. Some things just need to be overlooked." Jensen began violently coughing again. "Now you need to leave me alone. I got a busy day planned."

O'Hara and Ernie let themselves out of Jensen's house and walked across the street to O'Hara's car. Ernie turned to O'Hara. "If I ever get like that just do me a favor and shoot me."

"Same for me." O'Hara cocked his thumb and squeezed his trigger finger. "He was a righteous cop once. But he isn't the first old cop I've seen that burned himself out and stopped thinking about the right way to do things. They get so they just think about the result and justify everything else."

"Are we that much different?" Ernie said quietly.

"Partner, I know you are. I hope I am. Because if we're not, then for us looking at Mike Jensen is like looking in a mirror and seeing the future."

Chapter 52

O'Hara walked back to the crime lab and stood silently for a minute watching as Andy stared into a microscope. He had the message on his answering machine. Andy had found something. Finally, he cleared his throat and Andy's head popped up. The forensic analyst pushed back the mop of blond hair hanging over his forehead and grinned. "Well, I want you to tell me that I'm the king of forensics."

"And that would be because why?" O'Hara wasn't in a patient mood but he needed Andy, and if he had found something he was entitled to crow a little bit.

"Because not one in ten guys could have done it, but you have me."

"Right, we have you, king of forensics. Okay, tell me what you got."

"I found blood on that stuffed rabbit. Not much. Whoever touched it picked it up around the neck. There was blood down in the fold. I'm guessing the rest of it was rubbed off, but I found it. King of forensics."

"Is there enough there that you can identify who it came from?"

"The toy was filthy. The kid who had this must have dragged it everywhere but there was enough blood to do a DNA test. It was very degraded, but I was able to retrieve mitochondrial DNA."

"What's that?"

"As blood or other tissue deteriorates and degrades because it's biological in nature, bacteria attack it, destroying some of its distinctive characteristics. Typically, the last part of human remains are bones and hair, sometimes just degraded bits of blood, but if you are very good, which I am by the way, you can retrieve mitochondrial DNA. It is the mother of DNA."

"The mother?"

"Yes, because it's carried by the mother and passed on through her. In degraded blood samples, which this is, the most likely DNA trace that will be found is mitochondrial, which is one portion of the total DNA that would be found in a properly preserved biological sample. We can get it from old bones found years after the person dies, for example. We compare the mitochondrial DNA known to come from the mother or someone linked to the mother and see if it compares to the person we are testing in order to see if they are related. I could compare the mother to the remains of a suspected missing child or I could compare a child's to what are believed to be the remains of a mother or a sister or brother. That's one of the reasons we take DNA samples from soldiers and if they are missing we can link them if they are found years later. That is if you can give me maternal DNA samples to test against. Either get me a whole sample of the blood of persons you suspect or get me a sample of a person maternally linked. In other words, from their mother or a sister or brother. And of course, being king of forensics I can do this from a saliva swab if you can only get that."

"So, if we get the child's DNA sample you could tell if the blood came from someone she was related to, such as her mother, if her mother was the victim?"

"That's right. But the blood sample I found was mixed. Whoever picked up that stuffed toy had the blood of other people on their hand. I can't tell whose blood until I get samples to test against, but I can tell you it was from three different people."

O'Hara's immediate reaction was consistent with the surprise in his voice. "Three? What do you mean? You found blood traces from three different people?"

"That's right. Whoever picked up that toy had blood from several people on their hands, not a lot, but enough. I can guess that since it's a murder scene, some of the blood is from the victim but whoever had the victim's blood on their hands also touched the blood of somebody else or maybe were bleeding themselves. So, whatever happened, at least three people bled and that blood was on the hands of the person who picked up the toy. I have to do some more tests. First you get me the samples. I take it the little girl's mother was the victim?" Andy hesitated, then asked what he suspected. "This is the Harker case, isn't it?" O'Hara didn't respond. Andy pressed the issue. "I thought that case was closed."

"Like I said, this is a personal favor between us and nobody else. Nobody. Agreed?"

Andy was silent, his eyes focusing on O'Hara, squinting before answering. "Agreed. But if there are any questions I say you asked, okay? Then you explain why you asked—and you owe me."

"Is there anything else?"

"Well, I can't be absolutely positive, but I would say there's a high probability that one person was black."

O'Hara's jaw tightened. It was like a dark cloud crossed over him. "What do you mean black?"

"I mean black—African American. The genetic markers have patterns and those patterns show up in higher percentages in different ethnic or racial groups. That's how they do genealogical tracing. I mean very few Americans are just one ethnic or racial group. We're mutts. Well, you're a mutt. Nothing personal but I'm not a mutt. I'm a Russian."

Andy saw the scowl building on O'Hara's face. He made an immediate concession to avoid O'Hara's well-known intolerance for humor at his expense, sensing that there was something he wasn't seeing. "Well, maybe a little bit of a mutt. I'm probably related somewhere to Genghis Khan. I'm sure it would be somebody famous." Andy laughed and pushed the hair off his forehead. "But if the parents had mixed ethnicity, you can kind of backtrack and tell the probabilities of ethnic and racial history or you can tell that the genetic history is very specific to a region. It would be better if I had the father's but so far, I'm sure one of the people was African American or at least part. Was one of the suspects black?"

"I'm not ready to answer that yet. I owe you. Now explain to me how I get the samples." It had already been a long day. He needed to get back. Jamison was waiting for answers and he didn't have any good ones to give. He had to get those samples and he didn't want to deal with that explanation. But he also had to have answers from a man he'd talked to already and who had misled him multiple times. That wasn't something you did with O'Hara. Not if you were hoping for a good outcome.

〜

Ernie had waited until O'Hara finished with Andy before going in to talk to Jamison. He had decided to wait on the issue of who Tommy Sample's father was until his options ran out. It was a family matter that he not only respected, he knew it would probably stagger Jamison.

The two detectives went over Jensen's statements with Jamison, and then O'Hara dropped the bombshell that the blood on the rabbit included the blood of a black man. That could only mean one person, Clarence Foster.

Jamison's reaction was more subdued than either investigator expected. All that had happened was that more questions had been created. Until they got back the DNA comparisons there was nothing to which they could definitely point. Jamison was very familiar with the use of mitochondrial DNA, having attended multiple courses on it as well as used it in a murder case several years before where the body was discovered in a highly decomposed state.

He turned to O'Hara. "We need a sample of Harker's blood and I'm guessing that the coroner will probably have that or a tissue sample of some kind. Okay, Ernie, you go get a swab from the inside of Christine's cheek. Check with Andy on the proper way to do it but I know it isn't very technical. Just make sure you do it carefully. We can compare that to the blood on that stuffed toy for her mother's blood." That leaves Foster and either Dolores or Tommy Sample. See if Dolores will cooperate but if not, then let's get it from her grandson, Tommy. That should work." Both investigators glanced at each other but said nothing while Jamison continued. "As for Foster, before we go back and requisition that son of a bitch, I want you to check in the Department of Justice files to see if they've already done a DNA analysis of him."

O'Hara waited until Jamison was finished before asking, "What do we do about Mike Jensen? He might call Gage or even Cleary. We can't keep this whole thing quiet much longer."

"I don't think Jensen is going to call anybody. If he does, he does and I'll deal with it. But we know he covered up a murder and we know he concealed those tapes. Going to Gage isn't going to help him because they'll just blame him. You check back with him and remind him to keep his mouth shut if he has any plans of making this work out. I'm not sure yet what we do with him but for right now we remind him that you're his best friend. We're going to need him if this gets any uglier and he's going to need us."

Ernie asked, "Anything else?"

"I'm going to go talk to Paul Carter."

"Foster's lawyer?" O'Hara exclaimed. "Why would you want to do that?"

"Because he's the one who tipped me off about there being other interrogations with Foster and I want to know if there's anything else."

"Boss, you do realize he'll just tell Foster to stop talking to us."

"Bill, I saw Carter in court this morning. He already knows about you talking to Foster and he knows you didn't read him his rights. We don't need anything from Foster to nail him on killing Sample. He isn't going to admit it anyway. We need him on the rest of this. I need to know what's in my father's file on Foster and Carter has that."

Chapter 53

Carter sat in a dark booth at the back of the Cosmo. He waved Jamison over. There was a beer in front of Carter and a second one already on the table. Jamison nodded toward the second beer. Carter said, "I ordered for you. It's still cold. The waitress just brought it." Carter tapped his fingers on the table, waiting for Jamison to open the discussion. It was almost part of the lawyer DNA. If the other lawyer wants something from you, wait until they get around to telling you what it is before you offer anything.

"Thanks for seeing me," Jamison said. "I hear you did a good job on that Rodriquez rape case."

"I still lost."

"That doesn't mean you didn't do a good job. It just means he was guilty."

"Yeah, I had to take a shower after the verdict. Son of a bitch creeped me out every time I sat next to him."

"But you'll still argue for a new trial and a lesser sentence, right?"

Carter grinned. "That's my job. I don't have to like them, just defend them." Carter resumed tapping his fingers on the table, waiting.

Jamison deliberated before speaking. "Paul, off the record. I know that your client gave a statement to Gage and Cleary that he didn't know who killed Lisa Farrow because he was so drunk. And I know that interview disappeared. Alton Grady never saw it. Nobody saw it. But there's more here. I know your client killed Richard Sample and I'm guessing that's what he admitted to you. I'm not asking for any big reveal. I'm telling you right now that we can prove that, just so you know where you stand. How much do you know about the Harker case?"

"I read the file, the police reports. And now I know for sure that Harker didn't get a fair trial. Pretty serious stuff. Deliberate suppression of evidence in a capital case."

Jamison wasn't going to be baited. He left out disclosing any information about Sample. "The little girl had a stuffed toy, a rabbit. There's blood on it that our forensic guy recovered. We don't have the match yet but we do know that it includes the blood of a black man. My guess is that it's going to be your client's blood."

Carter's eyes narrowed. "What do you want, Matt? My client didn't kill Lisa Farrow. I'm convinced he was so drunk he didn't remember what happened but he's not a murderer. I've defended plenty of those guys."

"He killed Sample."

"Maybe he did and maybe he didn't, but you know what I mean. Whoever killed Lisa Farrow was one sick, cold-blooded son of a bitch. What he did to that woman and leaving that little girl in that house? It turned my stomach. Foster isn't that kind of guy. You and I've both seen those guys and that isn't Clarence. He's a two-bit criminal. Tell me what you really want."

"I need to know, Paul, is there anything in my father's file that shows that he thought or knew that somebody else killed Lisa Farrow?"

Carter's head rocked back. "Wait, where's that coming from? Like who? Are you saying you think that Harker didn't commit that murder?"

"No, but I need to know. Is there anything in that file that would indicate that my father thought that somebody else committed the crime?"

Carter was silent for almost a minute as he deliberated with himself over what to say. Finally, he broke his silence. "Your father knew that Foster had given a statement that wasn't in the reports. He knew that Foster told Gage and Cleary that he was so drunk he didn't know who committed that crime." Carter hesitated before continuing, weighing his breach of attorney-client privilege. He could see that anguish building in Jamison's eyes. "Matt, your father had no way of knowing what Foster did or didn't do. Getting immunity for Foster protected him from a charge of being an accessory or maybe even aiding and abetting a murder. You know as well as I do that defendants seldom tell the whole truth to their lawyers. I would have done the same thing."

"I can't discuss everything with you, Paul. But I don't think you would have done the same thing."

"Meaning what?"

"Meaning if you had evidence Harker was innocent or didn't get a fair trial, you wouldn't have let him be convicted of a crime he didn't do."

First shock and then compassion crossed Carter's face. "Matt, you think your father had reason to believe Harker was actually innocent?"

Jamison didn't answer. Instead he said, "You going to show me my father's file?"

"You know I can't do that, Matt. I've already crossed too many lines. What I told you is between us. I'm not going to give you anything that might hurt my client. Don't ask unless you're willing to give immunity."

"No immunity, but I'm not saying we're going to do anything about Sample either. We'll see." Jamison stood up and threw a five-dollar bill on the table. "Thanks Paul, I owe you."

"No, you don't owe. I'm sorry I couldn't help you more. Good luck, Matt."

⌐⌐

When he came back into the office Jamison had a note on his desk to see O'Hara. He walked down to find Ernie and O'Hara talking quietly. O'Hara said, "There were still blood and tissue samples from Harker, so I got what they said Andy would need for a DNA test. I checked and there wasn't any immediate family. There's a cousin who lives in Ohio. Apparently, Harker's mother had a brother who had a son. I called. He wasn't happy to hear anything about Harker but he said if we needed it he would give us a sample, so I made arrangements for that just in case. Anyway, it's going to take a couple of days for the results to come back. But we have a little problem with the rest of it."

Ernie interjected. "Yeah, I got the sample from Lisa, but Dolores isn't around. House is locked up tight and there were some newspapers on the porch, so she hasn't been there for a few days."

"So, we get it from Tommy, her kid," said Jamison. "That should do it. I don't really want to talk to her anyway. You said her kid's a lawyer in the public defender's office in Sacramento. I'll go with you. Maybe he knows something. He'll know he'll have to give us a sample one way or the other."

Both investigators looked at each other. Ernie shrugged. "Suit yourself, but it isn't necessary. I can do it."

Jamison shook his head. "I need to get out of the office. Call ahead and make arrangements." He picked up a vibe from Ernie that he wasn't interested in company. "You got a problem with me going?"

"No problem." Ernie glanced over at O'Hara. "Okay, I'll make the calls."

"Bill," Jamison asked, "can you go back to Mike Jensen? I want to know exactly what he and my father discussed, and I want to know more about Cleary."

"I don't think he's going to be very cooperative, Boss."

"Use your charm."

⤚

Ernie was unusually quiet on the drive to Sacramento. Tommy Sample, "Tom" as he now referred to himself, was in trial. He had asked why they needed a DNA sample from him and Ernie said it had to do with the murder of Richard Sample. He didn't imply that Richard was Tommy's father. He didn't know what exactly Tommy Sample knew but he thought it was unlikely that Tommy thought Richard was his father as opposed to the Mike Sample listed on his birth certificate. He was pretty sure none of the rest of the history of the Harker case had been shared with Tom. He was more worried about the reaction of Jamison and whether he should say anything. He decided against it. He could be wrong although all his instincts told him he wasn't.

Jamison and Ernie walked into the waiting room of the Sacramento Public Defender's Office. They both stood out like a red light on a dark night. The people in the waiting area turned their heads away, reading "cops" simply from the way they looked. Ernie asked for Tom Sample and said they had an appointment. The receptionist said he was still in court and they might have to wait a considerable period, but they were welcome to have a seat. Both men decided to go to the courtroom, rather than wait.

Tom Sample was standing and speaking to the judge when they walked in. He began pacing behind the counsel table as he spoke. Ernie almost instinctively took in the features of people. Tom Sample was a little heavier than Jamison and his hair was lighter, but it was clear to Ernie that he was looking at someone who could easily pass for Jamison's brother. Whether it was clear to Jamison he didn't want to ask.

Ernie shifted his gaze to his left. Jamison's jaw was locked tight and Ernie could see his face drained of color. Ernie whispered, "You want to wait outside?"

Jamison cleared his throat and wiped at his eyes. "No, I'm going to stay and watch. We need to get the DNA."

Tom Sample finished and picked up his file while his client was led out the back door of the courtroom, presumably to a holding cell or a chain gang of other men going back to the jail from their court appearances. His eyes scanned the courtroom and stopped when he saw Jamison. Tom looked at him with a quizzical expression, and then dropped the file into his briefcase and walked toward the front door of the courtroom.

Jamison caught up with him. "Tom Sample? I'm Matt Jamison, Tenaya County District Attorney Office. My investigator contacted you about taking a DNA sample?"

Sample kept staring intently at Jamison. "Right, let's go to my office and you can explain what all this is about." He walked ahead while Jamison and Ernie followed.

Jamison and Ernie sat down in the small cluttered office. Files were stacked on the floor and on the side of the desk. "Not like the DA's office, I'm guessing? Somehow the county always treats DAs a little better than public defenders, but I guess that goes with the territory. So, what have you got on my brother's murder? It's been a long time. And how is a DNA sample from me going to help?" Sample kept staring at Jamison's face. "My mother told me that you talked to her. So why don't you tell me what this is really about? She said you think Richard may have killed somebody. Is that it?"

Ernie started to answer but Jamison cut him off. "We have blood at a crime scene from almost thirty years ago. We need to know whether it's Richard's. The only way we can do that is to get a DNA sample from either your mother or you."

"Richard didn't kill anybody. I defend a lot of people, Mr. Jamison. My brother wasn't a murderer."

"We need to get the DNA sample to clear that up. Another man was convicted of the crime but questions have come up. The DNA will hopefully resolve them. I wouldn't have come to you except your mother wasn't at home and we need the sample quickly."

"My mother's on vacation." Sample didn't offer information as to where. "This has upset her and I don't want her bothered. I'll give you the sample. You could get it anyway and I'd just as soon this was all done quietly. My brother's history isn't a job reference I want passed around."

Sample pursed his lips before speaking further. "You're Roger Jamison's son, aren't you? I knew your father when I was a boy. He was a friend of my mother's. Maybe you didn't know that. I studied some of his cases in my trial practice class in law school. He was a great lawyer. It always surprised my classmates that I knew him. It must be hard to stand in his shadow."

Jamison didn't answer immediately. "I got out of his shadow a long time ago, Mr. Sample. Let's take care of the DNA. Ernie will swab the inside of your cheek."

Outside the public defender office, Jamison put his hands on the wall, breathing slowly. He had watched Tom Sample move around the courtroom. He recognized the mannerisms and the cadence of speech. He wasn't angry so much as numb. One more fracture in his father's pedestal. Thoughts of his mother flashed across his brain. What was he going to tell her? Then he thought about the man he had watched. What was he going to tell him? He realized Jensen knew, Cleary knew and Gage, his boss, knew. He suspected Ernie knew, and if Ernie knew then O'Hara knew. God only knew how many other people were aware. But it was clear what Cleary and Jensen had used against his father. It wasn't just the tickets. It was the existence of a son he had kept in the shadows.

The two of them drove back from Sacramento, miles passed silently before Jamison blurted out, "You knew, didn't you?" His voice was accusatory.

"Knew what?"

"Don't screw with me, Ernie. He looks just like me."

"I suspected. I wasn't sure. I looked at his birth certificate. Dolores isn't his grandmother like we were led to believe, and Richard wasn't his father, he was his brother. I didn't want to say anything. I figured it was best to let it stay buried if it could." Ernie reached over and put his hand on Jamison's shoulder. "I'm not sure what to say, Matt. What do you want to do?"

"Does he know?"

"You mean Tommy? I don't know. The man listed on his birth certificate is Richard's father, but he was long gone when Tommy came along. It wasn't hard to figure out. But I doubt if anybody ever told him. I'm guessing he didn't know. Whether he suspects now, I don't know either. The DNA will tell us, I guess."

While Jamison and Ernie were in Sacramento, O'Hara drove over to Mike Jensen's house. He needed to know what Jensen was going to do. When he walked to Jensen's front door, he heard, "It's open."

Jensen was sitting in the same chair he sat in each of the other times O'Hara had seen him, same glass with ice and bourbon, same overflowing ashtray. For the first time O'Hara saw a small oxygen cylinder on a little wheeled cart near the chair. It always amazed him that people would continue smoking even when they needed oxygen to breathe.

Jensen took a sip from his glass and inhaled deeply from the remains of a cigarette. The wheezing was noticeable as was the hacking cough that came with it as he blew out a stream of smoke. "You'll excuse me if I don't get up. So, Willie, what brings you back? You going to arrest me? Maybe you should just cuff me to my oxygen tank. I'm not much of a flight risk."

"I'm not going to arrest you, Mike. But I need to know something. Have you called anyone about this?"

"Meaning have I called a lawyer or have I called Bill Gage?"

"I know you well enough, Mike, to know you haven't called a lawyer."

"No, I didn't call Gage. What's the point? I wouldn't hurt you, Willie, and you've figured out that if any of this gets out a lot of people are going to get hurt. I'm no informant and I won't live long enough for you to try to make me testify. Is that it? You want to know if I plan to admit that I hid evidence and covered up a murder? I'm not sorry about what I did. But I did it and I'll face whatever the consequences are, but it won't be in any courtroom. You won't make me do that would you, Willie?"

"I wouldn't, but I don't control it."

"Well I do. It's got to end sometime, Willie." Jensen's hand moved under a folded newspaper and slipped out an old .38 detective special. He held it loosely, intently watching O'Hara.

O'Hara didn't move. "Mike, I don't believe you'd do anything that stupid."

"Don't worry, Willie. I'm not going to shoot you. But I will leave you with the mess." Jensen shoved the short barrel into his mouth before O'Hara could react. The sound of the gunshot reverberated through the small room. O'Hara had risen slightly but sat back down on the couch, staring at the remains of a man he had worked with. He didn't bother to check to see if Mike had been successful. It wasn't the first time O'Hara had seen the results of a fellow cop swallowing a gun. He suspected it wouldn't be the last.

Chapter 54

The news about Jensen shook Jamison. Without Jensen, all that was left was the DNA and the tapes. And a whole lot of still unanswered questions. He'd worked for a few days on an upcoming trial and tried to push the Harker case out of his mind. He wasn't successful. He still didn't know the DNA results. But there was one more person to talk to.

Jamison stood outside the entry doors to what was called impressively the Renaissance Plaza Building. But any renaissance was long past. The building could charitably be described as having "gone to seed" but it still held a group of tenants, mostly lawyers with marginal practices and one-person real estate operations that wanted to look more substantial than they were, at least if you only saw their address instead of what was at that address.

This was the location for the law offices of Walker Stevenson, formerly a judge of the Superior Court of Tenaya County, California, and now an attorney who couldn't sit down at a legal function without someone bringing up that he was the one who disregarded the jury's death sentence for Richard Harker. He had acted out of conscience when the mob was only interested in vengeance. To the uninformed and to those who did not have to take responsibility for sentencing a man to death, Walker Stevenson had committed the unforgivable. There would be no blood.

In the ensuing public furor and an election long on criticism and short on logic, Walker Stevenson lost his seat on the superior court. He now lunched in the back tables at bar functions with empty seats on either side of him, as close as you could come to being a legal pariah.

Jamison had debated talking to Stevenson but had decided he needed to know. Why did a highly regarded jurist set aside the death penalty in a case that cried out for the harshest punishment? It cost him his esteemed place in the legal community and relegated him to the bottom tier of lawyers. His act of conscience broke Walker Stevenson, and now the same case was breaking Jamison, although Jamison didn't flatter himself that he acted only from a sworn sense of responsibility.

Jamison walked out of the sixth-floor elevator, the bronze-faced doors, which retained an air of tarnished elegance. The hallway was lit by sconces that had not escaped the ravages of time. Here and there bare candle bulbs glowed, their glass covers long missing. It wasn't an appearance that invited confidence, unlike the rich carpets and paneled walls of uptown legal bastions.

Jamison couldn't help thinking that the price of Stevenson's apparent act of judicial principle had been high.

The varnish on the office door was cracked with age. The frosted glass window inset into the door read "Walker Stevenson, Esq. Attorney at Law." Jamison opened the door expecting to see the usual secretary acting as gate-keeper, but it was only one large room and sitting there staring at him was Walker Stevenson himself.

Stevenson didn't react or even seem startled. Apparently, he was used to people simply walking in on him without an appointment. Jamison doubted that his schedule required much advance notice. "Judge Stevenson, I'm Matt—"

"I'm not a judge anymore, but thank you for the consideration. And you are Matt Jamison, man of the hour for the current version of the Harker case."

"Yes, I mean, yes, I'm Matt Jamison."

"What can I do for you, Mr. Jamison?" Stevenson spoke quietly, the weari-ness well-worn into him. "I'm assuming you're here to ask the same question everyone involved with the Harker case gets around to asking: 'Why?' Is that it?"

"May I have a seat?"

Stevenson dismissively waved Jamison over to the only chair in front of the desk and moved the yellow legal pad in front of him. "Simple answer. I did what I thought was right. I did what I thought I could live with."

"I understand."

"I doubt that you do."

Jamison shifted uncomfortably in his chair. "Judge Stevenson . . ."

Stevenson smiled. It struck Jamison that the smile was with the corners of his mouth turned down, but there was something about it that seemed to be hiding a more insightful rationale. Jamison waited politely and then asked, "Judge Stevenson, it's important to me to know your reason. I can't let the Harker case go."

"You won, didn't you? What is it that you can't seem to accept?"

"I can't accept that winning was the right result."

"That never bothered your father. That's why you're here, isn't it? Your father?" Stevenson's eyes seemed to instinctively focus like those of a judge staring over the bench at a lawyer who was attempting to misdirect him.

Jamison didn't respond regarding his father. "Judge, the Harker case didn't seem like the kind of case to give mercy. You had to know when you refused to impose the death penalty that there would be a public furor."

Stevenson stood up and walked to the single window behind his desk. "I'm not sure that I expected what happened, but I did know that I couldn't live with the result otherwise. Every judge can count on his or her hands the cases that they never forget. They aren't the big cases or the flashy rulings. They're the cases where you wonder if you used your power wisely. They're the ones that keep you awake at night because nobody knows but you. The public doesn't understand that. Lawyers don't understand that. Not even your spouse understands that. Because you don't speak about it."

Stevenson kept staring out the window and talked as if there was someone on the other side. "I knew your father, you know. He was one of those people that burns like a meteor streaking across the night sky. Everybody wanted to be him. But I suppose you already know that. I imagine he had a lot to do with you becoming a lawyer."

"He had a lot to do with me becoming a lawyer, but it wasn't because I wanted to be him."

Stevenson turned slightly and shifted his gaze to Jamison. "Well, from what I've read and heard, you're apparently far more like him than not. But isn't that almost always true? We grow up either wanting to *be* like our father and not achieving it or *not wanting to be* like our father and looking in the mirror one day and realizing we are him." Stevenson appeared thoughtful. "The reason I did what I did, Mr. Jamison, *is* your father."

"I don't understand."

"I don't imagine you do. I've never told anyone this because both your father and I committed that we would never discuss it. If we did it would probably cost me my seat on the bench and your father his law license. We kept our word. In the end, it didn't make much difference. I lost my seat on the court, but that wasn't your father's fault. At least he kept his law license. In any event, I'm not going to break my word now—unless I know why you need to know. And even then, I make no promises."

Jamison measured his words carefully. "I don't think—no, I know—Richard Harker didn't get a fair trial."

Stevenson's eyebrows raised slightly. He tilted his head to the side. His eyes hardened to gray ice, staring at Jamison. "Are you saying I didn't give Harker a fair trial?"

"No, sir. I know you gave Harker a fair trial. I'm saying that I know evidence was concealed in that case, evidence you had no way of knowing about and evidence his lawyer, Alton Grady, didn't know about."

Jamison perceived from Stevenson's expression that his comment about concealed evidence didn't seem to surprise Stevenson, who quietly said, "Why now, Mr. Jamison? Richard Harker is dead and all the sins of that case are buried with him. Why now?"

"Because I need to know if my father did the right thing."

"The right thing? Is that it? I'm not sure what the right thing is in your mind but okay, yes, your father did the right thing. I like to think we both did the right thing, but what is the right thing is far more complicated than law school lectures on legal ethics."

Stevenson sat back down and leaned his head back, closing his eyes. "The right thing. When that verdict came in I fully intended to impose the death penalty. The crime was horrible and as far as I was concerned Richard Harker deserved no mercy. Your father defended one of the two primary witnesses, Clarence Foster, a little weasel who would have stepped on his mother's neck to steal someone's property. But it was a jury verdict and I believed Harker did it. I had no pangs of conscience or reservation about sentencing Richard Harker to death."

"Then why didn't you do it?"

"Most people, including many lawyers, do not understand that judges can't just set aside verdicts unless they have a good reason, a reason they can state on the record. There's only one area where it is all in the hands of a single judge and that is the imposition of the death sentence—whether to impose death or life. No judge wants to get it wrong. You have to live with yourself when you go home at night."

"What did my father have to do with that?"

"After the verdict and right before sentencing, your father called me and asked to meet with me at my home. He told me it was about the Harker sentencing. Normally I would have said no, but not to your father. We'd known each other a long time. He said it was urgent and he needed my advice. If a man like Roger Jamison needed my advice, then I knew it was important. He walked into my study and the first thing he did was ask for a drink. Then he told me that what he was going to do was put a burden on me and I could never speak of it. He told me that evidence had been concealed and that Harker didn't get a fair trial. I've been around a long time. I knew he had to have gotten that from Foster and he did. Don't you understand? Your father violated his attorney-client privilege. He disclosed confidential information. There are a lot of things I might criticize about Roger. I know far more about him than you might think. Perhaps far more than you know yourself. But he never stood in front of a judge and lied. I knew he was telling the truth and I knew that I could never use what he told me to grant a new trial.

"What was I supposed to say—that the lawyer for one of the prosecution's primary witnesses confidentially told me that the prosecution had concealed evidence? Not to mention that I had breached my duty not to discuss a pending case." Stevenson raised his gaze to meet Jamison's. "It isn't a pure process, Mr. Jamison. It's a process that we try to live up to. Human beings with faults apply the law. If I did disclose it, it would cost Roger his law license and it wouldn't change the situation. I couldn't grant a new trial based on what Roger said. He knew that. None of it would be admissible. The supreme court would reverse me in a heartbeat.

"There was only one way to ensure that Richard Harker would not go to the gas chamber with me knowing he didn't get a fair trial. I gave that to him. I believed he was guilty, but I gave him life. I couldn't have lived with myself if I hadn't done what I did and, I suppose, neither could your father.

"I'll never know whether that concealed evidence might have changed the verdict. There is a wide gulf between guilty, not guilty, and actually innocent. A lot of guilty people walk out the door having been found not guilty. That just means the prosecution failed to prove guilt. It doesn't mean they didn't actually do what they were accused of. Innocent is entirely different. I never believed Harker was innocent.

"Under the circumstances there was nothing I could do without evidence that could be used. If he was guilty, then I can live with what I did. If he was really innocent, then I have to live with that too. I don't believe Harker was innocent. So, the question becomes whether the verdict was a just result. The question you're wrestling with is what is a just result. And that's why you're here, isn't it, Mr. Jamison? I'm guessing you know that evidence was concealed by your office in the Harker case, don't you? And you know who did it. Now *you* have to decide—what is the right thing to do?"

Stevenson moved his mouth into a tight line, his age reflected in his eyes. "There is a certain irony here, don't you think, Mr. Jamison?"

"Irony?"

"Your father sat across from me and placed his burden on me. And now I sit across from his son and return that burden. Irony, Mr. Jamison. And now I'm also guessing there's nothing you can do either without destroying yourself. Just like your father."

Stevenson templed his hands in front of his face. "A piece of advice, Mr. Jamison. Richard Harker is dead. He didn't just take Lisa Farrow's life. Richard Harker took a lot of lives with him. But he's dead now. Sometimes it's best to let the dead rest quietly. There's no sin in that unless you have a career death wish. I can speak from personal experience."

Chapter 55

The next morning, O'Hara walked into Jamison's office with Ernie. "Andy called. He has the DNA results."

"What are they?" Jamison asked.

"He said he thought he should show you himself." O'Hara hesitated before adding, "I could tell from his voice that he thinks there's a problem."

⤳

Andy was firing a pistol into a large container of water. The sound reverberated through the room in part because there was no sound absorption material on the walls. He pulled up a strainer with a perfectly formed bullet and took off his sound-blocking headphones when he noticed the three men. "This is the gun that we think was used in the Owens murder." He rolled the bullet in a gloved hand, his voice triumphant. "If we have a match, then we have the murder weapon, and then we have the murderer." He could see the impatience on O'Hara's face. "You want to know whose blood I found on that pathetic stuffed rabbit. I told you, I am king of forensics. It's not easy to separate mixed blood samples to separate the DNA, but I was able to do it." Andy waited for positive feedback, but realizing it wasn't going to happen continued. "But I'm not sure it's going to help you. Easier if I show you." Andy shuffled around in a pile of paper on his desk and pulled up several sheets covered with what looked like a series of small dashes. "It's very simple, really. I don't mean the process, I mean the matching. You can see the patterns. First—"

O'Hara interrupted. "Just the results, please."

Visibly disappointed at not being able to show off his forensic expertise, Andy responded. "All right, like I said, the blood on the stuffed rabbit shows a direct relationship to the swab you gave me from Christine Farrow. Although it's all mitochondrial DNA, there's really no doubt it's from her mother, the victim. The DNA profile you gave me from Clarence Foster matches the DNA I found in the mixed blood on the toy, including the fact that the pattern fits someone of African heritage. If Foster handled the rabbit he had to have been bleeding or whoever handled the rabbit had both the victim's blood and Foster's blood on his hands.

"Here's where I ran into a problem. You gave me Harker's blood sample from his autopsy and you gave me blood from a Tom Sample and from an unknown fifth party. I would have expected to find Harker's blood. The blood I found was from the same matriarchal line as this Tom Sample, the mitochondrial DNA showed the relationship. They were both related to a mother or a grandmother common to them. The weird thing is the DNA you gave me from the unknown sample wasn't in the blood on the rabbit and it didn't have the same mitochondrial relationship, but the blood you listed as an unknown is definitely related to Tom Sample in some way, just not the same mother. Best guess would be through the father. Do you know who the father is? If you get me that it would help."

O'Hara interrupted. "And Harker's DNA?"

"It wasn't in the blood I tested from the stuffed rabbit. I'm not sure what that means to you but I can say that whoever left that blood on that rabbit had the blood of three people on their hands, the victim's blood, Foster's blood, and blood from someone related to Tom Sample. If Harker handled that rabbit, then I couldn't find his DNA. So that doesn't mean he didn't kill the victim. It's entirely possible the blood could have gotten on the toy at a different time. But it creates a question about the coincidence of all three blood samples being on the toy belonging to the murder victim's child and mixed together, which would indicate the mixed blood was placed on the rabbit at the same time. Is there anything else?"

"No, Andy," O'Hara said. "Like I told you this is off the books. No reports and no case number. You good with that?"

"Yeah, I'm good with that. It doesn't mean much with Harker dead. I'm guessing that whoever left that third DNA is dead too." Andy had a smug look on his face like he was now in on a secret. "I did look up a list of vics and a Richard Sample showed up from a bar killing almost ten years ago. Is that him? Is he related to Tom Sample?"

It was obvious Andy was fishing to try to insert himself into the investigation. He saw crime scene investigators on television running around like cops, although that wasn't reality. He just wanted to be a part of the street cred. O'Hara politely cut him off. "Not sure yet."

"Well, if that's him, then you would have a real shitstorm if Harker wasn't dead, I guess. Enough to cause you problems in a trial." Andy waited for an answer but the three men remained quiet. He knew enough to stop. "Don't worry, no report. But you owe me—and you will pay the king of forensics."

Jamison thanked Andy and led his investigators to a nearby empty office. He sat down heavily. "So, Sample killed Lisa Farrow. Christine said someone came in and touched that rabbit. That was probably Foster, who says he was so drunk he doesn't remember any of it."

"Or it could have been Sample and he had Foster's blood on his hands. But when Christine was hypnotized it sounded like there was a second man who came into her bedroom and touched that stuffed rabbit. Probably Foster." O'Hara added, "I've seen men do a lot of things when they were stone drunk and the next day they're blacked out, don't remember a thing that they did.

"Assuming Jimmy Stack is telling the truth. Rick Sample slipped up when he told Jimmy Stack that he would do the same thing to him that he did to Lisa Farrow in order to shut Stack up. That's what Clarence meant when he said he did the right thing. He knew he'd lied about Harker to save himself, but he believed Harker did it. He didn't have any pangs of conscience until Stack told him that Sample had actually been the murderer. So, killing Sample was how he made it right."

Ernie said, "Well, there's some justice in that, I suppose."

All three men absorbed the consequences of the blood tests, and then Jamison asked, "What about the fifth DNA sample? What did you tell Andy about where that came from and why we wanted it?"

Ernie said, "Like you told me, I gave Andy that swab I took from inside your cheek and told Andy it was an unknown that we wanted to compare with the swab we took from Tom Sample." Ernie could see the pain on Jamison's face. He paused before quietly saying, "Tom Sample is your brother."

O'Hara let the heavy silence fill the room before he asked a final question. "What are you going to do now, Matt? The only thing we can prove is that Gage and Cleary concealed evidence in order to ensure Harker was found guilty. And now we know that it's at least probable that it was Rick Sample who killed Lisa or else by some really weird coincidence that blood ended up on Christine's rabbit. I don't believe in coincidence."

Ernie's voice was almost inaudible. "If this is true, then Harker was innocent. That poor bastard spent almost thirty years behind bars and could have been executed. Now what? It's too late for Harker and there's nothing we can do to Sample. And then we got the other problem."

Jamison had been staring at his legal pad. He looked up when Ernie said, "other problem."

"There's something else? This isn't bad enough?"

"If this gets out, Matt, so will the information about your dad. You need to think about that. This isn't going to be a one-day article in the back pages of the newspaper. It's going to be front page and there's not a damn thing it can change in terms of Harker or Sample."

"What about Gage and Cleary? What about the fact that there's plenty of evidence now to believe that Richard Harker was innocent, and that evidence was suppressed to make sure he was found guilty?" Jamison's voice was a whisper.

O'Hara answered for Ernie. "More important, what about you? It won't be good. Dead is dead. Harker is dead. Sample is dead. This case is dead. Gage and Cleary aren't your problem. You need to drop this now."

Jamison didn't answer. He got up and walked from the room. This time O'Hara and Ernie let him walk alone. They knew he needed to work this out his own way.

〜

Jamison sat in his darkened office and stared at the manila envelope with the tapes of Foster that had been concealed. And then there was the forensic report. He picked up his phone and started to call his mother, then canceled the call. The phone wasn't the right way to do this and he wasn't sure whether she even needed to know if he decided to just put an end to the whole thing. He dialed another number. "Dr. Levy, I need to see you."

〜

Levy listened intently and without interruption until Jamison finished and looked at him with a question mark in his eyes. He took a deep breath and let it out slowly. "I'm not a lawyer so I don't know about any legal ethical responsibilities. But I do understand whether or not you can let this whole thing die. I think not."

"If I release these tapes people are going to want to know how I got them. Not to mention that O'Hara is right. My career will be over."

"Maybe, but people want to know a lot of things. That doesn't mean you have a responsibility to tell them. The only people you have a responsibility to right now are your mother, this newly discovered brother, and yourself. I think your first issue is what do you tell your mother, if anything? That depends on what you do with the tapes and how you do it. Let me ask two questions. First, what will be accomplished by disclosing the tapes? Second, if the tapes are disclosed, why does anybody need to know where the tapes came from?"

Levy paused, sensing Jamison's uncertainty as to the right course of action. Finally, he quietly added, "When I was in graduate school, the first thing one of my professors in human behavior said was, 'If good and evil are simply a matter of perspective, then what is morality?' He said that was what we would study. At the end, the only conclusion I could reach is that what is right and wrong isn't always that clear. It depends on the circumstances and sometimes on the consequences. You need to do what you believe is right and that is something only you can answer."

〜

Jamison drove aimlessly for over an hour, finally pulling up and parking at the curb of the destination he had been avoiding. He sat in the car for a few minutes, staring at the manila envelope. He had thought about a lot of things. It had been a long night. He could do nothing, but Levy was right, he couldn't do that and face himself in the mirror. He didn't have a career death wish, so making a public disclosure wasn't the right move, and even if it was the right thing, he was the one who would pay the highest price. By early morning he had decided.

He got out of the car and walked up to the offices of Samuel Gifford. Jamison waited in the reception area of what had once been the dining room of the aged home. Gifford walked out and extended his hand. "To what do I owe the pleasure. I notice you don't have your junkyard dog with you."

"You mean Detective O'Hara? I fed him before I came over. Do you have a moment?"

They walked into Gifford's office. Jamison took the available seat. The other one was covered with files. "Mr. Gifford, I would like to hire you. Are you available?"

The surprise on Gifford's face wasn't concealed. "I'm a criminal defense lawyer, Mr. Jamison. Do you need a criminal defense attorney?"

"I need someone who will handle a matter in the right way and will be discreet. Can you do that, Sam?"

Gifford took a moment before answering, measuring the man in front of him contemplatively. "Why don't you tell me what the problem is?"

Jamison fished a twenty-dollar bill out of his wallet and laid it on Gifford's desk. "Are you willing to represent me?"

Gifford's eyes narrowed to black slits. "I've never had a district attorney come to me for professional reasons. Why are you here?"

Jamison slid the manila folder across Gifford's desk. "I have a long story so tell me if it's more than twenty dollars' worth when I'm finished. But you can't use any of it unless we agree on the terms. Agreed?"

"I usually charge more but I'm willing to listen to this for the price of twenty dollars. Agreed."

Jamison slowly unraveled the story, including the fact that his father had a son that nobody knew about. Gifford was subdued and asked few questions until Jamison was finished. "So, what do you expect me to do with the tapes?"

"I expect you to do the right thing. The truth is still important. Richard Harker deserves that at the very least."

"What about your father?"

"If that comes out in the wash, it comes out, but it isn't going to come out unless somebody knows where to look, and even then, it's buried deep. It's about whether Harker got a fair trial. In the end, we won't ever know if he was really innocent, but we will know he didn't get a fair trial."

"What about Gage and Justice Cleary?"

"What's their motive for making their situation worse by telling the whole truth?"

"Good point." Gifford undid the clasp to the manila envelope and pulled out the tapes. He reached into a lower desk drawer and pulled out a tape recorder.

They listened in silence to the voice of Foster and Christine, as well as Jensen, Gage, and Cleary. "This wasn't in Alton Grady's file or the disclosure lists from the district attorney. It's obvious why." He pulled the tape out and put it back in the envelope. "I have a question."

"You want to know why?"

"I want to know why."

"You may not believe this, Sam, but I still believe that the system only works if you follow the rules."

Epilogue

Samuel Gifford made a motion to reopen the Harker case. Judge Williams denied it but not without the consequence of Gifford's explosive public declaration about the concealed tapes and an invitation to the press to listen to them. He declined to answer any questions about where he got them but referred the press to District Attorney William Gage and Justice Jonathon Cleary. Neither had any public comment, issuing statements that denied they had failed in their duties as prosecutors.

Jamison sat quietly in front of Bill Gage's desk, watching the broad back of the district attorney as he stared out the window at his fiefdom. Gage's summons had been waiting for him when he walked into the office. He could tell from Helen's voice that it wasn't a friendly invitation. Finally, Gage turned and sat down, his thick hands thrumming a drumbeat on his desk before speaking. "I suppose you don't know how those tapes came into Sam Gifford's possession, do you?" Jamison didn't answer. He knew Gage didn't expect him to.

Gage took a deep breath before continuing. "I told you before that to sit behind this desk you have to be able to make a lot of hard decisions, including political decisions. It isn't all black-and-white. You made a bad decision, Matt." Gage got up and walked back to the window. The conversation was over. Jamison stood up and walked to the door before he heard Gage make one more comment. "A man has to accept consequences for the choices he makes. Your father used to say that. You might remember it."

Jamison waited a moment before standing and walking out of the office. His only thought was the irony that Gage had chosen him to handle this case because Gage expected he would do what all lawyers do and stop when he won. Gage's mistake with him was in not realizing that he hadn't become a lawyer to do what lawyers do. He had become a lawyer to do what lawyers needed to do. Maybe that made him different than his father, and then again, maybe it didn't. He had to think about that. But one thing was reassuring. He was different than Bill Gage.

Within two days word leaked from the White House that Justice Cleary was no longer in the running for a seat on the Washington DC Circuit Court.

Rumor had it that Bill Gage received a call from the governor asking that he find a reason not to run for attorney general. He did, announcing that because of unnamed health issues he had decided not to run for statewide office or reelection. To the surprise of everyone he endorsed his assistant district attorney to replace him. Matthew Jamison wasn't mentioned.

About the Author

James A. Ardaiz is a former prosecutor, judge, and Presiding Justice of the California Fifth District Court of Appeal. From 1974 to 1980, Ardaiz was a prosecutor for the Fresno County District Attorney's office. In 1980 Ardaiz was elected to the Fresno Municipal Court, where he served as assistant presiding judge and presiding judge. Ardaiz was appointed to the California Fifth District Court of Appeal in 1988 and was named the court's Presiding Justice in 1994. Ardaiz retired from the bench in 2011 and remains active in the legal profession.

Ardaiz's previous books include *Hands Through Stone*, a first-hand nonfiction account of his work on the investigation and prosecution of murderer Clarence Ray Allen, the last man executed by the State of California, and *Fractured Justice*, the first Matt Jamison mystery novel.

CPSIA information can be obtained
at www.ICGtesting.com
Printed in the USA
JSHW021533260423
40887JS00001B/83

9 781610 353458